I0653249

Ethan Cadfael:

The Battle Prince

By
S.M Carrière

ISBN: 09 8669 7621

ISBN-13: 978-09 8669 7623

http://smcarriere.com

Acknowledgements and Apologies

The first thing I must do is apologise to all Welsh and Irish speakers for stealing and probably mutilating your respective languages. I hope I have not offended your sensibilities.

Thanks to all those people who knowingly or otherwise provided names or character references for everyone appearing in this tale.

I'd also like to thank my mother and father, both of whom I relied heavily on during and after the writing of this story. Thanks also to my Beta Readers (you know who you are), and to Laura Miller, whose skills at book cover design are remarkable.

Most of all, thank-you to Professors Birt and Kilmurray for introducing me to the world of Celtic Studies and Prehistoric Anthropology respectively, thus inadvertently providing fodder for my imagination.

I should also note quickly that this book was written prior to the new construction at Carleton University, and is accurate up until then. Also, to the best of my knowledge, at the time of writing, Carleton University did not have a lacrosse team.

For Jasmine, who puts up with my crazy like a champion.

Ethan Cadfael:

The Battle Prince

Prologue

*I*t all came down to this. Aerfyn, Battle Queen of the Pobl Gwir, sat upon her mount and quivered. The morning was damp. A chill had settled over the valley, covering the rolling grasslands in a thick, thigh-high fog. Beyond the valley sat an ancient, dense forest that concealed the enemy.

She knew they were there; watching her. She could feel their pallid eyes upon her.

The thought shot a shudder down her spine, sending her chainmail rustling. She shook the tension from her shoulders and searched the line of trees, nervously playing with the long strawberry blonde braid hanging over her shoulder.

Behind Aerfyn stretched the Pobl Gwir camp. Bright pavilions denoting the many houses of the Pobl Gwir who had rallied to her side at the beginning of the war dotted the slopes of hills behind the valley. Many of those houses had suffered greatly, decimated by the continual brutal advances of the Dynion Gors.

They called themselves the Fir Bolg. No matter their name, they were a most brutal enemy. Hailing from the swamps of Annwfyn, they were terrible beings. Taller than the tallest man, and many times slimmer, they gave the appearance of leather-bound skeletons. Pallid greyish skin stretched over bone and sinew as if sewn on by a cobbler who couldn't quite afford enough hide.

They painted their skin with peat dyes. Brownish stripes and chevrons decorated their grey skins in all the places that were exposed.

Their eyes were overly large and bulbous, protruding a little from their long, thin skulls. They were pale brown, so pale as to appear almost yellow. When the light caught them in the dark, they shone back red.

Yellow teeth filled their wide mouths, each tooth sharply pointed. When they grinned, it was as if death itself smiled.

For all their delicate structure, they were strong and wickedly fast; and vicious. Foul tempers matched their foul appearance.

Aerfyn closed her brown eyes briefly to rid herself of their terrible image. She opened them again and frowned. Still no movement from the forest. Surely they should have attacked by now?

"It's too quiet," Maelgoch said as he walked to the knoll upon which Aerfyn sat atop her mount. "They should have attacked by now."

Aerfyn bit her lip and nodded. She turned to her lieutenant with a frown. "Are the troops ready?"

"As ready as they're likely to be, my Queen." Maelgoch smiled grimly, pushing a lock of his dark brown hair from his equally dark brown eyes. Of a swarthy complexion not normally noted as handsome, Maelgoch's features were striking nonetheless. His appearance was such that his darker skin could easily be forgiven. Were it not for the scar that cut across his right cheek, he might even have been considered beautiful.

Aerfyn sighed. "Let us advance then. Perhaps we can call them out from their hiding places."

"As my Queen commands."

"Stop that, Maelgoch."

The lieutenant of the Pobl Gwir grinned. The grin slid from his face as the sounds of panicked screams from the very back of the camp reached his ears.

The charioteers who had been waiting patiently there for the signal to move had been attacked from behind, their vehicles in too tight a formation to turn swiftly enough to avoid bloody slaughter.

In a matter of seconds, the entire camp fell into chaos. Soldiers ran this way and that, their commanders screaming orders at them. The orders went largely unheeded.

Maelgoch swore and ran forward. Aerfyn turned her horse and drew her weapon. She kicked the beast into action and ran headlong into battle, calling her troops to her.

The sight of their Battle Queen galloping bravely forward with her sword drawn and her blonde braid flying behind her from beneath her helm brought the Pobl Gwir army to their senses. Their scattered flight turned into disciplined resistance and the surprise attack by the Fir Bolg quickly became a fully engaged battle.

They fought for hours, but the damage done by the enemy's ruse proved to be irreparable. Aerfyn had been separated from her army. Only Maelgoch had her in sight. Her horse, a sharp-witted beast of unrivalled skill, pranced and kicked, twisted and turned, all at his rider's most imperceptible command. The beast's ability to read both her commands and the battle around it was the only reason Aerfyn sat in her saddle.

She fought bravely, easily taking ten of the Dynion Gors as she struggled to return to her army. The fog that had began as a ground covering began to rise. Now reaching the horse's underbelly, Aerfyn had to keep her eyes peeled should one of the enemy try to use the mist as cover.

Pushed ever-farther back, Aerfyn hacked and hewed at the milling fiends around her. Swords and lances flashed out towards her mount. It ducked and danced away, neighing shrilly at the evil creatures around it.

No horse is immortal, though ancient tales may tell of one or two, and Cyngarch, the Queen's brave stallion, was tiring. The smell of blood and the threat of death could not keep the stallion's fire. It faltered a single step and one of the Dynion Gors plunged his lance through the beast's muscled chest.

Cyngarch reared, screaming in outrage and pain. Thrown from her saddle, Aerfyn landed hard on her back, knocking the wind from her lungs in a single, agonizing gust. Tears struck her eyes as she witnessed the silhouette of her brave mount through the mist, rearing high and lashing out with his front hooves. Another lance found his chest and the beast collapsed.

4

It was all Aerfyn could do to roll out of the way before Cyngarch crashed upon her. Anger took her then. She rolled to her feet, drew her long dagger and fought with all she had left. Fighting quickly became impossible, for the fog rose above her head, and all Aerfyn could see were looming shapes in the mist.

They came at her, one after another, the tall, hooded skeletons that were the Dynion Gors. One by one they were slain, but each battle cost Aerfyn much-needed ground, and no small amount of wounds. Each step backwards took her farther and farther from her army. Indeed, the sounds of battle faded into the misty distance.

Still the figures of the Dynion Gors materialized, coming at her, driving her backwards with each engagement. One warrior proved particularly troublesome. The fight lasted longer than Aerfyn's strength could. Blood-loss made her limbs weak and her head spin. She stepped back to avoid a blow from a heavy two-bitted battle-axe only to find emptiness beneath her foot. With a shriek, she toppled backwards and landed hard onto stone.

Fog floated thick and full about her, lit now with an orange glow. Aerfyn scowled. She smelled no smoke, yet a fire blazed steadily above her head. Groaning, she rolled over and struggled to her feet. A great noise filled the air. Deep booming sounds, not unlike what Aerfyn supposed the unsteady footsteps of a drunken giant must sound like, filled the air with a terrible racket.

Higher sounds in frantic rhythms floated over the top, accompanied by the distant sounds of chatter and laughter. Laughter?

Aerfyn stumbled towards the sound, weak from her wounds. Shapes loomed out of the fog. Aerfyn thought them Dynion Gors at first, but they were too short, too broad and strangely dressed.

One figure had wings. One looked like a cat, but walked upright. The cat held the arm of a strange, square-headed thing with pegs coming from either temple.

"Cymorth," she called, trying to chase them. "Cymorth."

The one with pegs on the side of his head smiled at Aerfyn and patted her on the shoulder. It was then that Aerfyn noticed he was a monster, with green skin and a face that had been stitched together and held fast by some cruel magic. He said something to her. Aerfyn could not understand him. He smiled again and walked on.

Figures in increasing numbers loomed through the mist. Monsters of every sort milled about, most of them heading in the same direction – towards the distant and bizarre booming noises.

The Battle Queen of the Pobl Gwir moved towards them to get a better look. She could not keep her balance. She stumbled far to the left and found herself in a forest of firs.

Disoriented and terrified, Aerfyn searched the foggy night for any sign of her troops.

"Cymorth," she croaked, tears streaming down her face. "Cymorth."

She could manage no more. Overcome by her wounds, Aerfyn fell to her knees. She wavered there a moment before toppling backwards, her weapons falling from her grip.

Blackness swallowed the fire in the fog.

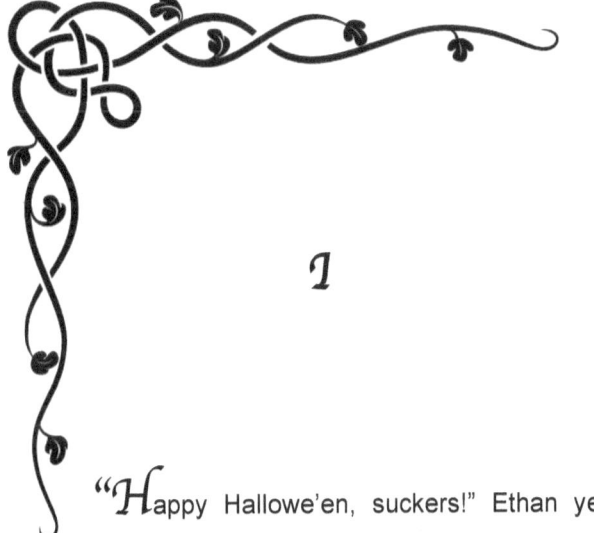

1

"*H*appy Hallowe'en, suckers!" Ethan yelled, the words muffled behind the wolf mask he wore. He tripped the weedy Asian kid who had been hurrying past. His teammates snickered as the boy scrambled to his feet and raced off, muttering to himself in Cantonese.

At twenty-one and flying through Ottawa's Carleton University on a lacrosse scholarship, Ethan Evans owned the world. Towering above almost everyone at an impressive six foot four inches and broadly built, he played a wicked midfield game, switching easily to attack should the team be down a man.

Black hair and striking blue eyes ensured that he was the darling of his year at Carleton. There wasn't a girl in any of his classes that didn't want him in their beds. Obscene numbers of girls, dressed up as playboy bunnies, begged him for a dance at the Hallowe'en party at Oliver's, the University pub-style hangout. He had nothing to prove.

He walked away from Carleton's Uni Centre with his lacrosse teammates towards Bronson Avenue, there to await the bus that would take them downtown for a more adult party.

"So," Harrison said with a grin. "Barrymore's?"

"Sure," Ethan replied in his usual I-don't-care-as-long-as-there's-booze-and-girls tone.

"Is Mitch coming?" Gordon asked.

"If his girlfriend lets him," Harrison replied.

Ethan scoffed. "Man, that girl's a bitch. I don't know why Mitch bothers with her."

"I heard she's got no gag reflex."

The group snickered.

"Yo, Ethan!" Mitch called as he jogged up the foggy path. "Ethan!"

"Man, where were you?" Harrison asked as Mitch slowed to walk beside his teammates.

"Sorry, guys. Wendy had a party at hers I had to attend."

"Could've told us sooner," Gordon grumbled. "We waited for you."

"She sprang it on me."

"Didn't you tell her you already had plans?"

"Of course I did."

"Yeah, course you did."

"Shut up."

"How'd you get away?" Ethan asked.

"Compromise," Mitch said with a shrug.

"See," Harrison said. "No gag reflex."

Everyone snickered and Mitch threw a punch at Harrison, who dodged neatly. The two chased each other for a while as the rest of the team strode along.

The fog was horrifically thick. It added much to the ambience of the Hallowe'en night, and the boys took full advantage of it, hooting and howling as they walked along; all keeping in character. The team had decided to spend Hallowe'en as a werewolf pack.

"I'm totally team Jacob," a very drunk freshman dressed as a mermaid said as she shuffled passed them.

Ethan snarled and leapt after her. She screamed and stumbled away, almost falling in her very restrictive tail. The boys laughed and continued on.

They talked mostly sports as they walked down the newly laid path. Only the presence of the lamps on their left indicated that they were on the path at all.

"Man, this fog is annoying," Mitch grumbled at last. "I can't see a thing." As if to prove his point, he stumbled.

"What the...?" he said as his teammates hooted their derision at him.

"Drunk already?" Ethan asked with a laugh.

"Shut up. I tripped on something."

"Oh, sure you did."

"No, I did!" Mitch walked back up the path, peering through the fog in an effort to locate the soft thing he had stepped on.

"C'mon, Mitch!" Harrison complained. "We're gonna miss the bus."

"Shut up," Mitch said. He stopped at about where he tripped and looked down.

Lying on the path, barely visible, was a long greyish thing. Mitch bent down to take a closer look. When he realised what had tripped him, he leapt backwards with a shriek.

The others fell about laughing, pausing in their laughter to mimic the high-pitched scream Mitch had managed to utter.

"Shut-up!" Mitch said. "It's a hand!"

"Eh?" Ethan walked forward to investigate. He knelt down and poked at the hand. The metallic rustle of chainmail answered his poking. "So it is."

"Is he all right?" Mitch asked.

"Who cares?" Ethan said, standing. "Probably just some idiot who couldn't handle his drink. C'mon, the bus'll be here any minute."

"I think we should make sure he's all right, first."

Ethan rolled his eyes. "Bleeding heart, honestly."

"Just, go in and check!"

"You found him. You go in and check."

Mitch stared at the small cluster of stunted firs that had recently been planted near the Campus' Bronson pedestrian entrance. In the fog, with a potential dead body, it seemed the most sinister place in the world at the moment.

"Yo, man. You go."

Ethan rolled his eyes. "Fine," he said. "Pussy." He turned back to the rest of the team, who hadn't moved. "Yo, Gordo, you've still got that flashlight?"

Gordon sighed and walked forward. He pulled the flashlight from his back pocket. "Seriously?" he asked as he handed it over.

"Shut-up," Ethan replied.

He unscrewed the top of the torch so it no longer displayed the image of a ghost and turned it on. He pointed it in the trees to reveal a body in chainmail with leather pauldrons, vambraces and an enamelled and embossed leather breastplate. The helmet was bronze looking, with a boar on the crest.

"Cool costume." Ethan stepped forward and nudged the body with his foot. "Hey, you all right bud?"

Other than the disturbance from being nudged, the hapless drunk didn't move. Ethan looked back.

"Well?" Mitch asked.

Ethan scowled and walked further in. He crouched by the body.

"Hey, Ethan," Harrison called. "I see the bus. C'mon, let's go."

"Hold up," Ethan called back. He reached down and pulled the helm off the head and nearly dropped the torch in surprise.

"Yo, it's a girl!" he called back.

"What?" Mitch said. He and Gordon exchanged a glance and edged into the firs together.

"Holy shit!" Gordon said, joining Ethan.

A young woman in full armour, with strawberry blonde hair that frizzed and escaped the long braid she wore, lay on the ground. Large, wide set eyes were closed beneath a smooth, white brow.

11

"She's kinda pretty," Mitch said. "Is she breathing?"

Ethan placed his fingers beneath the girl's nose. The faintest hint of warmth confirmed she was. He nodded.

The sounds of the bus roaring along Bronson reached the group.

"Yo!" Harrison yelled. "The bus is here!"

Mitch left the cluster of firs to spy Harrison and the rest of the team sprinting across Bronson Avenue just as the number four pulled up.

"Yo!" he called.

"We'll meet you there!" Harrison yelled back.

Mitch shook his head and, grumbling under his breath, went back to Ethan and Gordon.

"Well, the others have all gone to Barrymore's."

"Hey, look!" Gordon said, moving away a little. He picked up an object. "A sword. Man, it's heavy. Wonder if it's real?" He ran his thumb along the edge of the blade, and cut himself.

"Ow! Shit!" he said before plunging his bleeding thumb into his mouth. He dropped the sword back onto the ground and trudged back to Ethan and Mitch.

"You're so stupid," Mitch said. He turned back to Ethan and the girl. "Real armour, real sword. Wonder where she got this costume from? Wait. Dude. Is that blood?"

Ethan turned his attention back to the unconscious girl on the ground. He ran the light of the torch away from her face to her chest. A large gash in her breastplate oozed a dark liquid. Ethan tentatively reached out and touched it. It was warm and sticky and very red.

"Oh man!"

Mitch immediately pulled out his cell phone and dialed 9-1-1.

9-1-1, please state your emergency, a female voice on the end of the line said.

"Yo, there's a girl here and she's bleeding pretty bad."

All right sir. Please tell me where you are.

"Uh... Um... Carleton University, the Bronson pedestrian entrance. Please send an ambulance quick. She's hurt bad."

An ambulance has been dispatched. Please stay on the line, I'll talk you through some basic first aid.

"Uh... okay."

Is she breathing?

"Yeah. We think so."

Can you see the wound?

"Well... uh... she's wearing armour."

Armour?

"Yeah, like chainmail and stuff."

Okay. And you can't see where the blood is coming from?

"Hang on," Mitch said, placing his hand over the mouthpiece of his mobile. "Yo, man, can you see where the blood's coming from?"

"I can see it," Ethan said.

"Okay," Mitch answered. "He reckons he can."

He?

"Yeah, my friend Ethan. He's with the girl."

All right. Tell Ethan he needs to put pressure on the wound. It will help stem the blood flow.

"Yo, man," Mitch told Ethan. "You gotta stop the bleeding."

Ethan glared at Mitch.

"She said put pressure on the wound."

"Oh, man!" Ethan complained beneath his breath. All the same, he placed his hand over the gash in the armour and pressed. The girl shuddered, but did not wake.

"Hey, when is the ambulance going to get here?"

No sooner had Ethan asked then two police cars and an ambulance roared down Bronson, stopping before the pedestrian entrance to the campus. In a blur, Ethan was relieved of his duties by two paramedics and he, Mitch and Gordon were taken aside by the policemen.

"Is she going to be all right?" Ethan asked as he was dragged away from the paramedics.

"Don't know, son," the officer dragging him away said. "Come away now."

The three boys were taken to the police cars where a second officer waited. She left to investigate the scene as they arrived.

"Are we in trouble?" Gordon asked.

"We just need a statement."

Ethan, Gordon and Mitch stood despondently by the police cars in a close group while the officer took down their names, their ages and their version of the events that transpired that night.

"And it was you who tripped over her?" the officer asked, pointing his pen at Gordon.

"No, Officer," Mitch said. "That was me."

"So you're the one who found her?"

"Yes, sir."

"And you're Mitch, right?"

"Yes, sir."

"All right."

Ethan half listened as he watched the paramedics lift the girl onto the gurney and wheel her into the ambulance.

One paramedic approached. "All done here, Bill," he said. "There's a lot of blood on the ground, and a couple of weapons. She's barely alive."

The Paramedic turned to Ethan and smiled. "Lucky you found her when you did. She might make it yet."

"Weapons?" the officer who'd been taking the statements said in surprise.

"Yeah. A sword and a dagger."

"All right. Thanks, John."

The paramedic grunted. "You have a good night."

"Yeah, you too."

John jogged to the ambulance and clambered in. The driver pulled away and sped off down Bronson, sirens blazing, heading to the Ottawa Hospital.

"Oh, yeah," Gordon said meekly. "I found the sword and picked it up."

"And cut his thumb on it," Ethan said. "Idiot."

"Shut up."

"But you didn't see a dagger?" Bill asked carefully.

"No, Officer. Just the sword."

Bill grunted and made a note while his companion, returned from the scene, spoke into her walkie-talkie.

"Dispatch," she said with a thick French accent. "We need Forensics down here. Probable crime scene."

The radio crackled an inaudible response, but Ethan was no longer paying attention.

"Crime scene?"

"Everything's a crime scene until we decide otherwise."

"Jesus."

Bill raised an eyebrow at the three boys. "Werewolves?"

"Yeah," Mitch said. "We're a pack."

"Right. Look, this is suspicious, and since you're the ones who found the victim, we need you to stay close all right?"

"We live right here on campus, Officer, and it's the middle of the term. We're not going anywhere."

"All right, good. I need your contact details."

The boys gave them their details as more howling police cars pulled up, the roof lights flashing eerily through the dense fog. The police cordoned off the area and soon the foggy night was lit up with the bright flashes of cameras as Forensics painstakingly photographed the scene. One policewoman had a difficult time keeping the gathering horde of onlookers from coming too close.

"Right, that's everything," Officer Bill said with a tight smile. His crisp blue eyes examined each boy carefully. "You're free to go. We will be contacting you."

"Yes, Officer," Ethan said absently.

"You boys have a good night, now."

"You too," Gordon said. "Happy Hallowe'en."

Bill grunted. He got into his car and, lighting up the roof, roared off back to the station.

Ethan slapped Gordon on the back of the head. "Happy Hallowe'en?"

"What else was I supposed to say?" Gordon protested.

"Man," Mitch said. "You really are stupid."

"Whatta we do now?" Gordon said. "I mean, the others are all at Barrymore's, waiting."

"First thing I'm going to do is go home and wash this blood off my hands," Ethan said. "Then I'm heading to Mike's Place for a cold beer."

"Not going to Barrymore's, then?"

Ethan shook his head. "You really feel like dancing after finding someone who might have been murdered?"

"She's not dead," Mitch pointed out.

"Almost," Ethan said. "Jesus. I'm feeling a bit sick."

"Let's head back and get you cleaned up," Mitch said.

The three boys turned back and marched up the path to Dundas House, where Mitch and Ethan shared a room. They walked back in complete silence.

Once there, Ethan felt the need to take a full body shower and scrub himself vigorously. The other two simply changed from their costumes. Before long, they were sitting in the pub with a pitcher of Keith's Red between them.

Mike's Place, formerly the hangout for graduate students which had been taken over by anyone who could legally drink, had a typical small pub feel.

Tonight, however, it had a sad air.

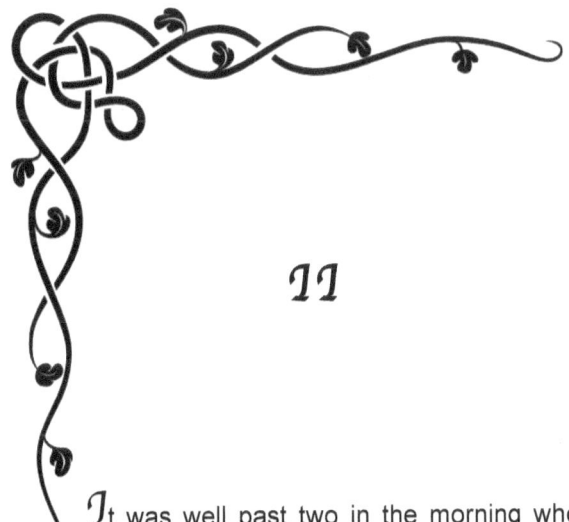

11

$\mathcal{I}$t was well past two in the morning when the police finished their work at the Bronson Avenue pedestrian entrance to Carleton University. Leaving the cordon up, they packed up and drove off, relieved to be out of the heavy, cold mist.

Officer Bill Jackman had just finished his paperwork when the squad cars pulled up. He went to the kitchen and filled a third cup of coffee.

"Long night," he noted to his partner.

Officer Boulduc, a petite blonde woman with a bright smile and a penchant for green eye shadow, shrugged. "It's a complete mystery. The girl's tracks indicate she arrived from the east, the boys from the north. There are no tracks but the girls leading to the scene from the east, and none at all but the boys leading from it. It's odd."

"Reckon they did it?"

"I haven't interviewed them, but it seems unlikely. You?"

"They seemed pretty genuine, not the killer type, you know?" Bill sighed and rubbed his forehead. "I have to wait to hear back from the doctors in any case. First word is it looks like a wound by a broad, thick, slightly blunt blade."

"What, like a sword?"

"Yeah, or axe."

"An axe?"

"That's what the surgeon said." Bill shook his head. "I hate Hallowe'en."

****

Biter Feargach sniffed the air. The fog still permeated everything, but this fog had a different smell. It was not the clean air of the field, or the heavy, mineral dense air of a swamp. It smelled... different. He was certain he wasn't on the battlefield anymore.

He looked up. A globe burned fiercely in the dark of night, radiating steady orange light throughout the fog. Nothing stirred, not even the air. He sniffed the air again, detecting the metallic, meaty smell of blood – and plenty of it.

He grinned a yellow, sharp-toothed grin from beneath his dark hood and crept forward. Behind him skulked Torthaí Searbh and Cath Drúis. The three Fir Bolg crossed the path. Biter Feargach stopped dead at the yellow and black ribbon that blocked his path. He sniffed it. Lingering traces of a strange scent that was neither Pobl Gwir nor Fir Bolg clung to the ribbon. It smelled otherwise foul.

Grumbling, Biter Feargach seized hold of the ribbon and tried to tear it. The material clearly was not fabric, or it would have torn in a neat line all the way down. This ribbon stretched and pulled, and remained stuck in whatever position he yanked it into. Biter Feargach bent down to peer at it with his enormous eyes. He blinked, poked it, then, pulling with all his strength, snapped the ribbon in two. It fluttered to the ground in silence.

He crept forward again, his companions scuttling nearby, scouting the surrounds.

He entered the small patch of firs and stopped still, disappointed. This was the place where the scent of blood was the strongest, and yet the missing Pobl Gwir queen was nowhere in sight. Growling, he went down on all fours and sniffed the area.

A large puddle of blood, long soaked into the ground with the strong smell of leather and steel and the unmistakable scent of the enemy queen dominated the fragrances on the ground, but there were other scents as well. Biter Feargach identified two males whose scents were the strongest.

His grin returned. They probably knew where the queen was. Striding from the clearing, he called softly to his comrades. They materialised from the fog instantly, answering his birdcall in silence.

"She's been taken," he said. "Two men. Follow me."
He got down on all fours again and crawled slowly around, trying to pick up the scent of the two males. He found them relatively easily. Slowly but surely, the three Fir Bolg crawled towards Dundas House.

****

"Fall back!" Maelgoch roared. "Fall back! The battle is lost!"

He almost needn't have said anything at all. The surprise attack by the Dynion Gors proved effective. The Pobl

Gwir army decimated, they had no choice but to retreat to the woods.

Chariots, cavalry and infantry alike fled back into the forest, leaving behind their fallen friends and pavilions, many of which were on fire, for the safety of the trees.

"To the forest! Regroup!"

Maelgoch scoured the retreating army, searching for some sign of his queen. She had been lost to the fog and vanished amongst the attacking Dynion Gors. He cursed himself over and over as he ran, still searching. He could discern no sign of her.

With no other choice, Maelgoch sprinted headlong into the woods, stopping at the line of trees to turn around.

"My Lord!" a soldier called. He tossed Maelgoch a bow and a quiver.

The line of archers were deadly accurate, and the Fir Bolg who had given chase quickly pulled back, allowing what remained of the Pobl Gwir force to escape into the trees.

"Tá tú aon rud!" the Dynion Gors army roared in victory. The roar became a chant that echoed in the ears of the defeated as they bitterly melted away.

"Bastards," Maelgoch growled as he retreated between the trees.

Aerfyn had wisely designated a meeting point in the event of defeat near Llyn Esus, a sizeable fresh water lake deep in the woods. The well-concealed clearing had been surrounded by a glamour, hiding it from even the sharpest Dynion Gors eyes.

The glamour had been raised by Gwalchgwyn, Aerfyn's father and a very powerful Dryw. The crude magic of the Dynion Gors would not be able to bring it down.

In that clearing, Gwalchgwyn waited anxiously. His thick white eyebrows rose when he saw the fleeing army burst through the line of trees. Many were heavily wounded; fear the only thing keeping them upright. Some collapsed moments before crossing the magical line that kept the clearing hidden from unfriendly eyes.

Many a warrior carried their wounded friends and several chariots were laden with the dead and dying. Some horses, either knowing or simply running instinctively with the herd, crossed the line without their riders.

Gwalchgwyn kept his eyes on those crossing into the clearing, searching for his daughter's fire-touched head. Maelgoch crossed the line, his expression grim.

Gwalchgwyn went to him. "Aerfyn?"

Maelgoch grimaced and shook his head.

The Dryw paled, but nodded. He turned to the wounded and, with the help of a few Iachawryr, tended to the wounded. He and the healers worked all night, trying to save as many warriors as they could. All through the night, Gwalchgwyn kept an eye out for his daughter. She never arrived.

When dawn's pale blossom lightened the sky, and the last warrior was tended to, Gwalchgwyn rose to his feet with a groan.

"Tylluan," he called softly, raising a bent arm. "Tylluan, come."

From the woods, a pale barn own flew into the clearing, landing with a barely heard flap of her wings on the Dryw's raised forearm.

"Tylluan, there are survivors of the battle lost in the woods. Find them and lead them to me."

The owl bobbed her head before taking off again. Gwalchgwyn watched her flight, ignoring Maelgoch's limping approach until the lieutenant spoke.

"I am so sorry, Great Dryw," he said. "I tried to find her."

"Tell me what happened."

"A surprise attack. The Dynion Gors came around us in secret and attacked us from behind. Aerfyn was separated in the fight. Cynfarch was slain, and she was thrown to the ground. Then a sudden fog that was taller even then the tallest of the enemy shrouded all. I fought hard to reach her. I got as far as Cynfarch's corpse, but Aerfyn was nowhere in sight. Forgive me."

Gwalchgwyn listened with a frown on his face. "Cynfarch was a brave steed. His loss is deeply felt."

"He was," Maelgoch agreed. "It took two lances to fell him."

Gwalchgwyn bowed his head. "I will say a prayer for him."

Maelgoch waited in silence as Gwalchgwyn muttered sacred words. When the Dryw raised his head again, the old man had tears in his eyes.

"His herd weeps."

"Great Dryw, if it pleases you, I offer my life as payment for Aerfyn."

Gwalchgwyn turned to Maelgoch and smiled slightly. "That will not please me. You are a brave warrior, Maelgoch, and now commander of our army. We need you. Besides, I do not feel Aerfyn is dead. Gone, yes, but not dead."

"I do not understand."

"Neither do I, dear boy. I shall sleep on it, I think. Tomorrow night, Tylluan will bring any others stranded in the woods, and I must be ready to heal them. You will also need rest. Sleep now. We are all safe behind the glamour."

It was as if Gwalchgwyn's words were a command. Maelgoch immediately felt sleepy. He nodded at Gwalchgwyn and found himself a patch of grass to sleep on. Using his chequered cloak as a blanket, Maelgoch curled up and dreamt strange dreams.

Dusk woke him, but he did not feel refreshed. He stood and went in search of Gwalchgwyn. The old Dryw sat against a large rock, snoring fitfully, near the shores of Llyn Esus. Maelgoch sighed and turned away.

"Approach, young commander," Gwalchgwyn said. He opened one eye and regarded Maelgoch with a grey gaze.

"Forgive the intrusion," Maelgoch said with a bow.

"You are wondering if Tylluan has found any others?"

Maelgoch nodded. "One specifically."

"Aerfyn is not found, but hark! Tylluan comes leading four brothers."

Maelgoch blinked in surprise when the pale barn owl hooted a greeting as she glided into the clearing to land softly on Gwalchgwyn's extended arm. She twittered and bobbed, to which Gwalchgwyn nodded gravely, before taking off again.

She passed over the heads of four brothers who stumbled gratefully into the clearing, to be helped by the roused iachawyr. The healers set to task immediately.

"They are well enough," Gwalchgwyn said, settling against the rock again. His talents were not yet needed.

"What did the owl say?"

"She spied two bodies on the south shore. Cousins. They died of their wounds in the day."

Maelgoch shook his head. "No sign of Aerfyn?"

"Not yet, no. Take heart. Tylluan's search is not yet over. Come, rest by me. I desire some company."

Maelgoch smiled a little and slid down the side of the rock. He watched the sunset dance upon the calm waters of the lake for a time.

"I cannot sense her," Gwalchgwyn said, his eyes closed and his voice distant.

"Dead, then."

"No. Not dead. I can sense the dead."

"Then what? Surely she could not have vanished into thin air?"

"Perhaps, perhaps not. This is the time of Wyl yr Hydref – the year ending."

Maelgoch sat up straight. "Surely not?"

"It does seem to fit, though, does it not? Gone, but not dead?"

"Oh no! We must do something."

"If it is so, and she has fallen through the divide, then there is nothing we can do. She must find her own way home."

"But –"

"No buts, Maelgoch. She is brave and quick of wit. She will be coming home."

"Can you see the future?"

"Which one?"

"Pardon?"

"Which future would you like me to see into?"

Maelgoch scowled.

"There are an infinite number of futures, my boy," the Dryw explained. "Each one is just as likely as the other, and each depends on what every single person does."

"Do they not behave in a predictable manner?"

"Oh yes, many people do, but there is a secret that no god wishes us to know."

"And what is that?"

"We wield a considerable amount of personal power, Commander. We can *choose*. Our decisions can and often do confound the fates."

Maelgoch eyed the Dryw suspiciously. "So we do nothing?"

"For now."

"I like it not."

"That is your own business."

Maelgoch growled a few curses under his breath. It should not have surprised him that Gwalchgwyn heard. The old man chuckled and closed his eyes once more.

The pair slept in fits and starts, woken every so often by Tylluan's arrival. Every time the owl flew into the clearing, she was followed by small groups of wounded warriors, men and women both, stumbling along as best they could. The owl also brought news of survivors who were too weak to walk. On hearing it from Gwalchgwyn, Maelgoch immediately organised rescue parties and under the cover of night, they set out to bring back the heavily wounded strays.

Gwalchgwyn was once again called to action, leaving his rock by the shore and tending to the wounded trickling into the clearing.

While he worked, the aged Dryw thought of his daughter, trapped in a strange world. He prayed that she would be able to find her way home.

****

"Yo!" Harrison called from across the classroom in the Loeb building as Ethan and Mitch entered.

"Where were you last night, man?"

Ethan and Mitch exchanged a glance. "We went to Mike's Place."

"What? Why?"

"Because we found an almost dead girl," Mitch snapped irritably. "While you lot went off to Barrymore's."

"Dude, we didn't know you tripped over a dead girl."

"You would've if you bothered to stay for five minutes."

"The bus was coming!"

"She's not dead," Ethan said with a sigh. "At least, she wasn't when the ambulance came."

He sat down heavily beside Harrison, Mitch sitting beside him. He'd been feeling queasy ever since discovering the girl en route to what was supposed to be a wicked Hallowe'en bash.

28

"You look green, man," Harrison whispered as the teacher walked in.

"I feel like shit."

Ethan struggled through the hour and a half lecture on John Locke. His mind continually revisited the girl, and the amount of blood she had lost. Sweat made his palm slick and he vigorously wiped it on his jeans, having the sick feeling that it was blood that coated his hand.

When the lecture ended, Ethan was the first one out the door. He ran to the bathroom and into a stall. Taking a deep breath, he pressed his forehead against the cool steel of the stall door. Calming himself, he straightened, rolled the tension from his shoulders and exited the stall.

A girl screamed.

With a sudden, horrified realisation, Ethan found himself in the ladies washroom. His cheeks flushed bright red and he froze, looking much like a deer caught in headlights.

"Get out!" the girl shrieked, lipstick half applied.

"I'm so sorry," Ethan said in a breathy rush before running out of the washroom.

"Dude, that's the ladies," Harrison said with a laugh.

"Man, I'm worried about you. Why don't you take the day off, all right? You can have my notes." Mitch's brow furrowed as he eyed Ethan.

Ethan nodded. "Yeah. Yeah, you're probably right. I'm a little out of it." He started walking towards Dundas House, his expression a little vague.

"I'll see you tonight," Mitch called after him.

Ethan raised a hand in acknowledgement.

Shaking his head, Mitch turned and went to his next lecture. Harrison followed, still chuckling.

Before Ethan had time to find his sense of direction, a blonde boy with thick glasses and a long face stepped in front of him holding a pen and pad.

"Hi," he said. "My name's Mark Crapp."

"I bet it is," Ethan mumbled.

"Sorry?"

"Nothing."

"I'm with *The Charlatan*, and I was wondering if you'd answer a few questions regarding the girl you found last night?"

"Wha...?"

"A report in the Ottawa Citizen this morning said the police thought the girl was attacked by someone wielding an axe. As the person who found the likely first victim of an axe-wielding psychopath, how do you feel?"

"Go away," Ethan growled.

The boy scribbled something down. "Are you afraid for your life, knowing there's some psycho on campus?"

Ethan pushed the boy. "I said go away!" he shouted, before marching away in a temper. Students scattered from his path.

"No comment," Mark Crapp said primly as he scribbled the words onto the notepad.

****

Aerfyn opened her eyes. Bright, mid-morning light shone through an enormous, glass-filled opening in the wall on her left. On her right, a very pale blue curtain hung from a steel rod. The ceiling was some bizarre mix of vaguely beige rectangular panels set into thin white lines that appeared to have no joins. One panel held a rectangular transparent box containing two long tubes that glowed with a bright blue-white light.

She scowled. Never before had she seen this magic. What thing other than the moon shone with such a light without even so much as a flicker? She took a deep breath. The air smelled strange, almost like stale piss, but not as sharp

Unable to cope with her strange surrounds, she closed her eyes again.

****

Constable Bill Jackman strode through the doors of Montfort Hospital purposefully. The hospital had contacted him and said that the Jane Doe that had been transferred there last night should be close to waking up. A nurse reported seeing the girl's eyes flutter open briefly.

It was enough. The lack of evidence was beginning to irk him, and he needed her statement. Besides, it gave him a good excuse to get away from doing paperwork. If he'd known how much paperwork was involved in being a police officer, he'd have opted for carpentry.

He made a quick stop at the Tim Horton's café in the lobby before heading up to the elevators. Over the few years he'd been a cop, he had become well used to this particular hospital. He'd investigated most of the emergency cases that ended up at Montfort.

"Hello, Bill!" a nurse greeted cheerily from behind the central desk on the third floor.

"Morning, Nancy," Bill replied with a smile. "She awake yet?"

"No. She had a look around this morning, though. Seemed a bit disoriented, unsurprisingly. I dare say she'll wake up again soon."

"I guess she didn't say anything, then?"

"No. What would she have said?"

"A name might've been nice."

Nurse Nancy laughed a musical laugh.

"I'll just go sit in the room, then," Bill said, and he did.

He unwrapped his bagel and took a bite. Leaning back on the chair, he cast his gaze at the girl in the bed. An I.V. dripped steadily into her right arm. He started, almost dropping his bagel, when he saw a pair of pale brown eyes staring right back at him.

"Hello," he said with a small smile.

****

Aerfyn stared. The man before her had kindly blue eyes and ash blonde hair. He seemed harmless enough, though he dressed strangely; entirely in black with strange sigils sewn onto the fabric. He wore a thick, black cloth breastplate, a nonsensical item. What good could cloth do against a sword?

He spoke. The word was unfamiliar – neither the language of the Pobl Gwir nor that of the Dynion Gors. Where could she be? The man turned his head and called.

****

"Nurse!" Bill shouted. "Nancy? She's awake!"

32

Nancy scurried into the room and met the confused and suspicious gaze of the young woman in the bed.

"Well, good morning, sweetheart!" she said brightly, her round face lighting up with a smile. "How are you feeling?"

The girl simply stared, a scowl painted on her pale face.

Nancy's smile slipped a little. She tried again in French. "Vous sentez-vous bien?"

The girl continued to stare.

Nancy and Bill exchanged a glance. "C'est correct," she said, moving to the bedside. "I'm here to look after you."

She checked the I.V. drip. Following her movements, the girl discovered she was connected to the drip and panicked. She cried out and reached over to disconnect herself. Nancy caught her wrist, and a hard struggle ensued.

"Atal!" the girl cried out in distress. "Atal!"

"Help!" Nancy cried out.

Bill was at the bed immediately, pulling the girl away from Nancy and holding her down. For someone who'd lost so much blood, she was surprisingly strong. She squirmed and cried out, both in pain and panic.

"Hold her! I'm going to sedate!" Nancy fled the room to fetch a syringeful of medicine. She returned shortly and injected something into the I.V. tube.

It didn't take long for the girl's panicked struggles to weaken and her eyes droop.

"Atal," she whispered as tears spilled down her cheeks. "At..."

Just to be on the safe side, Bill continued to hold her until he was certain she wouldn't start screaming again.

"The poor girl," Nancy said, her bun now in disarray. "Probably suffering from post traumatic stress."

"What the hell does 'atal' mean?" Bill demanded.

Nancy shrugged. "I don't know. It's not French."

"Damn it," Bill hissed. "Now I have to find an interpreter. Of course I do. This couldn't be easy for me. No."

"Well, at least you're not unconscious in some hospital somewhere." Nancy pressed her lips into a line and glared pointedly at Bill as she rearranged her hair.

"I'm taking her prints."

"You can't do that without her consent."

"She's unconscious, Nancy. She won't know."

"She's not under arrest, Bill."

"Whatever. If I can find out where she lives, perhaps a member of her family can interpret for me."

"Bill…"

"Shush."

Nancy rolled her eyes and left the room. The doctors would need an interpreter, and she intended to find one.

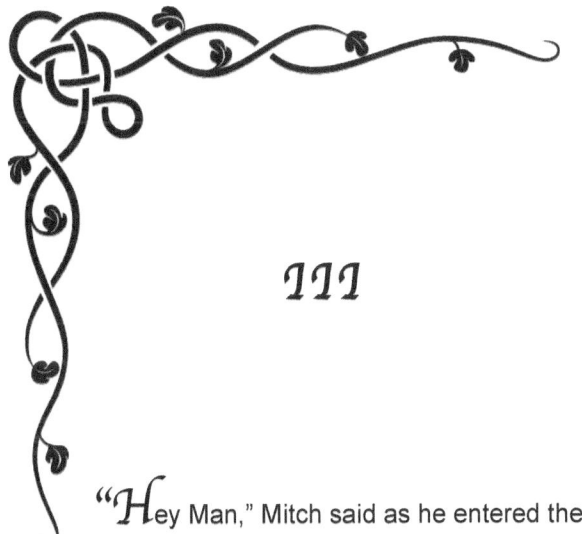

𝟑𝟑𝟑

"*H*ey Man," Mitch said as he entered the dorm room he shared with Ethan. "Sleep well?"

Ethan grunted. "Not really."

"Still sick?"

"A bit."

"You need to eat."

"Ugh! Don't mention food."

"C'mon, man. I'm taking you to the caf."

Ethan sighed and nodded. As much as his stomach rolled, he was hungry, and perhaps if he ate something, his stomach would cease to convulse. Together they walked in silence through the tunnels that connected the various buildings of the university.

Gordon rounded the tunnel corner and nearly slammed into them.

"Hey," he said.

"Hey," Ethan and Mitch replied in unison.

"I was on my way to find you guys. Did you read the Ottawa Citizen this morning?"

"No, why?"

"There's feature on that girl we found. The cops don't know who she is. She apparently doesn't speak English or French. The cops have put a call out to anyone who might know her identity."

"Oh, man!" Mitch breathed. "Poor girl."

"Yeah," Ethan agreed. "That really sucks."

"Has that cop called either of you?" Gordon asked, joining them as they resumed their walk to the cafeteria.

"No," Ethan said. "Why? Did he call you?"

"No. I just thought he'd be keeping us up-to-date. You know, since we found her."

"I bet we're probably suspects right now," Mitch said.

Gordon paled. "That'll be one phone call my mom would hate to get. 'Hey mom, love you lots, I'm going to jail.'"

"They can't arrest us," Mitch said. "They've got nothing."

"You sound guilty," Gordon teased.

Mitch threw a punch.

"Stop it," Ethan snapped. "It's not a joke."

"Whatever, man." Mitch put his hands in his pockets and sulked. They spent the rest of their journey in silence.

****

Biter Feargach growled bitterly. There were too many of them, like vermin under a log. He had managed to trace the scent of the two men to one building. Of the plethora of fragrances within, the queen's scent had not been among them. Now, he and his two comrades were wrapped in their grey-brown cloaks, nestled in the trees and shrubs across the road from the Staecie Building, unnoticed. He cursed the steady, cold drizzle as he pondered his next move.

Their cloaks served as something of a glamour. Fir Bolg magic allowed them to pass completely unnoticed, though not invisible, by the unwary eye - provided they remained completely still.

They had been there for two days. In the night, they travelled a little, searching for some way into the building without being seen. The loud, often drunk residents of the building foiled every attempt. All they could do was sit in the brush and wait.

Biter Feargach sniffed the air occasionally, trying to detect the scent of the two males he had picked up two nights ago. In the throng of often unwashed students, it was nigh on impossible.

Still, those two males were the best lead he had, and the quickest route to the queen.

****

Bill returned to the Montfort Hospital the following day, eager to try and talk to the very young Jane Doe. When he arrived the girl was very much awake, and had plainly been crying.

Nurse Nancy sat on her bed and sang softly to her, something the girl seemed to appreciate for she looked calmer now. Her large brown eyes noted Bill's arrival first. Nancy didn't bother to greet the constable until she finished her song. Then she squeezed the girl's hand and slid off the bed.

"Morning, Constable," she said.

"Morning. How is she?"

"Confused. Frightened. Lost. Poor thing." Nancy turned to the girl and smiled. "Nancy," she said.

The girl nodded in affirmation. They had been through this before.

Nancy went to Bill and put a hand on his shoulder. "William."

The girl looked at Bill and frowned. "William."

"So formal," Bill muttered.

"Well, it's your given name. You should be used to it," Nancy said primly.

Bill grimaced. "William," he said with a nod.

The girl touched her chest. "Aerfyn."

"Air-vin," Bill repeated. It was his turn to frown. He turned to Nancy. "What the hell kind of name is Airvin?"

"Look, it's the name she answers to. I just got her calm, so don't upset her, all right?"

"Does she understand English?"

Nancy shook her head. "But, we've been able to communicate pretty well regardless. Just use a lot of hand signals."

"What, like sign language?"

"No, you idiot. Just hand signals."

Bill shrugged. "Okay. If you say so." He smiled at Aerfyn and stepped forward. She shrank back in her bed a little and cast a glance at Nancy. The nurse smiled reassuringly.

"Hi," Bill said awkwardly. "Uh… who hurt you?"

Aerfyn stared at him with a scowl. Bill tried again, this time indicating on himself the position of Aerfyn's wound.

"Who did this?" he said slowly.

Aerfyn's hand went to her upper torso where the wound was and the spark of understanding hit her eyes.

"Clwyf," she said.

Bill looked at Nancy and back again to Aerfyn. "Who is Clwiv?"

Aerfyn made a sawing motion with her hand. "Clwyf, clwyf."

"She's talking about her wound, Bill," Nancy supplied.

"So 'clwiv' is the word for wound?"

"It looks like."

Bill rubbed his forehead. "This is a nightmare." He dropped his hand. "All right. Who 'clwiv'?" He made a similar sawing motion to Aerfyn.

The girl merely cocked her head. "Hoo-clwyf?"

"Um. Let's see." He dug around his pockets for the piece of paper with the photos of his three major suspects and handed it to Aerfyn.

She took it gingerly, and only after a glance at Nancy. She froze when she looked at the paper. The likenesses of three men were somehow painted on in such detail they looked as if they had been captured and put into tiny invisible boxes with an observation window. She reached out and touched each one. No paint came off on her fingers. She sniffed the paper and wrinkled her nose. She pulled it away from her face quickly.

Aerfyn flipped the paper over several times. She turned it upside down, held it up against the light, shook it and even tasted it before looking inquisitively up at Bill.

Bill pointed to one picture. "He clwiv you?" he asked making the sawing motion when he said 'clwyf' and pointing at Aerfyn when he said 'you.'

Understanding flooded across Aerfyn's features. She shook her head and handed the paper back to Bill.

"Dynion Gors."

Bill scowled. "Din-yon gorz?"

Aerfyn nodded. "Dynion Gors."

Bill turned the paper and pointed at the topmost picture again. Aerfyn shook her head. Bill pointed at the next one down. Again Aerfyn shook her head, her frown returning.

She was thoroughly annoyed when he pointed to the final picture. "Naddo," she said.

"Nah-tho," Bill repeated. "I'm guessing that means no."

"Naddo. Dynion Gors. Dynion Gors."

"Din-yon gorz. What is that? I don't understand!"

Aerfyn growled and snatched back the paper. She flipped it over and put it on her lap. "Cwilsen," she demanded of Nancy.

Nancy shook her head. "I don't understand."

"Cwilsen, cwilsen!" Aerfyn insisted holding her thumb and forefinger above the paper on her lap and wriggling her wrist.

Bill undid the breast pocket and pulled out a pen. He handed it to Aerfyn, who took it with a confused look on her face. "Lliw?"

"Here," Bill said, taking the pen and paper back. He undid the lid and scribbled a mark on the paper.

Aerfyn's face lit up. She took both back and tried to draw with the pen on her lap. The pen punctured the paper.

Bill dragged the bedside table across and put the paper on it. Aerfyn tried again with greater success. When the pen wrote, she seemed surprised, but didn't stop long to marvel at it.

Bill watched with interest as Aerfyn sketched a surprisingly detailed image of a strange, skinny man in a dark hood with long, pointed teeth and holding a double-bitted battle-axe. His face fell when he took the paper back.

"Oh dear," he said.

"What is it?" Nancy asked, moving to Bill's side to peek over his shoulder. The image was childishly drawn, but no doubt a monster of some kind.

"Oh dear," she said.

Bill sighed. He folded the paper, slid it into the pocket with the image of the three suspects, and looked sadly at Aerfyn. She seemed too pretty to be insane.

Sublimely unaware of her interviewer's disappointment with her, Aerfyn leant back on her pillows, a supremely satisfied smile hovering about her lips.

"Dynion Gors," she said as if it was perfectly reasonable.

41

Bill smiled tightly. "Thank-you, Airvin."

"William," she replied. She yawned.

"It's lunch time," Nancy said quietly.

Bill nodded. "I have to take this back to the station anyway."

Nancy nodded. "I'll get the psychiatrist down tomorrow."

"Good idea. I want to be there, though."

Nancy sighed. "What a shame," she said sadly, echoing Bill's sentiments precisely.

With the victim of the attack being a gibberish-speaking schizophrenic, this case was going to be the most challenging he'd ever encountered.

****

True to her word, Nancy made an appointment with a psychiatrist for the following day. Bill sat in the room with Nancy as he awaited the man. Aerfyn slept soundly. She looked stronger than yesterday, though Nancy had noted that she had woken screaming in the morning.

The psychiatrist arrived without ceremony. He was a small man, Bill noted, with a rat-like face that was nonetheless open and inviting. Evidently, he and Nancy knew each other well.

"Hello, dear," he said amiably, patting Nancy in a fatherly manner on her hand.

"Jeff," Nancy said. "Thanks so much for coming down."

"My pleasure, dear. I'm assuming this is the patient?"

"Yes."

"Right. Well, before I interview her, I'd like to interview you both, if you don't mind."

"Of course."

"Nancy first."

Bill watched as Jeff and Nancy left the room. With a sigh, he sat down on the chair in the corner and watched Aerfyn sleep. Insanity was a strange condition. Nothing about Aerfyn now suggested she was anything more than a recovering assault victim. Yet, Bill knew that when she woke she'd be speaking her made-up language and talking about the existence of monsters.

Some minutes later, Nancy returned and sent Bill out into the hall.

"Officer," Jeff greeted with a smile.

Bill simply nodded a greeting. A small sweat broke out on his brow and Bill silently chastised himself. He had stared down the barrel of a sawn-off and kept cool. Yet in the presence of a psychologist, he'd turned into a nervous wreck.

"It's all right, Officer. I'm not here to diagnose you."

"Sorry," Bill said. "I was nervous when they did my assessment for the force as well."

"Hm. Nancy said the patient had an interesting idea about who attacked her?"

"Yes. She drew some weird skinny man with sharp teeth and a battle-axe."

"Do you have the picture?"

Bill grunted and pulled out the paper from his pocket. He handed it over to Jeff who examined it for a while.

"And what did she call this creature?"

"Din-yon gorz."

"What now?"

"Precisely."

"I see. And in your opinion, she totally believed that this creature attacked her?"

"She seemed completely genuine," Bill said. "I don't think this is a prank by some bored teenager."

"Nancy told me they've run a full blood test and it came up clean."

"Yes."

"No drugs?"

"No drugs, no alcohol, nothing."

"Troubling."

"You're troubled? I have to try and find the person who attacked her. How am I supposed to go looking for a fictitious creature with a nonsensical name?"

Jeff snuffed a short laugh. "She was attacked on Hallowe'en, was she not?"

"Yes."

"Could this not have been a costume?"

"We're looking into it. No one on the campus recalls seeing someone dressed like this, and the major suspects until yesterday were all dressed as werewolves."

"Teammates, no doubt."

"Yes. How did you know?"

Jeff simply smiled and tapped his temple with one finger.

Bill rolled his eyes. "Right."

"Sorry to interrupt," Nancy said, sticking her head out the door. "She's awake now."

Jeff nodded. "Coming."

He entered the room and smiled at the girl who now sat upright and played with the plastic bracelet around her wrist.

"Hello," Jeff said.

The girl simply looked at him.

"Jeff," he said placing his palm flat against his chest.

"Aerfyn," the girl said, mimicking the motion.

Jeff smiled. The girl's serious, and curious, expression did not change. She observed him with keenly intelligent eyes. Jeff did much the same before saying, "Do you understand me?"

Aerfyn looked at Nancy with a quizzical expression before turning back to Jeff. She remained silent.

Jeff pulled out a map of Canada and laid it out before Aerfyn. She looked at it with a slight frown.

"Canada," he said, indicating the mass of land on the picture.

Aerfyn looked up. "Canada," she repeated slowly. "Canada, " she said again, pointing to the ground. Her voice held the constricted tone of disbelief.

Jeff smiled and nodded.

Tears welled in Aerfyn's eyes and she looked down at the map again. The land mass was entirely unfamiliar. The shape of the land, it's size and the dizzying number of strange markings that must surely have some important meaning made her heart sink. She was horribly lost in a land that was not her own. How was she supposed to get home?

"This has upset you," Jeff said. He made some notes in a small notepad. Aerfyn looked up.

"Cwilsen," she said, reaching out.

Jeff frowned. "Sorry?"

"It means pen, we think," Nancy supplied.

Jeff raised his brows and slowly handed Aerfyn his pen. Aerfyn took it with a small, grateful smile and flipped the map over. She scowled when the reverse side proved to be more markings.

Nancy scrambled to find a piece of paper. Aerfyn waited patiently until a sheet was placed before her on the bedside table. She bent over the table and scribbled quickly. Once finished, she handed the sheet to Jeff.

"Annwfyn," she said.

"An-noo-vin," Jeff repeated slowly. He looked down at the vaguely lupine shape on the paper.

"Jeff, Canada," she said with an affirmative nod. "Aerfyn, Annwfyn."

The mousy psychologist frowned and pointed at Aerfyn. "Aerfyn." He pointed at the map. "Annwfyn."

Aerfyn nodded.

Jeff smiled reassuringly at her and jotted down more notes. He then took out the drawing Aerfyn did yesterday and unfolded it. He put it on the table. Aerfyn's reaction was immediate. Her expression hardened significantly.

"Dynion Gors," she said in a tone of deep repulsion.

"This," Jeff said, pointing at the picture. "Hurt you?" He pointed at her.

Aerfyn cocked her head as she tried to puzzle out the words. She made two fists. "Dynion Gors," she said, moving her right fist. "Pobl Gwir – Aerfyn." She shook her left fist. Then she butted fists together.

"I see," Jeff said. He made notes, stopping briefly to rub one finger across his forehead. "Constable, am I correct in saying that Aerfyn's costume was, in fact, actual armour?"

"It was."

"And Nancy, the surgeon said the wound looked as if it was made by a slightly blunt blade like an axe, correct?"

"Yes," Nancy answered.

"Interesting."

"What is?" Bill asked.

"Well, she has her own language, and her own world inhabited with monsters with which she was or is currently battling. It appears that she is suffering from schizophrenia, and it might be quite severe, if she is no longer capable of distinguishing reality from the fantasy world she's created."

"So... now what?"

"Well, I would refer her to the Royal. It's a fine institution for the treatment of mental health issues. The problem there is that it's a short-term stay facility. Without somewhere to go..."

"We're trying to locate her family," Bill said wearily. "It's a little difficult when she has no I.D. No one has come forward to claim her so far."

"Poor girl. The best I can suggest for now is medication. I will write a prescription right away. I'll also write the referral to the Royal, but I'd advise against admitting her until her family can be located."

Nancy nodded. "Thank-you so much for this, Jeff."

"My pleasure." Jeff scribbled an illegible prescription on his pad, tore it off and handed it to Nancy. "Call me again if her situation changes. Schizophrenics can sometimes get quite violent."

"Of course."

"Well. Good day."

"Bye."

With that, Jeff vanished from the hospital room. Bill cast his eyes to the ceiling. "Great. Just great."

"It's not her fault, Bill," Nancy chided.

"Well, it's not mine either."

"Shouldn't you be writing this up, or something?"

"And that's the other thing – paperwork!"

Nancy smiled. "You think you have it rough. You should try being a nurse one day."

Bill grunted. "I should go."

"You probably should."

Bill smiled at Aerfyn before leaving the room. Nancy smiled at her and sat beside her on the bed. "I've visited the Royal," she said conversationally. "You'll like it there. It's a beautiful place. There's a lovely courtyard, and gardens, and things. The place is exceptionally bright and airy. Quite beautiful, actually. There's even a butterfly sanctuary."

Nancy kept her tone light and conversational, fearful that Aerfyn might guess that everyone thought her insane.

Aerfyn had been swift to pick up on the purpose of Jeff's visit, what it was he did, and precisely what he thought of her. Her quick mind ran through several scenarios and before Nurse Nancy had finished telling her of the wonderful space that was the Royal Ottawa Mental Health Centre, she had devised a plan of escape.

****

"Yo, man, did you read the paper this morning?"

Harrison asked, throwing a copy of the morning's Ottawa Citizen on the table in front of Ethan. The team sat at a large table in Oliver's on the first floor of the Uni Centre after practice. Harrison arrived much later, having had a meeting with an academic advisor.

Ethan scowled and pulled the paper towards him. The headline read: 'Jane Doe Victim Escapes Montfort, Could Be Dangerous.'

"Oh man," Ethan murmured. He picked the paper up and began reading the article in earnest.

"What is it?" Gordon asked.

"Yo, the girl we found has escaped the hospital last night. No one knows how. She was there one minute and gone the next. Apparently she's been diagnosed as schizophrenic and could be dangerous. She was supposed to be moved to the Royal."

"Holy shit!"

"I know, right?"

"Yo," Harrison said. "If there's a reward, we should go looking for her."

"Reward? This isn't the Wild West, you moron," Mitch said.

"They sometimes offer rewards."

"Well, there isn't one," Ethan said. "But there's a hotline number in case she's been sighted."

"Well call them and ask if there's a reward." Harrison grinned.

"Stop it with the reward stuff," Ethan snapped. "Jesus!"

Mitch's cell phone rang.

"That'll be the raging bitch," Gordon said.

"Shut up!" Mitch replied. He flipped open his phone and, rising from his seat, answered. "Hi, hon."

Everyone at the table rolled their eyes. They fell silent, eagerly eavesdropping on Mitch's conversation.

"I'm out with the boys. We had practice, remember?"

"Come home at once," Harrison said quietly, making his voice unnaturally high. Snickers erupted from the table. Mitch ignored them.

"No... No... Sweetie, I told you. We always go... No, I didn't! ... But I... Oh, c'mon... Babe? Are you crying? Oh, don't cry... Okay, I'm coming over. No... No... Don't worry. ...Yeah. I'll be there soon... Okay. Love you too. Okay. Bye."

As soon as Mitch hung up, the table erupted into mocking versions of him.

"Man, you are so whipped," Harrison crowed.

Mitch scowled. "Shut up."

"Bye, hon," Harrison said, his voice rising into a mocking falsetto again. "How are my balls, anyway? You're keeping them safe, aren't you?"

"Laugh all you want," Mitch said. "I'm the one getting laid tonight."

That shut everyone up. Grinning, Mitch started for the door.

"Hang on," Ethan said. "I'll go with."

"Dude, I know where the stop is. I don't need an escort."

"Yeah, well, I need the walk."

"Hey, if you see that crazy chick-" Harrison started.

"Shut up," Mitch and Ethan said in unison. They exchanged an irritated look, then started for the door.

The evening greeted the pair frostily. A damp wind whipped in from the east, carrying with it the threat of snow. Ethan pulled his brown leather jacket closed and zipped it up.

"Hey man," Mitch said. "Do you reckon they'll find her?"

"The girl you mean?"

"Yeah."

"Hopefully."

"I had an uncle who was schizophrenic. He ended up killing the neighbour's dog because he thought it was an alien spy."

Ethan scoffed. "Sorry man," he said after Mitch cast him an evil glare. "That's kinda funny."

"Dude, you suck."

"Yeah, but I don't swallow."

51

"The stop's here, man."

"Let's go to the Bronson one. I want to walk a bit."

Mitch shrugged. "Suit yourself."

****

Biter Feargach sniffed the air. He had decided to explore the grounds again now that it was dark. He stood in the small cluster of firs where the scent of the enemy queen still lingered. He had come back to think. There had to be a way to lure the males who knew where the queen was out from the reeking building in which they lived.

His mind had been on that very thought when the familiar scent of them reached his nose. He turned his head and went rigid, his large, bulbous eyes searching for them.

They appeared shortly after, deep voices talking quietly between themselves. One stood quite tall and broad. The other, several inches shorter and nowhere near as broad, strolled along beside him. They strode casually, unarmed and unaware. Biter Feargach grinned a sharp-toothed grin.

The naïve fools.

The Fir Bolg warrior did not stop to ponder what sort of idyllic world he must have stumbled into, where people need not walk about armed and armoured, constantly on their guard. He crouched down and slunk forward on all fours, watching the boys carefully as they walked past him completely oblivious to his presence.

He continued to watch as they turned right, walked to a strange shelter made of very clear glass and then stopped. There they leant casually against the glass walls.

Biter Feargach whistled low, calling his two comrades to him. After a few brief moments, they slithered carefully into the firs with practiced silence. Their commander indicated with a nod in the direction of the boys that he had found his prey. Together they exited the firs. Standing upright, the hoods of their cloaks hiding their faces save for their grinning, sharp-toothed mouths, they walked forward.

Biter Feargach unslung his axe.

****

Ethan leant against the outside of the bus shelter, one foot up and pressed against the glass. He shoved his hands in his pockets and closed his eyes.

"You all right, Man?" Mitch asked, his right shoulder pressed against the corner of the shelter.

"Yeah. It's just. I mean, that girl, man. She was hurt bad. What kind of asshole attacks a girl who's not all there, you know?"

Mitch shrugged. He felt someone tap his shoulder hard three times and glanced around. His first glance revealed three tall, skinny men in cloaks with hoods that hid their faces. The one closest to Mitch, who must have tapped him, held an enormous double-bitted axe.

Mitch didn't register the sight fully at the first glance. He frowned at the three men as if they were a minor annoyance before realisation made him jump, swear and spin around simultaneously.

"What?" Ethan asked, glancing over. "Shit!" He turned to face the three, cloaked men.

All three grinned, revealing yellow, sharply pointed piranha-type teeth. The foremost one hoisted his axe and swung it in a wide sweep at Mitch. Mitch jumped backwards, banging into Ethan, yet managing to miss what promised to be a nasty, slow death from spilled innards.

With a shriek, the other two hooded men leapt forward.

Ethan had never been in a fight before in his life. The only thing that kept him upright for the first two minutes happened to be his lacrosse training. It didn't help him for long, however. He found himself pinned to the ground, one of the cloaked creatures on top of him, holding him down with a strength that seemed disproportionately formidable for its slender frame.

Mitch fell immediately, and now struggled and screamed as one of the creatures held him down and the other with the axe stood over him.

"Áit a bhfuil sí?" the axe-wielding monster demanded in a deep, gravely voice.

Mitch just screamed.

"Áit a bhfuil sí?"

Ethan fell still as he watched. His mind turned blank, shock and disbelief taking over.

A pale figure wearing a light blue robe tied at the waist with twine flew through the air from Bronson, taking the axe-wielding beast to the ground. With a shriek, the creatures holding Ethan and Mitch released their prizes and went after it. Ethan rolled over and scrambled to his feet. He ran over to Mitch and helped him up.

The boys watched as the figure fought the monsters, a blonde braid flying as she ducked swiftly between bodies, lashing out skilfully with her fists and feet. Ethan recognised her right away. His jaw dropped.
Shock kept both boys where they were. They watched as

the girl fought. It was evident she knew how to fight well. The three monsters were kept expertly at bay.

The girl glanced over at them briefly, after kicking one of the creatures away.

"Ffoi!" she yelled.

"What?" Mitch asked Ethan.

"I think she means 'run.'"

The boys needn't be told twice. Terrified, the pair fled back towards Dundas House. Ethan stopped when he reached the tunnel beneath the O-train tracks, fear making his eyes wide. He looked back.

"Ethan!" Mitch called from halfway in the tunnel. "Come on!"

Ethan swore and started running back.

"Hey, man! Where are you going?"

"She needs help!" Ethan shouted back as he ran.

Mitch, still halfway in the underpass, hesitated. Instinct told him to run like hell. Friendship told him to go back and help. Torn between the two, he stood dumbly in the tunnel until, chastising himself furiously for being a coward, he turned and followed Ethan.

Ethan did not know how to use an axe or a sword, but he knew how to use a stick. He picked up a sturdy stick as he approached, pausing briefly when he reached the fight. The girl was bleeding above the eye, and the side of her adjusted hospital gown was covered in blood. Still, she fought as if she could not even feel the wounds.

"Hey!" Ethan yelled before coming down hard on the closest monster's head with his stick. The creature stumbled away from the fight. Ethan swung hard into the stomach of the next creature.

Though Ethan had contacted solidly, the beast seemed to hardly feel it. It grabbed the stick and wrenched it from his grasp. Tossing the stick aside, it advanced on Ethan, who backed slowly away. Behind him, the one he had struck on the head closed the distance, having recovered.

Mitch threw a rock with well-practiced accuracy, striking the one behind Ethan on the side of the head, before running at the other one with a roar, a stick in his hand.

Ethan retrieved his makeshift weapon, and turned to face the one Mitch had hit as it recovered and leapt forward.

The girl fought the one with the heavy axe, Mitch and Ethan both faced one each. The odds now even, the monsters seemed unsure.

"Come on, you ugly son of a bitch!" Ethan said through clenched teeth. "Come and eat my stick."

A high whistle from the one with the axe and the monsters fled.

"Yeah!" Mitch screamed after them. "That's right! You pussies!"

Ethan grinned over at Mitch, feeling suddenly exhilarated before turning to the girl. His smile fell.

She knelt on the pavement, not caring about the shattered glass that littered the ground beneath her knees, her head bowed, her breathing ragged and her hand pressed firmly on her bleeding side.

"Shit," Ethan said. He dropped his stick and ran to her. "Mitch, give me a hand."

Mitch turned and saw the girl. His lopsided grin vanished and he ran to her side. He and Ethan helped the girl to her feet. She managed to stumble forwards a few steps before falling again.

"Man, she's heavy!" Mitch said as he helped her into Ethan's arms.

"Yo, your jacket."

"What?"

"Wrap your jacket around her."

"What? Why?"

"Because she's covered in blood, and we're carrying her right onto campus, you dumb ass."

"What about your jacket?"

Ethan growled and placed the girl down again. She leant heavily against him, fighting to keep her feet. Ethan carefully removed his jacket and dressed her in it before picking her up again.

"Sooo drunk," Ethan said with a smile as another student passed on his way to the bus stop.

The student, having been there himself, grinned. "Lucky she's with her mates," he said in a thick Australian drawl.

"Yeah," Mitch agreed. "Lucky us."

Ethan shook his head at Mitch and strode off towards their room in Dundas House. A few concerned students enquired after her and Ethan's bright laugh assured them that she was just drunk as hell. It remained dark enough, and fellow students remained oblivious enough not to notice Ethan and Mitch's own wounds until they entered the brightly lit Dundas House.

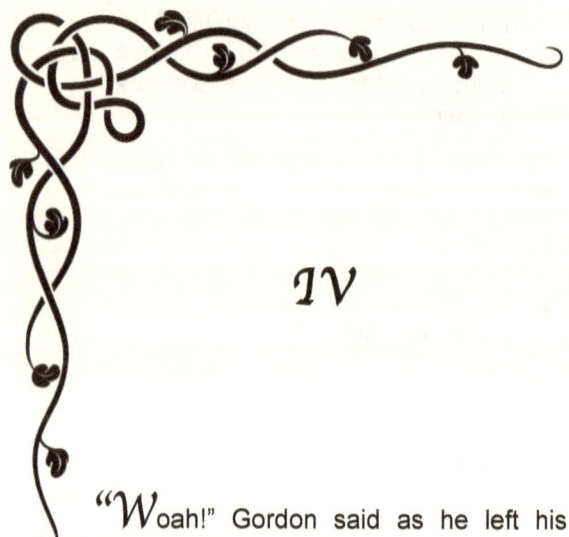

IV

"*W*oah!" Gordon said as he left his room. "What the hell happened to you guys? Wait... is that... is that the *crazy girl*?"

"Shut up," Ethan growled.

"Follow," Mitch said.

Bemused, Gordon followed his teammates to their room.

Ethan laid the girl on his bed. "Get my first aid kit."

"First aid?" Before Gordon had a chance to ask why, Ethan removed his jacket, revealing a spreading bloodstain on the girl's pale blue gown.

"Jesus!" Gordon breathed. "What the fuck happened?"

"We were attacked," Ethan said, taking the bag Mitch handed him.

The girl had put on her hospital gown backwards so it opened at the front before tying the twine. It made it infinitely easier for Ethan to access her wound. He started to undo the knot that bound the gown closed.

The girl's bloodied hand snapped over his wrist. Ethan looked up in surprise. The girl's pale brown eyes were opened and sharply focused on him.

He smiled slightly. "I need to get at this wound," he said gently. He touched the centre of the blood patch gently.

The girl slowly nodded and released Ethan's wrist. He finished undoing the knot and pulled the robe aside slightly. She was completely naked beneath, though Ethan tried hard to keep as much of her covered as possible.

What was revealed was a strong, muscular frame.

"Attacked by who?" Gordon managed when he recovered from the shock of what Ethan said, and the sight of what was revealed beneath the hospital gown.

"Attacked by what would be a better question," Mitch said. His voice trembled and his face looked dangerously green. He sank onto his bed and watched as Ethan cleaned the wound with a sterile pad and saline solution.

"What?"

"Precisely," Ethan said.

"I don't understand."

"I'm not surprised."

"Shut up."

"Look, they were tall, taller even than Ethan. And they were skinny, and kinda grey coloured. One of them had a battle axe."

"*What?!*"

"A battle axe, man. Straight out of Dungeons and Dragons. I mean, man were they ever freaky! They all wore hoods, and when they smiled..." Mitch shuddered.

"What? What happened when they smiled?"

"Fangs, man. A whole row of yellow fangs – like those fish from the Amazon. The ones that eat people."

"No freakin' way."

"It's true." Ethan put aside the bloodied cloth and examined the cleaned wound. "Well, it's the one she had when we found her the first time. It used to be stitched."

"The first... you mean... this is *the* girl. The one the cops are offering a reward for?"

"There is no reward," Mitch said automatically.

"You breathe a word of this, Gordo, and I'll have your scalp," Ethan snapped.

"He can do that, you know," Mitch drawled. "His great grandmother was a plains Indian."

"Ojibwa," Ethan said.

Gordon scoffed, but his disbelief melted when Ethan threw him an evil glare. "And for the record, they didn't scalp anyone."

Mitch grinned. "Whatever you say, redskin."

"You're an ass," Ethan grumbled. He turned back to the wound and dressed it with a polysporan smeared sterile pad held in place with micropore tape. "That's the best I can do for now."

"Yo, man. That girl needs a doctor. We should take her to hospital." Gordon eyed the girl suspiciously.

"No," Ethan said firmly. He turned to Mitch and Gordon. "Look, she saved our asses from those monsters."

"The cops say she's crazy – and dangerous!"

"They probably think she's crazy because she told them about those monsters. And I can guarantee you she is dangerous. She can fight like nothing I've ever seen."

"What are we going to do, then?" Mitch asked.

Ethan shrugged. "First, we're going to help her get better. Then we're going to get her back to wherever she came from. What we aren't going to do is turn her over to the police."

"And just how are we supposed to get her back to wherever she came from?"

Ethan shrugged. "I don't know, man! We'll cross that bridge when we come to it. For now, we've got to get rid of this hospital gown. Hand me a T-shirt or something will you?"

Mitch sighed. He went to Ethan's drawer and pulled out a simple black T-shirt with AC/DC in golden letters across the chest. He threw it at Ethan, who deftly caught it, then wrapped his arm around the girl and helped her sit up. It took a great deal of effort from both of them. Ethan looked at his friends with a frown.

"Turn around," he said.

"But – " Gordon complained.

"Turn. Around."

"Not fair," Gordon grumbled as Mitch grabbed his shoulder and physically turned him. The pair stared at the door for what felt like an age before Ethan said, "All right, you can turn around again."

They did and found the girl dressed and wrapped in a blanket on Ethan's bed. Ethan hurriedly stuffed the bloodied hospital gown into a hempen grocery bag. "We need to find a way to burn this," he said.

"Dude, I'm too tired to do anything more," Mitch said. "I'm calling it a night."

No sooner had he spoken than his cell phone rang. He took it from his pocket and stared down at it.

"Shit," he said. He flipped it open and, wincing, said, "Hi, hun."

Ethan and Gordon rolled their eyes simultaneously. Mitch strode into the bathroom to avoid their mocking remarks.

"I'm going to bed," Gordon said.

"Don't breathe a word. I'm warning you."

Gordon nodded. "My lips are sealed. Let me know if I can help, though."

Ethan nodded, but said nothing. Gordon left the room and Ethan went to the washroom.

"Out," he told a stricken-looking Mitch. "I need to shower."

Mitch left the washroom, still on the phone. "No babe, it's not like that. I went to the bus stop, but... Honey... Please stop crying."

Ethan shook his head and shut the door. "What a chump."

When he left the shower, Mitch was sitting on his bed, looking dejected.

"Everything okay?" Ethan asked, more from duty than any real concern. He wore nothing but his boxers. They were his version of pajamas.

Mitch shook his head. "She's really mad, man. I'm going to have to do something extra special now."

"Dude, you are so whipped!"

"She's upset, all right?"

"You've just had the snot beaten out of you, and she only cares about herself. You can do so much better, man."

"Shut up. Don't talk like that about her."

"Whatever, dude. Yo, you still have that blow-up mattress Harrison lent you when we went camping?"

"Yeah. It's folded under my bed."

"Can I use it?"

Mitch nodded absently.

"You'd better wash up. You look like hell."

Mitch nodded again. He chucked his phone on his bed and went to the washroom. When he finished his shower, Ethan had already blown up the bed and was laying on it, his hands behind his head as he stared at the ceiling.

"Night," Mitch grunted.

"Night," Ethan replied. Mitch flipped the light switch, plunging the room into darkness and crawled into bed. Somewhere down the hall, someone was blasting Michael Jackson. The heavy bass beats thudded through the walls. It mattered little to anyone in Ethan's room. All three were sound asleep in under five minutes.

****

The morning dawned cold and rainy. Maelgoch squinted up at the sky through the misting drops and sighed. Gwalchgwyn slept on, apparently not noticing. Tylluan, having arrived moments before the sky began to lighten, settled on the old Dywr's shoulder and preened herself.

"Still haven't found Aerfyn, I see," Maelgoch growled at her.

The owl turned her wide-eyed gaze away in a manner that felt suspiciously like deliberate insolence to Maelgoch. After a time, she nibbled gently at Gwalchgwyn's beard. The old man snorted awake.

"No... Faster... Huh...?"

"Morning," Maelgoch said, his voice as bleak as his expression.

Gwalchgwyn yawned and stretched, earning a titter of annoyance from the owl on his shoulder. "Sorry," he muttered to the bird. He squinted up at the sky. "Wonderful."

"If you say so," Maelgoch replied.

The owl twittered gently. Gwalchgwyn listened intently. "Well, now, that's interesting."

"What is?"

"Tylluan flew the battlefield last night. A wolf told him that the scent of Aerfyn ended rather abruptly a few feet from Cynfarch's body, and with it, the scent of three Dynion Gors. It seems we were correct in assuming she fell through the divide."

"And the enemy with her. Damn it!"

"There's good news."

"How can there possibly be good news?"

"The divide is still open."

"It is?"

"Yes. I think."

"You think?"

Gwalchgwyn shrugged. "I'm certain. Almost."

It was enough. Maelgoch stood and turned. "Olwen, Gawain, Peredur, to me!"

The three Captains, roused from slumber by the sound of their names, stood immediately and answered their commander's call.

"My Lord," they said in unison.

"Aerfyn is not found. The Dryw believes she has fallen through the divide, and that the divide is open still. Gather your weapons. We are going to find her."

"Not you," Gwalchgwyn said, still seated against his rock.

Maelgoch turned. "Pardon?"

"Not you, Commander. The army needs a leader, and you're it."

"Aerfyn's the Commander of this army."

"Only if she returns."

"But —"

"You are staying."

Maelgoch gave a look that conveyed his annoyance to his chosen comrades.

"Fear not, noble leader," Olwen said. "We shall embark upon this quest, and bring the Battle Queen home."

"Tylluan will lead you to the divide," Gwalchgwyn said, finally struggling to his feet. "Follow her, and you shall not be lost. But be warned, warriors of the Dynion Gors have fallen through also. Be on your guard."

Olwen nodded. "We shall, Great One."

"Then prepare. You shall leave at dusk."

The three men bowed and left.

"I should be going with them," Maelgoch grumbled.

"You dedication to my daughter is touching. But you must remember the needs of all the Pobl Gwir. Our very existence hangs in the balance. Should the Dynion Gors win the next battle, I fear we shall be lost and the Blessed Isle shall fall."

"That will never happen," Maelgoch scoffed.

"Let us hope."

****

Aerfyn opened heavy eyelids to find herself staring up at an unfamiliar white ceiling. It was not the ceiling of her pavilion, nor that of the strange place from which she had escaped. It took her several moments to recall precisely what had happened and where exactly she was.

She sat up slowly, wincing in pain as the cut at her side changed shape to accommodate her movements. On the floor beside her bed, sleeping soundly on his stomach and snoring loudly, lay the kind blue-eyed man who had carried her here. On the only other bed in the room slept the brown-eyed stranger who had helped the blue-eyed one.

She observed them both before leaning against the wall at the bed's head and dozing off.

Some time later, noises of movement woke Aerfyn and she saw the blue-eyed man get up and rub his short, dark hair. He stretched, revealing taught muscle, and stood. He turned around, saw Aerfyn looking at him and twitched so violently it threw him back half a step.

"Jesus!" he said.

Aerfyn smiled and he, recovering quickly, smiled back.

"Aerfyn," she said, touching her chest just below her collarbone. The man's smile broadened.

"Ethan," he said, mimicking her motion. He pointed at the still sleeping stranger. "Mitch."

Aerfyn smiled again.

The man named Ethan turned to the man named Mitch. He pulled Mitch's pillow out from under his head.

"Wha...?" Mitch said sleepily.

The man named Ethan said something nonsensical to the man named Mitch.

"Uh-huh," Mitch replied, putting his head down again and starting to snore.

Ethan beat him repeatedly with the pillow until Mitch woke properly and sat up. He rubbed his eyes and looked at Aerfyn.

"Hi," he said.

Aerfyn cocked her head at him. "Aerfyn," she said, indicating herself. "Mitch." She pointed at him.
Mitch looked at Ethan questioningly.

Ethan said something else, to which Mitch shrugged in acceptance. Aerfyn watched them both carefully. She knew them not, and though they seemed sympathetic towards her, she could not be sure that they weren't in league with the people who ran the place from which she escaped.

The best plan for now was to simply wait and observe.

****

Mitch found Aerfyn's unwavering gaze unnerving. "So..." he said. "How are you feeling?"

The girl cocked her head again, a slight frown on her face.

"I don't think she speaks English, dude," Ethan said, throwing Mitch's pillow back onto the bed.

Mitch shrugged. "It was worth a shot. So, what now, genius?"

Ethan shrugged. "I don't know. Maybe she's hungry. Want to go get breakfast?"

Mitch grunted. "Why don't you get breakfast?"

"Dude, it's not that far away."

"So it shouldn't be a problem for you."

Before Ethan could retort, a soft knock at the door announced a visitor. Ethan scowled and went to the door. He looked through the peephole and the tension left his shoulders in one great rush. He opened the door and Gordon walked in, carrying a tray of food and hot drinks from Tim Horton's.

"Figured you'd be wanting breakfast," he said with a smile. He stopped dead when he found the girl awake on Ethan's bed, watching him with interest.

"Hi," he said awkwardly.

"Gordon, this is Aerfyn," Ethan said. "Aerfyn, Gordon."

"Hi," Gordon said again.

Ethan rolled his eyes and took the tray from Gordon.

"Dude, she is *hot*!" Gordon said in a harsh whisper.

"Shut up!" Ethan snapped back.

"What's for breakfast?" Mitch asked.

"Bacon breakfast sandwiches and hot chocolate," Gordon said, seating himself on Mitch's bed.

Ethan put the tray on his computer desk and pulled out the hot chocolates. He handed them around. Aerfyn took hers gingerly. She sniffed it before observing the others removing the dark brown lids. She followed suit. Ethan tossed the wrapped breakfast sandwiches to his teammates, handed Aerfyn hers before settling on his computer chair with his.

Aerfyn copied the boys carefully. She watched them eat before taking a nibble of her sandwich. She chewed thoughtfully before taking a larger bite. Either the food agreed with her palate, or she was simply too hungry to care. Either way, she ate faster than any of the boys and was happily licking her fingers by the time Ethan had finished his.

"What's the plan now?" Gordon asked.

"Well, we should find out where she's from if we're to return her there," Ethan said.

"What she needs is clothes. She's only wearing your T. She can't walk around like that," Mitch said.

"Who said she'll be walking around?"

"So you what? Mean to keep her captive in this room? C'mon, man. Even I think that's a little sick."

"She's not well enough to move is all I meant."

"Yeah, but what if we have no choice? What if those monsters strike again? Or if the cops swing by?"

Mitch thought a moment. "Point," he said. "I'll call Wendy."

"No!" Ethan and Gordon said in unison.

"Sorry man," Ethan explained when Mitch looked startled. "I know she's your girl and all, but I don't trust her."

"Come off it, man. What's she gonna do?"

"Turn us all in," Gordon said.

"She wouldn't."

"Isn't she really mad at you?" Ethan asked. When Mitch sullenly refused to answer, he added, "She might."

"Great. Now what?"

"I can call Jazz," Gordon said. "I mean, they look like they're roughly the same size, and Jazz is really good at keeping secrets."

"Jazz? Your friend from the Gonq?" Mitch asked.

"Yeah."

"The Gonq?" Ethan asked.

"Algonquin College," Mitch said.

"Ah. She won't blab?"

"No."

There was a short, thoughtful silence from everyone in the room. Ethan nodded. "Call her."

Gordon nodded and pulled out his cell phone. "Hey!" he said brightly. "Look, I need a massive, massive, massive favour...No, like, massive...Do you have any spare clothes that you think you can give away? ... Look, I can't tell you why, but seriously, I need your help on this... You do? Man, Jazz, you rock! Can you bring them over? ... Yes, now... Look, I don't want to tell you over the phone... Bring over some clothes and I'll explain

70

everything, I promise... I'll buy you chocolate... No, just the clothes... Man, you will never believe me... Okay I'll see you soon... Thanks again, Jazz. You're awesome... 'K. Bye."

Gordon hung up and slipped the phone into his back pocket. "We have clothes."

"In the meantime, we need to find out where Aerfyn's from, and how to get her back there." Ethan swung around on his computer chair and turned his laptop on.

"And just how do you expect to do that?" Mitch asked.

"Mitch, you draw, right?"

Mitch shrugged. "A little."

"Do you think you could draw one of the things that attacked us last night?"

Mitch blinked. "I'll give it a shot. Chuck me my pencil case, will you?"

Ethan rolled his chair to Mitch's desk, grabbed the pencil case on it and threw it to Mitch. Mitch deftly caught it, and then reached under his bed for his sketchpad. Before long, he was bent over the pad, scribbling away.

Gordon simply sat on the bed, feeling utterly useless. He twiddled his thumbs until he noticed Aerfyn watching him with her unnervingly shrewd eyes. He smiled at her. She cocked her head.

"There," Mitch said. He held up the pad for everyone to see.

The sketch was a quick, anime-style drawing that nevertheless looked remarkably like the creatures that had attacked them the previous night. Ethan grabbed the pad from him and went to Aerfyn. He handed it to her and looked at her expectantly.

She looked down at the drawing, then up at Ethan with a questioning expression. Ethan pointed at the drawing. Aerfyn looked back down.

"People," Ethan said, indicating everyone in the room. He pointed at the drawing again.

"Dynion Gors," Aerfyn said quietly.

"Dynion Gors," Ethan repeated.

Aerfyn nodded. She pointed at the drawing. "Dynion Gors. Dynion Gors."

Ethan nodded. He went to his laptop. "All righty, Google. Work your magic."

He opened his web browser and then stopped. "Dynion Gors. How is that spelled?"

"Try d-i-n-y-o-n-g-o-r-z," Mitch suggested.

"Okay. That goes nowhere. There aren't even any suggestions."

"What about d-i-n-i-o-n-g-o-r-s?"

"Nope. Same. No results."

"Well, maybe they're two different words. Try d-i-n-y-o-n g-o-r-s," Gordon said.

"It's asking if I mean 'dino gyros.'"

Mitch scoffed and Gordon threw him an evil look. "Try swapping the 'y' and 'i' around," he suggested.

"D-y-n-i-o-n," Ethan said as he typed. "G-o-r-s-. Ah-hah! Here's something. All the sites that come up have something to do with Welsh."

"What, the grape juice?"

"Not Welsh's, Welsh. As in the language. Look here," Ethan pointed at the screen and read slowly and painfully as he tried to pronounce the Welsh words. "Y Tylwyth Teg Stole From Us. Dynion Mwyns Nemesis. The sixth result is about Welsh Witchcraft."

"So, what? She's a Welsh witch?" Mitch asked.

"Well, she might be Welsh. Google Translate here we come!" He pulled up the site and typed in the words. "Bingo. Dynion means men. And Dynion Gors... Bog men. Bog men. Those monsters are called bog men. Okay, Google, magic time again."

Ethan typed 'Bog Men' into the search engine. "Huh."

"What?" Mitch and Gordon asked, moving over to the computer.

"Look at the first result."

Gordon squinted and leant in. "'Murdered "Bog Men" Found With Hair Gel, Manicured Nails. The bodies of two Iron-Age murder victims have been recovered from peat bogs in Ireland.' Ireland?"

"National Geographic," Mitch said, looking at the website provided beneath the link.

"Iron Age," Ethan said. "Dude, that Bog Man had an axe."

"So, what are you saying? She's a Welsh woman-warrior from the past?"

Ethan shrugged. "Maybe."

"All right, this is just too weird for me," Mitch said, returning to his bed. "I mean, this is ridiculous. Are we supposed to believe that some girl fell through some sort of wormhole and just happened to land on frikkin' Carleton University Campus in the middle of frikkin' Ottawa?"

Ethan and Gordon exchanged looks.

"I don't know," Ethan said. "But I mean to find out."

"It's just not possible."

"Dude," Ethan said. "Monsters are supposed to be impossible."

"Well, let's examine the facts," Gordon said. "We find the girl, heavily injured. She's wearing real armour, with real weapons. The surgeon reports to the cops that it looks like she'd been attacked by someone with a weapon like an axe. It cut through her armour, for Pete's sake. Then, you two get attacked by monsters, one of which has a... What the hell kind of axe did you draw anyway?"

"I don't know what it's called, but it looked just like that," Mitch snapped.

"Right, then you two are attacked by monsters, one of which wields an axe straight from Dungeons and Dragons. She comes in, having escaped the hospital, and kicks ass. Then she tells you the name of the creatures that attacked you in a language that just happens to be real, not gibberish."

"My head hurts," Mitch complained.

The conversation was interrupted by a rapid knock at the door. Gordon peered through the peephole and smiled before opening the door.

"Hey, Jazz," he greeted.

"Hey." Jazz was a petite strawberry-blonde with large, blue eyes and a bright smile. "So here are the clothes." She handed Gordon a plastic bag filled with clothes. "What's the huge big secret you can't tell me over the phone?"

Gordon pulled Jazz into the room and shut the door. "Jazz, this is Ethan and Mitch."

Each one waved as his name was mentioned.

"Hi," Jazz said. "What happened to you guys? Nice bruises."

"We'll tell you later," Ethan said.

"And this," Gordon said, turning Jazz towards Ethan's bed. "Is Aerfyn. She's the secret."

"Hi," Jazz said.

Aerfyn cocked her head at Jazz.

"Aerfyn," Gordon said. "This is Jazz."

Aerfyn looked seriously at Jazz. "Thisisjazz," she said.

"No, no," Ethan said. "Jazz."

"Jazz," Aerfyn repeated.

"What, is she retarded?" Jazz asked Gordon.

"No, she's Welsh, we think. She doesn't speak English."

"That's stupid. Wales is in Britain."

"We think she's from the past," Ethan said. "Like, Iron-Age past."

Jazz turned to him with a look that informed him he was clearly insane. "Okay... Several flaws with that argument. I'm pretty sure Wales didn't exist in the Iron Age and even if it did, they wouldn't be speaking modern Welsh."

"Hah!" Mitch said.

Ethan looked utterly crestfallen. "Well, maybe she's from a different dimension, then. Somewhere where they speak Welsh, and still fight with swords and shit."

"What the hell are you talking about?" Jazz asked.

Gordon left it to Ethan to fill Jazz in on all the details. Mitch interrupted if he felt Ethan left anything important out. When they'd finished, all three boys looked at Jazz expectantly.

"You're making that up."

"I swear to God, we're not!" Ethan said. "Look, we need to get her back to wherever she's from. She saved our lives, Jazz. It's the least we could do."

"You're all insane. I'm going."

"Wait! Jazz, wait," Ethan said. Jazz reached the door before pausing and turning around.

"What if we're not?" Ethan asked. "What if it's possible, and she did somehow fall into our world from somewhere else? What if we're the only ones in this whole world who can help her?"

Jazz hesitated, her hand on the door handle.

"You have to believe us."

Jazz released the door handle. "I can't believe I'm about to say this, but all right. Suppose you are right. What now?"

"Well, you could help dress Aerfyn. She's wearing one of my shirts right now, and that's about it."

"And," Mitch grumbled. "We need to find someone who speaks Welsh."

"They teach Welsh at the University of Ottawa, you know," Jazz said, snatching the bag of clothes back from Gordon.

Ethan looked surprised. "Do they?"

"Yeah. They have a Celtic Chair and everything. You should go speak to him. He should know all about this mythical crazy stuff."

Ethan turned on his chair and immediately went to the University of Ottawa website. "Huh. So they do."

"How do you know this stuff?" Mitch asked.

"My roommate. She's really big into the whole Celtic thing. She took a couple of classes there."

"Does she speak Welsh?"

"No, but the Chair is from Wales."

"Dr. Gwilym Davies," Ethan read. "Office hours, Mondays through to Thursdays 1pm to 4pm. Friday's 9am to 11am. What day is it today?"

"Wednesday," Gordon said.

Jazz went over to Aerfyn and smiled. "I'm going to help you get dressed," she said slowly. She opened the bag and laid out the clothes. She pointed at the clothes and then at Aerfyn.

The strange girl understood right away. She nodded and tossed the blanket aside. Ethan's shirt came to the middle of the thigh. All the boys stared.

"Turn around," Jazz said primly. Grumbling under their breath, the boys turned around.

Shaking her head, Jazz helped Aerfyn from the bed and walked her into the bathroom. The boys turned back around when the washroom door clicked shut.

"Dude," Gordon said to Ethan. "If I were you, I'd totally tap that."

"Shut up," Ethan replied.

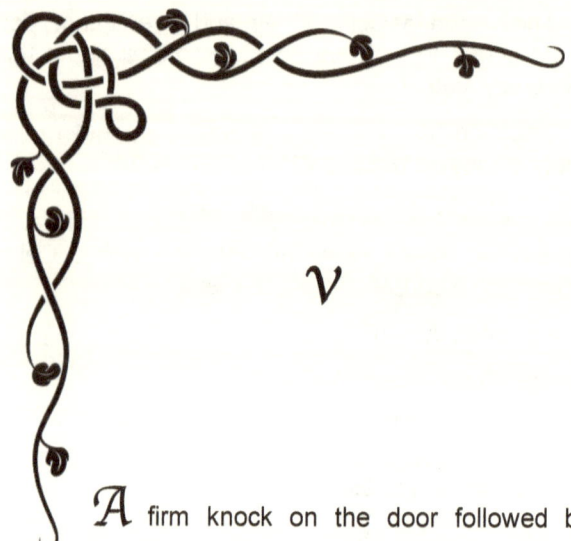

$\mathcal{V}$

$\mathcal{A}$ firm knock on the door followed by two others in close succession ended the conversation. Frowning, Gordon went to the peephole and peered out. He slammed his back against the door, looking stricken.

Cops! he mouthed.

"Oh shit!" Ethan said. He and Mitch exchanged a panicked glance.

The police knocked on the door again. "Ethan, Mitch?" a man's voice said from the other side of the door. "It's Constable Jackman. Open up."

"Jesus," Ethan said. "Open the door, Gordon. Quick."

Gordon obeyed. "Hey," he said through the slight opening he created. "I'm Gordon."

Constable Bill Jackman raised his brows. "Hi Gordon. Are Ethan and Mitch in?"

Gordon looked back into the room and then back at the Constable. He had with him a very tiny blonde policewoman with green eye shadow.

"Yeah," Gordon said.

"May we come in?"

"Uh…"

"Let them in Gordon," Ethan called from his chair at the computer. "Dumb ass."

Gordon obediently opened the door wider. He walked stiffly to Mitch's computer chair and sat down.

"Sorry, Officer," Ethan said.

"You boys look like hell," Constable Jackman said, observing their bruised and scraped faces.

"We got into a scrap," Ethan said.

"Really? About what?"

"Nothing," Mitch said.

"About what?" Officer Jackman repeated in a tone that made it clear he expected an answer.

"Wendy," Mitch said.

"His girl," Ethan said.

"Mitch's girl?"

"Yeah. She's a bitch."

"Yo, shut up!" Mitch snapped.

"Come off it, man."

"Don't talk about her like that!"

"Dude, if none of your friends like her, then there's something wrong."

"I'm warning you!"

"You could do so much better."

"I said, shut up!"

Officer Jackman cleared his throat. "I'm here on official business, so if you don't mind, can you keep your personal issues out of it for now?"

Ethan shrugged. "Sure."

"Fine," Mitch grumbled.

"Look, we've been canvassing the campus, looking for that girl you found on Hallowe'en."

"Yeah, I read in the paper she escaped the hospital. Nice work." Ethan grabbed the stress ball he kept on his desk and started tossing it up in the air and catching it again.

"Some students have said they recall seeing you carrying a girl matching her description here last night."

"Uh…" Mitch said.

Just then, the toilet flushed and Jazz stepped from the washroom. "Oh, hello," she said amicably.

"Hi," Officer Jackman said.

"I'm Jasmine."

She walked forward and handed Ethan his black shirt. "Thanks for helping me out last night," she said.

"Feeling better?" Ethan asked, trying not to sound as relieved and grateful as he felt.

"Yeah. I might even be able to eat something without throwing up."

Ethan scrunched his shirt into a ball and threw it into his laundry basket. He turned to the two police officers. "Anything else?"

"Nope," Officer Jackman said, a little disappointed. "I think that solves that mystery." He pulled business cards from one of his many pockets. He handed one to everyone in the room. "Look, if you do happen to see her, call me immediately all right? She might be dangerous. She's suffering from schizophrenia and needs help."

"Sure thing," Ethan said taking the card and smiling up at Constable Jackman.

He and his partner turned and left the room. As they did so, the argument between Mitch and Ethan started again. Mitch stormed from the room after the two officers, slamming the door shut and leaning his back against it.

"You take it easy, now," Officer Jackman said.

"Yeah." Mitch replied. He watched the two officers walk down the hall.

****

Police Constable Bill Jackman was silent as he walked beside Officer Boulduc back to their squad car.

"Well, there goes that theory," Officer Boulduc said cheerily.

"Does it?" Bill asked.

"They had an alibi, Bill."

"Yeah, yeah. I know. Still, there's something about those boys. My Spidey senses are tingling."

"Your 'Spidey senses'? Seriously?"

"What?"

81

"Get in the car. Dweeb."

Bill opened the door and slid into the passenger seat as Officer Boulduc opened the driver's side door.

They were quiet during the drive back to the station. Bill stared absently out the window, his mind going over the details of the boys' room. He stiffened slightly as he recalled a drawing on one of the beds, a drawing the looked suspiciously like the drawing Aerfyn had done while in hospital.

Officer Jackman pulled out his notepad and scrawled down a note. He smiled the rest of the journey back to the station.

****

The door opened so suddenly behind Mitch that he nearly fell backwards into the room.

"Yo," Ethan said from his desk chair. "Are they gone? By the way Jazz, that was one hell of a save."

Mitch glared at Ethan. He nodded curtly and went to his bed, leaving Gordon to close the door behind him.

"What's your problem?" Ethan asked.

"Don't you ever talk about my girl that way again!" Mitch snapped.

"Whoa," Ethan said. "It was your idea to use her as the thing we fought about. Don't blame me."

"You know what? Whatever. I'm done here." Mitch grabbed his coat from his chair and stormed from the room.

"Dude, where are you going?"

"For a walk." Mitch slammed the door behind him for a second time. He pulled on his coat and left Dundas House.

"Dude, you were kinda harsh," Gordon said.

"Whatever," Ethan replied. "We were supposed to make like we'd been fighting. Besides, she *is* a two-faced, manipulative harpy."

"Wow," Jazz said.

"Yo, is Aerfyn all right?" Gordon asked.

"Shit," Jazz said. She turned and opened the bathroom door and walked in.

Aerfyn had been hiding in the shower, and it was there she remained, hugging her knees to her chest. She looked up, startled, when Jazz whisked aside the shower curtains. Jazz smiled down at her and she relaxed.

With a great deal of help from Jazz, Aerfyn stood and walked from the washroom. Her movements were achingly slow, the gash in her side causing considerable pain.

The boys stared as Aerfyn hobbled in, leaning heavily against Jazz. She wore boot-cut jeans and a black racer-back shirt.

"She's too broad-backed for the bra I brought," Jazz said by way of apology.

"No, don't worry. That's totally cool," Ethan said.

Jazz helped lower Aerfyn onto the bed. The strange girl swung her feet up and, wincing, settled herself against the pillows.

"That reminds me," Ethan said, reaching for his first aid kit. "I need to take a look at that gash."

"I'm going shopping for her," Jazz said. "She's going to need a coat of some sort if she's going to go outside. Not to mention a bra and a supply of underwear."

"She doesn't really need a bra," Gordon said.

Jazz gave him a glare that could have melted the polar caps.

"Here," Ethan said, standing up. He reached for his wallet and pulled out some money. "Here's a fifty."

"Wha...?"

"You shouldn't have to spend any money over this. You've already helped a huge amount, what with saving our asses from the cops, and all."

"I've got a twenty," Gordon offered.

Jazz took both. "Excellent! I'll be back in a bit."

"Thanks again, Jazz," Gordon said as he showed her to the door.

"Yeah, well. You owe me."

"I will make it up to you, I swear!"

"You better!" She threw a bright smile around the room and then vanished down the hall.

Ethan turned his attention to Aerfyn. He lifted up her shirt. She stared up at the ceiling and refused to look at him. She winced when he pulled the pad off.

"Well, the good news is that it doesn't look infected."

"Oh, man!" Gordon said when he looked over. "That's just gross!"

Ethan shrugged. "It's not that bad, you pussy."

"Dude, that's super gross."

Ethan rolled his eyes. He took out another couple of sterile pads and his bottle of saline solution. He cleaned and redressed the wound before smiling up at Aerfyn.

"All done." He pulled her shirt back down and covered her over with his blanket.

"Diolch," Aerfyn said.

"You're welcome," Ethan replied.

Aerfyn smiled at him before closing her eyes. She fell asleep almost immediately.

"So, what's the plan now?" Gordon asked.

"I'm going to see this Professor Davies guy this afternoon. We have to find out how to get her back home. If Jazz is right, he should know a thing or two about where she comes from."

****

Maelgoch watched Olwen, Peredur and Gawain vanish through the trees with a resigned sigh. He hated sitting in the clearing, hiding behind a glamour while his friends risked their lives to cross behind enemy lines and rescue their queen.

As much as Maelgoch disliked the adventure, Olwen, Peredur and Gawain were thoroughly excited. They had grown up listening to tales of accidental wanderings into other worlds, of the hero's exploits in that world, and the triumphant return. They conveniently chose to ignore the tales when the adventurer never returned at all.

They grinned to each other as they set off after the barn owl, Tylluan, armed and ready to face whatever magical beasts lay beyond the borders of their own world. More importantly, they were looking forward to the glory and honours they would receive when they returned with their

Battle Queen. What noble warrior would turn down such an adventure?

The woods were dark, almost purple, in the fading light of dusk. The changing leaves shuddered in the chill breeze, some giving up in the face of inevitability and falling silently to join their brethren on the forest floor.

The three adventurers were silent as they trod on the wet leaves. Only the quiet hiss of chainmail belied their movements. Tylluan flew through the woods, flitting from branch to branch and pausing often so her slower companions could follow. The barn owl paused now at the edge of the expansive plain where the last battle had been fought.

The crows had left the field, leaving it to the wolves, though there were few enough of those.

The owl turned her head, the large yellow eyes seeing everything that stirred in the deepening dark. Then, Tylluan spread her wings and glided across the field, coming to land silently on the pommel of a sword that someone had thrust into the ground.

After a brief hesitation, the three adventurers followed, keeping low to the ground and running swiftly. They stopped at the sword. Tylluan preened a moment before taking wing once more. A short glide, and the owl vanished rather suddenly from sight. Peredur, Olwen and Gawain looked at each other, shrugged, and ran forward, vanishing from the field as if they were ghosts.

****

Tua Bhuail grinned a wicked grin. His yellow fangs dripped with saliva. He watched the three Pobl Gwir warriors cross the battlefield from the safety of the trees. He saw them vanish from sight and immediately knew they had gone in search of the Battle Queen.

He turned back and nodded to his warriors. The chosen twelve, armed with various cruel-looking weapons and ill-fitting, stolen Pobl Gwir armour, nodded at their chieftain and slunk silently across the field. Pausing briefly at the sword to sniff the air, the twelve Fir Bolg vanished.

Tua Bhuail chuckled.

****

Tylluan glided over the battlefield, high in the starry sky so that she appeared little more than a shadow to those below. No one paid heed to shadows in the night. She observed the twelve Dynion Gors as they followed the three adventurers into the other world.

Turning her wing, she flew for Gwalchgwyn. The aging Dryw would need to know. The three adventurers were not alone. Their mission just became a desperate fight against time and numbers.

****

Professor Gwilym Davies stared down, dumbfounded, as he endeavoured to read through what might just be the worst grammar he had come across since he'd started teaching. Shaking his head, he threw the essay aside and rubbed his face. He'd tackle the marking tomorrow, he decided. As of the moment, he felt like playing solitaire.

Professor Davies was a typical Welshman in more than just name. Tall and lean, his dark brown hair was now peppered with grey. His brown eyes sparkled with mischief, even when he was not being mischievous, giving the impression he knew something everyone else did not.

He was passionate about his native language and his native country. He lived now in Canada only because, in his youth, he had fallen in love with a Canadian girl and, having obtained his doctorate, found a job in Ottawa. It was a pleasant enough city and, though his affair with the Canadian girl did not last, his job as tenured professor made it nearly impossible to return home.

Determined to share his passion, he began teaching everything he could in the field of Celtic Studies. It began first with the languages and literatures, but had since, after a great deal of effort on his part, expanded out to the archaeology, anthropology and mythologies of the broad swath of cultures designated 'Celtic.'

Now, not only was he a tenured professor, but the Ottawa Celtic Chair, and he'd managed to squeeze a Celtic Studies minor programme from the university administration. There was much to be proud of in his career as a university professor.

This latest batch of essays, however, had him questioning his life choices.

He'd only just opened up the solitaire game on his computer when a knock on his half-opened door made him turn.

"Come in," he said.

A tall, broad youth whom he'd never seen before stepped into the room.

"Are you Professor Davies?"

"That's what it says on the door," Gwilym said with a cheeky smile and a lilting Welsh accent.

The boy smiled back, a little uncomfortably. "Do you have a moment?"

"Of course. Take a seat."

Ethan sat down on the chair across from the professor's desk. Papers and books were piled every which way on the desk, the archaic monitor barely visible through the stacks. Several tea towels were pinned to the walls. One depicted traditional Irish recipes, while another boasted several useful welsh phrases, the one in largest print read 'Mae fy hofrenfad yn llawn o lyswennod.'

"It says, 'My hovercraft is full of eels,'" Gwilym said, his eyes twinkling.

"Uh… useful," Ethan murmured.

A small, hand-drawn poster of a national Eisteddfod from the 70's sat on the far wall, as well as a framed portrait of St. David. Above the computer, a detailed map of Wales had been tacked to the wall.

The Professor himself looked so much like a caricature of a professor, Ethan almost laughed.

Short, salt and pepper hair that looked like it hadn't seen a brush in the better part of a week stuck out every which way from the Professor's head. Einstein himself would have been proud.

The Professor wore round, gold-framed glasses that accentuated his straight, sharp nose.

A brown tweed jacket, boasting tan elbow patches, hung on a coat rack near the door.

"Are you in one of my classes?" the Professor asked.

"Uh, no, actually. I go to Carleton."

"Really? Well, what can I do for you, uh…?"

"Oh, sorry. Ethan. Ethan Evans."

"Evans? That's a good Welsh name." The professor's accent was still surprisingly thick.

Ethan smiled. "Yeah, my great grandfather. Anyway, I was wondering if you knew anything about Bog Men?"

Professor Davies thought for a moment.

"I was just doing some research and I fell across them and was wondering if you knew anything."

"A fair amount as it happens. Bog Men have been found all across Europe, and the British Isles is no exception. It seemed there was a pan-European cult that required, what are likely, sacrifices. Some of them were criminals, though one or two seem to be aristocracy of some kind -"

"Oh, no, I meant more in myth."

"Myth?"

"Yeah, like, monsters, or something."

"Monsters?"

"Yeah. Like, are there any monsters in Welsh myth that you know about?"

This took the Professor by surprise.

"Well, no, to be honest. Much of what we know of Welsh myth comes from *The Mabinogion*, a collection of Welsh tales that dates back to the Middle Ages." The Professor sucked in his breath audibly through the sides of his mouth, as he was prone to do when getting excited. "There are a few early poems that allude to an early beginning for the Arthurian legends, such as the *Y Gododdin*. Well, one version of it, in any case. Incidentally, the Arthurian legends make mention of giants, and even a giant boar. Are those the kind of monsters you are referring to?"

Ethan looked utterly crestfallen. "Oh. So, no mention of Dynion Gors?"

"Well, Dynion Gors is the direct translation for bog men, though I've never heard of the term in my life."

"Oh."

"You look thoroughly disappointed."

"These monsters would be like people, only... well... horrid looking. Grey skin, uh, big, bulging eyes. Yellow fanged teeth?"

"That sounds something like the Fir Bolg of Irish myth."

"Fir Bolg? What are they?"

"Well, the name literally means stomach men. They were supposed to have existed in Ireland before the Irish. They were involved in a colossal battle, which ended in a stalemate, so the myth goes."

"That sounds about right, actually. So these things, they're Irish?"

"Yes, that's right."

"But she spoke Welsh," Ethan muttered to himself.

"Is that helpful?"

"Yeah. I think so. Oh, another thing, Professor. Are there any stories of people going into, you know, other worlds?"

"Oh goodness, yes."

"There are?"

"Many, many tales, both Welsh and Irish. Though it's the Irish tales that describe it best. There are tales of heroes going to islands filled with nothing but women, or filled with sheep that on one half of the island are white, but as soon as they cross into the other half, turn black. That kind of thing. To be honest, the concept of adventuring into other worlds is not a uniquely Celtic thing. There are examples of such occurrences in many different cultures."

"And, how would someone get there?"

"Across water, most of the time. Though, there are places such as caves that are supposed to be entrances."

"So, it's kinda like Narnia."

"Well, yes, only less Christian allegory, I imagine."

"Huh."

"Why so much interest in the Otherworld, if I might ask?"

"I just find it fascinating. Hang on, *the* Otherworld?"

"Yes. In myth it's said the 'faeries' or the Tuatha de Dannan live there. We think that it's a mythical place where the dead end up when they leave this world. The best example would be in Arthurian legend, when King Arthur is mortally wounded, he's collected by a woman – a Fae woman – in a boat, and taken to the other world where, we are told, he lives in peace and prosperity forever.

"The Otherworld is supposedly where the dead go. It's not well recorded as to where it is or what happens when you're there. The tradition of the Land of the Dead survives well into modernity. Hallowe'en, for example."

"Eh?"

"Well, Hallowe'en is when the divide between worlds supposedly falls and, for a night or two, the dead return to the land of the living. It's an ancient celebration dating back to the Iron Age, probably well before. In Irish it's called Samhain. We only have the Irish name, but it was likely a pan-Celtic celebration."

"So this divide between worlds, it only comes down once a year – at Hallowe'en?"

"That is the tradition."

"Oh man!"

"Are you all right, Ethan? You've gone rather pale."

"Uh... Yeah... Low blood pressure. Listen, thanks so much for your time."

"You're very welcome. It's lovely to chat with someone who is genuinely interested. You should consider taking our Celtic Studies minor, if it really interests you."

"Yeah, sure." Ethan stood. "Thanks again, Professor D."

Professor Gwilym nodded and Ethan vanished from his office.

"Professor D," Gwilym said as he turned back to his game of solitaire. "I like that."

****

"Hey," Gordon said as Ethan entered the room.

Mitch sat on his bed, reading and Gordon was on Mitch's laptop, playing a violent online role playing game. Aerfyn slept on in Ethan's bed.

"Yo, you look upset." Gordon paused his game. "What did the prof. say?"

"We are so screwed," Ethan said.

Mitch looked up with a frown. "What? Why?"

"OK, get this, there is a place, Professor D. called it the Otherworld, right? Imagine Narnia, right? Well, apparently every year, once a year, the divide between this world and the Otherworld collapses, right? But only for one night – Hallowe'en."

"Shit!" Gordon said. "So we can't get her home?"

"Not until next year."

"Brilliant," Mitch said, throwing the book down. "Now what do we do, genius?"

"I don't know," Ethan replied, ignoring the sneer in Mitch's voice. He sank slowly on his computer chair and watched Aerfyn sleep. "I really don't know."

"What about the monsters?" Gordon asked.

"Professor D. knew nothing about them. When I described them, he said it sounded a little like the monsters in Irish myth, only they're called the Fir Bolg, and that translates as stomach men, not bog men."

"Maybe they're the same, just different names."

"Well, everything else seems to fit, so, maybe."

"We should turn her in," Mitch said.

"What?" Gordon and Ethan demanded incredulously in unison.

"No way," Ethan said. "They think she's nuts. All they'll do is lock her away."

"And that's bad because?"

"Because those monsters are still out there," Ethan said. "And they're still after her, probably still after us."

"Armed guards, free meals, a gym. Prison seems like the safest place to be for her."

"You are cold," Gordon said. "C'mon, man. She's injured and you said it yourself. You owe her your life."

"Yeah, yeah," Mitch grumbled. "It's just. A year, man. How are we supposed to keep her hidden for a year?"

94

The dilemma silenced the room for a solid five minutes before a rapid knock lifted the oppressive hush. Mitch answered the door, and let Jazz back into the room. She smiled at the gathering, carrying a large number of shopping bags with her.

"Good afternoon!"

"Good God!" Ethan said. "What the hell did you buy her?"

"You can get a lot on a budget if you know where to look," Jazz replied. "I figured she'd need some basic stuff like toothpaste and a brush and hair elastics and stuff as well."

"Oh, man! Someone's a thinker. Thanks, Jazz," Gordon said with a bright smile.

Jazz began pulling out an assortment of clothes, including a warm long coat and a stylish hat to match. "Courtesy of Value Village," Jazz announced. She also pulled out brown tall boots with a short, broad heel.

"Nice boots," Gordon noted picking one up and examining it.

"Italian leather," Jazz said. "Five bucks, would you believe it?"

"Sweet!"

"I also have two sweaters, a few pairs of socks, two packets of underwear, a few shirts and a second pair of jeans. She'll last the whole winter with this wardrobe."

Gordon wrapped his arms around Jazz' shoulders. "You rock!"

"Yeah, I know. How's she doing?"

"She's been asleep since this morning," Mitch said, eyeing the scene over the top of his book.

"Poor thing. Hey, Ethan, any luck with the U of O prof?"

"Yeah, I think so."

"Oh, here's a kicker," Mitch said. "According to the professor, there's a legend that on Hallowe'en the divide between worlds comes down and things can cross over. Did you know it only happens for one night, once a year?"

"No way!"

"Way," Ethan said. He sighed glumly. "She won't be able to go home until next year."

"No *way!*"

"Way," the boys answered.

"So... what are you gonna do?"

"No idea," Ethan said. "We're going to have to find a place to hide her until next Hallowe'en."

"Hang on," Jazz said. She flipped open her cell phone and pressed it against her ear. "Hey, it's Jazz," she said when a voice answered on the other end. "Listen, you know about Celtic stuff, right? ... What do you know about Hallowe'en? Uh huh... Yeah... Uh huh... Huh? Oh, no reason. Just trying to settle an argument... Yes, that helps a lot. Thanks for that. O.K... see you later tonight, then." She hung up and slipped the phone into her pocket. "All right, so, my roommate says that Hallowe'en is derived from a really ancient festival called Samhain."

"Knew that," Ethan said.

"Now, we only celebrate one night, but she says she remembers reading that the celebration was either three days or three weeks long, she couldn't remember which."

"Well, which is it? 'Cause that's kind of important," Mitch said.

Jazz shrugged. "She couldn't remember."

"For now, let's hope for the best, and assume that it's three weeks and she can still go home," Ethan said. "In the meantime, we're going to have to find a place to hide her in case it isn't, and she does end up having to spend a year here."

"Any idea where to start looking for this doorway to her world?" Mitch asked.

"Professor D. said that this Otherworld was accessible usually by crossing water, or in certain caves."

"Dude, this is the Outaouais. There are like, a thousand bodies of water around here."

Ethan shrugged. "It's a step closer than we were."

Jazz started packing away the clothes. "Well, that's something. I'll keep prying my roommate for info. Maybe she'll be able to dig something up."

Aerfyn's eyes fluttered open.

"Oh!" Jazz exclaimed. "Good afternoon!"

Aerfyn smiled shyly at her. She was please to note that she was still where she had fallen asleep. Her friendly captors hadn't handed her over. That was something. Her stomach rumbled.

"Dinner time, much?" Gordon asked.

"Oh shit, yeah," Ethan said. He grabbed his wallet and stood. "I'll go get us dinner."

"Dude, just order a pizza or something," Mitch said.

"I kinda feel like Chinese," Gordon said.

Ethan rolled his eyes. "Which is it, pizza or Chinese?"

"How about Greek?" Jazz asked with a shrug.

The boys blinked stupidly at her.

"I'm up for Greek," Gordon said.

"Yeah, actually. Me too," Mitch agreed.

"Greek it is. What does everyone want?" Ethan put down his wallet again.

"Chicken gyro," Jazz said quickly. "No peppers."

"I dunno," Mitch said. "Whatever you guys are getting is fine."

"Chicken souvlaki platters it is," Ethan said. He spun on his desk chair and logged into his laptop. The food was ordered in a matter of minutes.

An hour later, they were sitting around the residence room, happily munching on dinner.

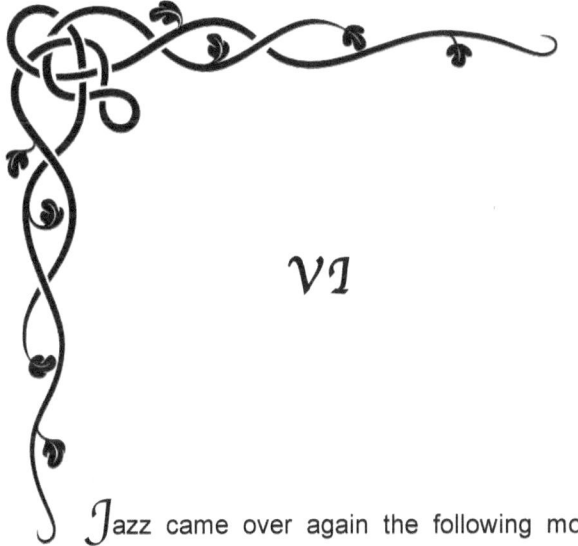

$\mathcal{VI}$

$\mathcal{J}$azz came over again the following morning.

Between jobs, she had a lot of spare time on her hands and, if she was being perfectly honest with herself, the very possibility of Ethan's theory being correct had her so excited she could barely sleep.

She entered the room to find Ethan pouring over a map of the Outaouais, munching down on a bagel from Tim Horton's. Aerfyn was again asleep on Ethan's bed. No one else was in the room.

"Morning," Jazz said.

Ethan jumped. "Dude! Don't do that! How'd you get in?"

"The door was open."

Ethan scowled.

"Where is everyone?"

"Mitch and Gordon went to class."

99

"Don't you have class?"

Ethan shrugged. "This is more important right now."

Jazz smiled and sat on the end of Ethan's bed. The motion woke Aerfyn. The young woman opened her eyes slowly.

"Morning," Jazz greeted cheerily. She pulled a wrapped bagel from her patchwork bag and handed it to Aerfyn. "Here, breakfast."

"Thanks," Ethan said.

Jazz shrugged.

Ethan stared back down at the map. "Man, this is pointless! There's nothing!"

"What are you looking for?"

"Professor D. said that the entrances to the Otherworld would be a lake or a cave or something. There's nothing near where we found Aerfyn."

"Well, maybe during Hallowe'en you don't need a lake or cave. It sorta … just happens."

"That's not helpful."

"Maybe you'll find it if you go back to where she was found."

"It's a high traffic area," Ethan said with a sigh. He flopped onto his desk chair. "If someone had vanished through the divide, it'd be all over campus by now."

"Maybe it shifts?"

"Oh God, I hope not. Then it'd be impossible to find!"

"Except by those who know where it is," Jazz said in her best pirate imitation.

"What?"

"Pirates of the Caribbean?"

Ethan stared at her blankly.

"When Jack Sparrow is talking about where the Black Pearl ... Oh, never mind."

Aerfyn finished her bagel. "Rwyf am i ymdrochi," she said softly.

Jazz cast an enquiring look at Ethan, who shrugged. "What?"

"Ymolchi. I Ymolchi." Aerfyn waved her hands in small circles over her face and forearms.

"Oh! A shower!" Jazz jumped to her feet. "Come on," she said, beckoning Aerfyn.

Hesitantly, Aerfyn pulled the blankets from her and left the bed. Movement, though still painful, looked easier today. She moved slowly to Jazz, who grabbed a towel and led her into the washroom.

"Here," she said, pointing to the shower in which Aerfyn had hid yesterday.

Aerfyn scowled.

Jazz pulled back the shower curtain and pointed at the tub. Aerfyn simply scowled and stared, so Jazz pointed to the round, sundial-shaped diverter on the wall. She grabbed a hold of the handle and turned it. Water started streaming from the tap. Placing her hand in the water, Jazz waited for the temperature to warm before pressing the knob in the centre of the diverter. The tap stopped streaming and a fraction of a second later, the showerhead began spewing water.

Aerfyn was dumbstruck. With an open mouth, she stared incredulously at the water streaming from the shower.

Jazz smiled at her. She raised the towel she held and placed it on the closed toilet seat. Aerfyn nodded at her and Jazz left, closing the washroom door behind her.

"Well, it's as if she's never seen a shower before," Jazz noted.

"She probably hasn't." Ethan rubbed his face. "I don't know how to help her."

"Well, let's start with how to hide her first, all right?"

Ethan nodded. Just then, Mitch entered the room.

"Hey," he said unenthusiastically. He tossed his books onto his bed. "The girl in the shower?"

"The girl has a name, Mitch," Ethan said.

"Whatever. Anything new, genius?"

"Dude, get over it all right? Stop sulking."

"Whatever."

"Uh, maybe I should leave you boys be," Jazz said.

"No!" Ethan said. "Don't. Aerfyn seems to like you and I don't know how to handle... uh... girls' stuff."

"Girls' stuff?"

"Yeah... you know..."

Jazz rolled her eyes. "So, any idea where to hide her?"

"Nope. Somewhere out of town, though. Maybe I'll go see the professor again today. He might have some brilliant ideas on how to get people back across the divide."

"I'm not babysitting, man," Mitch said. "Wendy and I are going out this afternoon."

"Whatever," Ethan said. "I'll figure it out."

"Good. I'm going over now. See you later."

Ethan grunted and watched Mitch leave. "What time is it?" he asked Jazz.

"About ten, why?"

"Great. Three hours."

"Wanna play cards?"

"Sure. Why not?"

****

Bill stared down at the drawing Aerfyn had done of the creature she called Dynion Gors.

"Looks a bit like a muscular Gollum," Constable Genevieve Boulduc noted from over Bill's shoulder.

"Who?"

"From Lord of the Rings?"

"I didn't watch it."

"Seriously? It's a good movie."

"It's twelve hours long."

"You're not supposed to watch it all at once."

Constable Jackman shrugged.

"Still no sign of her?"

"It's like she fell off the face of the earth," Bill said. He put the drawing back down on his desk. "I still think those boys have her."

"Come on, Bill. They had an alibi."

"She was lying."

Genevieve rolled her eyes. "Of course she was."

Bill fell silent for a time. "Hey, do you think monsters could exist?"

"Well, anything's possible, I suppose. But monsters? I really don't think so. She was probably attacked by some freak in a costume on Hallowe'en and has turned it into something supernatural in her head."

"Yeah. Probably."

"You don't sound convinced. Don't tell me you believe in monsters."

"No. No, it's not that. It's just…"

"Just what?"

"Something's off. I can't put my finger on it, but something is definitely off."

"Okay, Spiderman." Officer Boulduc handed Bill a mug of steaming coffee. "Caffeine break."

"Thanks," Bill muttered.

"You look exhausted."

"Haven't been sleeping."

Officer Boulduc raised her brows, expecting more to follow. Bill simply shrugged when he noticed. "It's nothing."

"Sure."

"Seriously. It's nothing."

But it wasn't nothing. Nightmares had plagued Officer William Jackman since he had seen the drawing Aerfyn had done. Tall, slender creatures in black hoods chased him through the deserted streets of downtown Ottawa.

One had an axe.

****

"Where are we?" Olwen asked as his run came to a stop. They had lost sight of Tylluan some time ago and now were running through woods.

"I've found a path!" Peredur called from a few feet ahead.

Shrugging, Olwen and Gawain trudged to Peredur. Sure enough, a thin, well-trodden path wound its way through the trees.

"So," Gawain said. "Left or right?"

Peredur squinted up through the foliage. "I don't recognise these stars."

"Wonderful, so navigation is out of the question."

"Even if we could navigate, we have no idea where Aerfyn is. The question 'left or right?' would still stand."

Olwen sighed. "So, now what?"

"Well," Gawain said. "Gwalchgwyn said the laws of our world are roughly the same as the laws of this one. Rain falls downward, trees grow upwards. The sun should still rise in the east and set in the west. If we wait until dawn, we can at least get a bearing."

"I don't like the delay," Olwen growled. "Aerfyn could be in serious trouble."

"I dare say she can handle herself."

"Hey, look! An owl!"

Olwen and Gawain turned to look at where Peredur pointed.

"That's not Tylluan," Olwen said.

"No, but it's an owl," Peredur said.

The owl leapt off the branch upon which it sat and sailed silently overhead. The three adventurers watched it land on a branch of a far tree, then turn its brown head to look back at them.

"That's a sign," Peredur said. "We go left." Without waiting for agreement, Peredur started walking.

"I wish I had his faith," Gawain muttered as he followed.

"Cheer up," Olwen said, smiling in the dark. "It is an adventure after all."

Gawain simply growled.

****

Itheann Beanna, leader of the twelve, narrowed his bulging eyes. The other eleven Fir Bolg waited patiently behind him, waiting for his signal. The three Pobl Gwir he stalked had paused to talk amongst themselves. It seemed as if they had no plan.

Stupid little people, he thought to himself. *No wonder we're winning.*

After a time, the small group of Pobl Gwir turned down a narrow trek and trudged down it.

Itheann Beanna signalled his warriors, and they flitted through the shadows, silent and unseen after the Pobl Gwir. Those foolish men would lead the twelve Fir Bolg straight to their Battle Queen, and when they did...

106

Itheann Beanna grinned to himself. The odds were three to one. There was no way the Battle Queen was escaping – not alive.

****

Professor Gwilym Davies was not any more impressed with the essays than he had been yesterday. Thankfully, the one he currently had in front of him used correct grammar. If only the student cared so much about spelling.

A knock at his door pulled his attention away from the essays. The young man from yesterday stood awkwardly in the doorway.

"Well," Gwilym said, sucking in air. "If it isn't Ethan Evans."

"Uh... hi."

"Come in. Sit down."

"Thanks." Ethan did so. "I'm really sorry to bother you, Professor D."

"That's all right. A welcome distraction, actually. More questions today?"

"Yeah. It's probably going to sound pretty crazy, actually."

"Oh good. Normal is thoroughly boring." Gwilym's eyes twinkled merrily.

"Uh. Right. I was just wondering if you knew any places where, you know, someone could pass into the Otherworld."

"There are a number of locations in the U.K. where such myth is atta –"

"No, I mean, like, here. In Ottawa."

Professor Davies leant back in his chair. "In Ottawa?"

"Yeah."

"There are no such places. Not in Ottawa."

Ethan slumped. "I was afraid of that."

Professor Davies had dealt with a lot of nutters in his lifetime, but Ethan Evans was the most surprising. He seemed perfectly normal otherwise. "Why?" the professor asked, not sure he wanted to know the answer.

"You'll never believe me."

"Try me."

Ethan shifted uncomfortably in his seat. "All right," he said at length. "Do you remember the big hoo-rah on Carleton's campus on Hallowe'en – the wounded girl they found?"

"I read something of it the papers."

"Well, I'm one of the guys who found her."

"Indeed? Go on."

"All right. Well, this girl, she's... well... special."

"Special how?"

"I think she's from ... somewhere else."

Silence followed as the professor's quick mind jumped immediately to Ethan's meaning. "You mean to tell me you think she's from the Otherworld."

"Um... yeah. I guess."

"I... See."

"I told you you wouldn't believe me. Look, she was wearing real armour, and carried real weapons, and the surgeon said she'd been hit with an axe or something similar, and she doesn't speak English, only Welsh, well, I think it's Welsh, and she's the one who told me about the Dynion Gors, and I believe her because they attacked me and my buddy, Mitch, and she saved our asses, and we really need help hiding her while we figure out how to get her home."

Ethan talked so quickly it was all Gwilym could do to keep up with him. "Woah, woah, slow down, Ethan."

Ethan stopped talking and took a deep breath.

"Look, she's here, if you want to talk to her yourself."

"She's here?"

Ethan nodded.

Gwilym couldn't hide his curiosity. "Bring her in."

Ethan went to the door. He opened it and poked his head out. "Jazz," he said, waving someone in. He stepped aside as two young women entered.

One seemed normal enough, wearing jeans and a Nordic sweater. The other was slightly slimmer, slightly taller and wore a tan, three quarter length pea coat with the hood drawn up. When the door shut, the coat-wearing girl reached up and took her hood down.

She was beautiful. Red gold hair hung in shimmering waves down her back and intelligent, curious brown eyes looked at Gwilym.

"Professor D," Ethan said. "This is Aerfyn."

Gwilym rose to his feet. "Bore dda," he said gravely.

The girl relaxed significantly and a relieved smile crossed her face. "Byddwch siarad fy iaith! A ydych yn Pobl Gwir?"

Professor Davies almost fainted. His greeting had been a test. He did not expect her to pass it. "Pobl Gwir?" he asked.

The girl's smile slipped a little. "Yna nad ydych yn. Byddech yn gwybod y Pobl Gwir os oeddech."

"Gwelaf. Gwelaf. Yr wyf yn Gwilym. Dywedwch wrthyf amdanoch eich hun."

Aerfyn sat on the chair and started speaking rapidly to Gwilym. Jazz and Ethan stood by the door and exchanged a confused glance.

The conversation lasted quite a while. By the end of it, Professor Davies had gone quite pale and shook a little. He looked up at Ethan with wide eyes.

"Is it true that these Dynion Gors attacked you?"

Ethan nodded. "Man, they were so weird. Ugly, and skinny, you know, but super strong. One had a massive axe. That's why I'm trying to help her out, you know? I figured I owe her one."

Gwilym seemed to shrink. "It's not possible."

Aerfyn cocked her head at him. "Ddim yn eich pobl yn gwybod am y rhwystr?"

"Mae'n dim ond chwedl bell," Professor Davies replied.

"Yna byddwch yn gwybod unwaith, ond wedi anghofio."

Gwilym nodded absently.

"I'm sorry, but, what?" Ethan asked.

"She just asked if we did not know about the barrier between worlds. I told her that to us it was nothing but distant myth."

"And she said?"

"That we knew once, but forgot." Professor Davies was still in shock. He stared into space a moment. "I can't believe this. This is some bizarre dream, or you're putting me on. Or you're all insane."

"Professor, please," Ethan said. "I know it sounds crazy. I know you don't believe us, but I've seen these things. They genuinely did attack us. We genuinely owe Aerfyn our lives."

"It can't be."

"Can you tell us what you two were talking about just before?" Jazz asked.

"I told her to tell me about herself."

"And?"

"And, according to her delusion, she's the commander of the army of the Pobl Gwir – the True People. A year ago, the leader of the Dynion Gors – Bog Men – came forward with a marriage proposal for her. Both she and her father refused him and in a rage, he declared war. They've been fighting ever since. Aerfyn here says she was in a battle when she fell through the divide. When she woke next, she was in, as she puts it, a 'strange healer's pavilion.'"

"The hospital," Ethan said.

"I expect so. She's remarkably self-aware for someone with delusions."

"Professor D, I swear to God that I was attacked by monsters. There were three of them. One had a huge axe."

"So she said. This is a prank, isn't it? Which one of my students put you up to this?"

"It's no prank," Ethan said. "Look, the cops are after her. These monsters, the Dynion Gors, are after her... please Professor, we need somewhere to hide her until I can find a way to get her home."

"No. Absolutely not! If she is being hunted by the authorities, it's for good reason. She needs proper care."

"She needs to go home."

"Gwilym," Aerfyn said gently. "Fy mhobl angen i mi."

Gwilym looked at her. Aerfyn was young, and very pretty, and her expression was deadly serious. Her brown eyes were both sad and sharp. Everything about her belied absolute confidence in herself. If warriors existed they would probably hold themselves as she did.

"I..."

"Professor," Ethan said urgently. "Just imagine, for a moment, just imagine that everything she's described, everything I've described is actually possible. Imagine it was you who fell into some other world in a freak accident. Imagine waking up in a place you don't know, surrounded by people you don't know, machines you've never seen before. Imagine how lost and alone you'd feel, how much you could use a stranger's kindness at that moment. Please, I am begging you. Help me get her home."

Gwilym was moved, and every fibre of his being begged for the adventure, but his mind could not let go of reality so easily. He rubbed his cheek as his gaze shifted back and forth between Ethan and Aerfyn. Ethan looked painfully uncertain, almost desperate. Aerfyn looked calm and composed. Both stared at him, waiting for a response.

"This isn't happening," Professor Davies mumbled. "This isn't happening."

"Please, Professor," Ethan said.

Aerfyn leant in. "Beth oedd ei fod yn gofyn ichi?"

Gwilym burst out laughing.

"What?" Ethan asked.

"She just asked…" Gwilym shook his head. "She's putting a lot of trust in you, Ethan Evans. She just asked what it was you were asking for."

Ethan looked at Aerfyn. She smiled back.

"Tell her we're trying to get her home, but we need somewhere to hide her, somewhere safe, while we figure out how."

"Am rywle i guddio chi hyd nes y gall fynd â chi adref."

In an instant, Aerfyn was out of her chair. She threw her arms around Ethan's chest and pulled him into a tight embrace. "Diolch yn fawr," she whispered.

"Uh…" Ethan said, unsure of what to do. He hesitantly put his arms around Aerfyn and rubbed her back in awkward strokes.

"You're welcome," he said.

A small sob told Ethan that Aerfyn was crying. He pulled her in closer.

"Hey, hey… it's okay It's going to be all right. We'll get you home, Aerfyn. We'll find a way. I swear it." He looked over at Jazz, hoping for some advice on what to do with the sobbing girl.

Jazz just smiled secretively and shrugged at him.

Gwilym sighed. "I can't believe I'm about to say this," he muttered to himself. "I have a cottage up past Blue Sea Lake. It's fairly isolated, and most all of the cottagers have gone home for the season. Not too many people are around. She should be safe from prying eyes there."

Ethan's jaw dropped. "Seriously? Really? You'll let her stay there?"

Gwilym nodded. "But if I find this is all some sort of terrible joke, God help you all!"

In a matter of minutes, everything had been arranged. Jazz left the office to collect Aerfyn's things, such that they were, and returned shortly thereafter. Professor Davies placed a sign on his office door stating that he wasn't feeling very well and that he would not be holding his regular office hours.

Ethan, Aerfyn and Jazz all piled into Jazz' car and Gwilym went to his. The tiny convoy made their way out of the city.

During the entire two hour drive, Aerfyn examined the inside of the car, tapping on the windows, pushing against the frame, playing with her seatbelt and, more often than not, leaning over the front passenger seat to glare at the road ahead. Once or twice, she muttered something darkly.

Jazz and Ethan exchanged amused looks. Ethan almost burst out laughing a few times. It had been the same when Aerfyn first entered Jazz' car to come to the University of Ottawa. Though then she had been much more alarmed and almost panicked when the engine roared to life and the car started moving forward. It had taken Ethan a long while to calm her down, and even then, Aerfyn remained agitated.

At the moment, her agitation had cooled and curiosity had taken over. Ethan could only imagine what was going through her mind at the moment.

"Do you think she's thinking about horseless carriages right now?" Ethan asked Jazz.

Jazz shrugged. "I'd be thinking about it if I were her."

Ethan grinned.

They drove on in the hazy afternoon light. Several small townships came and went as they followed Professor Davies' car down the winding Quebec roads. Long stretches of mountainous terrain populated by nothing more than maple forests wearing their autumnal vestments filled the car windows. Aerfyn enjoyed the view enough to stop pondering about what magic lay behind the vehicle in which she rode. She pressed her palm against her window and stared out at the coloured forest a small smile on her face.

This was terrain that was, if not the same, at least similar to her home. Her smile faded slightly at the thought of home; her father and her friends, either still fighting or dead upon the field. She knew not which.

Biting her lip, Aerfyn faced forward again and bowed her head.

Roughly fifteen minutes past the township of Kazabazua, Quebec, Professor Davies turned off the paved road onto a grey gravel road. The road from there grew steadily worse, and Aerfyn's anxiety returned. She braced herself against the roof and side of the car as it bounced and bobbed its way along.

The road grew narrower yet and switched from gravel to brown dirt, pitted with potholes and miniature gorges etched by run off from heavy rains. On all sides, the trees pressed in close, their spindly branches scraping on the tops of the cars.

Jazz' car, an ancient Sunfire, was not equipped to deal with the conditions of the road. It lurched savagely from side to side, the shocks doing nothing for the heads of the passengers, which were continually bumped against the roof as the vehicle scraped over rocks and banks of various kinds.

"Jesus," Ethan said the third time his head hit the roof.

"Sorry," Jazz muttered. "It's a little bumpy."

"Thank-you, Captain Obvious."

"Your face is obvious."

"What? That doesn't make any sense!"

Jazz chuckled to herself.

The drive lasted a further ten minutes before Professor Davies' car crawled to a halt in a vaguely rectangular clearing. Jazz pulled up beside him and all three piled out of the car. Aerfyn required some assistance and looked quite ill.

"What?" Jazz said when Ethan threw her an irritated glance after Aerfyn had slid out of the car and stumbled unsteadily away from it. "My driving isn't *that* bad."

Ethan looked around. Trees grew thick here, but between them, he caught a glimpse of a small wooden house.

"Is that it?" he asked Gwilym, nodding in the direction of the house.

"Yes," Gwilym answered. "Come on, I'll take you on the tour."

Ethan collected Aerfyn and they all trudged up the barely visible path to the cottage. The cottage itself was larger than Ethan had guessed. It contained a fairly decent sized kitchen with an adjoined dining room, two bedrooms, and a large balcony that overlooked the lake through the trees.

Ethan took Aerfyn through and the pair stood on the balcony, watching the late afternoon sun dance upon the lake.

"It's beautiful here," Ethan said when Gwilym and Jazz joined them. He breathed in deeply.

The air smelled like water, and maple and cedar. It was clean and crisp. A few late birds twittered here and there, accompanied by the occasional call of a crow.

"My girlfriend and I would come here often," Gwilym said. "Before the split. I barely make it out here now."

"Is it safe, do you think?"

"I doubt very much anyone would disturb Aerfyn here. Like I said, most everyone leaves the lake in the winter."

"Will it be warm enough?" Jazz said, turning back to eye the cottage.

"There is a wood stove in each of the bedrooms, as well as the dining room, and all the windows are double glass and sealed tightly. If she has to live through the winter here, she should be all right."

"Let's hope it doesn't take us that long," Ethan murmured. "So... I can come up every Thursday and on the weekends. I have no classes."

"I can come up with you on the weekends," Gwilym said. "But I've obligations at the University during the week."

"I can come up Thursdays as well," Jazz said. "And Tuesdays. But I'm working at the cinema until my next gig."

Ethan nodded. "Well, that's three days out of four. Not the end of the world. Still, I'd feel better if she wasn't alone so often."

Gwilym turned to Aerfyn. "Ni allwn aros yma gyda chi drwy'r amser."

Aerfyn nodded. "Rwy'n deall."

"Byddwn yn dod pryd bynnag y gallwn."

Aerfyn nodded again. "Byddaf angen gleddyf."

Gwilym blinked in surprise. "Uh…"

"What?" Ethan asked.

"She says she will need a sword."

"Yeah. That makes sense."

"It does?"

"Well, to defend herself in case the Dynion Gors find her. Of course, the problem then lies in where the hell to find a frikkin' sword."

"Kutters," Jazz said. "In the Merivale Mall. They sell all kinds of swords."

Ethan and Gwilym stared at Jazz.

"How the hell do you know all this stuff?" Ethan asked.

Jazz shrugged. "My roommate. She's into all this kind of stuff."

"How much? Do you know?"

"I don't, but I don't think they come cheap."

Ethan nodded. "I'll ask my dad if he'll loan me some cash. I'll pick some up and bring it with me on Thursday."

"And if they find her before then?" Gwilym asked.

Ethan chewed his lip. "I don't know."

"I have a solution," Jazz said. "I will go down tomorrow and pick up some weapons. I'll give you the bill, and you pay me back."

"Wait," Gwilym said. He pulled out his wallet. "Here, let me write you a cheque. How much do you think you'll need?"

Jazz shrugged. "I don't know. Maybe two hundred?"

"I'll give you five, you can pay me the difference if there is any."

"Dude," Ethan said. "That's really good of you, but…"

"No arguments. I make more than the pair of you combined."

"Yeah, but, you don't even really believe us."

Professor Davies shrugged. "I'm undecided. But, what the hell? If you're right, and all this is real, I'd gladly pay more for the privilege of having met someone from there."

Jazz accepted the cheque. "Listen," she said. "Thanks so much."

"Just pay me back when you can," Gwilym replied with a shrug.

"What about tonight?" Ethan asked.

"Well, I have to get back to my dog," Gwilym said. "He gets grumpy when I am out late."

"I should head back too," Jazz said. "Especially since I have to get to Kutters tomorrow."

Ethan nodded. "Well, I can miss another day of class. It's not like I've been all week. I'll just say that I was ill or something. Besides, Mitch'll give me his notes."

Gwilym smiled at Aerfyn and told her that Ethan planned to stay the night with her, but Jazz and himself had to return to the city. Jazz would return on the morrow with weapons, and Gwilym would return two days following. Aerfyn looked at Ethan, then nodded.

They all walked back to the cars and Aerfyn thanked both Jazz and Professor Davies profusely before they both drove off. She turned to Ethan after the cars vanished from sight, smiled a little, then returned to the balcony to watch the water.

Not knowing what else to do, Ethan wandered into the kitchen to see if there was any food for dinner. As it happened, Gwilym kept a good store of non-perishables and soon Ethan was cooking a large portion of Kraft Dinner.

****

Out on the balcony, Aerfyn watched the water and listened to the birds in the trees.

"Can you hear me, Papa?" she whispered into the wind. "Are you there?"

Only the breeze gave her reply. Aerfyn shook her head in an effort to fight the tears that had formed at the corners of her eyes. She pulled her jacket closer around herself.

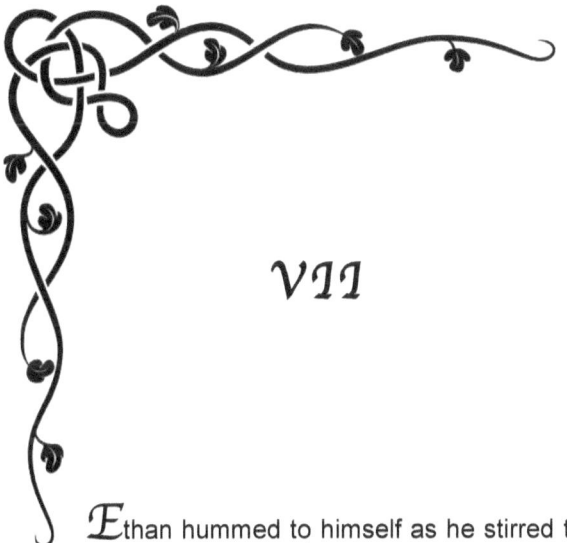

VII

*E*than hummed to himself as he stirred the pot of bubbling powdered cheese, macaroni and water. From the kitchen he could see Aerfyn leaning against the railing of the balcony, enjoying the fading sun. October had been unseasonably warm this year. November, however, brought with it its typical chill. Those trees that had not yet lost their leaves were likely to lose them this week, leaving nothing but a bleak scene of grey until the snows came and made everything beautiful again.

It was Ethan's third November in Ottawa. As a child of British Columbia, he found that the cold had taken some getting used to. However, once the snows arrived, it made the cold bearable. He wondered if it ever got as cold where Aerfyn was from as it did here, and if not, how on earth she would cope with the inhospitable weather soon to strike Ottawa?

As it was now, many of the trees still had their golden and red leaves, and she seemed quite comfortable in her jeans and leather jacket.

Ethan breathed deep. The smell of burnt food filled his nostrils.

"Shit!" he swore, ripping his eyes off Aerfyn and back down at the food he was supposed to be cooking. He grabbed a tea towel and took the pot off the archaic stove and placed it in the sink. He shook his head, turned off the stove and fetched bowls to put the macaroni and cheese into.

When the steaming food was cool enough, Ethan popped some into his mouth to test it. The burnt flavour was barely noticeable, though he'd have one hell of a task before him when it came time to scrub the pot out. Throwing the tea towel over his shoulder, he picked up the bowls and went to the balcony.

"Here," he said gently as he placed the bowl on the railings beside Aerfyn.

Aerfyn looked down at the bowl, then up at Ethan. She smiled gratefully for the warm food and dragged the bowl in front of her. She waited for Ethan to begin eating before she started. Ethan was unsure if it was intended as a mark of respect or if she was concerned that he'd poisoned the meal.

He watched carefully as she took her first bite. She pulled a face.

Ethan laughed. "Not to your liking?"

Aerfyn smiled and played with the contents of her bowl a while before taking another mouthful. The taste seemed to grow on her. It was that, or she was far too hungry to care about taste at the moment. In any case, she ate quickly.

Ethan smiled as he watched her as she finished her bowl.

"K.D," he said, pointing with his fork at the food in his bowl.

"K.D," Aerfyn repeated.

Ethan grinned and nodded. "Do you want more?"

Aerfyn cocked her head.

"More?" Ethan asked, pointing to her empty bowl, and then to his half-full one.

Aerfyn shook her head with a frown. She didn't understand.

Ethan hurriedly finished his bowl and took Aerfyn's from her. "Come," he said, indicating the cottage with his head. Aerfyn followed him inside.

He went to the kitchen sink and began refilling his bowl. He offered it to Aerfyn, who took it with relish. Grinning, Ethan filled the other bowl and the two went to the table. They sat and ate in comfortable silence. When they were done, and the pot was empty, save for the crust of burnt food at the bottom, Ethan rinsed the dishes and set them aside.

By that time, it was quite dark outside. Aerfyn retired to a chair, found a snow globe and entertained herself. Ethan watched her from the kitchen sink before deciding he should probably scrub the dishes. It took him the better part of two hours to scrub the pot clean. By that time, Aerfyn had fallen asleep, curled up in the ample seat of the chair.

Ethan smiled to himself as he dried his hands. He went over to Aerfyn and shook her shoulder gently. Aerfyn's body moved, but her eyes remained shut.

Sighing, Ethan picked her up from the chair and took her to the second bedroom. He laid her on the bed and covered her over with the many blankets that had been folded at the foot of it.

He stood by the bed a moment and watched Aerfyn sleep. She looked impossibly young with her eyes shut. Eighteen, perhaps; not much older than a high school student. Shaking his head, Ethan walked from the room and turned the light off. He sat down on a chair and tried to think of something else. Try as he might, however, his mind always turned back to Aerfyn.

Sighing to himself, he left the chair and went to bed. The stillness of the night made it impossible for him to sleep. He tossed and turned, trying to think of his lectures rather than Aerfyn. After what felt like hours, Ethan finally drifted into sleep.

The morning dawned bright and cold. Ethan shivered when he tossed the blankets aside. He left his room to find the cottage silent. He checked on Aerfyn. Her bed was empty. He left the room and ran out onto the balcony. She was not there either. In a panic, he dashed back into the cottage, threw on his jacket and, forgetting his boots, raced out to check the surrounding woods.

He rounded the corner of the cottage and nearly ran right into Aerfyn. He frowned at her. She, in turn, smiled up at him. In her hand she held a rope upon which was affixed four freshwater fish of various sizes, already gutted and scaled. In her other hand, she held a spear with three porcupine quills attached at the end.

Ethan blinked.

"Bwyd bore," Aerfyn said. She walked into the cottage with the fish. Ethan followed her. Aerfyn took the fish and laid them on the kitchen counter. Ethan had an idea. He left the cottage again to collect the firewood stacked neatly against the south side. He returned, filled the wood stove in the dining room with tinder and wood and started a fire. He went to the kitchen to fetch a skillet and some salt.

Aerfyn watched with interest as Ethan placed the large skillet on the wood stove and left it there. It did not take long to heat up. Seasoning the fish with salt and pepper, the only seasonings Gwilym had at the cottage, Ethan threw them whole into the skillet, two at a time. He covered the skillet over and left them to cook.

He beckoned Aerfyn over. She went to him, her curious expression unchanging. Ethan picked up the box of matches he had used to start the fire. He removed a match and held it up.

"Match," he said.

Aerfyn nodded. "Match," she repeated.

Ethan smiled. He struck the match against the side of the box. Aerfyn jumped backwards when the head flared. She stared at the match in wonder. Ethan blew the match out and handed her the box.

"You try," he said.

Unsure, Aerfyn opened the box and extracted the match. She placed it on the side of the box. Ethan laughed.

"No," he said, turning the box over. "This side, where this red stuff is."

Aerfyn nodded. She placed the match and struck it, trying to emulate Ethan. The head broke off, unlit, and flew into the air, getting lost in one of the cracks in the floor.

Ethan laughed again. He took the box from her and showed her once more. Scowling Aerfyn took the box back and tried again. This time the match flared. She dropped the match in shock. Ethan jumped back before stomping on the match to put it out.

"Please don't burn the place down," he said.

Aerfyn might not have understood the words, but it was perfectly clear she understood the sentiment. Pale, she nodded and tried once more. This time, she managed to hold onto the match when the head flared. She watched it in fascination, before blowing it out.

Ethan smiled. He would cook and clean while he was here, but she needed to be taught how to take care of herself for when he was not. He figured a wood stove would be easier to deal with than an ancient, difficult oven. Any civilisation that used swords must know about fire.

But perhaps not matches.

Aerfyn struck another match, her face lighting up when the head flared. Ethan laughed and snatched back the matches.

"That's enough, you pyro," he said, grinning. He placed the matches in the hand-turned terracotta bowl on the shelf by the wood stove and returned to making breakfast.

They ate well that morning, polishing off the fish at a leisurely pace. Once Ethan had done the dishes, Aerfyn went back outside. Curious, Ethan followed. He watched Aerfyn stalk around the trees, her eyes on the ground, her pale brow furrowed. She ducked down and picked up two sizeable sticks, examined them briefly and then looked back at Ethan. She smiled and beckoned him over.

He walked over, his hands in his pockets. Aerfyn threw him a stick, which he deftly caught, and then readied her own as if she were holding a sword. Ethan understood. He placed both hands at the lower end of the stick and copied her.

There were five major strokes Aerfyn showed Ethan, and five corresponding major blocks. Ethan and Aerfyn drilled them for almost an hour. She led and Ethan copied. The drill changed to Aerfyn attacking and Ethan defending, and then again to Ethan attacking and Aerfyn defending. They went through each of the five attacks and blocks in sequence, spending most of the morning out in the trees, drilling together.

Fit already from lacrosse training, and a fast learner, Ethan picked up the lesson fairly quickly. It was more fun than he thought possible. His imagination ran wild as he attacked and defended in turn. He was suddenly ten years old again, and an imaginary knight of an imaginary realm training to defend his king and castle against imaginary fearsome invaders.

The thoughts painted a lopsided grin on his face as he blocked and attacked and blocked again.

Their play ended when the sound of a car pulling in drew their attention.

Jazz had arrived, a large bundle in her arms. "Hey," she called when she caught sight of Ethan and Aerfyn approaching through the trees.

"Good morning," Ethan said.

"Morning? It's one o'clock."

"Is it? Already?"

Jazz looked up as she slammed the boot of her car shut. She had pulled out four long rectangular boxes and had a bunch of swords wrapped in a towel in her arms.

"Here," Ethan said, dropping his sword. He grabbed the bundle from Jazz. "Let me help."

"Thanks," Jazz said with relief. She picked up two boxes and Aerfyn silently did the same. They trudged into the cottage.

"All right," Jazz said, opening a box. "Now, I'm not sure what kind of sword she'd want, so I picked out a bunch."

"How could you afford all this?"

"They have my credit card. None of these are paid for yet." She opened the first box to reveal a hand and a half sword – a simple design with an oval pommel – still in its very plain scabbard. Aerfyn carefully removed it from the box and drew the sword, testing its weight and balance. She sheathed it again as Jazz opened another box.

This box contained a single-handed long sword of equally plain design. It was lighter and faster than the other sword, yet a little wider at the hilt. Aerfyn seemed to prefer it. She held onto it as the third box was opened.

A long, thin, single-handed sword with an ornate brass pommel in a wooden scabbard was revealed. Aerfyn picked it up, but placed it down again nearly as quickly. She shook her head.

"That was quick," Ethan noted.

"All right, now this one was called the 'Celtic War Sword.' I figured that if she was Welsh, she might want something Celtic. The Welsh are Celts, right?"

Ethan shrugged. "I dunno."

"Well, it was a new sword for them. I figured I'd give it a try, at least."

It proved to be the best possible choice. Aerfyn tested the weight and balance, a thoughtful look on her face. She placed the sword down and tested the other one again. It took her several tries before she decided to go with the Celtic War Sword.

"Yes!" Jazz said. "I win!"

Ethan laughed. "What are all these, then?"

"They're called 'wasters' apparently. They're blunt swords used for practice."

"How much did that run you?"

"Nothing. My roommate gave them to me, said they were freebies from her trainer."

"Sweet! Can I have one?"

Jazz shrugged. "I guess so. There are, like, six here."

"Sweet!"

The wasters were all the same – simple single-handed swords without scabbards. Many of them were notched and nicked, but were otherwise whole and unbroken. Ethan pulled out two of the least damaged and handed one to Aerfyn. She took it with a smile.

"I brought some sandwiches," Jazz said. "Figured you'd be wanting some lunch."

"Oh! Yes please!" Ethan said.

"I'll be right back." Jazz left the cottage to fetch the food from the car.

Aerfyn observed her new sword, evidently pleased. She smiled brightly at Ethan before returning to testing it. If

Ethan had doubted her story before now, the skill with which she handled the blade would have convinced him. He watched her a moment before Jazz returned carrying a cooler. He cleared off the dining table and soon all three were seated and happily munching on freshly made sandwiches.

"So, what did you guys do this morning?"

"It's so cool!" Ethan exploded, glad to have someone to talk to about the morning's activities. "Aerfyn showed me how to use a sword! We've been drilling all morning." Ethan's blue eyes sparkled and he waved his hands about animatedly as he spoke.

Jazz grinned. "Cool."

"Oh my *gawd*, you have no idea!"

Aerfyn watched amused as Ethan explained the intricacies of what he had learnt this morning to Jazz. Though she could not understand his words, she knew by the motion of his hands precisely what he spoke of and she could tell by the excitement in his voice and the way he bounced on his chair that he was enthusiastic about the morning's lesson. His boyish excitement was endearing.

Jazz remained for most of the afternoon and, enticed by Ethan's enthusiasm, she even consented to taking sword-fighting lessons with him. Before long the three of them were running amidst the trees, applying their newly acquired skills against one another.

They had so much fun that Jazz completely forgot the time and ended up trudging back to her car after the sun had set. Ethan elected to stay for Friday and the weekend. He figured missing one more day of lectures was not going to kill him.

The night was spent by the opened potbellied wood stove, wrapped in a blanket with a steaming cup of tea. Aerfyn seemed content to sit in silence and watch the flames, but Ethan desperately wanted to talk to her; to ask her age, her thoughts, her dreams. He watched her watch the fire, an unintended smile painted on his face.

****

Peredur scratched his head. "All right," he said, uncertain. "Left again?"

The three adventurers stood on the side of a very wide road. Three chariots could easily have moved side by side along it.

Gawain swore. "What is the point of all these paths and roads? I thought they were designed to connect places. These just seem to be here for no reason."

"Perhaps there are great distances between places in this world."

"That's ludicrous. More than a couple of day's ride? The people of this place must be fond of sleeping out of doors."

"Do you hear that?" Peredur asked, turning his attention to the right.

"What kind of animal is that?" Olwen asked, stepping up to stand on Peredur's right.

"Whatever it is, it's getting closer."

The distant whining roar grew in volume rapidly.

"Lamps," Gawain said.

It seemed to the three men that no sooner had they spotted the twin lights, than the lights roared past at phenomenal speed, the roar increasing and then

131

decreasing in tone as the strange thing whipped by.
The wind off the thing was so strong, Peredur had to take a step to right his balance after it passed.

"What the hell kind of beast was that? Gawain said.

"I don't think it was an animal," Peredur said. "There was a person sitting inside it."

"I saw nothing."

"I saw him," Olwen said. "There was definitely a person."

"So, what then? Some sort of magical chariot?"

"It seems so. What beast would follow a road so closely?" Peredur asked.

"Or have a person ride in it, rather than on it?" Olwen added.

Gawain grunted. "So, these people are in possession of powerful magic. Wonderful. Let's hope they're on our side."

"I suppose we head in the direction the chariot was headed," Peredur said.

"Why?"

"Well, wouldn't you want to go to where someone was headed, rather than where they were coming from at this time of night?"

Olwen shrugged. "It's as good a direction as any. Let's go."

The three men, careful to keep off the road, started walking.

****

Biter Feargach sniffed the air. The Pobl Gwir queen and the tall, broad boy had been gone for a long time now.

Only the slightly thinner man remained. That was not what had Biter Feargach sniffing the air, however. A northern wind brought a familiar scent to his nose, barely detectable amidst the almost overpowering smells of this city.

It was there, nonetheless. His fellows had found their way here, and were somewhere north of himself. He turned to one of his companions and said, "Stay and watch. Our brothers are here. I will go find them."

The woman nodded and Biter Feargach and his other companion vanished from the bushes, making their way north.

****

Mitch flipped the business card of Police Constable Bill Jackman over and over in his hand. He sat in the darkened residence room he and Ethan shared, alone and wondering where the hell Ethan and Aerfyn had gotten to. Had they been abducted by the Bog Men?

Police Constable Bill Jackman was only a call away. All Mitch had to do was call and he would have his friend back.

But what if Ethan didn't want to be found? What if he'd hidden Aerfyn away and stayed with her?

With a sigh, Mitch slipped the card back in his wallet. He spun on his desk chair and stared up at the ceiling.

****

Constable Bill Jackman, on the other hand, stared down at the drawing Aerfyn had done. He'd been working the graveyard shift for the past couple of days.

"Dynion Gors," he muttered to himself. "What the hell kind of rubbish language did she make up?"

"Hey, Spiderman," Officer Boulduc said as she marched into the office. "Hear about the robbery on Bank and Fourth?"

Bill simply grunted.

She peeked over his shoulder after she filled her mug with coffee. "Still on that?" she asked.

"I can't get it out of my head," Bill said. "She really seemed so earnest."

"Yes, but crazy people don't know they're crazy. She probably fully believes in these monsters."

"Probably."

"Uh, all cars, this is dispatch," a voice crackled over the radio Bill had on his desk. "We've had reports of three men in armour marching downtown. Latest report on Wellington in front of Parliament Hill. Be warned, they are armed with... uh... swords."

"What the...?" Bill said. He grabbed the walkie-talkie.

"Dispatch this is Constable Jackman. Say again, please?"

"Three men seen in armour on Wellington in front of Parliament Hill."

"No one touch them," Bill said through the radio. "They're mine." He jumped up and, grabbing his baton from his desk, raced out the door.

"I'm coming too!" Officer Boulduc said. She left her mug on Bill's desk and ran out after him.

By the time Bill and Genevieve arrived on the scene, the three men were surrounded by squad cars. Royal Canadian Mounted Police and Ottawa Police Service both stood before their cars, their guns and tasers drawn.

The three men, fully armed and wearing enamelled leather and steel armour, stood with their backs against one another, their swords drawn and held steady. For men that were about to be shot, they seemed suspiciously calm.

Bill got out of the car and approached cautiously.

"Bill," an R.C.M.P. officer with grey hair and a large gut greeted.

"Bob," Bill replied.

"You wanted these?"

"In connection with another case I'm working on."

"The crazy girl."

"Yup. That one."

"Good luck, sir. These bastards are speaking gibberish."

Bill walked forward, taking out his badge. "Good evening," he said to the three men.

All of them turned to look at Bill, only one held his gaze. The other two turned back to keep an eye on the others surrounding them.

"Noswaith dda," the man in armour said. "Yr wyf yn Peredur. Rhydym yn chwilio am Aerfyn."

"What the f...?" an officer said.

Bill, however, recognised one word in the jumble of gibberish spewing from the man's mouth.

"Aerfyn," he said.

Peredur frowned at Bill. "Aerfyn. Aerfyn yw ein brenhines."

Bill approached slowly. "Aerfyn," he said again, pointed back towards his squad car. Peredur glanced briefly at it.

"Dangos i mi," he demanded. "Dangos i mi Aerfyn!"

One of the others muttered something to Peredur, who nodded. He glared at Bill. "Dangos i mi Aerfyn!"

The man's tone became increasingly agitated. Bill stopped approaching.

"Okay there, boss," he said. "Just calm down. I will take you to Aerfyn."

Peredur stepped forward menacingly, his sword still at the ready. That was enough of a threat for the gathered policemen. One shot his taser, but the end failed to gain purchase on Peredur's armour. There was one zap before the taser fell uselessly to the ground. It was enough of a zap, however. The electric charge dispersed through the armour the man wore with enough force to make him yelp and jump. The distraction enabled Bill to charge forward.

He batted the man's sword aside and rugby tackled him to the ground. Shouts erupted and the gathered officers managed to take down the other two in the confusion. The armoured men struggled and shouted in their bizarre language as the officers held them down and cuffed them. They shouted and yelled as they were dragged to Bill's squad car and forced inside.

"You sure you want them?" Bob asked as he shut the door.

"Yup," Bill answered. "I think they're connected with the Jane Doe that was found at Carleton U. last week."

"Suit yourself," Bob said. "Better you than me."

Bill grinned. He and Officer Boulduc jumped back into their squad car and drove back to the station.

****

Watching the three Pobl Gwir get themselves into trouble was more than simply entertaining. Itheann Beanna could not contain his grin as he watched from the weathered copper roof of Centre Block on Parliament Hill. He squatted, perfectly still, looking very much like one of the grotesques of the quasi-gothic architecture of the building upon which he sat.

His Fir Bolg cloak kept him from being seen by all except those who were looking for him, and no one was looking for him.

The Pobl Gwir were blissfully, and idiotically under the impression they crossed the divide without being spotted and the strange men who rode inside the magic chariots probably didn't even know the Fir Bolg existed.

It was all too amusing.

His amusement faded, however, when the three adventurers were shoved into one of the magical chariots, and it sped away. Unleashing a tirade of whispered curses, Itheann Beanna watched the chariot's flashing lights for as long as he could before having to content himself with waiting for the other natives of this world to disperse.

It was well into the exceedingly cold night before Itheann Beanna thought it safe to clamber down from the rooftop. He whistled once, very lowly, and all twelve Fir Bolg stirred and clambered down from their various positions on the roof.

****

137

Peredur twisted his wrists, trying a figure a way out of the cuffs, but the steel was not giving and his wrists were starting to hurt.

Olwen turned to him. "Well, that went exceedingly well."

"Oh, hush," Peredur growled.

Wedged between Olwen and Gawain in the back of the magical chariot that needed no horses, he was very uncomfortable.

"At least we know one thing," Olwen said.

"What's that?"

"He recognised Aerfyn's name. He might know where she is."

The other two fell silent and Peredur stopped struggling.

"Only one problem," Gawain noted sourly. "They don't understand a word we're saying."

The silence that fell upon the three adventurers became melancholic.

Bill watched them in the rear-view mirror as Genevieve drove to the station. Whatever gibberish they were speaking, they seemed to understand one another perfectly. They also acted very much like brothers, or at least people who've been friends for a very long time.

Of the three, Peredur looked the youngest. The other two seemed roughly the same age as one another. One had dirty blonde hair that fell in wavy locks around his shoulders and a long reddish blonde moustache.

Peredur had shorter, much curlier, dark brown hair and was clean-shaven. The other one was shorter than both his companions, but much broader with a long black braid and a full, though neatly trimmed, beard.

They looked like they just stepped into reality from some online role-playing game.

"World of Warcraft, much?" Genevieve asked.

Bill grunted. "Maybe that's where they got their ideas from."

"What's up with all the freak show?"

"I don't know. Is it a full moon?"

Officer Boulduc laughed.

One of the unidentified men leant forward. "Rhaid i chi ddeall," he said. "Aerfyn mewn perygl. Mae'n rhaid i ni ddod o hyd i'w."

"Okay, boss," Bill replied. "Just relax there. We'll get this all sorted out."

The man slumped back, and Peredur leant forward. "Aerfyn. Aerfyn. Mynd â ni i Aerfyn."

Bill didn't answer. The frequent repetition of the Jane Doe's made-up name was troubling. Had they all escaped from some institution? Was this all an elaborate prank for some new reality show?

Peredur shook his head and leant back again. "Eich mam yn gafr, ac mae eich tad yn llyffant," he muttered.

His comment earned muffled chuckles from his companion. Officers Jackman and Boulduc exchanged glances and drove the rest of the way in silence.

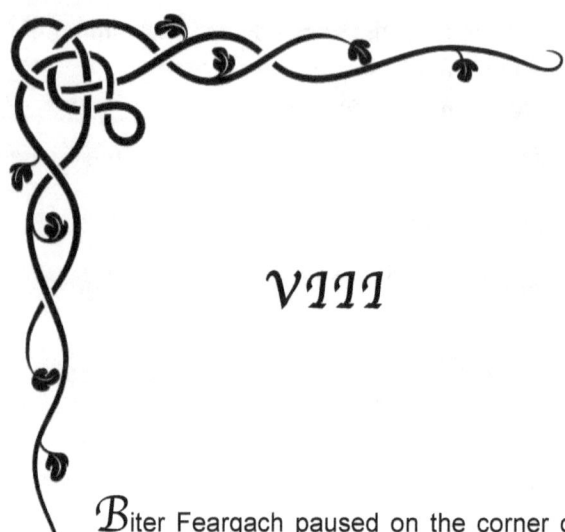

VIII

Biter Feargach paused on the corner of Bank and Wellington streets and tested the air with his nose. He and his companion had run, swift as deer, from Carleton University to here without being seen. Still as posts now, the pair were protected from sight. Not that there was anyone around this part of downtown at two o'clock in the morning.

The scent of the other Fir Bolg was very strong here. Biter Feargach whistled into the still night air. He stood in silence and waited. To his right, a low, long whistle answered.

Biter Feargach smiled and moved to the right. Using low whistles and his nose, he found his way to Itheann Beanna and the rest of the twelve.

"Well, now," Itheann Beanna said. "This is unexpected."

"My Lord," Biter Feargach said with a low bow. "I did not expect to find my brethren in this world."

140

"Nor I. How are you here?"

"We followed the Battle Queen. We've been here for days."

Itheann Beanna's eye lit up. "The Battle Queen? Have you found her?"

Biter Feargach nodded. "There are two men who have sheltered her. We've kept watch on them, waiting for the time to strike. However…"

"However?"

"Earlier this week, one of the men and the Battle Queen left their shelter and are yet to return. Only the one man is there now."

"You lost her?"

"I don't know."

"Well, do you know where she went?"

"No, my Lord."

Itheann Beanna cuffed Biter Feargach on the side of his head. "Then you lost her, you idiot!"

Rubbing where he'd been struck, Biter Feargach swallowed back a sharp retort. "Forgive me, my Lord."

"Luckily for you, we may have a way to locate her."

"My Lord?"

"There are three Pobl Gwir warriors who we've followed here. They were sent, no doubt, to rescue their commander. They will know where she is."

"Where are they?"

Itheann Beanna hesitated. "We're not sure."

"So, you lost them?"

The Fir Bolg lord raised his hand to cuff the mouthy captain again. He grimaced in macabre satisfaction when the soldier flinched. His hand dropped and he turned.

"The flashing magic chariot went that way," he said. "My scouts have told me that there are many people there, however. I'd rather not be seen."

"Then come with me," Biter Feargach said. "For that road looks relatively straight and the road I came up on is virtually deserted."

"Then lead the way, Captain," Itheann Beanna said.

Biter Feargach nodded and skulked to the lead of the pack of now fourteen Fir Bolg warriors. They slunk like cats through the deserted streets of downtown Ottawa, stopping only when they encountered someone nearby, relying on their cloaks to keep them hidden from view.

****

The station was very quiet, as it ought to have been at two o'clock in the morning. Constable Jackman, with the help of Officer Boulduc and a few of the other officers on the graveyard shift took the cuffed men in armour inside for processing.

"I hate paperwork," Bill growled as he filled out the forms. "Why is there so much damned paperwork?"

"Because we live in a bureaucracy," Genevieve said.

"I didn't become a cop to fill in forms all damned night." Bill flexed his wrist and stretched his fingers.

"No, you became a cop because you like to shoot stuff, right?"

Bill rolled his eyes.

"Come on, all country boys become cops just to own a gun, right?"

"All country boys already own a gun," Bill replied.

"Sure, in Texas. And probably Alberta. But a boy from Toronto? Really?"

"I'm from outside of Markham. And I had a shot gun," Bill said.

"Did you shoot tin cans with it?"

"Damn straight."

"Wow. Yet you seem so sophisticated, Spiderman."

"Shut up."

Genevieve laughed. "That's going to take a while. Coffee?"

"Yes, please."

****

"You know," Olwen said cheerily from his holding cell. "As far as dungeons go, this one is quite comfortable. Clean, you know?"

"Olwen," Gawain said from his cell.

"Mm?"

"Shut up."

Peredur sighed. "So much for thrilling adventure. We have to get out of here."

"And just how are we going to achieve that, genius?" Gawain said.

"I don't know."

"'Let's go left,'" Gawain said in a high-pitched mockery of Peredur's decision earlier.

"If you knew better, why didn't you speak up?" Peredur answered defensively.

Olwen sighed. "All right, you two. This is not the time to start fighting amongst ourselves."

Gawain and Peredur clamped their mouths shut.

"That man knows Aerfyn," Olwen said. "What we need to do is figure out a way to make him understand our mission."

"Good luck with that," Gawain grumbled.

"Let's just all demand Aerfyn whenever he comes to speak with us. We'll say nothing else. Perhaps then he'll understand."

Peredur nodded. "At the very least, it'll buy us time enough for us to figure a way out of here."

"Yeah. Good luck with that too."

"Shut up, Gawain."

****

Gwalchgwyn sighed. There had been nothing but late autumn drizzle all day, and he pined for some sunshine. Maelgoch broiled like a thundercloud as he sat beside the aged Dryw. For three days there had been no word of Peredur, Olwen and Gawain, and he didn't like it.

"Be still, Maelgoch," Gwalchgwyn said. "Time moves differently in each world. Perhaps for them, it's only been a few minutes."

"A great deal can happen in a few minutes."

"Yes, and no."

Maelgoch rolled his eyes. "Yes and no," he childishly repeated.

Gwalchgwyn chuckled. "A brave warrior indeed, but wisdom escapes you."

"Sometimes I think wisdom escapes you."

Gwalchgwyn laughed. "Take this time to rest, Maelgoch. We will be fighting again soon enough."

At that moment Tylluan flew into the clearing to deliver her latest report. She twittered and chirruped excitedly, even hopping up and down at one point before the noise ended and Gwalchgwyn gave her a piece of rabbit he'd been saving.

"And?" Maelgoch asked.

The Dryw sighed. "The three adventurers have been captured by the natives of that land. Worse still, the Fir Dynion Gors are in pursuit. Luckily for Aerfyn, neither party has managed to locate her yet."

"*Lucky?* We have to send in a rescue party for Olwen, Gawain and Peredur!"

"Be still, Commander," Gwalchgwyn said gently. "Events may yet prove to be in our favour."

"How can this possibly work to our favour?"

"Patience, Maelgoch. That's what you need. Patience"

Swearing a blue streak, Maelgoch stalked away from the Dryw. He took up a training sword and picked a willing training partner. Before long the Commander of the Pobl Gwir army and his partner were fighting one another in the centre of the clearing.

****

Ethan woke suddenly, certain he'd heard the metallic clang of swords meeting. He found himself asleep on the floor of the dining room in Professor Davies' cottage, his blanket twisted around himself. Aerfyn was also asleep, curled into Ethan's side for warmth.

Ethan smiled to himself. Though he desperately needed to stretch, he remained as still as possible so as not to disturb the sleeping girl. The sound of clashing swords echoed in the still morning air from across the lake. This time, it woke Aerfyn as well. She sat up and frowned out the window to where the lake glittered in the early morning light.

All sounds ceased.

That didn't stop Aerfyn from struggling to her feet and walking out to the deck. Grabbing her jacket from the back of a dining room chair, Ethan followed.

Aerfyn stood still, leaning her weight against the railings of the deck, listening for the sound of fighting once more. The sounds had faded into silence, and now only the muted calls of crows waking up could be heard.

Ethan wrapped Aerfyn's jacket around her. "Come inside for some breakfast," he said gently.

Aerfyn looked up at him with tears in her eyes. "Gallai Rwyf wedi tyngu llw Clywais ymladd cleddyf."

Not understanding a word, Ethan simply nodded and, shivering, led her back inside. He set about making a fire in the potbellied stove in the dining room. Aerfyn sat at the table and stared out the window, distracted.

Ethan had been so busy making the fire that he hadn't heard the car that pulled up. Professor Davies' entered the cottage carrying two very full bags of groceries with him, taking both residents by surprise.

146

"Good morning," he said, his Welsh lilt particularly strong. "Bore dda."

"Bore dda," Aerfyn answered distantly.

"Is she all right?" Gwilym asked.

"I heard sword fighting this morning from across the lake. So did she, I think. She's probably feeling homesick."

"Ah. Aerfyn, beth fyddech yn hoffi i frecwast?"

"Frecwast?"

"Yesterday morning she held up fish and said 'bwyd bore,' if that helps any," Ethan said.

"Ah! Hoffech chi gael unrhyw beth gyfer y bwyd bore?"

Aerfyn smiled faintly and nodded. "Os gwelwch yn dda."

"Well, there's a difference." Gwilym started unpacking the bags.

"What is?"

"They don't use the word breakfast. It's morning meal, instead."

"Bwyd bore means morning meal?"

"Yes. Well done!"

"Well, it was either that or 'fish.'"

"Fish is pysgod."

"Pysgod."

"Very good. I'll have you speaking Welsh in no time."

"My great grandfather would be proud."

Gwilym snorted a short laugh and pulled out a packet of whole-wheat crumpets, butter and honey. He pulled the toaster out from under the sink and plugged it into the oven. After popping in two crumpets, he turned to the cupboard under the sink and pulled out a kettle.

"Coffee?" he asked Ethan.

"Yes, please!"

"It's only instant I'm afraid."

"That's more than all right."

Having finished lighting the fire, Ethan went to the kitchen, pulled out some cutlery and placed it on the table, along with the butter and honey. Aerfyn sniffed each in turn, before redirecting her attention outside again.

"It had occurred to me too late that there was little food in the house," Gwilym said conversationally. "So I went shopping."

"That's all right. Aerfyn caught 'pysgod' yesterday."

"Did she now? How?"

"That spear thing in the corner there," Ethan said, indicating Aerfyn's three-pronged spear leaning against the deck railing outside. Gwilym scowled at it.

"Huh," he said.

"What?"

"Well, I don't recall seeing that in the archaeology."

Ethan shrugged.

The toaster popped the crumpets out so violently, they flew clear of the toaster and landed on the kitchen counter.

"Oh damn!" Gwilym said. "I forgot it did that." He picked up the hot crumpets, put them on a plate and placed the plate in front of Aerfyn. She smiled up at him and picked up the honey. She gave herself an ample helping of honey on each crumpet, then happily ate while Gwilym moved about the kitchen.

Ethan couldn't help but smile at her contented face.

"So, anything exciting happen while I was away?" Gwilym asked, sitting down at last once everyone had their crumpets.

"Well, Aerfyn is teaching me how to fight with a sword," Ethan said. "It's ridiculous fun."

"Is she now. I'd like to see that!"

"Hey, Professor D?"

"Yes, Ethan?"

"Do you actually believe us? Do you really think it's possible that there's another world?"

Gwilym looked at Ethan seriously. "To be perfectly honest, I'm still not sure I do believe you both. I'm still expecting to wake up to find this a long, very bizarre dream, or that you're all having me on. Still, Aerfyn's Welsh is understandable, more or less. And you certainly seem convinced."

Ethan shrugged. "I sometimes wonder if it isn't because I really, really want it to be true. I mean, I haven't been excited about the world since I was a kid, pretending to be a superhero. When did we lose the magic, do you think?"

Professor Davies smiled. "Some of us never have. We just pretend it's academics."

Ethan laughed. "You know, my kid sister used to tell me all about the faeries she'd seen at the bottom of the garden. She was so breathless and excited, it was hard not to believe her, you know?" Ethan shook his head sadly.

"How old were you both?"

"She was four, and I was eleven. She was my half-sister, actually."

"Was?"

"Yeah. She and my mum died in a car accident. A drunk driver ploughed into them on Christmas Eve a few years ago."

"I'm so sorry," Gwilym said.

Ethan shrugged. "Not much to be done about it now, is there? My step-dad and I don't talk much, and frankly, it was just easier to get out of there as fast as possible, so I came to Ottawa for school."

"Where are you from?"

"Bear Lake, B.C."

"Ah. That's quite a ways away."

"Yeah, well. It's not so bad."

Gwilym packed up the plates and went to the kitchen to take care of the kettle that had begun to squeal in complaint. He made coffee for everyone. He placed milk and sugar on the table before handing out the mugs of steaming instant coffee.

He watched carefully as Aerfyn pulled her gaze from the window and took a sip. She screw up her face and, forcing herself to swallow, gagged audibly. She glared at Ethan when he laughed and watched with interest as he took two small spoons of sugar and put them into his coffee.

"Siwgr," Gwilym said, smiling.

Aerfyn frowned and, taking the sugar pot, dipped her finger in. She nervously tasted the granules of sugar on her finger, before taking several spoonfuls and dumping them into the coffee.

"Milk?" Ethan asked, handing her the milk jug.

Aerfyn pulled a face, and drank her coffee black and very sweet. Finishing her cup, she pulled another face. The dregs were far too sweet now.

Ethan laughed brightly. Aerfyn stuck her tongue out at him.

After the dishes were cleared away, Gwilym went outside with his guests to observe as Ethan continued in his sword-fighting lessons. Skill of any kind is difficult to fake, and it could not be disputed that Aerfyn was very skilled with a blade in her hands.

Ethan tried in earnest to strike Aerfyn, but found himself unable. He was hit, tripped, kicked and slapped around for the better part of an hour, before he finally dropped his sword in defeat.

Professor Davies laughed and clapped.

"Oh man!" Ethan said, panting. "That's hard work! You want a go, Professor D?"

"Oh... well... I... sure."

Not even a man with greying hair could resist the urge to be a knight for an afternoon. Ethan grinned, handing Gwilym his sword and heading to the deck to watch. He grinned madly as Aerfyn began her instruction.

Able to communicate with her, Gwilym had an easier time of it than Ethan did, but his age and occupation worked against him. It took him a little longer to learn than it did Ethan, and when it came time to apply the knowledge, he struggled.

For her part, Aerfyn did not seem to mind instructing either Ethan or Gwilym in the art of swordplay. She smiled and laughed often, her brown eyes sparkling.

The afternoon passed in this amusement. Ethan and Gwilym took it in turns to fight Aerfyn. Though she fought most of the day, she seemed less tired than either Ethan or Gwilym. Eventually, Gwilym could not even lift the sword, so he retired to the cottage to prepare dinner. He watched from the kitchen window as Ethan and Aerfyn continued, smiling to himself when Ethan got frustrated, tossed his sword aside, and tackled Aerfyn.

Even that did not work. Aerfyn bested him, pinning him to the ground and holding the waster's blunt edge against his throat.

"No frikkin' way!" Gwilym heard Ethan exclaim. He laughed and turned back to the oven. Dinner was going to be frozen pizza.

It was a meal Aerfyn heartily enjoyed. She and Ethan ate so much between them, Gwilym was forced to put a second pizza in the oven. The three talked over a pot of tea while they waited for the food to cook.

Through Professor Davies, Ethan was able to ask every question of Aerfyn he'd been dying to in the last couple of days. Aerfyn was eighteen, he discovered, and unmarried. Her father was an old man, by her standards, of fifty-three and powerful; something like a priest, Gwilym had to explain.

She was the daughter of a very famous warrior-queen, who also happened to be the Chieftain of her tribe. When her mother died, rule of the tribe went to her older brother, but he was killed in the first battle with the

Dynion Gors. Now Aerfyn ruled not only her tribe, but had command of the coalition of tribes that now fought against the vast army of men from the bog.

"They're taking orders from an eighteen-year-old girl?" Ethan asked Gwilym incredulously.

"I don't think there is the same stigma attached to being female in her world as there is in ours, you know."

"Yes, but, grown men, taking orders from a girl."

"What? It happens in the military all the time."

"Yeah, *now* it does, but it took us a while to get there."

"There is precedent in the Iron Age for this, you know."

"There is?"

"Well, yes. Boudicca."

"What?"

"Who."

"Pardon?"

"Who, not what. Boudicca was a woman. Queen of the Iceni Tribe in southeastern Britain, she led a revolt against the Roman occupation of Britain in 60 or 61 A.D. It was very nearly successful. By all accounts, she was the commander of that army."

"Holy crap! No way!"

Gwilym's mouth quirked. "Way."

Ethan was silenced for a time. He chewed his food and looked thoughtfully at Aerfyn. She returned his gaze with a steady one of her own. When it felt awkward to still be looking at her, Ethan turned back to Professor Davies.

They chatted well into the night.

****

Peredur sat on the strange collapsible steel chair before the equally flimsy steel table in the small, brightly lit room with a long mirror on one wall. His armour had been removed, and all he had on were his trousers, his undershirt, and his sleeveless gambeson, spotted now with the rust from his chainmail. In truth, it was something of a relief to be able to remove the steel and leather from his person, but he felt nervous that someone might run him through at any moment.

The door to the room opened, and a man dressed entirely in black stepped inside. He was clearly wearing armour of his own, though how fabric could possibly help him confused Peredur no end.

The man looked at Peredur, his steel blue eyes curious and suspicious both.

"Aerfyn," Peredur said, crossing his muscular arms across his chest.

The man in black raised his eyebrows. He threw a manila folder on the table, the loose papers sliding out a little.

Peredur looked at it briefly before turning his attention back to the man. "Aerfyn," he said again.

The man scowled. He pointed to himself. "Bill."

Peredur hesitated. They had all agreed to speak only Aerfyn's name until the strange inhabitants of this world led them to her. He shrugged. What could telling this man his name hurt?

"Peredur," he said slowly.

"Pere-deer?" the man named Bill repeated.

Peredur nodded. He leant back on the chair and said, "Aerfyn."

154

The man took the chair across the table from Peredur and sat down. He observed Peredur in silence.

****

This would be a difficult interrogation, Bill decided. The man clearly did not or chose not to speak English. Peredur sat, looking confident and slightly angry, his arms folded across his chest. Still, Bill could tell from his posture and the set of his shoulders that Peredur felt threatened and unsure.

The door opened and Officer Boulduc walked in. "The psychiatrist is here," she said.

Bill nodded. "Take him in to observe."

"You got it, Spiderman."

"Stop that," Bill said, smiling nonetheless. He gave Genevieve two minutes to enter the observation room before leaning forward. He flipped open the folder he had thrown on the table, revealing the drawing Aerfyn had done of her monster.

Peredur's stern gaze fell onto the drawing. He tensed, leant forward and picked it up. "Ydi hi yma?" he asked, an edge to his voice. "Ydych chi wedi gweld hi?"

Bill scowled. "Look, save your crazy language for another time. I'm starting to get annoyed."

Peredur scowled back. "Nid wyf yn deall yr hyn yr ydych yn ei ddweud."

Bill put his finger on the paper. "Name it."

Peredur's scowl deepened. He leant back again and folded his arms. "Aerfyn," he said.

Bill sighed. He pointed at Peredur. "Peredur," he said. He pointed to himself. "Bill." He pointed to the picture and looked expectantly at Peredur.

Understanding crossed Peredur's face with comedic visibility. "Dynion Gors," he said, pointing at the drawing. "Dynion Gors. Maent yn ein gelyn."

Bill turned around and frowned at the one-way window. He turned back to Peredur. "Thank-you," he said brusquely. He left abruptly, leaving a very confused Peredur behind.

Bill entered the observation room and found Jeff and Genevieve. "So, doc," he said. "What do you make of that?"

"Interesting."

"Yes," Bill said flatly. "It's very interesting. But your interests don't help my investigation. I need a little more to go on than 'interesting.' Are they all the same kind of crazy?"

"They all could be schizophrenic, yes," Jeff replied. "However, this is extremely organised. Schizophrenic expression is usually much more individualistic. One person might be concerned about the spider-people living under bridges, for example, while another is certain that alien spies inhabit the family pet and so on. Never before have I seen or even heard of many schizophrenics believing in the same alternate reality."

"So, what, this is an elaborate prank?"

"It could be, though this Peredur fellow seems very sincere."

"A good actor, then."

"Possibly."

"Why me?" Bill said. "I would be the one stuck with a crazy escapee and her crazy friends – or normal idiots who are just pretending, and making my life unnecessarily difficult."

"Try a scare. He's young – can't be more than sixteen. They're relatively easily scared straight," Officer Boulduc suggested.

"Before you try that," Jeff said. "I'd like to make a few enquiries."

"Be my guest," Bill said. He remained in the observation room as Jeff left and entered the interrogation room.

"Good morning," Jeff said amicably.

Peredur scowled at him. "Aerfyn," he said, his tone irritated.

"Yes, yes. You want to see Aerfyn, I know." Jeff placed a briefcase on the desk and opened it. He pulled out a number of thick squares of card and some pens.

"So," he said conversationally. "You're from Annwfyn, then?"

Peredur twitched and looked sharply up at the doctor. "Rhydych yn gwybod am Annwfyn? Ydych chi'n gwybod sut i fynd yn ôl yno? Mae'n rhaid i chi ein cymorth ni! Mae'n rhaid i ni ddod o hyd i Aerfyn ac yn chymryd ei chartref. Os gwelwch yn dda!"

Jeff looked at Peredur, who spoke rapidly and in earnest. The young man's eyes were pleading, and his voice agitated. He spoke animatedly, waving his hands about in an effort to make himself understood.

"Uh-huh," Jeff said, making a note in his pad.

Peredur stopped talking to observe Jeff writing. He frowned and tilted his head as he looked at the markings on the paper. Jeff held it up for him to see. Peredur stared at it, but looked confused.

"Writing," Jeff said.

An idea struck Peredur. He extended his hand towards the pen and pad. Jeff handed them to him. Peredur pulled the pad to him and scratched at it with the pen. He paused briefly to try and figure out how the pen worked. Failing, he shrugged and continued.

When he handed Jeff back the pad, Jeff found it covered in drawings of stick figures. The page was divided in two. On one side, many stick figures holding swords faced a horde of other stick figures with a variety of weapons. One stick figure, quite obviously a woman, if the oversized circles for breasts were any indication, stood very near the line that divided the two halves of the page.

"Dynion Gors," Peredur said pointing to the horde of stick figures on the far left of the page. He pointed at Aerfyn's drawing and then back. "Dynion Gors," he repeated.

He pointed at the other horde of stick figures. "Pobl Gwir," he said. He indicated himself. "Pobl Gwir."

He placed his palm on the half of the page with the two armies of stick figures. "Annwfyn," he said.

Then he pointed at the female stick figure. "Aerfyn." He crossed her out violently, then circled a similar figure on the other half of the page.

"Aerfyn," he said. Then he circled three stick figures with weapons. "Olwen, Gawain, Peredur," he said.

He dragged his finger from the Annwfyn side of the paper to the other side. He pointed at Aerfyn on the right hand side of the page and dragged his finger back to the Annwfyn side.

"Dwedwch wrthyf eich bod yn deall."

Jeff smiled. He thought he understood. Taking up his pad, he smiled at Peredur and left the room. Peredur spread his hands in an exasperated, unspoken demand to know what was going on. It remained unanswered as Jeff entered the observation room.

"Well?" Bill demanded.

Jeff triumphantly showed him the pad.

"Beautiful. I think my two-year-old niece did something similar."

"Don't you see? It's their story."

"How so?"

"All right, so, this is Annwfyn, where they're supposedly from. This scribble down here is Aerfyn, the girl you're chasing. These are the two armies – the Pobl Gwir and the Dynion Gors, right? According to Peredur over there, Aerfyn somehow ended up over here and he and his two companions, whose names are Olwen and Gawain, by the way, left here to find her and bring her back home, to Annwfyn." Jeff indicated the figures on the page as he spoke, dragging his finger across the page and back again.

Bill stared blankly at the psychiatrist. "And?"

"And it's obvious, isn't it?"

"Is it?"

"It's clearly a reality they created together. Look, they're probably all from the same institution and became friends there. As their friendship formed, so did their shared reality. The enemy they're fighting with is probably just the staff at the institute and they've turned them into the army of monsters they've called the Dynion Gors in their

159

mind. The Pobl Gwir would be all the patients at the institute.

"Aerfyn, if that is even her real name, escaped the institution, and these three followed her to bring her back, turning it into a rescue mission in their minds. You see, to them, the institution is a home overrun with monsters, with whom they are currently at war."

"Huh," Bill grunted. "Kinda like the movie 'Sucker Punch.'"

"Didn't see it," Officer Boulduc and Doctor Jeff said together.

Bill shrugged. "Wasn't bad."

"There is a slight flaw in the theory," Genevieve said. "The police are usually notified of any escapes from these places. None have been reported. Then there's the issue of them wearing actual armour and holding actual weapons. I mean, we tested the swords. They're sharp."

"Swords and armour can be purchased."

"By crazy people who've just escaped an institution?"

Jeff shrugged. "The alternative is that there really is a place called Annwfyn, and they really are fighting monsters."

Bill sighed. "May I have that drawing?"

"I will fax you a copy," Jeff said. "For now, I suggest you interrogate the other two. If you don't mind, I'd like to as well."

"I'd very much appreciate it if you did."

****

Peredur was taken back to his cell. He went without a struggle, figuring he'd get farther with his captors if he

160

cooperated with the small things. He sat on his bed and watched as Olwen, and then Gawain were taken to be questioned.

"Hey," Olwen whispered as he shuffled past. "Did they torture you?"

Peredur shook his head. "No."

Olwen looked so relieved it made Peredur chuckle.

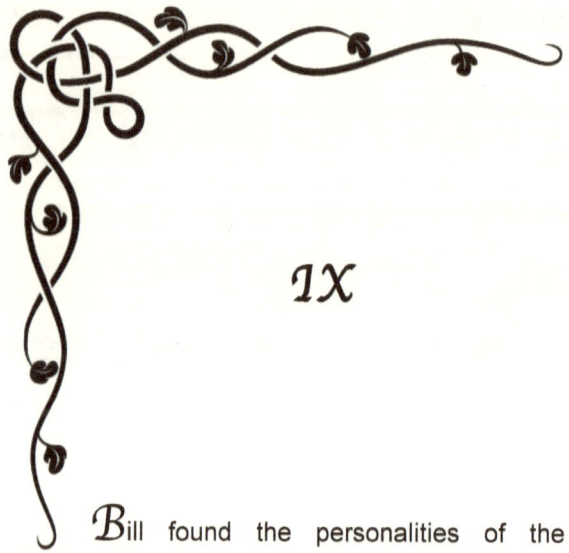

IX

$\mathcal{B}$ill found the personalities of the three companions to be so different from one another, they might have stepped straight from the pages of a comic book. Peredur had been earnest and very serious. Olwen was the comedic one. He happily introduced himself, grinned often, made jokes that only he could understand and therefore find funny, and behaved in a generally relaxed manner. Yet behind his good-natured mannerisms, beneath each smile and sparkle in his eyes lay a glint of hard steel.

He gave no information, and his first word in answer to everything Bill said or did was, "Aerfyn."

The last of the three, Gawain, proved to be positively surly.

If he were one of Snow White's dwarves, Bill mused to himself, he'd be Grumpy, only significantly more intimidating.

He sat and scowled, his arms folded across his barrel-like chest. Largely silent, he'd interrupt Bill's questions every so often simply to demand, "Aerfyn," in a growl.

He showed no surprise that Bill knew his name. He showed no emotion when Bill displayed Aerfyn's drawing of the Dynion Gors, or when he was shown Peredur's drawing of their supposed mission.

Of the three, Gawain was by far the most frustrating to deal with. Bill lost his temper. He slammed his palms on the table. "Look you pompous miniature bear of a man, I want answers! Saying 'Aerfyn' is not going to help you any!"

Gawain rose slowly from his chair and placed his hands on the table just as slowly. Staring Bill in the eye, he pointedly growled, "Aerfyn."

Bill gave up. Taking his folder and his mug of coffee, he stormed from the interrogation chamber to his desk, leaving some of the other officers to take Gawain back to his cell. Gawain looked positively smug as he was led away.

"Bastard," Bill grumbled as he watched Gawain walk by. He turned back to his desk and logged onto his computer.

"You all right there, Spidey?" Genevieve asked mildly.

Bill rubbed his eyes. "That was the longest four hours of my life," he said.

"You were supposed to be off-duty three of those hours ago."

"I had work to do."

"You're going to do more?"

"Yeah. I'm going to call around and see if any nut houses are less a few nuts."

"No. You're going to come out to breakfast with me, and then you're going to go home and sleep. You look like hell."

"Thanks," Bill mumbled. He glanced at his waiting computer before sighing and shutting it down.

"Cora's?" Officer Boulduc asked.

"Sure," Bill said. "Why not?"

****

To say that Itheann Beanna was frustrated might have been the biggest understatement in the long, convoluted history of the Fir Bolg. Not only had they lost track of their quarry, but they had no way of picking up their scent.

The fragrance of the horseless chariot they rode in smelled virtually the same as every other horseless chariot the Fir Bolg came across, and they had come across many.

The idea of following the sound of the chariot's blaring whistle had also proved to be fruitless. It sounded often, in various places around the city, moving quickly, and then stopping before even being sighted. It was as if the damned chariot could disappear and materialise at will.

The fourteen Fir Bolg searched fruitlessly all night and, once the morning began in earnest, had to retire to the rooftops. There were simply too many people moving about down below to make staying on the ground feasible. They might have been protected from sight by their cloaks, but they were still present. All it would take is one person to bump into them and the glamour would be broken.

No, better by far to be on the roof where they would remain hidden. Also, a number of pigeons lived up on the rooves of this city. They were easy targets for the hungry Fir Bolg, being neither especially bright nor especially cautious.

Itheann Beanna sat on the ledge of the tall building on the corner of Rideau and Dalhousie Streets in downtown Ottawa. He watched the people scurry about below, noting with interest that there were many horseless chariots that were very large indeed and seemed capable of holding an infinite number of people in their steel bellies. When the chariot stopped, people poured out like vermin escaping a sinking ship.

The Fir Bolg lord's lip curled in disgust. All around him, the city sprawled into what seemed like eternity. How on earth was he to find the three Pobl Gwir warriors in this mess of twisted steel and stone?

A blue-striped white vehicle pulled up immediately below. He watched with a growing smile as a man and woman emerged from the chariot. They smelled familiar, and Itheann Beanna quickly realised that they were the very two who had captured the three Pobl Gwir the Fir Bolg were hunting.

The pair entered the very building upon which Itheann Beanna and his Fir Bolg now sat. The smile turned sour when Itheann Beanna realised that he and his warriors would have to descend into the very busy streets, or miss their chance at finding their prey.

He turned back and summoned Biter Feargach to him.

"That chariot, the riders were the same who captured the three Pobl Gwir we seek. You must go down and ride it. Where it stops is where they are kept. Find that place, and report back to me. Do not return until you have found it."

"But the streets are filled with people! Our cloaks will not be able to conceal me from them all."

"Then I suggest you be careful," Itheann Beanna snarled.

Biter Feargach bit back a retort. Glancing around and realising he'd garner no support from Itheann Beanna's warriors, he swallowed and scampered over the edge.

He moved painfully slowly in an effort to keep hidden, crawling down the wall of the building head first, his cloak hem wrapped tightly about his ankles so it didn't fall down over his head. It felt like an age before his clawed hands touched the pavement, and even longer for him to right himself and move to the chariot.

With the same painfully slow movements, he circled around the chariot and tested the handles of what were obviously the doors. Each one moved up, but the doors remained stubbornly closed.

Locked.

Having no other option, Biter Feargach crawled slowly onto the top of the chariot and clung onto the lamps affixed there. Not a single person even so much as batted an eyelid at Biter Feargach's presence. Most looked down at the ground as they marched by, oblivious to all and sundry. Others talked to one another as they walked, unheeding of all else.

Biter Feargach spared a moment to ponder on the luxury of their surrounds – that they could be so oblivious of the world around them and not fear for their lives. He probably didn't even need his cloak. None in this city would see him regardless.

No sooner had the thought occurred, than the chariot riders dressed in black emerged from the building. They were talking to one another, just as unheeding of him as the other people.

The female pressed down on a black thing in her hand, and the doors magically unlocked. Both got into the horseless chariot, the male stopping to brush some snow from the top of the car, a finger's breadth away from Biter Feargach's hand. The man did not even see the Fir Bolg warrior clinging to the lights.

The chariot roared and shook, and in a few moments, they were gliding smoothly along the road. Biter Feargach smiled a yellow-fanged grin. He carefully took note of the direction the car drove. It seemed simple enough – forward then left.

Following that road, the chariot turned into a parking area with one or two identical chariots. The two people in black left the car and headed inside.

The building was squat and ugly, all corners and sharp edges – not like the circular buildings the Pobl Gwir favoured or the artfully sculpted mud huts of the Fir Bolg. It was also relatively busy.

A fair number of people milled about just inside the doors that opened of their own volition. Some sat on chairs provided, others queued in long lines on the left-hand side, where other people dressed in black sat behind strange, see-through barriers. If this was the dungeon where the three Pobl Gwir warriors were kept, it was a strange dungeon indeed.

Biter Feargach slid carefully off the chariot and retreated to the bushes near the road to observe. Pulling his cloak around him, he sat on the ground and waited until dark, when it was relatively safe to roam around freely again.

****

Bill took his time in the shower. The hot water felt good. The breakfast and now the shower served to relax his tense shoulders. His mind, however, still ran at break-neck speed. The issue of the missing woman, Aerfyn, and now the sudden appearance of three more loonies, who happened to speak the same language, all dressed in real armour and carrying real weapons had his thoughts in a jumbled, nonsensical mess.

He knew his task was simple – find the girl, gather the evidence. The detectives would do the rest. Still, he'd found himself drawn deeper in than he liked, and he didn't much like the detective assigned to the case any way. The man was notoriously lazy.

When Bill was out and dressed, he met Officer Boulduc at the lockers.

"Uh-oh," she said.

"What?"

"You have that look on your face."

"What look?"

"The 'I'm thinking of doing something' look, when you should be getting ready for a nice long sleep."

Bill shrugged. "I'm thinking, that's all."

"Precisely."

Bill grinned. "Whatever."

"Promise me you'll go home and go to bed."

"I promise," Bill said. He meant it. He desperately needed sleep, and he often did he best thinking in the minutes before he fell asleep.

"Good."

Genevieve and Bill walked to their cars together. Officer Boulduc waited for Bill to drive away before climbing into her car. Sighing, she pulled out of the Elgin Street Station parking lot and headed home.

****

Sunday morning dawned pleasantly. The sky displayed brilliant plumage as the sun made its lazy way upwards. Aerfyn had woken a few moments before the dawn. Creeping past Ethan, who slept on the couch now that Professor Davies had arrived, she pulled her jacket on and crept out onto the deck to watch the sunrise.

Dawn had always been her favourite time of the day. In the days before the war, she would climb onto the roof of Caer Avallach and watch the day bloom. The only other person up at that time was the baker. The air was filled with the sounds of the earliest birds, and the scent of wood smoke and freshly baked bread.

Aerfyn would sit and listen as the rest of the city started to wake. The low brass bell would announce the change of the guard, and from her section of rooftop, she watched the short ceremony where the tired sentinels of the night gladly relinquished their watch to the guards of the day. They marched so wonderfully in time, the career soldiers – second born sons and daughters of important households all.

The blacksmith would start his forge just as the milkmaids wandered into town, calling out their wares. The knife-grinder would follow suit and soon the marketplace before the high palisades of Caer Avallach would bustle with activity as children ran errands for their parents, apprentices and servants for their masters, and squires for their lords.

Training began not long after, and the sounds of metal striking metal, horses thundering past targets and the soft twang and hiss of bows releasing their arrows would fill the martial quadrant of the fortress.

Then Aerfyn's mother would call her to the morning meal. If the morning's hunt had been successful, then the morning meal would be a feast of boar or deer, fruits of all kinds and warm, honeyed porridge. If not, the fishermen provided ample fish for their table.

After breakfast, she and all the first born sons and daughters of the noble houses would gather in the courtyard for training. They, having pledged their allegiance to Caer Avallach and her Queen, would train all day to become the newest in the ranks of the honoured guard, the Knights of Caer Avallach.

These men and women were the highest rank a person could hope to achieve, save for the Queen herself, and the Dryw. Those living in and around Caer Avallach afforded them the greatest respect. As such, they were expected to act with the greatest honour and be the fiercest fighters the fortress had in her service. With a mother as celebrated as her own, Aerfyn had a great deal to live up to.

Ever since she could remember, she worked hard to please both the Lord Marshall, who trained the Knights of Avallach, and her mother. Both were hard on her, but both expressed their delight with her successes.

It had been a devastating blow to lose her mother. Aerfyn had been sixteen when complications during childbirth took her mother and her baby brother from her in one fell night of blood and screams. A week later, the grieving girl had been crowned Queen of Caer Avallach.

A year away from earning her place within the order of the Knights of Caer Avallach, she continued her training. A week before the knighting ceremony, the king of the Dynion Gors, a ragged but fierce nation of men living in mud shelters in the bogs of Annwfyn, came forward with a proposition of marriage.

Aerfyn, backed by her father, the Dryw, had refused. Outraged, the king of the Dynion Gors declared war.

The entire body of royal advisors had underestimated both the size and strength of the army of the Dynion Gors. After several separate engagements, the Pobl Gwir were forced into a fighting retreat.

Or, at least, they had been when Aerfyn vanished from the field.

She watched the sunrise sadly, wishing that she had accepted the king's offer. She would gladly bear a lifetime of cruelty if it would save her people from the torment of conquest. She bit her lip. She had no way of knowing the outcome of the last battle she fought.

Perhaps they were all dead, and the gods had spared her life by sending her into this world. Perhaps they lived, but under the tyrannical rule of the Dynion Gors king. Perhaps they had come out victorious after all, but grieved the loss of their queen.

Whatever the case may be, she would not rest until she returned home to her people. If the Dynion Gors now ruled from her seat in Caer Avallach, she would gather what fighters remained to her, and fight to win it back. If her people had been victorious, then all the better. She could resume her life.

She looked back at the cottage. But what of Ethan? He had been kind to her; he had sworn to aid her and, with fierce bravery worthy of any Knight of Caer Avallach, he had fought beside her to drive the Dynion Gors away. Aerfyn found, rather surprisingly, the thought of returning home and leaving him behind was horribly bittersweet.

She turned back to the sunrise and closed her eyes, enjoying the warmth of the sun as his golden rays broke over the horizon.

"Morning," Ethan said from behind her.

Aerfyn turned and smiled. Behind them both, Professor Davies shuffled about the kitchen, preparing breakfast. Though his doctor would rage at him, he decided bacon and eggs were in order. He hummed 'God Save the Queen' as he worked.

The smell of frying bacon brought Aerfyn and Ethan back inside. Aerfyn smiled gratefully when Gwilym wished her a good morning, and indicated that she should sit. Ethan set the table and he and the professor talked as breakfast hissed and spat on the stovetop.

****

Mitch had decided that if Ethan did not return by the end of the day, he'd call Constable Jackman and tell him everything. In the meantime, he spent the day wandering the Rideau Centre with Wendy, nodding at her inane gabble and pretending to be interested in what her second cousin once removed did when he was last on the farm. The truth was, unless he was drunk, his girlfriend was terribly boring.

Then again, Mitch thought, so was he. He'd never once stepped foot outside of Canada, let alone North America. Travel did not interest him all that much. Neither did school, if he was being perfectly honest. He just drifted through life, relying on chance to make his decisions for him. That was why, he supposed, Wendy was now his girlfriend. He didn't really choose it – she did. And that was that.

Mitch didn't regret the decision. Wendy was exactly what he needed – strong-willed and bright; someone who could kick his arse into shape and who could tell him what he needed to do next. He was perfectly clueless otherwise. He didn't understand why his friends resented her.

Smiling, he put his arm around her shoulder and strolled into the artificial light of the shopping mall in downtown Ottawa.

Just three blocks away, Itheann Beanna shifted his weight. Soon, the Fir Bolg lord thought to himself. Soon, he would be presenting the Pobl Gwir queen to his king. The honours that would follow would make everyone envious. He scratched his cheek and squinted up at the sun.

That is, if Biter Feargach hadn't erred. Again.

****

Lord Marshall Rhydderch squinted up at the grey sky and sighed. For a week the sky had wept a soft drizzle. That was a bad sign. Everyone knew the earth responded to events. If she wept, then things probably went badly in their fight against the Dynion Gors, upsetting the natural order.

That, and there had been no sign of, nor any message from Queen Aerfyn or her brave lieutenant, Maelgoch. Still, the battle should have ended some days ago, and the Dynion Gors had not marched on Caer Avallach, meaning that perhaps their army had been broken on the field. That was something at least.

Behind him, Caer Avallach continued in her routine as if everything was perfectly fine. The career soldiers took their posts at each changing of the guard, the marketplace bustled with life, and the new generation of hopefuls had arrived and begun their knightly training.

Still, the day sat ill with Rhydderch.

He watched the line of trees that extended in a bountiful forest beyond the still lake that surrounded the sizeable isle upon which Caer Avallach sat – The Blessed Isle, it was known to most. If the Dynion Gors were to attack, they would make their approach through that wood.

Rhydderch grimaced. That would get them uncomfortably close to the glamour that protected the Blessed Isle. The glamour was designed to obfuscate the fortress, making it difficult to find. However, if they already knew where to find it, then nothing save the lake and the fortress' own defences were all that could save her.

The lake was a boon. Masters of the bog they might be, the Dynion Gors could not swim. Their only chance of making it to the Isle was to cross on rafts. Knowing the Dynion Gors, the rafts would be crude, blockish things that would be difficult to manoeuvre, unlike the elegant and swift lake boats of the Pobl Gwir.

Still, by sheer numbers alone, they could cross and land, and then Lord Marshall Rhydderch would be responsible for the lives of everyone on the Isle. At least, until Caer Avallach's knights returned.

If they returned.

A sentry cried out, and the horn of Caer Avallach sounded. The Dynion Gors had been sighted, flitting through the trees as they approached the fortress. Lord Marshall Rhydderch turned on his heel.

"All hands down!" He bellowed. "Open the gates! Evacuate the city!"

Pandemonium ensued. The citizens of the Blessed Isle were unused to attacks. They had been living an idyllic life for as many generations as anyone cared to remember. Several women screamed as they grabbed their children and fled their homes, leaving their husbands to gather food stocks and any other items they felt necessary. Goatherds and shepherds and their yapping dogs struggled to get their flocks behind the walls of the fortress speedily, without their herds becoming mixed.

For all the chaos down below, the career soldiers and knights in training handled themselves well, aiding all they could to hurry into the castle, and keeping the citizenry from trampling one another in a panic. For the most part, the citizens of the Blessed Isle were agreeable and orderly, even if it didn't look like it from atop the gatehouse.

If Caer Avallach had all her knights, then the city's walls could be defended and only the countryside need be evacuated. As it stood, with the army away from home, Lord Marshall Rhydderch had only enough men and women at arms to protect the fortress proper.

He watched with dark brown eyes as the Dynion Gors gathered on the lake's far shore, milling about in confusion. The glamour, for now, held.

There could be no mistaking the King of the Dynion Gors. He strode through the trees with an arrogant air, boldly walking into view. Upon his hooded head, he wore a brass crown inset with polished wood, stained red by the waters of the bog. Its many sharp points ended in spearheads, razor sharp and glinting evilly in the dim light.

"Tá a fhios agam go bhfuil tú ann!" he bellowed across the water. "Dearbhófar do chathair sruthán!"

"Not before your army does," the Lord Marshall growled in return.

He ran his fingers over his red-brown beard, speckled now with the pale signs of aging, and narrowed his eyes as the Dynion Gors retreated into the woods to make their rafts. Sighing, Rhydderch looked up in time to see the small figure of a barn owl gliding silently overhead. He nodded up at it. *The Dryw, at any rate, will know of the peril of Caer Avallach.*

Lord Marshall Rhydderch closed his eyes and bowed his head in brief prayer.

Lady of this Island, and Maiden of the Lake, as you did in life, protect the Blessed Isle and her people until your daughter and rightful Queen returns to us.

He opened his eyes. "Hurry, my Queen," he whispered. "We are in dire need now."

****

Maelgoch paled as Gwalchgwyn relayed the news.

"We must do something," he said quietly. "We can no longer afford to sit and wait for our queen."

Gwalchgwyn nodded. "The Blessed Isle is more important, it is true. On the bright side, the glamour worked."

Maelgoch glared at the aged Dryw before he burst out laughing. "Oh, aye," he said. "It worked so well, the Dynion Gors army marched right by us to attack the very place we were trying to protect."

"They must have assumed that we made a full retreat and are now sheltered behind Caer Avallach's stone walls."

Maelgoch nodded. He became thoughtful. "It does offer us some advantage, however."

"Oh?"

"We can take this army from behind. Pressed between the fortress and our forces, the Dynion Gors will break."

Gwalchgwyn smiled. "Aerfyn did well to chose you as her lieutenant."

"Who defends Caer Avallach?"

"Your lord father," Gwalchgwyn replied.

Maelgoch nodded. "Good. There's no one better, and it isn't simple family pride which says so."

"No indeed. There is good reason Aerfyn's grandmother made him Lord Marshall."

Maelgoch grimaced. "And what of Aerfyn?"

"She will find her way to us," Gwalchgwyn said. "She will have to."

"If Peredur, Olwen and Gawain find her, they will bring her here, and we shall be gone."

"Tylluan will remain to guide them to us," Gwalchgwyn said. He rubbed the owl's breast affectionately. "Won't you, my sweet?"

The bird on his shoulder twittered in annoyance and shifted her weight. Gwalchgwyn smiled. Maelgoch looked from the bird to the seer and back again before saying, "There is much I would give to have the ability to speak to birds."

"There is much I have given," Gwalchgwyn said sadly.

Tylluan, tiring of the conversation, took to wing to settle upon the rock that Gwalchgwyn had taken to leaning against in rest. She twisted her head to look back at Gwalchgwyn. Maelgoch could have sworn to the gods that the bird frowned at the Dryw before preening herself.

"Well, my boy," Gwalchgwyn said quietly. "Let us prepare. Caer Avallach's need is dire."

Maelgoch nodded and turned to address the waiting, and very bored, army.

"My friends," he began. "Caer Avallach and the Blessed Isle are under attack. Come my brothers and sisters. We have waited for our queen long enough. It is time now to end this war."

Wearily, the Pobl Gwir army stood and gathered their weapons and armour. Once armed, their countenance changed. Their faces grew hard and their stances determined. The Blessed Isle was threatened and they, the Knights of Caer Avallach, were her best hope.

The horses that remained were quickly groomed and dressed. Mounted and on foot, the army of Caer Avallach moved out from the protected clearing to surprise the enemy from behind.

****

Biter Feargach rejoined Itheann Beanna and his men shortly after nightfall.

"I've found the dungeon," he said.

"Have you truly?"

Biter Feargach narrowed his bulging yellow eyes. "No, I've switched allegiances and am now leading you into a trap by telling you I know where the dungeon is."

Itheann Beanna cuffed Biter Feargach hard on the side of the head, prompting snickers from the others. "That's enough of your lip," the Fir Bolg lord growled.

Biter Feargach refrained from retorting, though he did resort to sticking his forked tongue out at his commander when the latter turned his back.

Slowly and carefully, the Fir Bolg warriors crawled down the side of the building and onto the street. In this part of downtown, traffic was relatively high, despite the frigid temperature. Thanks to the freezing weather, however, most people walking had their eyes firmly on the ground, hoods and hats tight over their heads, limiting their vision. The Fir Bolg, moving slowly and carefully, were able to make their way about unhindered.

The street Biter Feargach took them down was no less populated. Growling savagely about the number of people milling about, Ithean Beanna decided to take the rest of the way on the rooftops.

"You'll want to stay on the right, then," Biter Feargach said. "The dungeon is on the right hand side of the road."

Grunting, Itheann Beanna led the way up the side of a building and onto the roof. They moved much faster now, scurrying over and leaping between the roofs like oversized rats. A few times, where the distance between roofs proved too great, they were forced to return to ground level. In those cases, Itheanna Beanna led them down the nearest perpendicular street.

"Beyond this small wood," Biter Feargach said. "That building there. That is the dungeon."

Itheann Beanna scowled. "Are you certain? It looks unlike any dungeon I've ever seen."

"And the rest of these buildings look so very familiar, do they?" Again, Biter Feargach earned himself a cuff on the side of his head.

"One day you'll learn to control that mouth in the presence of your superiors." Itheann Beanna looked around. "There is a castle there." He pointed.

"The dungeon is here. The male and female drove here in their cloth armour, and left again driving different magic chariots and no longer dressed in armour."

"So all we know for certain is that this is a guardhouse of some kind."

"The Pobl Gwir were taken in a white screaming chariot. All the white screaming chariots come here and go no further. Where else would they be?"

Itheann Beanna grunted. "We will watch." He made a signal with his hand and three Fir Bolg warriors broke from the group to scout the building and surrounds. The rest of the Fir Bolg dispersed, settling in the young trees that surrounded the building, or on the roof, or in the bushes across the street. They wrapped their cloaks tightly around themselves and fell still, their bulbous eyes continually scanning the building and their noses occasionally testing the air.

No one walking past the Elgin Street Police Headquarters saw even a hint of the Fir Bolg.

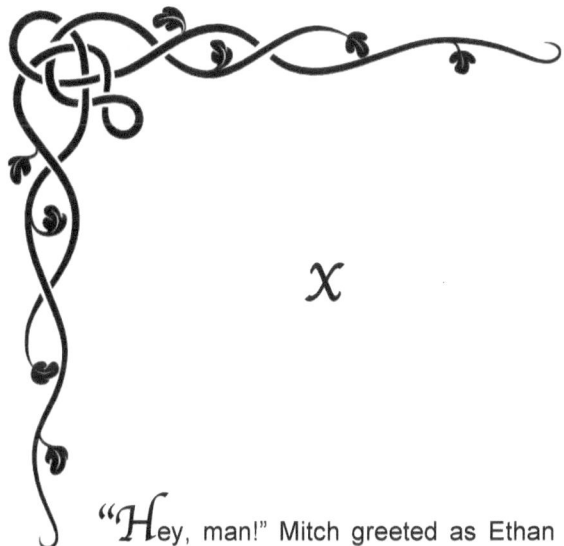

$\mathcal{X}$

"*H*ey, man!" Mitch greeted as Ethan opened the door to their residence room. "Where the hell have you been?"

"Found a place to hide Aerfyn. Spent the weekend there."

"Yeah? Where is it?"

"Up past Kazabazua somewhere. How was your weekend?"

Mitch shrugged. "Good. Spent it with Wendy."

Ethan grunted.

"What, no smart-aleck comment? No snide remark?"

"Hey man, I just came off an awesome weekend. Don't try to pick a fight, O.K?"

Mitch shrugged. "Thanks for leaving a note, by the way. I was this close to calling the cops and reporting you missing."

"I'm touched. Wanna go to Oliver's? I want a beer."

Mitch nodded. "Yeah sure."

The pair grabbed their wallets and headed down to the student bar. Ethan knocked on Gordon's door as they passed.

"Yo, Gordo!" he called through the door. "We're heading down to Oliver's. Coming?"

"In a minute." Gordon answered, his voice a little higher than usual and muffled by the door.

"Okay. See you there."

"So," Mitch said as they walked through the tunnels towards the Uni Centre. "What did you do all weekend?"

"Oh, man! It was *amazing*!" Ethan's eyes sparkled as he excitedly explained what he'd learnt about Aerfyn, and how she had taught him swordplay.

"I can't wait to go back!" he said. "It was so much fun."

"So you and her didn't...?"

"Didn't what?"

"You know."

"Man, you're getting as bad as Gordon!"

As if on cue, Gordon ran to them through the tunnel. "Hey guys!" he said. "Yo, Ethan. Where the hell were you all weekend, man? You missed the extra practice."

"Shit! Dude, I'm so sorry. I forgot all about it."

"Ethan was in the woods with Aerfyn," Mitch said.

"Seriously?" Gordon asked. "Did you… you know?"

"Jesus, guys! Get your minds out of the gutter! No, I didn't 'you know.' I learnt swordplay."

"Is that a euphemism?" Gordon asked.

Ethan smacked him playfully on the back of his head. "That's a big word for such a small brain," he said.

Gordon tried to hit Ethan back, but the latter dodged effortlessly. The pair chased each other down the tunnel, leaving Mitch behind.

"Children, children," Mitch called out. "Calm down!"

Ethan and Gordon stopped running. Gordon smacked Ethan on the shoulder. Ethan immediately put Gordon in a headlock.

"Hey!" Gordon complained, struggling. "No fair."

"All's fair in love and war, my friend," Ethan answered. "Now smell my pit!"

Gordon struggled harder, while Mitch and Ethan laughed. At length Ethan released Gordon and the three resumed their walk to Oliver's.

"Yo, man," Gordon complained. "You really need a shower!"

Ethan shrugged and Mitch laughed.

Shortly thereafter, the three friends and teammates sat at a table in Oliver's, sharing a pitcher of Keith's Red and listening to Ethan tell all about his weekend with the strange woman, Aerfyn.

Gordon leant over to Mitch and whispered, "Somebody's in love."

Mitch grinned.

For much of the following week, life returned to normal. On Thursday, Jazz arrived to drive Ethan out to the cottage for the day. Grinning like an excited fool, Ethan ran into the car and they drove off together. Neither of them noticed that the lone Fir Bolg sentry left to watch the boys in Dundas House had clambered onto the top of the car.

****

Thursday morning, Bill slid into his car and drove to the Elgin Street station. Officer Boulduc arrived at the same time. He smiled at her as she climbed out of her car.

"Morning, Officer," he greeted.

"Hey there, Spiderman. What's up?" Genevieve pulled out a tray from Tim Horton's and handed Bill a large coffee. She tossed him a bagel as well. "You need to eat breakfast."

"Yeah, okay, Mom," Bill said. "Ugh, it smells like swamp here."

"The paper mill across the river, I imagine. Wind must be blowing in from the east."

Bill grunted. As he sipped his coffee and looked over the morning's emails, Bill's mind was on the several arrests he had made that week. None of them, however, were in connection to the biggest puzzle of his career.

The drug bust on the corner of Bank and Somerset had been particularly pleasing. He and Officer Boulduc were the only uniforms in that sting. There had been three undercover officers as well. Bill envied them, except that one earned a knife in his gut. Officer Enge was recovering well, however.

There was something satisfying about making arrests, but the three mad men currently in the holding cells still

184

weighed on Bill's mind, taking away much of his satisfaction.

"Morning, Officer Jackman," Detective Chartrand said as he walked passed.

"Hey, Luc. Any news on the crazy case?"

"Nope. The three morons have reverted to saying 'Aerfyn' over and over, and the surly one has stopped speaking altogether. You?"

"Nothing on my end. What say you and I go talk to the Carleton boys again? I still reckon they know where the girl is."

"Sure. Hey, did you hear?"

"What?"

"Some idiot busted the top floor windows last night."

"Break and enter?"

"Just vandalism, I expect. There's nothing on the tapes though – just the smashing window. And nothing's missing."

Bill grunted. "No, I didn't hear. Any idea who?"

"Nope. Detective Shore is on that one. I'm surprised you didn't hear about it. It was all over the news and the police radio."

"Yeah, well," Bill said. "Someone convinced me to unplug for my days off."

"Hey," Genevieve said from her desk. "Not my fault someone decided to do something stupid on your weekend."

"Whatever. Carleton after lunch, Luc?"

"Sounds good. Give me a call when you're ready to head off."

"Sure thing."

With that, Detective Chartrand marched off, walking past the water cooler and never seeing the tall, slender figure in a dark hood that stood perfectly still behind it; not even when that figure grinned.

****

Mitch was not expecting police at his door, yet again. He opened the door and allowed them in. One was a plain-clothed officer.

"Hi Mitch," Officer Jackman greeted. "This is Detective Luc Chartrand."

"Uh... hi," Mitch said, shaking the offered hand of the detective.

"Am I in trouble?"

Detective Chartrand raised his eyebrows. "Is there a reason you would think you are?"

Mitch tried a smile. It looked as forced at it felt. "No, it's just... well... I wasn't expecting the cops to just show up... again."

"Well," Bill said easily. "No one expects the Spanish Inquisition."

Mitch stared blankly at him.

"Never mind," Bill grumbled. "Ethan not in today?"

"Uh no. We've no classes today so he took off."

"Really? Where to?"

"I dunno," Mitch said. "I'm not his mother."

"Okay there, boss," Bill said. "Calm down. It was just a question."

"Sorry," Mitch mumbled. "Cops make me nervous. Hey, you find the crazy girl yet?"

Bill smiled. "No. That's why we're here. You haven't seen her, have you?"

"Uh, no."

"Are you certain?"

"Yes, I'm certain. I think I'd remember seeing a crazy girl running around in armour, don't you?"

"She'd be in a pale blue hospital robe, actually," Detective Chartrand said, looking carefully around the room.

"Oh. No. I don't recall seeing that either."

"Uh huh."

"Yo, don't you need a warrant or something before you go snooping through our stuff?"

Detective Chartrand threw an easy smile at Mitch. "Of course. Do you mind answering our questions?"

Mitch shrugged. "No."

"Your friend, Ethan is it?"

Mitch nodded.

"Have you noticed any unusual behaviours? Does it seem like he's keeping secrets all of a sudden?"

"What? No, man. He's the same as ever."

"So why don't you know where he is right now?"

"What, like you know where all your friends are twenty-four seven, do you?"

"It never occurred to you to ask?"

"Why would I? A man's entitled to his privacy."

"Fair enough. You do understand that withholding information is a punishable offence, don't you?"

Mitch paled a little, but shrugged casually. "Yeah. Look, I'm answering the questions as best I know."

"Your friend Ethan, has he done anything out of the ordinary, something not routine for him?"

"He went to see some University of Ottawa professor last week."

Luc raised his brows. "Who?"

"I dunno. Some guy with a really weird name like Davis or Davies or something. Yeah, I think that's it, Professor Davies."

"All right. That's all we need for now," Luc said. "But we need you at the station to make a formal statement."

"I thought the statement I signed last time was enough."

"It was for that time. We need more now."

"Man, do I have to?"

"Not going would cast suspicion on you and Ethan both."

Mitch sighed. "Shit."

"Bring your wallet. You'll need I.D."

****

Professor Davies did not appear surprised at the appearance of the two police officers at his door later that afternoon.

"Is it one of my students?" he asked wearily, though his heart thudded violently against his ribs.

"You have particularly troubling students, Professor?" Detective Chartrand asked after the brief introductions.

"Some of them, if their essay writing skill is anything to judge by. Besides, why else would police show up at my door?"

"Your name was mentioned as part of our investigation into the disappearance of a schizophrenic patient from the hospital over a week ago. One of the suspects approached you."

Gwilym blinked in mock ignorance. "I read about that in the papers. I was unaware that any of my students were suspects in the case, however."

"Not a student of yours, a Carleton University student. His roommate said he'd visited you last week?"

"Oh, yes. A tall lad, dark hair, blue eyes, broad. His name was Ethan, I think."

"That's right."

"A suspect in a criminal investigation, really? He seemed perfectly amicable."

"Why did he see you?"

"To talk about our Celtic Studies programme, I imagine. We talked Celtic myth for a bit."

"Celtic myth?"

"Well, yes."

"Why?"

"Why?"

"Yes, why was he talking to you about Celtic myth?"

"Extraordinarily, gentlemen, some people have interests that are purely academic. Perhaps he was just interested? What, may I ask, has this to do with the missing girl?"

"We're not sure yet. Listen, do you mind coming down to the station to make a statement and answer more questions?"

"I do, as a matter of fact. These are my office hours, and it's getting on midterm time. My students will be expecting me to be here, and I have papers to mark."

"All right," Bill said in a bright, friendly tone. "We can either arrest you all official-like, or you can come to the station and make a statement."

"Arrest me? On what charge?"

"Oh, I don't know. Obstruction of justice? I'll make something up."

Professor Davies looked between the detective and the officer for a moment in silence. Sighing, he stood and picked up his tweed jacket. He scrawled a note on a scrap of paper and left the room with the policemen.

"This is very inconvenient, I'll have you know," he said as he tacked the note up on his office door.

"You can make a formal complaint after the investigation if you like," Bill said. "I'll have the paperwork drawn up for you."

"Do."

Ethan, Jazz and Aerfyn spent the entire day training, pausing for lunch and an early afternoon snooze. Their laughter rang clear over the misting water of the lake for much of the day.

Though Aerfyn could not speak Ethan's language she could make herself understood readily enough. The three had so much fun, they quite forgot about dinner until well and truly after the sun vanished from the sky.

Professor Davies had left plenty of food, however, so Jazz treated Ethan and Aerfyn to her culinary expertise. Soon, they were heartily chowing down on pepper steak and roasted vegetables. Talk came easily.

It was the goodbyes that were difficult. It was painfully clear that Aerfyn had been terribly lonely. She stood at the parking spot and watched the car drive off, a miserable expression on her face.

"Poor girl," Jazz said as she drove.

"I know," Ethan replied, looking back. "Maybe I should just quit school and stay with her until this is all sorted out."

"Are you crazy? That's the stupidest idea I've ever heard!"

"What? Why?"

"She's going to be gone in about a week, if you ever figure out how to get her home. Then what are you going to do?"

Ethan shrugged. "I dunno," he replied, sulkily. He scowled. "I don't know how to get her back home either."

"Yeah, well, you'd best figure that out. You've already missed the three day window, and we're living on a prayer that it is actually a three week window. You've got little over a week, pal."

"Shut up."

Ethan spent the rest of the drive in silence, his arms folded across his chest and his brow furrowed in thought.

****

Officer Genevieve Boulduc sat in the car and chewed on her B.L.T. as she watched the entrance to Dundas House in what must be the single most boring stakeout in the history of stakeouts.

"Any sign?" Bill's voice crackled over the radio.

Genevieve sighed. "It's the same as the last five times you asked, Spiderman," she growled. "I will call you when I see something."

No sooner had she said the words than a beat-up red Sunfire pulled up in front of Dundas House, and Ethan stepped from the passenger side.

"All right, he's here. Going in," Officer Boulduc said into the radio. She put down her sandwich and, still chewing, walked across the parking lot.

"Ethan Evans?" she asked.

Ethan turned and looked surprised. "Yes?" he replied in a guarded tone.

"I'm Officer Boulduc. We met a week ago."

"Yes, I remember. Vaguely."

"You mind coming down to the station for questioning?"

Ethan froze. "What?"

"You too, missy," Officer Boulduc said to the driver of the car. "Out of the car."

192

Jazz stepped out. "Is something the matter?"

"You're that girl from the other day."

"Yeah. I was in the toilet when you dropped 'round."

"All right. You both, in my car."

"Are we under arrest?" Ethan asked.

Officer Boulduc smiled tightly. "See, the thing about arrests is they're all official. It goes on your permanent record, and means a whole lot of paperwork for us. We'd much rather you just come down to the station for questioning, that's all."

"So, we're not under arrest?"

"Do you want to be?"

"Uh, no."

"Good. Now come with me please, we have some questions for you regarding the missing assault victim."

Jazz and Ethan exchanged a look, but obediently followed the officer to her car and crawled in.

****

Mitch sat quietly by Officer Jackman's desk as the latter scrawled on some forms.

"Right," the officer said, perusing the form. "I think that's everything I need to fill in. You do the rest."

"What's this for?" Mitch asked suspiciously as he took the form from Bill.

"It's two things, a personality profile, and then the information we need to perform a background check."

"A background check?"

"Calm down, Mitch. It's routine."

The fact of the matter was this was far from routine. Bill was just buying time until Ethan arrived. Detective Chartrand wanted to see the reaction they had when Mitch, Gwilym and Ethan all saw each other at the station. Then they would each be questioned.

"We're here," Officer Boulduc's voice crackled over the radio. "Bringing them in now."

"Them?"

"Yeah, he was with that girl from the other day."

Bill shrugged. "Good, actually."

"I figured as much."

"Would it kill you to use official language?" Detective Chartrand asked as he breezed past Bill's desk on his way to interrogate the professor.

"Yes, sir, sergeant, sir," Bill barked with a lopsided grin.

"Smart ass."

Bill looked at Mitch, who was still holding the form. The boy looked pale and unnerved.

"Don't mind him," Bill said gently. "He's always a pompous ass."

"Where's he going?"

"Oh, to interrogate the professor your friend Ethan went to talk to."

Mitch's already pale face turned slightly grey.

"You all right?"

"Yeah, yeah. It's just... look, is Ethan in some kind of trouble?"

"That remains to be seen. Now, fill out the form, please." Officer Jackman held up a pen.

Mitch took it with a trembling hand and bent over the edge of the desk. Bill watched him like a hawk as he slowly filled in the form, so distracted that he barely even knew what he was writing.

Bill smiled.

At that moment, Officer Boulduc appeared, Ethan and Jazz in tow. "Here they are, as promised. Now I'm handing them off and going home."

"Paperwork," Bill said.

"Tomorrow. Better yet, you do it. I've stayed overtime long enough, don't you think?"

Bill sighed. "I hate paperwork."

"Yeah, join the club. See you tomorrow, Spidey."

"Yeah, yeah. Have a good night."

"Ciao."

With that, Officer Boulduc left, heading for the showers. Bill looked between Mitch and Ethan, the pair having matching expressions of surprise as they stared mutely at one another.

"What's going on?" Ethan asked slowly.

"It's really very simple, Mr. Evans." Bill leant back in his chair and laced his fingers behind his head. "In one of the interrogation rooms right now, your friend, Professor Davies, is being questioned in connection to the missing assault victim you found on Hallowe'en. You see, I'm pretty sure you know where she is, and unless you fess up, you're all going to prison."

Ethan stiffened. "I don't know what you're talking about."

195

Bill raised his brows. "Oh no? You know, Detective Chartrand came with me this afternoon to pick up Mitch here. He noticed a bunch of bloodied sterile pads in your garbage bin. The little black thing beneath your computer desk there. Now, I know you boys were in a fight, but nothing that would've bled like that. The girl, on the other hand…"

"A friend of mine skinned his knee," Ethan said quickly.

Bill raised his eyebrows. "All right. Who?"

"Pardon?"

"I need the name of your alibi, Ethan."

"Uh…"

"For Christ's sake, Ethan. Just tell him," Mitch said.

"Shut up, man!" Ethan snapped.

"Look, we saw her, all right?" Mitch said. "Last week. We were waiting for the bus when these things jumped us."

"Things?" Bill asked.

"You're going to think we're crazy."

"Ethan, Jazz – it is Jazz, right? Mitch, come with me. Everyone. Let's go."

Unable to do anything else, they all walked down the hall. Bill put Mitch in one room, Ethan and Jazz in another. Ethan turned and glared at Bill as the policeman shut the door on their interrogation room.

"Mitch, you dumb son of a bitch," Ethan growled to himself. He kicked one of the folding chairs and started to pace.

Jazz, silent and in shock, sat down at the table and closed her eyes.

"Mum is going to kill me."

****

"Alrighty, Mitch," Bill said. "Start from the beginning. These 'things' attacked you."

"Look, it was just Ethan and me, right? I was going to my girlfriend's house. I never made it. These things… they looked like people, except tall and skinny, and they had, like, razor sharp teeth, man. They looked like piranha teeth, right? Anyway, there were three of them. This one guy had an axe, right? Like, a massive, massive axe. And he, like, fully swung it at me! Anyway, we got into a scrap when the girl with the funny name –"

"Aerfyn."

"Yeah, her. She comes out of nowhere, in nothing but a hospital gown and tackles the one with the axe. And then they're fighting. Like, kung fu or some weird shit. By the way, she's really good at fighting. Anyway, it scares the three things off, and Ethan, like, well, he, like, he felt like he owed her, right? So he promised her he'd help her out, all right?"

"Could you describe your assailants again for me, please?"

"You know Gollum, from, like, Lord of the Rings? Like that. Only taller. And meaner. He had a frikkin' *axe*!"

Bill cleared his throat. Was there something in the water that was making everyone crazy?

"All right, so talk me through what happened next."

Mitch sighed. "Ethan brought her back to our residence room and took care of her. She had a nasty cut in her side that had been stitched, but the stitches had come undone in the fight, right? When she woke, we quickly

197

found out she couldn't speak English. So we got the name of the creatures that attacked us. Dynion Gors, she said they were called. Anyway, we googled it. Turns out, Dynion Gors was Welsh for Bog Men. Dude, we were attacked by the thing from the black swamp!"

"Welsh?"

"Yeah. Welsh. Who knew, right? So, now we knew she spoke Welsh and we find out from Jazz that there's this dude at University of Ottawa who's Welsh and he teaches Welsh and shit. So Ethan goes down to talk to him, like, twice."

"And?"

"And this is where shit gets really weird, all right? Ethan comes back and says he found out that like, the Celts, they had, like, this myth, right? And the myth says that around Hallowe'en the divide between this world and the Otherworld falls, right?"

"Hold up. What other world?"

"I don't know. *The* Otherworld, man! Look, the way Ethan said the Professor described it was that it was like Narnia, right? Anyway, turns out that's where Aerfyn is from, and we're all, like, trying to help her to get back."

Bill looked down at his notepad and tried to collect his thoughts. "So, what you're saying is that this girl is from, what, an alternate universe, and you're trying to get her back home?"

Mitch nodded. "Yeah."

"Oooookay, then."

"I told you you'd think we're all crazy."

"Yup. Uh-huh, I do." Bill opened a file and pulled out three photos. "Do you recognise these men?"

Mitch took the photos and stared at them. "Nope. Never seen them before in my life. Loving the moustache on that dude, though. Who's he supposed to be? Hulk Hogan?"

Bill grunted. "You are certain you've never seen them?"

"Positive, man. I've seen a lot of crazy these past two weeks. These three aren't part of it."

"Thank-you," Bill said. He gathered up the photos and left the room rather abruptly.

Mitch sat back in his chair. "Great," he muttered.

Ethan and Jazz were next on the list. Bill entered their room and greeted them by saying, "Before you think of a whole bunch of lies to tell me, Mitch told me everything. If you're not going to jail, you're going to the nuthouse." He unceremoniously threw the file he carried on the table. The mug shot of Peredur slipped out.

Ethan picked it up.

"This guy's wearing armour," he said. He looked up at Bill. "Dude, this guy is wearing armour!"

"Thank-you, I know. I made the arrest."

Ethan looked back down at the photograph. "Is he here? Like, in the building?"

Bill scowled. "None of your business. Now, let's get to it shall we?"

"Dude, you have to take me to him."

"What? No! Sit down, shut up, and answer my questions."

"Dude, you don't understand. He's one of them!"

"One of who?"

199

"One of Aerfyn's warriors."

"What?"

"Look, you know everything Mitch knows, right? So you have to know that Aerfyn, she's like, a queen and they're fighting a war with the Dynion Gors. She fell through the divide between her world and ours, and she needs to get back home, 'cause, well, she's fighting a war. Look, man. They've obviously come to rescue her. You gotta let me talk to them!"

Bill stared. "You're all crazy."

"Whatever. I know it's hard to believe, but if you saw this girl fight, you'd know it right away. She's not from here, and she needs help."

"Yes, she does need help. And so do you."

"No, not like that. Jesus! This is insane."

"Yup, you said it."

"Do you smell that?" Jazz whispered to Ethan. Ethan stopped his attempts at making Officer Jackman understand and sniffed the air.

"Dude, did you fart?" he asked the police officer.

"What? No!" Only Bill could smell it now too. "It's probably from the paper mill across the river."

The sound of shattering glass and an almost-feminine scream broke Bill's glare. He turned towards the door.

"Stay here," he said.

Ethan and Jazz nodded, their eyes wide in identical expressions of fear and curiosity.

Bill got up and left the room, drawing his gun as he did so. The smell of stagnant water was stronger out here in the hall. He turned to look up the hall, and froze.

Detective Luc Chartrand lay on the floor, eyes open and blank, a pool of deep red blood spreading below him. The lower half of the detective remained in the interrogation room. Bill edged forward slowly. He rounded to corner, his gun held before him.
His jaw dropped.

Three tall figures in dark grey hooded robes were in the room, the two way mirror smashed in. One held Professor Gwilym Davies aloft by the throat. The man struggled against his captor as he slowly choked.

"Hey!" Bill yelled. He fired two shots at the one choking Gwilym. The creature dropped the professor with a high-pitched shriek. All three fled the room via the shattered mirror. Bill ran in and helped the professor to his feet.

"Are you all right, sir?"

"Dear God, they're real," Gwilym wheezed.

Another cascade of shattered glass and a scream sent Bill and Gwilym running back to Ethan and Jazz' interrogation room. There, Ethan defended against two of the creatures, holding them back with a chair.

Bill didn't even get to fire one shot. As soon as he arrived, the creatures shrieked and fled.

Ethan slowly put down the chair and grimaced. "Now do you believe me?"

"Shut up. C'mon. Let's get you all out of here."

"Help meeeeeeeeee!" Mitch yelled as he ran past the interrogation room, four more creatures dogging his heels.

"Hey!" Bill yelled as he ran out of the room and aimed his gun. The creatures broke off their pursuit and disappeared around corners. Mitch joined the group huddled close to the police officer.

"Thanks," he said.

Bill nodded and listened. The station was silent.

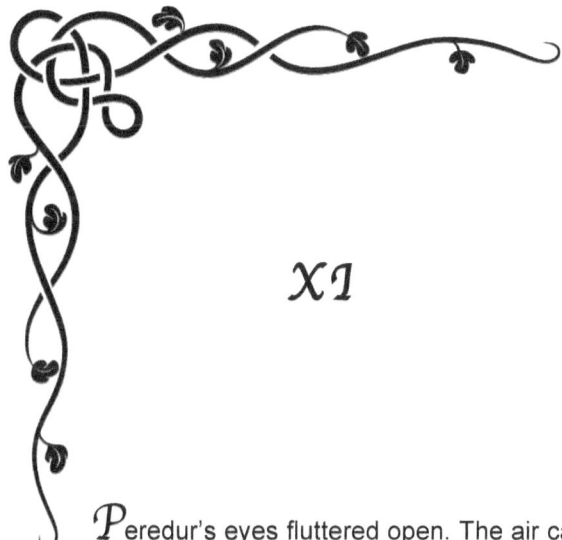

XI

$\mathcal{P}$eredur's eyes fluttered open. The air carried a familiar earthy stench.

"Uh-oh," he whispered.

"Peredur," Olwen whispered from his cell. "You smell that?"

"Please tell me that they aren't here," Gawain said.

"They're here," Peredur answered.

"What did I just tell you?"

Olwen scowled. "We need our weapons."

"Never mind our weapons, we need out of these cells. Damn it, we're sitting ducks locked up like this!"

"Hey!" Peredur yelled, knowing there was an officer down the hall, reading some sort papery cloth thing. "Hey! You need to let us out of here! You're all in danger! Hey!" He shook the bars. "Hey!"

Down the hall, Police Constable Bob Vachon put down his paper.

"Hey!" One of the prisoners shouted. "Mae angen i chi adael i ni allan o fan hyn! Rydych chi gyd mewn perygl! Hey! Hey!"

"Eh there. Quiet, la. I'm trying to read here, la," he called down the hall in a thick Quebecois accent.

When the prisoner simply shook the bars and screamed, "Hey!" Officer Vachon sighed and stood. "Tabarnaque! Arrête, la!"

Officer Vachon did not make it three steps from his desk. A sword, jagged and not quite sharp, punctured his chest clean through. Behind him, the wielder of the weapon laughed quietly as Bob's legs gave way and he fell to the floor.

"Hey!" Peredur yelled. "I am trying to save your life!"

The sudden appearance of a Dynion Gors warrior at the bars made Peredur leap backwards.

"Ró-dhéanach," the warrior snarled.

Peredur dropped his eyes to the bloodied sword in the warrior's hands. He swallowed.

"You bastard," he said. "He had nothing to do with your damned fight against us!"

The warrior of the Dynion Gors grinned and slid his sword slowly through the bars. The blade was nowhere near long enough to reach Peredur.

Seizing the opportunity, Peredur stepped to the side and kicked the blade on the flat. It snapped neatly at the hilt.

"Bastaird!" the warrior snarled, leaping backwards in surprise.

Three loud bangs sounded, startling Peredur enough to drop him to his knees and cover over his ears with his hands. The cloaked warrior stumbled, then collapsed, black blood spreading beneath him.

Peredur uncurled himself and walked forward. "What the…?"

The sudden appearance of the man who had captured the three adventurers made Peredur jump backwards once more. The man fiddled with the keys in the lock and the door slid open. He smiled a short grimace at Peredur before moving to Olwen's cell. Peredur cautiously stepped out.

"Here," someone said to him, holding out a sword.

Peredur looked. A man in his early forties, wearing the strange garb of the natives of this world held out Gawain's sword. Behind him stood two strong young men and a tiny young woman with large, blue eyes.

"That's Gawain's," Peredur said. He pointed to his own weapon. "That's mine."

"Of course, excuse me." The man handed Peredur his sword. "I'm Gwilym, by the way."

"Peredur. Thank-you for my weapon."

Olwen stepped out of his cell and watched a moment as the man in black unlocked Gawain's cell.

"Olwen," Peredur said, taking a sword from Gwilym. He tossed it over. Olwen deftly caught it and wrapped the belt around his waist.

"Thanks," he said. He tilted his head at the four people behind Peredur. "Who are they?"

"Gwilym," Peredur said, indicating the oldest man. Everyone else understood the gist and spoke their own names.

"Ethan."

"Mitch."

"Jazz."

"Bill," Officer Jackman said as Gawain stepped past him. The Pobl Gwir warrior paused long enough to glower at him from under heavy eyebrows.

"Peredur," Peredur said, indicating himself. "Olwen, Gawain."

Gwilym almost choked. The names were well known to him from early Arthurian myth.

"What's the plan now?" Peredur asked Gwilym.

"Uh…" replied Gwilym.

Bill raised his eyebrows as Professor Davies turned to him. "What's the plan?" he asked.

"We get the hell out of dodge," Bill said.

Gwilym dutifully translated.

Peredur nodded. "Os gwelwch yn dda yn mynd â ni i Aerfyn."

Gwilym nodded. "We're going to get them to Aerfyn," he said to Officer Jackman.

"Sounds good to me," Bill said with a shrug. "Where is she?"

"At my cottage."

Bill blinked in surprise before saying, "All right. Let's get going then, shall we?"

The group turned and headed towards the parking lot where Bill's squad car sat waiting. Bodies of policemen met them at almost every turn.

"Jesus!" Ethan breathed. "Did they kill everyone?"

Bill didn't answer. With his gun drawn, he led the way through the building.

The attack was swift and sudden. Twelve Dynion Gors set upon the group, their cruel weapons nowhere near as terrifying as their savage smiles. The struggle was brief, but vicious. Bill dispersed the bog men with a few well-aimed shots from his gun, and the group fled the building.

"Shot gun!" Ethan yelled when they reached the squad car.

"Me too!" Jazz squeaked. She dove in the front passenger side door after Ethan, landing on his lap.

"What the…?" Ethan said.

"There's no room in the back."

Ethan turned. She was right. The three Pobl Gwir adventurers and Gwilym were crammed into the back seat like sardines in a tin. Mitch took refuge on the floor. Gawain smugly rested his feet on Mitch's back.

"Bastard," Mitch grumbled.

"Everyone in?" Bill asked.

"Yup," Ethan, Gwilym, Mitch and Jazz answered in unison.

"Bring the noise," Ethan said as Bill flipped the switch and the lights and siren screeched to life.

Bill and Jazz gave him a look.

"C'mon. Hot Fuzz? Please tell me you've seen that movie?"

"No," Bill answered grimly. He pressed his foot on the accelerator.

"Well," Ethan said lamely. "It's funny as hell."

The Dynion Gors had gathered around the car. When the siren sounded and the lights flashed, they jumped back in surprise. It lasted but a second before they began a desperate sprint in pursuit.

"Jesus!" Ethan said. "They're running after us!"

"They won't be able to keep up," Bill said.

"I'm not so sure," Ethan replied, craning his neck around. "Uh, can you go faster?"

Bill looked up in his rear view mirror. "You cannot be serious," he breathed. Reflected in the mirror were twelve hooded figures, and they were gaining.

Officer William Jackman pressed his foot on the accelerator. The sirens did their job at keeping the traffic out of the way, for the most part. The squad car was on the highway before long.

"Can you still see them?" Bill asked his cramped passengers.

"Uh... nope. No, I... AH! I see them! I see them!" Ethan said. "Shit, they're fast!"

"Son of a ...!" Bill accelerated more.

"I don't wish to be a bother, but if you're looking to get to my cottage," Gwilym said. "You're going the wrong way."

Bill let loose a string of profanities that would shame a sailor. He sped down the Queensway at break-neck speed until he could find an exit.

"There!" Ethan shouted. "You missed it."

Bill gritted his teeth and edged the car over.

"There!" Ethan shouted again.

Bill pulled the car over suddenly, and it went screeching down the exit ramp. A neat, three block turn, and they were back on the highway going the other direction.

****

"That was senseless," Biter Feargach mumbled to himself when he found himself on the same road, but going the other way. The Fir Bolg had chased the car off the road upon which many cars travelled, followed it around once it was off, only to find themselves back on the road again, this time going the other way.

A quick grin from one of other warriors spurred Biter Feargach on. They ran as fast as their slender legs would carry them.

"This chariot is fast!" the one who grinned at Biter Feargach said to him.

"Just run," he growled in return.

The grin turned vicious and the Fir Bolg warrior faced forward again

Now it was a race.

****

The squad car screamed down the road. Patches of ice made the driving difficult and incredibly dangerous. Bill, however, had a great deal of experience driving like a maniac. He had, in his misspent and very bored youth, spent many days just driving around in gravel parking lots in terrible weather and often drunk.

Still, the practice made him the best driver on the force now, most especially in dangerous conditions. He drove on, faster than anyone else in the car felt comfortable with.

"Are they still tailing us?" he asked.

"I don't know, it's dark out. I can't see any movement. No wait. Yup. They're still there. They've fallen behind a bit, though."

"Good."

"That means you should lose them by the time you get to the exit," Gwilym said.

"You know, Professor D," Mitch said from the floor. "You sound awfully calm."

Gwilym simply shrugged. "Keep calm and carry on," he said.

They drove on in relative silence.

****

A hot bath with a full glass of Australian red wine had been the plan since this morning. Genevieve Boulduc filled her glass as the tub filled with steaming water. The apartment soon filled with the smell of lavender and patchouli. At her feet, her two ferrets chattered up at her, begging for a treat.

"Oh, all right, then." She padded barefoot to the fridge and pulled the treats from the top of it. In her living room, the television rattled off some facts and figures on the economy section of the news broadcast. She tipped a small amount of the treats onto the floor and, taking up her glass and turning off the kitchen light, she slipped into the bathroom.

She turned the tap off, slipped out of her dressing gown and stepped into the tub. Her muscles immediately relaxed. What the water and scented bath gel didn't achieve, the wine did. Officer Boulduc took a sip and closed her eyes.

Thank-you, Ian, a reporter on the television said. *I am standing outside the Ottawa Police Headquarters here on Elgin Street.*

Genevieve opened her eyes.

Just two days ago, the top floor windows of the building had been smashed in what police then described as a senseless act of vandalism. Tonight, the story takes a darker turn. Early this evening, the headquarters were attacked again. All the officers and support staff in the building have been killed. Among the dead are Police Constable George Poulton, Staff Sergeant David Perkins and Detective Luc Chartrand and one officer, Police Constable William Jackman, is missing, as are three suspects in the Hallowe'en assault on Carleton University's campus.

"What the...?!"

Genevieve leapt from the tub and ran into her living room. Naked and dripping wet, she stared at the screen, dumbfounded. The news displayed the Elgin Street Headquarters. The entire building had been cordoned off and gurney after gurney laden with black body bags were filing from the station and into ambulances.

No word yet as to who might be responsible. The entire police force, and the city of Ottawa, are still reeling from this unprecedented slaughter. More news to come when it breaks. I'm Rebecca Thompson for CBC News, Ottawa.

The wine glass Officer Boulduc had in her hand slipped from her grasp and shattered on the floor. The sound of smashing glass brought her sharply back to reality. Ignoring the mess, she ran to her room and searched her pockets frantically for her mobile phone. She dialed Bill's number. It rang thrice, before going to Bill's voicemail.

You've reached Bill. You know what to do.

"Bill! Bill, you bastard, pick up! Um, look. What happened at the station? It's all over the news. I'm heading there now. You'd better be there."

Genevieve hung up and, making a conscious effort to control the panic that threatened to take over, she hurriedly dressed. She skipped past the spilled wine, which her ferrets happily lapped up, and raced out of the apartment.

****

"Oh no! No! No!" Bill said as his eye caught the petrol metre.

"What?" Ethan said.

"We're running on empty! Damn it, Bob! You said you'd filled it! Son of a–"

"House!" Ethan said, pointing at houselights that shone in the distance through the naked trees.

Bill swerved rather suddenly into the narrow, leaf-strewn unpaved lane. Halfway to the house, the engine gave up.

"Shit," Bill said.

"We'll have to push," Ethan said, unbuckling the seatbelt that wrapped around both him and Jazz.

Mitch groaned.

"Come on," Jazz said cheerily. "It's not that far to the house."

Everyone exited the car. Jazz ran around to the driver's side and jumped in. Bill drew his gun, Peredur his sword and they watched the darkening woods as everyone else pushed.

****

Joseph Bille thumped down the stairs and threw his backpack on the floor beside the table, spilling its contents.

"Yo," his older brother, Elroy, said. "Don't mess up the place. I just cleaned."

'The place' was an abandoned farmhouse on a property, long overtaken by trees, that had neither been demolished nor claimed. The brothers Bille found it by accident one night after skipping school to go exploring. For a long time, it was their clubhouse. Now it was their gang hideout.

Their gang was really nothing more than a few guys who hung out occasionally to drink, smoke, play cards and pretend to be hardened criminals. Other than a few scuffles with rival gangs outside of nightclubs in the Byward Market, the boys who gathered at the farmhouse were generally well behaved.

"Whatever," Joseph said. He flopped on an armchair and leant his head back.

"Rough day at school?"

"Yo, man, Ottawa U is crap. Man, I don't know what I'm doing in the business programme. Should've gone for general arts."

"Don't tell mom, she'll freak. You know how much she wants you to do good in school. She never got the chance in Somalia, you know."

"You know I got in trouble 'cause I wasn't wearing a suit. What the hell, man? I'm in university, not some cubby buddy. I shouldn't have to wear a damned suit."

Elroy shrugged. "You're lucky to be in university at all. I didn't have the grades. Here." He put down his cards and grabbed the bottle of whiskey sitting on the table. He tossed it to his brother, who caught it deftly. Elroy quickly followed that with a plastic cup. Joseph wasn't expecting that and the cup bounced off his forehead.

The men around the table guffawed. Joseph threw them an evil glare. He picked up the cup and poured himself a generous helping of Crown Royal.

Elroy, in the meantime, picked up Joseph's school bag and tossed the books back in. A pack of cards fell to the floor. Elroy picked it up and looked it over.
"Yo, what's this?"

"Nothing," Joseph said quickly, jumping up to take back the cards.

"N-n-n-no," Elroy said, holding his brother back reading the card packet.

"Yo, man," Joseph complained.

"Magic: The Gathering?"

"Give it back."

"What the hell is this?"

"It's nothing. Just a game friends and I play at school."

"Yo, man," Zachary said from his place at the poker table. "Toss it here."

Elroy did, tossing above Joseph's head. Joseph jumped for it but missed. He went for Zachary, but Elroy held him at bay.

"You know who plays this? Nerdy white kids with thick glasses and lisps who'll never get laid."

"Shut up," Joseph said. "There's a club, all right?"

"You know this shit?" Elroy asked.

"Yeah, man." Zachary nodded. "They all sit around a table in robes and pretend to be elves and wizards and shit."

"What?"

Joseph cringed. "It's not like that."

"Go long," Gracen said and he leapt from his chair and ran through the door into the kitchen. Zachary threw the packet of cards to Gracen, who shook it at Joseph.

"Come and get me, Paladin," he teased.

"That's not funny," Joseph said. He gave chase nonetheless, and was soon running ragged through the house as Gracen, Zachary and Elroy taunted him.

"Come on wizard," they teased. Or, "Come and get it, elf-boy!"

"Yo, man, give it back," Joseph whined every so often.

The game was interrupted by three firm knocks at the door. Gracen, who did not hold the cards at the moment, went to the window to check.

"Yo," Elroy whispered to Zachary. "What's a Paladin?"

"Shit!" Gracen said suddenly from the front window. "It's the cops!"

Three more firm knocks followed by, "Hello? Is anyone home?" sounded at the front door.

Gracen, after getting the affirmative nod from Elroy, opened the door a crack. "S'up?" he said through the crack.

"Uh," the policeman on the other side of the door said. "Sorry to disturb you, sir, but I was wondering if you had any gas?"

"Gas?"

"Yes. Uh... rather embarrassingly, I'm out of fuel for my car and could use a fill-up, if you've any to spare."

Gracen shut the door. *Is he for real?* he mouthed to Elroy. Elroy shrugged. Gracen opened the door a crack again. "We don't have any, sorry."

"Look, there are four cars here. Do you mind if we siphon off some from one of the tanks? I'll pay. We're in a bit of a hurry and could really use the help."

"Yo, let the white man in," Elroy said.

Gracen shrugged and opened the door.

"Thank-you!" the policeman said with marked relief. He and his rather large entourage walked in. One man, last through the door, walked in backwards, sword drawn. Gracen closed the door behind him and eyed the sword in disbelief.

"I'm Police Constable Bill Jackman. These are my friends, Ethan Evans, Professor Gwilym Davies, Jazz, Mitch, Peredur, Olwen and Gawain."

"Yo, you're O.P. What are you doing this side of the river?" Elroy demanded.

"Never mind O.P, what's with the sword?" Gracen said, still eyeing Peredur in disbelief.

"It's a very long story, and we're in a hurry. Is it all right if we siphon off some gas?"

An ungodly shriek from outside made everyone inside jump. Two more members of the group drew swords and turned to face the front door and windows.

"What the...?" Elroy said, his eyes going wide.

"Was that...?" the policeman asked.

"Dynion Gors," the lean swordsman with the dark, curly hair said grimly.

"Fuck," the man named Ethan said. "How the hell did they keep up with us?"

"Look," Officer Jackman said, turning very serious. "You are all in terrible danger. We're being pursued by... well, it doesn't matter. But they're dangerous, and out for blood. You need to get to your cars and get the hell out of here. I'm commandeering a vehicle on official police business."

"Yo, man," Elroy said. "You can't take our cars!"

Another shriek, closer this time echoed into the night.

"There's no time to argue. Get into a car, and get as far away as possible. I'm taking the truck that's out there, though."

"Yo –" Elroy started.

Bill grabbed him roughly at the collar. "Look, those things out there are out to kill, so if you want to be dead before morning, then by all means argue with me. I'm taking the truck, do what you want. Keys."

Elroy nodded to the pile of keys on the poker table.

"Which ones?" Bill asked.

"With the dollar sign key chain," Elroy mumbled.

Bill released him and grabbed the keys. "Let's go," he told the group.

They went to the front door. Bill put his hand on the door handle and turned back.

"When I count to three, I'm going to open this door. You four," he indicated Elroy, Zachary, Joseph and Gracen. "Head out to one of your cars and get the hell outta dodge. I'll provide cover fire, while the rest go to the black truck there."

Gwilym very quietly translated for the benefit of the three foreigners. They nodded, swords still drawn.

"Ready?" Bill asked. Everyone nodded, Elroy's protests silenced by the general air of fear that had settled over the group.

"One... Two... Three!" Bill opened the door and the four gang members were out first, heading straight for the silver Mazda 3 nearest the door. Everyone else followed, sprinting fast to the truck. Professor Davies and Jazz shared the passenger side of the cab, leaving the driver's side to Bill, who followed the group, gun at the ready.

The thirteen Dynion Gors fell upon them from the trees like a swarm of demonic bats, shrieking and hissing. Joseph had just made it to the car, when he felt his brother leave his side suddenly. He turned to find Elroy surrounded by the hooded attackers. In a blink of an eye, Elroy's throat opened and gushed blood.

"Elroy!" Joseph screamed. He left the car to go to his brother's aid.

"Joe!" Zachary called from the front passenger side.

"Screw this!" Gracen said. He started the car and drove off.

Bill started the truck and began to drive as well when Peredur noticed Elroy's capture and killing, and Joseph's subsequent abandonment. He leapt from the tray of the truck and ran to Joseph. Bill slammed on the breaks.

It was a struggle to get Joseph away from the Dynion Gors. Peredur hauled the grieving man, who could only shout his brother's name to the tray. Ethan, Olwen and Gawain helped haul him into the tray in between fighting off warriors of the Dynion Gors.

Peredur followed, only to have his ankle grabbed at the last. He was pulled backwards off the truck.

"Peredur!" Olwen screamed.

Peredur got to his feet. He stood grimly between the truck and the remaining ten Dynion Gors warriors.

"Ewch!" Peredur said.

"Dim," Gawain replied.

"Ewch! Ewch! Fe wna i gynnal i ffwrdd. Ewch!"

Olwen and Gawain exchanged a look.

The Dynion Gors attacked. Making the decision for the two warriors, Ethan banged the top of the cab and the truck was off, roaring down the long laneway as fast as Bill dared in the rough conditions.

"Dim!" Gawain screamed. Olwen and Ethan both had to hold him back as the Poble Gwir warrior struggled to exit the tray. "Peredur! Peredur!"

They rounded the corner and Peredur was lost to sight, fighting valiantly as the Dynion Gors swarmed over him. Silence fell over the truck as Peredur's brave sacrifice

219

settled in. Bill had watched in his rear view mirror, Gwilym and Jazz doing the same. Bill clamped his jaw grimly and drove on as tears slid silently down Jazz' cheeks.

In the tray, Olwen sat beside Gawain, his hand on the broader man's trembling shoulder. Gawain knelt at the back of the tray, staring blankly into the night, his cheeks wet with tears.

"Ffwl," Gawain whispered. "Twpsyn dewr."

"Bydd yn byw bendithio yn y byd a ddaw," Olwen said gently.

Gawain closed his eyes and bowed his head.

"Yo, man," Mitch said. "That was way too close."

Not knowing what else to do, Ethan went over to Joseph. "Hey," he said. "Sorry about... uh..."

"Elroy," Joseph whispered.

"Yeah."

"He was my brother."

"Oh, man. I am so, so sorry."

"What were those things?"

Ethan glanced back at the road. "Not entirely sure. These guys call them Dynion Gors, which in Welsh means Bog Men."

Joseph looked at Ethan, confusion writ large on his features.

Ethan sighed, settled in beside Joseph and told him the whole story.

"Woah, woah, hold up," Joseph said. "So Narnia is real?"

"No. Well, yes. Well, sort of. The place itself isn't real. I mean, these guys don't come from Narnia, but the idea is similar. It's another world, in the same way Narnia is another world. I mean, there's no Aslan or anything."

"Holy shit!"

"Yeah, tell me about it. I'm Ethan, by the way."

"Joseph. Joseph Bille."

Olwen turned sharply. "Gwilym!" he barked.

Ethan looked up. Some distance away, barely visible through the trees that lined the road, flashes of pale flesh indicated the Dynion Gors were in hot pursuit.

Ethan pounded on the cab.

"Step on it!" he called through the window. "We've got company."

"Son of a bitch!" Bill spat. He accelerated, pushing the truck for all it was worth.

"They can run," Joseph noted wryly.

"Yeah, and they're wicked with a blade," Ethan said.

Gawain stood. "Dewch i gymryd i ni, rydych drwg lyffantod!" he bellowed out into the darkness. "Mae gen i ddyledion i'w talu'n," he growled quietly after.

"What the fuck did he just say?" Joseph asked Ethan, who shrugged.

"I don't speak Welsh." He tapped on the cab window. "Did you catch that Professor D?"

"I think he said, 'Come get us, you evil toads!'" Gwilym replied.

"And afterwards?"

221

"What?"

"What did he say after that?"

"I didn't hear anything after that."

"Kay, thanks."

Ethan turned back to Joseph and shrugged. They settled in for a long and melancholic journey to Gwilym's cottage.

A short hour later, Bill pulled the truck up to the parking spot for Gwilym's cottage. Everything was pitch black.

"That can't be a good sign," Ethan whispered. His heart beat rapidly with sudden worry for Aerfyn.

"They can't have gotten here before us," Gwilym said as he jumped out of the cab. "She's probably just asleep. Did anyone think to bring a torch?"

"A what now?" Joseph replied.

"That's flashlight in Brit-speak," Jazz said.

"Oh. Right."

"Here," Bill said, taking his flashlight and handing it to Gwilym.

The professor led the way through the woods to the cabin. He stopped dead as the light of the flashlight hit the back door.

The door creaked in the breeze, hanging by one, twisted hinge. The doorframe had shattered and come away from the rest of the cabin.

"Oh no," Gwilym murmured.

"No!" Ethan said sharply, running forward.

"Ethan!" Bill said. "Stop this instant!"

Ethan did not heed Bill's order. He ran forward, chased by Bill, who unholstered his gun.

"Ethan!" Bill said again. He caught Ethan just as he stepped through the door to the kitchen and reached for the light switch. Ethan looked at Bill in surprise. Bill shook his head and pressed his finger against his lips. He turned back to the others who stood awkwardly outside.

"Professor," he said in a harsh whisper. "My flashlight."

Gwilym walked forward and gave the constable his flashlight back.

"Stay behind me," Bill said.

The soft hiss of swords sliding from their sheaths was the only answer Bill received. He walked forward slowly, his gun at the ready.

The interior of the cabin was a complete mess. Smashed porcelain and glass littered the floor, crunching underfoot. Pictures hung askew on the wall, while others lay on the ground. One, a map of the lake, had a deep slash down its centre. The group stepped carefully into the dining room to find the dining table splintered and several chairs broken.

Bill carefully checked the two side rooms, finding them both empty, before moving out to the deck. He checked carefully.

"All clear," he said, holstering his gun again. "Looks like the girl is gone, and so's her attacker."

"We have to find her!" Ethan said.

"You think?"

"Like, now!"

"Quiet, Ethan, and give me time to think."

The group fell silent, watching Bill expectantly.

Overhead, a pale barn owl glided silently across the starry sky.

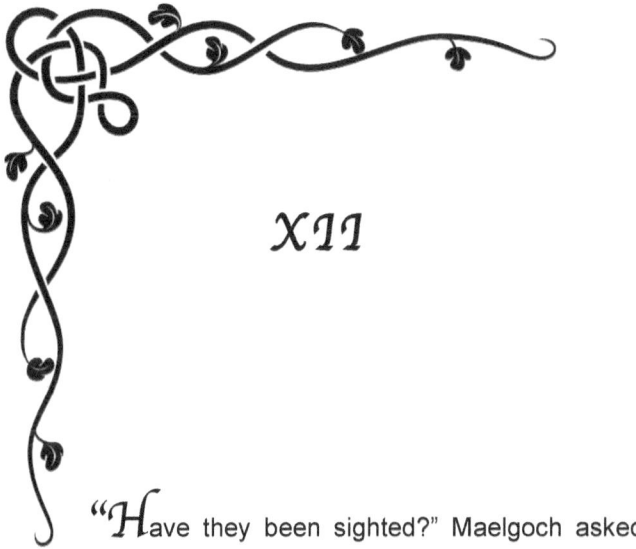

XII

"Have they been sighted?" Maelgoch asked Gwalchmai.

The Dryw nodded. "Their camp is on the southern side of the lake. It looks as though they're building rafts and siege engines."

"We should attack before they've completed their task, my Lord," Cai said.

"We can't," Maelgoch replied. "Not until we've gained a better measure of their strength and strategy. I will not walk into battle blind again."

Cai gritted his teeth. "Mighty Dryw, is there word of my brother and his companions?"

The aged seer shook his head. "Tylluan is yet to return, Lord Cai, and I fear my sight ends at the divide between worlds."

The young lord sighed and shook his head. "I grow weary of waiting."

"We all do," Maelgoch said. "Still, wait we must."

****

Across the lake, the shining fortified city and the magnificent Caer Avallach sat silent and waiting. The first strike of the Dynion Gors would not be long away, and the soldiers and squires left to defend the walls were prepared.

Though terrified, not a single warrior within the fortress doubted the abilities of the man who led them. Rhydych patrolled the wall, keeping his keen brown eyes trained on the far side of the shore.

"All is in place, my Lord," a page said.

Rhydych grunted. "Good. They will be fighting blind for the first while, and will be relying on sound to tell them when the outer wall has crumbled. That should buy us some time, at least. Gods but that the knights were here!"

"They'll be here, my Lord Rhydych. They will come."

Rhydych looked down at the boy and smiled. "Oh, to have the faith of youth," he murmured.

"My Lord?"

"Nothing. Return to your station. The Bog Men will attack soon enough."

"Yes, my Lord." The page ran off.

"Too young," the Lord Marshall mused to no one in particular. "Too young to know the horrors of war."

Rhydych resumed his pacing and watching. His thoughts were with his son, Maelgoch, who rode out with the rest of the Knights of Caer Avallach in defence of their queen and, like the queen herself, had not been heard from since.

He recalled himself as a youth, a boastful, arrogant boy who was as beautiful as he was talented. The then Lord Marshall, Powys, had brought him down hard. It had been a humbling ten years of training, but that made the medallion he earned – the sigil of the Knightly Order to which he now and forever belonged – all the more worth the earning. For all his boasting in the early days, he had never known true self-pride until he stood with his brothers and sisters, newly made knights all.

Maelgoch had not been like him. Truth be told, he'd been much more like his mother. Though a solid rival in looks and talent to his father, his view was darker; grim and unyielding. No one was as hard upon Maelgoch as the boy himself.

As Lord Marshall, Rhydych had not been easy on his son. As a father, though, he constantly worried that his son was taking things too hard upon himself. It was well that he did, however. Maelgoch graduated from training the top of his peers, and was awarded special commendation for it. He had been given the honour of the seat next highest to the queen at the celebratory feast. He had laughed and smiled more that night than Rhydych remembered him doing his entire life.

Beside him, the young queen, resplendid in a gown of red and gold, kept Maelgoch entertained. They had trained together, and were fast friends. It was Rhydych's hope that they would one day marry. Such a union would produce children of such beauty and prowess, it would be sung of for thousands of generations. Surely it could not be otherwise.

Yet, for all Rhydych knew, all the promise and life that had been encapsulated in his son might well have been snuffed out, cut short by the cruel blades of the savage Dynion Gors. Perhaps his son's body lay on the battlefield even now, stripped of flesh by the carrion birds and wolves.

Rhydych forced the thought from his mind. He would not believe it until he saw it for himself, even if the very fact that the Dynion Gors were on the shores of Y Llyn Gwydr gave evidence as to its likelihood. Maelgoch could not be dead. Rhydych's first born was alive. The Lord Marshall was certain of it.

He sighed.

The war horns on the towers of Caer Avallach sounded their baleful warning. The Dynion Gors had begun their attack. Rhydych braced himself as the first thudding booms of catapult-thrown boulders crashed heavily into the outer wall of the city of Y Ynys Bendigaid.

"Come soon, Knights of Caer Avallach," Rhydych said softly. "I fear we cannot hold out without you."

****

"I swear to God if they've hurt her, I'll kill them!" Ethan fumed. He stood with the rest of the group on the deck of Professor Gwilym's cottage, with only Officer Jackman's flashlight to see by.

"Shh!" Bill said. He looked up sharply. "Did you hear that?"

Heads swivelled around as the others tried to catch the sound. Bill frowned. "There. Something's dripping."

"A tap inside maybe," Mitch offered helpfully.

Bill shook his head. He moved slowly towards the sound and stopped dead at the far end of the deck. The others followed. Bill shone the light on the floor of the deck, where a pool of dark liquid slowly spread, seeping into the wood like sinister lacquer. Bill squatted and pressed his fingers into it. It was cold, and smeared dark red on his fingertips.

"Blood," Bill said.

A few more drops fell onto Bill's thumb. He shone his torch up at the roof. A slow, steady drip of the dark blood trickled from the corrugated iron roof.

"Get me a chair."

Jazz ran over to the patio table and dragged over one of the flimsy plastic chairs. Bill stood on it and hauled himself up just high enough to peer over the eaves. He moved the flashlight. The light hit something crumpled and bleeding on the roof. Bill lowered himself down again.

"There's a body on the roof," he informed the waiting crowd.

Gwilym translated for Olwen and Gawain.

"Aerfyn's?" Ethan asked, stricken.

"I don't know. I'm going to go up for a closer look. Boost?"

Ethan nodded mutely. He cupped his hands together. Bill put one booted foot in the hand-stirrup. On the count of three, Bill pulled and Ethan lifted. Officer Jackman made it easily onto the roof. He walked slowly over and knelt by the body.

"Please don't be her," he whispered. He turned the body over and jumped backwards as a pair of overly large, glassy pale green eyes stared up at him. The skinny creature dead on the roof was not Aerfyn, but a warrior of the Dynion Gors.

Bill walked back over to the edge. "It's not her," he said. He heard Ethan sigh with relief and smiled.

Something hit him with a powerful tackle, and suddenly he was on the deck, winded and disoriented. He stared up in disbelief as the pale, angry face of Aerfyn stared down at him, a kitchen knife at his neck.

"Aerfyn!" Ethan said, grabbing her and hauling her off Officer Jackman. "Aerfyn! It's me!"

It took the young woman several breaths to realise who she faced. Her eyes went wide. "Ethan!" she breathed.

Ethan nodded. He wrapped his arms around her to hug her when her weight gave way. The pair toppled to the ground.

"Aerfyn?" Ethan enquired as he pushed himself into a sitting position.

Aerfyn's eyes fluttered open. "Cymorth," she whispered hoarsely.

It was only then that Ethan noticed she bled heavily from her side – her stitches torn again, no doubt – and from her shoulder. He swore and picked her up.

"Inside," he ordered everyone as he strode inside the cottage. They followed.

"Hey!" Bill protested from the ground. "What about me?"

It was Olwen who turned back to help the police officer to his feet. The pair went into the cottage.

"Where's your first aid kit?" Ethan asked Gwilym.

"Uh... I don't have one here."

"What?"

"I'm sorry! I don't do anything up here that would require one!"

In the distance, a chilling shriek echoed in the night. Everyone turned towards the sound.

"Shit!" Ethan said. "Shit! Shit! Shit!"

A tapping at the window brought Bill's eyes back out to the deck. "Uh, guys," he said.

"Get me towels or something," Ethan ordered, ignoring the policeman.

"Guys," Officer Jackman said again.

Gwilym got up and raced to the linen chest in the master bedroom. He pulled out some towels and an old pair of leggings that once belonged to his ex-girlfriend.

"Here," he said, handing them to Ethan. Working quickly, Ethan made makeshift bandages out of what he'd been given.

The shriek sounded again, much closer this time. It gave everyone pause before Ethan returned to work, double time. Aerfyn's eyes fluttered open again. She frowned at the group.

"Olwen?" she croaked. "Gawain?"

Olwen took Aerfyn's trembling hand. "Rydym ni yma, fy frenhines," he said gently. She smiled slightly before losing consciousnous again.

Olwen turned to Gwilym. "Mae'n rhaid i ni gael iddi ei thad," he said.

"What?" Ethan asked.

"He said we must get her to her father," Gwilym replied.

The tapping at the window continued.

"Yeah? And how are we to achieve that?"

Gawain left the group huddled around Aerfyn momentarily. He returned with the swords he had spied lying around the litter in the cabin.

"Guys!" Bill barked.

"What?" Ethan barked back.

Bill pointed. Everyone looked to find a pale-faced barn owl tapping its beak insistently at the window.

"Tylluan!" Olwen said, his face breaking into a smile.

"Daft name," Gwilym muttered.

"It's an owl," Ethan said, not understanding.

"Precisely," Gwilym said.

"What?"

"Dilynwch Tylluan," Olwen said to the group.

"What the hell kind of crazy mumbo-jumbo are they speaking!" Joseph said.

"He said we should follow the owl," Gwilym replied.

"Aw, no! Hell no! I am not following some bird through the woods with those things on my arse! Hell. No."

"Do you have a better idea?" Ethan hissed as another shriek and a low whooping noise reached the group.

Joseph was silenced. He looked back into the dark cottage nervously.

"All right," Ethan said, deciding. "Let's go." He stood, scooped Aerfyn up in his arms and went out onto the deck. The owl flew to the railings, then to a tree nearby. It turned its head to look directly behind it, then flew to the next tree.

Ethan followed, glancing around as he did so. He froze as he spied the party of Dynion Gors gathered at the tree line. Their large eyes caught the faint light of night and seemed to glow slightly. Everyone stopped behind Ethan and looked across.

"Hell no!" Joseph said, louder than he intended.

"Ffoi!" Gawain shouted.

The word did not need translation. Everyone fled, sprinting headlong into the woods. One of the Dynion Gors shrieked, and the Bog Men were after them. Bill stopped and turned. He loaded a fresh clip into his gun.

"Bill!" Ethan shouted.

"Go! I'll draw some of them off. Give you a chance. Go! Go!"

Ethan, pained, nodded and continued to run, Olwen and Gawain at his side, their weapons drawn. Bill ran north of the group and behind the thick trunk of a maple.

****

Hero was not the word William Jackman would ever have used to describe himself. He was not any braver than the next man. He didn't join the Ottawa Police for a chance at a medal. He just wanted to make a difference. He gritted his teeth and checked his surrounds. From where he was he could make out the truck.

He fired some well-aimed shots into the rabble of Dynion Gors that chased Ethan and his group. Three fell. That was enough to draw the collective attentions of the Dynion Gors.

"Hey!" Bill shouted, waving his arms to ensure that he was seen. "Hey you ugly, overgrown toads! Come get me!"

Five warriors broke off.

"Shit," Bill said. He bolted for the truck, firing behind him as he did so.

In the longest five-second sprint of his life, Bill reached the truck and got in, slamming the door shut just as the first of the Dynion Gors reached it. The window shattered as the blade of an axe went through. Bill ducked to the side, turned and fired three shots right into the warrior's face. It shrieked as it fell backwards.

Sitting up, Bill started the truck, shooting at the Dynion Gors as they attacked. Hitting one several times in the chest. With two down, the engine roared to life. Bill spun the truck around and zoomed off. He checked his rear view mirror to ensure the three remaining warriors were giving chase. Fortunately, they were.

Unfortunately, they were gaining. Fast.

One leapt onto the tray just as Bill joined the main road. He pulled the handbrake and spun the wheel, throwing the warrior off. He released the handbrake and put his foot down. The truck barely bounced as it rolled over the fallen Bog Man.

He pulled the same trick to take down the last two warriors of the Dynion Gors, hitting them hard with the edge of the tray. Bill grimly ran back and forth over them as well, ensuring that they would never again get up.

All was quiet when he finished. The only sounds were the rumble of the diesel engine and Bill's own ragged breath. He looked around, checking every mirror for any sign of any more Dynion Gors. There was none. He closed his eyes.

"Good luck, Ethan," he whispered before putting the truck in gear and heading out to find a payphone.

****

The fighting retreat employed by Olwen and Gawain proved effective. When he felt he could no longer carry Aerfyn, Ethan would hand her off to either Olwen or Gawain, and, in return, would take their weapon and fight.

They followed the barn owl. Ethan didn't have time to pause and marvel at how they were suddenly on a battlefield, the corpses of horses and warriors hungrily devoured by the wolves that now scattered before the fleeing group.

There was no time. If he was not labouring under the weight of the unconscious queen at full sprint, he was fighting back tall, slender monsters so the others could increase the distance between them and their foes.

It was exhausting. Ethan's muscles screamed in agony at each changeover, freedom of movement becoming equally as painful as the burden of a body. His lungs burned raw, and a disturbing watery wheeze had started to accompany each exhalation.

Still, he ran and he fought until a creeping numbness took over. Everything became unreal, as if he was in a dream and aware he was dreaming. The pain faded, as did conscious thought. Everything turned guttural, instinctual; every movement performed without thought.

The screech of the barn owl the group followed, and the twang and whistle of arrows flying past, brought Ethan back to reality in a single, painful instant. He stumbled as

235

an arrow whizzed past his ear, thudding into the throat of the foe who had very nearly run him through.

He was caught by a strong youth wearing green enamelled armour. The youth took Aerfyn from him and indicated with his head to follow. Ethan did, free of both Aerfyn and the obligation to fight, Ethan sprinted behind the youth into the trees, passing a row of archers as he did so.

It did not take long for the five pursuing Dynion Gors to be defeated. They lay in bloody heaps upon the battlefield, their bodies bristling with arrows.

Ethan slowed as the youth he followed slowed. He almost fainted, landing on his knees as he fought for breath. Olwen and Gawain collapsed beside him. Ethan had not even been aware that they were anywhere near him. He looked around.

Jazz and Professor Davies were standing, leaning against one another as they struggled to recapture their breath. Joseph and Mitch were together as well, both curled over a large boulder near the shores of a lake, emptying the contents of their stomachs.

A noise made Ethan turn back. He saw first an expertly crafted pair of greaves. He looked up. A tall, lanky youth with light brown hair and bright green eyes looked down at him.

"Ydych chi'n dda?" the youth asked.

Ethan stared up at him helplessly, still panting. The youth nodded. He patted Ethan on the shoulder and turned to Olwen.

"Peredur?" he asked.

Olwen, not yet strong enough to speak, simply panted and shook his head.

"Marw," Gawain said grimly.

The youth blinked, sudden tears striking his eyes. He clenched his jaw and nodded curtly.

"Mae angen i ni symud. Caer Avallach o dan warchae. Maelgoch yn gwersylla tu ôl i linellau'r gelyn."

Gawain nodded. With the aid of the youth, he stood and helped Ethan to his feet. The youth went to Olwen and helped him up, then stood in front of Ethan and extended his arm.

"Cai," he said.

"Ethan," Ethan replied, grasping Cai's forearm.

Cai smiled, managing to look miserable while doing so, and then left to fetch the horses that grazed near the lake. Ethan approached Jazz and Professor Davies.

"You okay?" he asked them.

"I'm going to be sick," Jazz mumbled, before turning and doing just that. Blood trickled down her back from open claw-marks.

"Jesus!" Ethan cried. "You're hurt."

"It's nothing," Jazz said. "Just a scratch. Oh God." She threw up again.

Professor Davies looked a little green around the edges, but held himself together admirably. "I haven't run like that since I was twenty," he said with a brief smile.

"That guy there," Ethan said, nodding towards the broad-shouldered youth leading the horses forward. "His name is Cai. I think he's the leader here."

Gwilym nodded. "It wouldn't surprise me."

Mitch and Joseph, having emptied their stomachs of all possible contents staggered over to Ethan. "Fuck you for dragging me into this," Mitch said.

Ethan could only respond with a consolatory pat on the shoulder.

"Where are we, man?" Joseph asked.

"Joe," Ethan said. "Welcome to Narnia."

He turned and saw Aerfyn being loaded onto a makeshift stretcher near the lake, then turned to Cai, who had walked to his side.

"Will she be all right?" he asked.

Gwilym dutifully translated.

"Mae'n edrych yn llwn. Dim ond ei thad hi bellach yn cymorth," Cai replied, keeping his surprise at an outsider knowing his language to a minimum.

Gwilym nodded. "He says that it's looking bleak. Only her father can help her now."

Ethan swallowed.

"Mae angen i ni symud." Cai handed the reigns of a horse to Ethan, who took it slowly.

"Uh... I can't ride," he said.

Gwilym translated. Cai raised his eyebrows and said something to Gwilym, who replied. Cai shook his head in disbelief. "Olwen!" he called.

Olwen jogged over and after a brief conversation, mounted the horse. He extended his hand to Ethan.

"Hyd," he said.

"Go on then," Gwilym said. "Up you get."

Unsure, Ethan took Olwen's hand and, with help, mounted behind the man.

Gawain extended the same courtesy to Jazz. Cai took Professor Davies upon his mount, leaving Mitch and Joseph to share a horse. Neither had ever ridden so much as a pony and so Cai led the horse as if it were a pack mule, tugging it behind his mount by the reigns.

In a tensely quiet procession, the mounted warriors and the archers filed out of the clearing.

Scouts came and went as the procession moved through the woods. Ethan watched with interest as they reported to Cai before rejoining their fellow archers.

Gwilym and Cai spoke in quiet undertones in Welsh, leaving Ethan feeling jealous of all the Professor was learning. It was sunrise when the procession arrived at the crest of a forested hillock overlooking a clearing crowded with an entire army of Aerfyn's people. Thousands of curious eyes turned towards Cai and his party.

"Holy shit, man," Joseph said to Ethan. "It's Prince Caspian!" He indicated a tall, lean man with dark brown hair and eyes and slightly darker skin than many of his companions.

"What? No it's not."

"It is too! Look!"

"It does look kinda like him," Mitch noted.

"What? No way! Caspian was blonde."

"Hell no!" Joseph said. "He was just like that guy."

"In the movies," Mitch prompted.

"Oh," Ethan said. "Well, in the books he's blonde."

"What the hell, man? I'm black. I didn't read those books. Those are white peoples' books."

"Oh, but not white peoples' movies?" Ethan countered.

Joseph clamped his mouth shut. The Prince Caspian doppelganger strode forward.

"Cai," he greeted before the stretcher bearing Aerfyn came into view. He froze. "Aerfyn!" He ran to the stretcher.

He examined her a moment before spinning around, his dark eyes narrowing. "Beth ddigwyddodd?" he demanded.

"Dim ond un yn siarad ein hiaith," Cai said.

"Dilynwch," Prince Caspian said.

Cai sighed and dismounted, helping Gwilym off his horse as well. Taking that as their cue all the riders dismounted. The horses were collected by young boys and led away. Gawain and Olwen smiled at their guests and indicated for them to follow the path of the Prince Caspian doppleganger as he stormed through the camp.

They soon found themselves gathered in the only uncluttered part of the clearing — a small alcove surrounded by ash trees and weeping willow. Standing there, in slightly muddied robes of white, stood an old man leaning heavily on a stick. A familiar barn owl preened herself on his shoulder.

"Dryw," Prince Caspian said, bowing shortly before the aged man. He indicated the stretcher. The old man's eyes grew wide and, dropping the stick, he stumbled towards the stretcher.

"Aerfyn!" he croaked. He stroked the young woman's pale face. He turned back to the group. "Beth ddigwyddodd? Ble mae Peredur?"

"Mawr," Gawain growled. "Ddewr."

"Dewch," the old man said. "Gadewch i mi wella fy merch. Yna byddwn yn trafod."

The stretcher was set down in the alcove, and everyone was ushered out of sight.

****

Constable Pierre Laporte of the Sûreté du Québec sat in his cruiser and watched the empty highway as he bit into his bagel. There was no one on the road at this time of night, but he was out here regardless, sitting in the speed trap. He picked up his steaming coffee and brought the cup to his lips.

A truck roared past with enough speed to rock the cruiser.

"Tabar... noosh!" Pierre cursed as scalding coffee spilled onto his lap. He spasmed in pain, put down the coffee and pulled out of the speed trap, sirens blaring.

****

Bill grimly ignored the shards of glass in his thigh and face and the blood that trickled from a gash in his head and a cut in his arm, and drove full speed towards Ottawa.

What he could not ignore were the sirens and flashing lights behind him. It took him a moment to realise that he was being chased by the S.Q.

"Thank God!" he said, pulling over immediately.

"Bonsoir," the officer said moments before reaching Bill's window. Once there, he froze. Whatever he had been expecting that night, it was not an officer of the Ottawa Police Service wounded, driving a monstrous truck with a shattered window.

"Col... line!" he breathed. "Qu'est-ce qu'y se passe? Ça va?"

"I don't speak French," Bill said, the shock finally setting in.

"Are you all right, sir?" the officer said in heavily accented English. "What 'appened?"

"It's a really long story. I need you to contact Ottawa Police headquarters. I need to get a hold of my partner, Constable Genevieve Boulduc."

"What's your name, sir?"

"Police Constable William Jackman, Ottawa Police."

"All right. Sit tight. I am calling de ambulance also."

"Whatever floats your boat, boss."

Officer Laporte ran back to his cruiser and picked up the radio. "C'est Laporte. J'ai besoin d'une ambulance pour un homme du O. P. Oui, c'est vrai. Il est en choc. Merci." He put down his radio mic and walked back to the car.

"That sounded informal," Bill said with a crooked smile.

Officer LaPorte shrugged. "We all know each udder pretty well. You mind telling me what 'appened, dair?"

Bill opened his mouth, then clamped it shut. "Gang attack," he said finally. "Some crazy group carrying axes and swords. They attacked H.Q. in Ottawa and they chased me and four witnesses to a witness' cottage."

242

"It's not your jurisdiction, you know. Why didn't you call it in?"

Bill shrugged. "There was no time."

"I don't know how you do tings in Ontario, dair, la, but if you were one of ours, you'd be in big trouble."

Bill laughed. "Yeah, I think I am in pretty big trouble in Ontario as well."

The sounds of sirens filled the air. Bill looked down the road expecting to see an ambulance. What he saw were three O.P.S. squad cars and a number of Mounted Police cars. They squealed to a halt in front of the truck. Genevieve stepped out of the foremost car and ran to the truck.

"Bill!" she said. "What the hell? Are you all right?"

"I'm fine," Bill said. "A little shook-up, is all."

"Were you at the station when it was attacked?"

Bill nodded.

"What happened?"

"I don't know. I was interrogating the suspects in association with the Hallowe'en vic. There was a scream and when I went out, Luc was dead in the other interrogation room. I ran in and one of the suspects was being attacked with an axe by this tall man in a hooded cape."

Officer Boulduc's eyes went wide.

"I fired some shots, gathered the witnesses and got the hell out of there. Everyone was dead, Gen. Everyone."

"Okay Spiderman. I know. I saw. It was a massacre. It doesn't explain what you are doing out here, and why you didn't call for back-up, by the way."

Bill nodded. "They said they knew where the girl was... I wasn't thinking straight."

"You saw the girl?"

Bill nodded. "Another one of the hooded people got there first. She was in pretty bad shape."

"Where are they now?"

Bil shook his head. "I don't know. The hooded men... they were after the girl and her friends. There were, like, fourteen of them or something. I drew some off so the others could get away."

"Get away? To where?"

"Back to wherever they came from."

"Bill, you're not making much sense. You need to tell me where they went."

"Into the woods. I don't know."

"Christ," Genevieve said. "No S.O.P. at all! What the hell were you thinking?"

Bill smiled wanly. "There wasn't time for standard operating procedure, Gen. There was nothing standard about this at all. As to what I was thinking, I was thinking, 'They're all dead, and I'm being chased down.' That's what I was thinking."

"All right, I need their last known whereabouts."

"Professor Gwilym Davies' cottage. It's right on a lake."

"Address?"

"I don't know. I just drove. Gwilym gave directions. It's back that way." Bill pointed with his thumb.

The ambulance arrived.

"Helpful." Officer Boulduc said. She stormed to her car and picked up the radio mic as the paramedics ran to Bill.

"You there, Toby?"

Protocol, said a male voice on the other end.

"Shut up. I need an address on a secondary residence for a Dr. Gwilym Davies, PhD. A cottage on a lake?"

Give me a second… Yup. OK. Got it. Sending you the directions now.

"Right… got it! Thanks."

So… how about dinner. My treat?

"Protocol, Toby."

Six?

Officer Boulduc smiled, hung up the mic and walked to S.Q. Officer Laporte. "Pardonnez-moi, je suis constable Geneviève Boulduc de la O.P.S. Nous sommes en pursuite des suspects du massacre récent à la station de police de la rue Elgin et nous voulons la pleine coopérations de la S.Q."

"Vous l'avez."

"Merci. Avez-vous des chiens?"

"Oui."

"Bon. Faites l'appel." She turned and walked back to Bill. "You are in so much trouble, Bill. I can't even…"

"Don't."

"Right. Look, I'll do what I can."

"Don't do that either. Look, just do what you need to do. And so you know, I killed seven of those bastards. Two at the station, five at the cottage."

Genevieve frowned. "The only bodies at the station were the dead Officers and staff, Bill."

Bill scowled. "That can't be right. There should be two of... them – one wearing a grey hooded cloak and carrying an axe."

"There was a cloak and an axe, and some bits of random leather, but no body."

Bill sank back in his chair. "That... that's not possible." He stiffened. "That means... what? I'm suspect number one?"

Genevieve shrugged. "I don't know. So far, it looks as though everyone was killed with either a pipe or some sort of edged weapon. Not a single shot fired, except for yours, of course. There's a mountain of evidence to be analysed, but nothing's going to come through for a couple of days yet."

"Do you... do you think monsters could be real?"

Genevieve frowned at Bill. "What?"

"We're all done here," the paramedic said.

Genevieve nodded. "Take him away, then." She looked at Bill. "I will see you later, O.K?"

Bill nodded. He let the paramedics guide him to the ambulance.

"Nous sommes prêts," Pierre said.

Officer Boulduc nodded and got into her car.

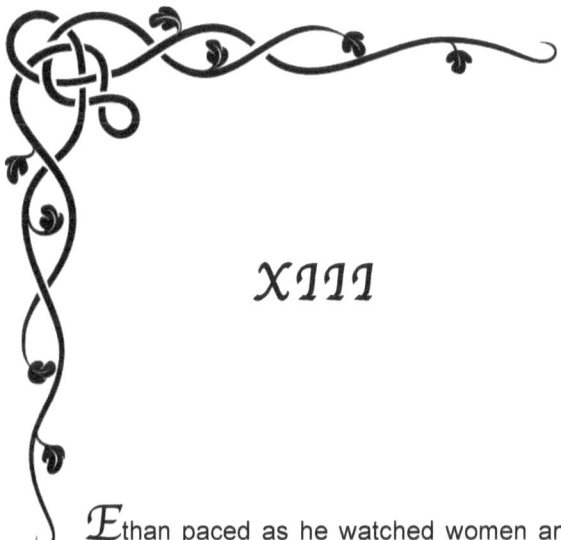

XIII

Ethan paced as he watched women and men in white robes scurry to and from the alcove, bringing supplies and medicines, and taking away bloodied towels and cloths.

"Sit, Ethan," Professor Davies said gently.

"Can't."

"Pacing won't help her."

"But it helps me."

Gwilym sighed and nodded.

"I don't understand. We're in this ... Narnia," Joseph said. "How did we get here? I mean, one minute we were running through the woods in Canada, and then suddenly we were running through the woods in Narnia. I mean, we didn't even have no wardrobe or nothin'."

"This isn't actually Narnia, you know," Ethan said with a faint smile.

"Whatever. The question stands."

Ethan shrugged. "I don't know how it works." He looked expectantly at Professor Davies, who could only shrug.

"The stories never detailed how," he said.

"I hope she's all right," Jazz said. She had also been watching the parade of healers scurry to and fro.

"Man, I am starving," Mitch said.

Ethan glared at him.

"What? I am!"

The conversation ended there. Ethan continued to pace, and everyone else sat in glum silence as the sun steadily rose overhead.

Before midmorning, the stretcher bearing Aerfyn was carried from the alcove and the tall, aged man in white approached the group. He stopped before them and leant on his tall stick. Tylluan flew from the trees to land atop the staff and began her preening.

"Yo, is he a wizard, like... you know, Gandalf?" Joseph whispered to Ethan.

Ethan shrugged, watching closely as the Prince Caspian look-alike walked forward and bowed.

"Dryw," the man said. "Sut mae hi?"

"Dryw?" Gwilym whispered.

"What?" Joseph asked.

"Well, these people are speaking modern Welsh, but Dryw is an old Welsh word. It means something like 'seer.' Some people think it is the root of the modern word 'druid.' I think this man is their spiritual leader."

"Wow."

Ethan glanced briefly at Gwilym as he spoke before turning back to watch the old man and the young man converse. After a moment, the old man walked forward, Tylluan twittering in protest as the stick moved.

"Pa un ohonoch yn yr arweinydd?" he asked.

Gwilym translated.

"I nominate Ethan," Mitch said. "He's the one who got us all into this mess."

"Well, Ethan?" Gwilym asked. "Will you act as spokesman?"

"How can I? I don't speak the damned language!"

"I'll translate."

Ethan sighed and looked at the motley group before him. He nodded mutely.

"Mae e'n," Gwilym said, pointing at Ethan. "Ond nid yw'n gallu siarad eich iaith."

The old man cocked his head and observed Gwilym. "A sut mae'n eich bod yn methu?"

"Yr wyf yn Gymraeg."

The man frowned. "Dydych chi ddim yn dod o'r wlad hon."

Professor Gwilym blinked before understanding. "Rhif. Fy bobl galw eu hunain yn y Gymraeg; o Gymru."

"Ahhhh. A chi yw'r unig un sy'n gallu siarad?"

Gwilym nodded.

"Ni fydd hynny'n ei wneud."

Gwilym smiled a little. The old man stepped forward and pressed the tips of his forefinger and middle finger against Ethan's forehead, between the eyes. Ethan scowled and stepped back.

"Ow!" he complained, rubbing his forehead. "That hurt!"

"Ah, but the rewards were well worth it, do you not think?" the old man said.

"I'll take… hey! I understood you!"

"That was the design."

Ethan blinked. "How did you do that?"

The man smiled and tapped his nose. His grey eyes twinkled merrily. He moved past Ethan and did the same to everyone in the group who was not a native of the land. Soon everyone was rubbing their foreheads and grumbling.

"You may have a headache," the old man said to the group as he returned to Ethan. "But that will pass in a day or so."

"Aerfyn," Ethan said. "Will she be all right?"

"She lost a great deal of blood, and the wound in her side has been opened three times now. Risk of infection is high."

Ethan's heart sank.

"But," the old man said. "She is a stubborn girl, and very strong. She may yet survive. At least her wounds will keep her from the upcoming battle. Chances of survival are greatest when you aren't on a field facing an army of people who want to kill you. I am Gwalchgwyn. I am Aerfyn's father."

The surprise Ethan felt at that announcement was plainly evident. His eyes went wide and his mouth fell open a little. "Oh. Uh. Nice to meet you, sir."

"Just Gwalchgwyn will do. This is Maelgoch, Aerfyn's lieutenant and commander of the Knights of Caer Avallach in her absence."

"The Knights of Caer Avallach? Aerfyn's fortress, right? On the Blessed Isle in the middle of the Glass Lake?"

"You know this?"

"Aerfyn told me. With Gwilym translating, of course."

Gwalchgwyn's sparkling eyes turned to Gwilym. "I assume you are Gwilym?"

Joseph listened in eagerly as Gwilym and Gwalchgwyn talked. He turned to his companions. "Yo. This is just like in Stargate when SG1 get those chips implanted in their heads that automatically translates alien languages!"

"Stargate?" Mitch asked. "Seriously?"

"What?"

"Dude, you are such a nerd!"

"What? There was a kick-ass black guy in it."

"Oh yeah? What was his name?"

"Teal'c," Jazz said absently.

"Yeah," Joseph said. "He was cool. See, he used to be a commander for the Gould, but he helped SG1 escape capture and fought with them to free his people."

"That was a good episode," Jazz said.

Mitch looked between Jazz and Joseph a moment before lifting his brows and saying, "Wow."

"Yo, who was your favourite?" Joseph asked Jazz.

"Colonel O'Neill."

"Yeah, he was cool. For a white guy."

The conversation ended abruptly when Ethan whistled and said, "Guys. Guys!"

They turned to him in surprise. Ethan beckoned them over.

"These are my friends Mitch, Jazz and Joseph," he said to Gwalchgwyn, indicating each person in turn. "Everyone, this is Gwalchgwyn, spiritual leader of the Pobl Gwir and Aerfyn's father."

"Hi," everyone said awkwardly.

"And this is Maelgoch, Aerfyn's lieutenant and now commander of the Knights of Caer Avallach."

Maelgoch nodded a greeting. "Thank-you for returning our queen to us. You must be anxious to return home. Stay for a while. I'll have you escorted back to the divide after you are fed and rested."

"Wait, what?" Ethan said, his smile falling from his face as if he'd been slapped.

"Y Ynys Bendigaid is under siege, Caer Avallach threatened. Come the morrow, what remains of the Knights of Caer Avallach shall engage the enemy from behind in hopes of breaking the siege."

"Oh man," Mitch said. "Glad to be going home then."

"No!" Ethan said. "No way. I did not brave a platoon of Bog Men to be sent home now. I'm staying."

Maelgoch's mouth twitched with the threat of a smile. "This isn't your fight, Ethan."

"The hell it's not!"

252

Maelgoch's expression became serious. "This isn't your land. These aren't your people. Aerfyn is not your queen."

"She is now," Ethan said.

"Woah, woah, woah," Mitch said. "Ethan, can I talk to you a moment?" He dragged Ethan aside. "Are you insane?" he demanded of his friend. "You cannot be serious about staying!"

"I've never been more serious in my life, Mitch."

"Dude! You have lost your mind! This isn't a movie, Ethan. You could die!"

"I know that!" Ethan snapped. "Don't you think I know that? But Jesus, Mitch, for the first time in my life, I have an opportunity to make a difference."

"You want to make a difference? Do charity stuff – back home in Canada."

"Dude, no! I'm staying here, all right."

"What? Why? Because of the girl?"

"The girl has a name, Mitch."

"Oh, come off it! Seriously? Because of the girl. That's why you're going to stay? I mean, damn it, Ethan! You can't fight!"

"I can! Aerfyn taught me, okay?"

"No. No, it's not okay Look, forget about her, all right? She's a queen. You're just some guy."

"Would you forget about Wendy?"

"That's different."

"Yeah? How?"

"I love Wendy."

"And I love Aerfyn!"

Mitch blinked and straightened, looking at Ethan with an expression akin to that of a recently labotamised madman.

Ethan stuck out his chin. "I'm staying, Mitch. You do what you want."

"Fine!" Mitch said. He turned on his heel and stalked off. Ethan watched him go before walking back to the group.

"The others can go home if they wish. But I'm staying."

Maelgoch looked him over. "No," he said.

Gwalchgwyn placed his hand on Maelgoch's shoulder and the latter clamped his mouth shut.

"Come here, boy," Gwalchgwyn said. He took Ethan a step to the side and looked him over critically. After a moment of gazing at Ethan's defiant expression, he nodded curtly. "Then stay. Aerfyn will be glad of it, I am sure."

"With all respect, Dryw," Maelgoch started.

Gwalchgwyn raised a hand and Maelgoch fell silent, glowering angrily at Ethan."I have armour that will fit you, I think," the old man said. "Can you use a sword, boy?"

Ethan shrugged. "Aerfyn showed me a little."

"I don't think he appreciates the danger he's placing himself in, Gwalchgwyn," Maelgoch growled.

"Perhaps, perhaps not," Gwalchgwyn replied, not taking his eyes off Ethan. "But it is still his decision to make."

"And I get no say? I am commander of this army!"

"Yes, you are. And it's an army that is nowhere near the strength it used to be. Every warrior helps."

"He doesn't know how to fight! He's as much a danger to us as he is to them!"

"Hey!" Ethan said. "I can do it!"

Maelgoch gritted his teeth and gave Gwalchgwyn a pointed look. Gwalchgwyn smiled.

"I know you are unsure, Maelgoch," he said. "But I have a good feeling about this one."

"Hey," Joseph said. "I'm staying too."

"What?" Maelgoch said.

"Yeah. I'm staying."

"For the love of the gods!"

"Hey, man! Those bastards killed my brother. I've got some payback to deal out. I'm staying."

"Do you know how to use a sword?" Gwalchgwyn asked him.

"Uh. No. But I can learn. I mean, I'm a fast learner."

Maelgoch looked at Gwalchgwyn and shook his head. Gwalchgwyn smiled at Joseph.

"Then we must teach you."

"Gwalchgwyn," Maelgoch said. "We haven't the time."

"Nonsense. Aerfyn cannot be moved as of yet. There is time enough to give basic training to these boys."

"Fine, but you're training them!"

Gwalchgwyn smiled. "Very well."

Ethan and Gwalchgwyn turned to Jazz and Gwilym. Gwilym shook his head.

"If I were twenty years younger," he said. "Nothing could have stopped me. Now..."

"Hey," Ethan said. "That's okay. You've done more than enough. Without you, we never would have gotten Aerfyn home. We'd probably all be dead. You're a hero."

Gwilym smiled slightly.

"Me too," Jazz said sadly. "I mean, this stuff is cool to read about, but there's no way I could fight for real."

Ethan nodded. "Yeah. That part is kinda terrifying."

Jazz smiled sadly. "You know, you're all right, Ethan Evans."

"Thanks," Ethan mumbled.

Gwalchgwyn clapped his hands. "You must be hungry and in need of sleep. Come, a pavilion has been prepared for you, and food is ready to be eaten. Follow me."

Gwilym, Ethan, Jazz and Joseph followed Gwalchgwyn away from the edge of the encampment into the throng of soldiers and knights preparing for battle.

Maelgoch watched them go with a sour expression. He sighed, shook his head and went to where Cai, Olwen and Gawain sprawled on the grass. He sat down.

"You can't blame the lad for falling in love with her," Olwen said. "She's a beautiful girl."

Maelgoch grunted. "Let's hope his skills are as keen as he is."

Olwen barked a short laugh. "How much time do you think you have to train them?"

256

"Not enough to keep them from getting killed," Maelgoch answered.

"Ethan might surprise you yet," Gawain said quietly. "There is strength in that boy."

"I don't doubt his strength, or his resolve, or even his affections. It takes ten years to train a knight." Maelgoch sighed. He looked over at Cai.

The young lord sat cross-legged, his head down. He played absently with the grass at his knees, pulling blades up from the ground, then tearing them into strips.

"Lord Cai," Maelgoch said gently.

"Yes, my Lord?" Cai said, not looking up. The tightness in his voice gave away the tears he struggled to keep hidden.

"I am sorry for your loss. Peredur was a brave and faithful warrior. I know he meant a great deal to you."

Cai closed his eyes. "Peredur was brave. And faithful. But before these things, he was my brother. My brother, Maelgoch."

At this, Cai broke down sobbing. Maelgoch shuffled along the ground until he sat beside the grieving youth. He placed a firm hand on Cai's trembling shoulder.

"We will make them pay, Cai," he said softly. "They will pay."

****

The guest's pavilion was a large, octagonal tent set up roughly near the centre of the encampment. Inside, a low table with cushions for chairs sat at the centre. It had been laden with bowls of steaming soup, platters of still-sizzling meats, loaves of bread and a large bowl filled with fruits. Cutlery was limited to a spoon and a single, sharp knife.

The food smelled incredible and everyone piled into the tent as fast as they could. They sat at the table and waited.

"What are you waiting for?" Gwalchgwyn said. "Eat, before the meat goes cold."

Ethan was the first. He grabbed the bread and tore himself a healthy chunk. Ripping a smaller chunk, he dipped the bread in the soup and ate it.

"Mmm!" he said in approval. "Delicious!"

His example spurred the others. It was not long before they were all devouring the soup quickly. Ethan had just carved himself a slice of what smelled like goat when a young page led Mitch into the pavilion. Everyone froze in sudden discomfort as Mitch and Ethan locked eyes.

Ethan nodded at Mitch. Mitch nodded at Ethan.
It was enough. The discomfort dispelled, Mitch sat down to eat and everyone else resumed their feasting.

Gwalchgwyn quietly excused himself with a small smile and twinkling eyes as young pages carrying terracotta pitchers wandered in.

"Metheglyn, sir?" one boy asked Ethan.

"Methe-what?" Ethan asked.

The boy blinked. "It is a drink, sir, made with honey and beer."

Ethan shrugged. "Sure. Why not?"

The boy smiled and poured Ethan a cupful. Ethan sniffed it. "Smells like honey," he said before taking a sip. "Mmm! It's good!"

He was awarded a top-up from the boy before the page went about filling the cups of everyone else who begged for a drink.

"Thank-you," Ethan called after the page when he left to fetch more metheglyn.

"Man, this is good!" Jazz said. "It combines my two most favourite things – beer and honey."

Ethan looked thoughtful. "It's really interesting. I wonder why they don't sell this stuff down at the L.C.B.O."

"They probably do," Mitch said. "The big one on Dalhousie has practically everything. Did you know there's such a thing as green ginger wine?"

"Huh."

"I'll have to check it out," Jazz said. "My roommate's been hunting for mead for a while now. She'll probably want to try this as well."

"What the hell is up with your roommate? Is she from the Stone Age or something?" Mitch asked.

Jazz shrugged. "Iron Age, probably."

Mitch snorted a laugh and turned back to the feast before him. Conversation flowed easily after that. There was much talk and laughter as everyone ate. It soon died away, however, when excess of food and physical exhaustion took over.

Jazz was the first to seek somewhere to lie down. She didn't need to search far. Soft cushions and blankets had been set up around the edge of the pavilion. Jazz happily collapsed into one and fell immediately to sleep. Not long after, everyone was fast asleep.

They slept most of the day away. It was very late afternoon when Cai entered the pavilion and started waking everyone. He looked as miserable in the afternoon as he did that morning.

His green eyes were made greener still by the red rims that indicated tears had recently been shed. Gwilym offered Cai a sad smile and got one in return, but no words were exchanged.

Gwalchgwyn arrived shortly thereafter. "Good evening," he said amicably.

"Hey," Ethan greeted. He winced as he stretched. His muscles ached.

"It'll be worse in two days," Mitch noted.

Ethan grunted.

"Ethan and Joseph," Gwalchgwyn said. "I have armour and weapons for you." He beckoned to the pages waiting outside. They scurried in, bringing the items with them – a jumble of steel, leather and cloth that included clothing for them both.

Not caring about the many pairs of eyes in the pavilion, Ethan hurriedly changed. The clothing was surprisingly comfortable. Ethan shrugged into loose-fitting pants and a light, loose shirt with a mandarin collar. His feet were a little too large for the boots supplied, so one page vanished to find a larger pair.

"All right," Ethan said, looking at the jumble of armour. "How does this work?"

"Gambeson on first," Gwalchgwyn said.

"Eh?"

"The gambeson."

Ethan stared blankly at the Dryw. "The what?"

The page attending Ethan smiled a little. He picked up the gambeson – a sleeveless, collarless, padded shirt.

Ethan blinked. "So this is called a gambeson?"

Gwalchgwyn nodded.

"Cool." Ethan put it on and the page adjusted the laces at the sides so that it fit better. He handed Ethan a chainmail shirt. Ethan wordlessly slipped it on. It fell to the middle of his thigh and about three quarters of the way down his arm.

"This is going to get warm, fast," Ethan said.

"You will be too busy trying to survive the battle to notice," Gwalchgwyn said.

"Thanks."

Next came the breastplate. It was, in fact, a thin piece of steel, covered over in hardened leather that had pieces cut out so that steel glinted in the gaps between the tendrils of the swirling pattern of the leather. The leather itself was painted in places with enamel.

"Looks pretty sweet," Mitch said, sounding almost jealous.

Vambraces to protect the forearms in exactly the same materials and design followed. A sturdy, leaf-shaped blade was strapped to Ethan's hip by way of a double wrap belt. The page that had been sent for boots returned, and Ethan put them on. Greaves that matched the vambraces and breastplate were placed over his shins. Lastly, a steel and leather helm was placed on his head.

"Well?" he asked, spreading his arms wide and turning around slowly. "How do I look?"

"Yo man!" Joseph said, only dressed in his new underclothes. "That is COOL!"

"Yeah," Mitch agreed. "You look... out of a movie, or something. Unreal. Looks good."

"Yup," agreed Jazz. "Pretty bad-ass."

Gwilym simply grinned.

Ethan smiled and took off the helm. "You go," he said to Joseph.

Joseph didn't waste time. He hurriedly dressed into his armour – a similar design but different pattern and colours. When he was dressed, he modelled his armour as if on a catwalk. Ethan laughed and clapped.

"Man, this is so cool!" Joseph said. "Elroy would laugh at me, but I used to dream of being a knight. Now look at me!"

"Very cool," Ethan agreed, grinning broadly.

"The divide will not be open much longer," Gwalchgwyn said. "Cai and his troops will escort you to it."

"We'll go with," Ethan said. "Say our goodbye's there, I guess."

Mitch shrugged. "I guess." He put his hands in his pockets.

"Hey man, you want my jeans?" Ethan asked suddenly. "Don't think they'd be very fashionable here."

"Nah. Keep 'em. You might end up needing them one day."

Ethan nodded.

"So," Jazz said brightly in an effort to break the awkward silence. "We should probably get going."

"We should," Cai agreed. "It's a long way there, and a long way back."

Ethan sighed. "All right then. Let's go."

The group filed out of the pavilion with Ethan in the lead. He stopped dead when Maelgoch stepped in his path.

"Hi," Ethan said.

"Aerfyn is awake," Maelgoch said bluntly. "She's asking for you."

Ethan turned around. "You guys mind waiting a bit?"

"Nope," Mitch said.

Turning back to Maelgoch, Ethan said, "Lead the way."

He followed Maelgoch to a white pavilion. The commander of the Knights of Caer Avallach pulled back the cloth entrance and ushered Ethan inside. Ethan stepped in.

It took a moment for his eyes to adjust to the sudden dark. When they did, he found three beds. Two were empty. One, at the back of the pavilion, had Aerfyn lying on it. She lay, propped up by a mountain of cushions. She smiled weakly at Ethan.

"The armour suits you," she said.

Ethan smiled. He looked down at himself. "You think so? I kinda like it." He walked forward. "How are you feeling?"

Aerfyn pulled a face. "Like I've been dragged behind a horse for days. I probably look it too."

"No," Ethan said. "You look beautiful."

The warrior queen flushed slightly. She looked down, but could not conceal the smile Ethan's words had painted on her face. Ethan sat on the bed and took Aerfyn's hand.

It seemed impossibly small and delicate for someone who, he knew, was capable of killing monsters.

"You have done so much for me already," Aerfyn whispered. "You don't have to stay."

"I want to stay."

"Have you ever fought in a war, Ethan?"

Ethan frowned and shook his head.

"I would never wish it on anyone. The terror, the pain... it's hell."

Ethan smiled again. "Who knew? A fearsome warrior-queen, with the heart of a doe."

Aerfyn laughed, wincing in pain as she did.

"Careful."

She glared at Ethan. "Thanks. Ethan, this is my fight..."

"Don't start. Maelgoch already tried. I'm staying, Aerfyn."

The young queen sighed. She looked Ethan in the eye and, noting the bright, fervent light of conviction, nodded. "Very well. But do not say I didn't warn you."

"I wouldn't dream of it."

Aerfyn smiled. It was a sad sort of smile. "I am keeping you. You should go."

Ethan nodded. "I'll be back before you know it."

He gave Aerfyn a squeeze on the hand and rose. Casting one last smile at Aerfyn, he left the pavilion and, ignoring the glower that Maelgoch threw in his direction, went back to his friends.

Maelgoch entered Aerfyn's pavilion. She smiled at him. He sighed.

"That boy knows nothing, my Queen."

"He will learn, Maelgoch."

"He said you started teaching him sword craft. Is he any good?"

Aerfyn shook her head. "Not really," she said. "But he has potential."

Maelgoch sat on Aerfyn's bed. "He is in love with you, you know. It's painfully obvious."

Aerfyn smiled sadly.

"Do you love him?"

The question took Aerfyn by surprise. "We've been through a great deal together."

Maelgoch scoffed. "He's not one of us, Aerfyn."

"I know," Aerfyn replied. She looked down at her hands.

"Father had hopes for us."

"I know that too."

The commander sighed. "We'd have made beautiful children."

Aerfyn smiled. "Yes."

"So..."

"I would marry you, Maelgoch. If you truly wanted, I would."

Maelgoch smiled. "And what do you want, my Queen?"

"To be happy."

"And would Ethan make you happy?"

Aerfyn bit her lip and nodded.

Maelgoch nodded. "I thought so."

"Maelgoch..."

"Hush, my Queen. It's all right. I mean, it hurts, but much of that is pride, I think. Father will be disappointed, though."

"I do love you, Maelgoch. You must know that. Just..."

"Not as you love Ethan, I know. I love you also."

Aerfyn's eyes filled with tears.

Maelgoch laughed. "Why are you crying?" he asked.

"Because you are a good man, Maelgoch. You deserve to be loved better than I can love you."

Maelgoch wrapped strong arms around Aerfyn. "It is enough that you love me at all. Do not fear for me, Aerfyn. I will be loved."

Aerfyn let herself fall into Maelgoch. She smiled at his words. "Because you're pretty," she teased.

"Hey, enough of that." Maelgoch released Aerfyn. "Sleep now. It will be a few more days before we're ready to attack, and you need your rest."

"Thank-you, Maelgoch."

"Sleep well, my Queen."

He stayed by Aerfyn's bed until she fell asleep. It was no great length of time at all. When he exited the pavilion, Gwalchgwyn stood before him.

"You handled that very well, my Lord," Gwalchgwyn said with a smile. His eyes sparkled with mischief.

Maelgoch narrowed his eyes. "Thanks," he said suspiciously.

"Just so you are aware, your future looks decidedly brighter now."

"Is that so?" Maelgoch asked, disbelief colouring his tone. He looked at Gwalchgwyn's smiling face and twinkling eyes. "What's she like?"

"You'll see."

Maelgoch laughed and walked away. "You're crazy, old man," he said as he left.

"That is often said of the brilliant."

Maelgoch laughed again.

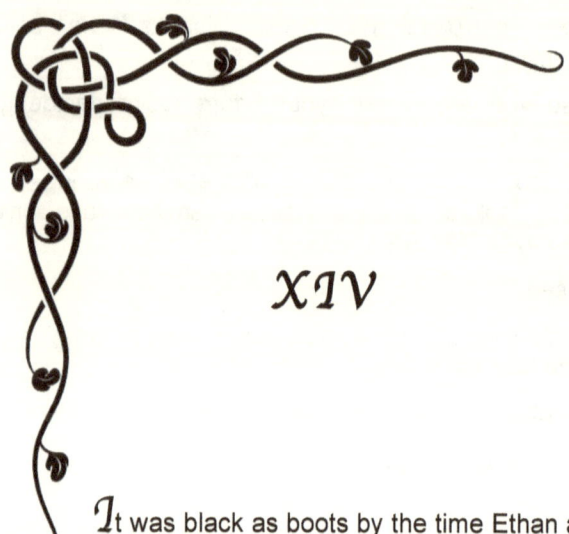

XIV

*I*t was black as boots by the time Ethan and his friends crossed the battlefield to where Tylluan perched on the pommel of a sword stuck in the ground.

"It is here," Cai said. "In the woods there."

Everyone stared at the line of trees that marked the end of the field. No one moved.

"Did you hear that?" Mitch said.

"No," Ethan said.

"It sounded like dogs."

"Hey, is it just my imagination, or is that mist rolling in," Gwilym said.

Cai turned and nodded. "The divide. Mist had risen when Aerfyn disappeared from the field. Gwalchgwyn thinks that the mist is a sign of the rising and falling of the divide."

"So what you're telling us is that the divide is now closing?"

"I suppose so."

Mitch, Jazz and Gwilym exchanged glances.

"I suppose that means we ought to go, then," Mitch said.

"I'd say so," Cai replied.

Ethan laughed. He extended his hand to Mitch. "I will miss you," he said.

Mitch took Ethan's hand. "Yeah. I'll miss you too. What the hell am I supposed to tell everyone?"

Ethan shrugged. "I vanished into thin air."

"Yeah. Sure. Well, see ya?"

"Maybe," Ethan said, a mischievous grin crossing his face. "I might come visiting one Hallowe'en."

"That'd be real nice." Mitch smiled sadly, then stepped away. Jazz stepped up and gave Ethan a hug.

"Thanks for everything, Jazz," Ethan said.

"Thank-you. I'll never forget it."

"Indeed," Gwilym said, shaking Ethan's hand. "Life will seem so very dull compared."

Ethan nodded and smiled. Everyone said their goodbyes to Joseph, who chewed on his bottom lip in an effort to keep the tears at bay.

A hissing whistle caught Ethan's ears.

"Down!" he yelled, dropping suddenly to the ground.
Without hesitation, everyone followed suit and three arrows sailed overhead.

"Go!" Ethan shouted to his friends. "Run! We'll hold them off!"

They didn't need to be told twice. Mitch, Jazz and Gwilym got to their feet and sprinted for the forest. Ethan, Joseph, Cai and Cai's men jumped up and unsheathed their weapons.

Mitch looked behind him just once as he hit the line of trees that marked the forest. Ethan and the others were embroiled in a fierce fight with a large contingent of Dynion Gors.

"Good luck, man," Mitch whispered before turning and running again.

****

Officer Genevieve Boulduc scoured the forest. It was growing dark, and there was no sign of the missing boys. The dogs had followed their scent trail for a kilometre from the cabin, but had, apparently, lost it rather suddenly. They milled around, sniffing the ground, returning to where they lost the trail to sniff, and leaving again to wander about aimlessly. Several whined in confusion.

"I don't understand it," Officer Laporte said. "It's as if they just... poof!... vanished."

"Hey," Officer Boulduc said. "Did you hear that?"
"Hear what?"

Genevieve narrowed her eyes and stared at the darkening woods. She heard it again, faintly on the breeze:

"Run!"

"This way," she said. Taking up her flashlight, she started running towards the sound. She slid to a stop just before

270

a gully through which ran a bubbling stream, choked now by a carpet of fallen leaves.

Running directly towards her were Mitch, Jazz and Professor Davies, clearly in distress.

"Police!" Officer Boulduc said, leaping over the gully. "Stop! Police!"

"Oh, thank God!" Mitch said, relief written all over his features. He fell to his knees and put his hands in the air. "Thank God!"

Jazz and Professor Davies followed suit. They all panted and were covered in sweat and grime.

"Thank God you're here," Mitch continued. "Man. Oh man!"

"Mitch Campbell, right?" Officer Boulduc asked.
Mitch nodded.

"Mitch, where's Ethan and the girl?"

Mitch hesitated. He looked around, catching Jazz' eye as he did so. "Man. Oh man. I don't know. They were right behind us."

It wasn't entirely a lie.

"What do you mean?"

"We must have gotten separated."

"Why were you running, Mitch?"

"They were chasing us."

"Who?"

"I don't know. Tall men in grey cloaks. Jesus! Ethan! Ethan! Where are you, man?"

Officer Boulduc helped Mitch to his feet.

"You gotta find him," Mitch pleaded. "I mean, what if they got him? Ethan!"

"Okay, okay. Take a deep breath."

Mitch nodded and did. Officer Boulduc took a few steps past Mitch and shone her flashlight into the woods. Mitch looked over at Jazz and grinned.

Nice, Jazz mouthed.

"All right," Officer Boulduc said, turning back. "There's no sign of them." She put both her hands up to stop Mitch's imminent outburst. "I'm going to take you back to the cabin to the paramedics. They're going to check you out, and then I need to get statements from you. Okay?"

Mitch nodded slowly.

"Got this?" Genevieve asked Officer Laporte.

"Got it," he answered. He whistled and the police dogs and their handlers began scouring the area for any hint of Ethan and Aerfyn.

With a sinking feeling, Officer Boulduc led the three witnesses to the paramedics.

****

The battle was brief, lasting only half an hour, but it was fierce. Ethan and Joseph fought instinctively. Joseph flailed wildly as he defended himself, but for all his ungainly motions, he came out without a single scratch.

Ethan had a black eye, but that was it.

Cai lost two of his men, but remained unharmed himself.

"Bastards," he panted. Then, "The camp!"

Giving Ethan and Joseph the horses of the two fallen knights, Cai turned his party for the encampment and left the battlefield at a full gallop.

Ethan found the horse's rhythm easily, having some practice the day before. Joseph had greater difficulty, bouncing all over the place like a battery-powered yo-yo on a very short string.

"Move with the horse," Ethan called over when he noticed Joseph, white-knuckled and grimacing as his horse raced on.

"What?" Joseph screamed back.

"Move with the horse. Just relax."

"Don't you tell me to relax!" Joseph yelled.

Ethan laughed.

"Screw you, it's not funny! I'm going to die!"

"No you're not! Just relax."

Sounds of battle ahead drew everyone's attention, and distracted Joseph enough for him to ease into his horse's rhythm.

"To me!" Cai called.

He spurred his horse forward and the animal leapt on, its ears pricked and keen.

Cai drew his sword, prompting everyone else to do the same. They attacked from behind, crashing into the attacking battalion of Dynion Gors. The Bog Men were not expecting the reinforcements. They scattered like cockroaches before the fierce onslaught of Cai's troops.

Ethan searched the scene for Maelgoch. "Cai!" he called. "Where is Maelgoch?"

273

Cai searched, but could find no sign of his commander. Without him, the knights were directionless.

"I can't find him!" Cai called back.

"Hold on here!" Ethan said. He turned his horse. "Joe!"

Joseph turned his horse and the pair galloped around the camp. Ethan raised his sword.

"Knights of Caer Avallach!" he bellowed. "To me!"

The knights responded instinctively. They fought their way to Ethan.

"My Lord," one of the knights said. "Give me two battalions. I'll take the left flank."

Ethan nodded. The knight shouted something, and a hundred knights arranged themselves behind him.

"You!" Ethan said, calling another knight over. "Take command of the right flank."

"My Lord, I haven't –"

"Just do it! Worry about experience later."

The knight nodded. He shouted orders, and knights formed up behind him.

"Joe," Ethan said. "You and I have the middle. We'll meet Cai at the centre."

Joe nodded grimly. Ethan raised his sword, and the knights surged forward, cutting through the Dynion Gors. Pockets of knights from throughout the embattled camp joined in the tidal wave that crashed upon the enemy.

The force of Dynion Gors broke beneath the wave of steel and horses. Sandwiched between Cai's men and the rest of the knights, they had nowhere to go. They were slaughtered to the last reeking warrior.

Ethan dismounted the moment Cai called victory.

"Maelgoch!" he yelled. "Commander! Maelgoch!"

Ethan raced through the camp, hoping for some sign of him. A soft moan caught Ethan's attention. On the ground, before the entrance to Aerfyn's pavilion, Maelgoch lay on the ground, a spear through his left hip. Ethan swore and ran to him.

"Commander! Maelgoch!"

Maelgoch opened his dark eyes. "Ethan," he breathed. "Thank the gods."

"Come on, up you get."

With Ethan's help, Maelgoch stood, fainting from pain and blood loss.

"Aerfyn!" Ethan called wildly.

"Ethan? Is that you?" Aerfyn called back from inside the pavilion.

"I'm coming in."

Half-dragging Maelgoch, Ethan entered the pavilion. Aerfyn was still on the bed, but had her sword drawn. Thanks to Maelgoch's brave defence, none of the enemy made it inside.

"Maelgoch!" Aerfyn said. She dropped her sword and tried to get out of her bed. Still weak and trapped by blankets, she fell flat on her face. Ethan chuckled.

"It's not funny," Aerfyn said, her voice muffled by the rug pressed against her face.

Ethan laughed harder. He lowered Maelgoch on a bed. "Looks nasty."

"I'll live," Maelgoch said.

"Right." Ethan grabbed some cloths and folded them up. He pressed them on Maelgoch's hip around the spear, causing him to cry out in pain.

"Sorry," Ethan said. "Here, put your hand on it. Maintain pressure. It'll help slow the blood."

Gritting his teeth, Maelgoch did so. Ethan turned and helped Aerfyn back onto her bed. "You, missy, need to stay put."

"Is that an order, Ethan?"

Ethan grinned. "Me? Order a queen? Never."

Aerfyn smiled.

"I'll fetch your father." Ethan needn't have suggested it. Gwalchgwyn appeared at that moment, rushing into the pavilion and straight to his daughter's side.

"Aerfyn," he said. "Are you all right?"

"I'm fine, father," she said, though she looked anything but. "Well, as good as can be expected. They did not enter the pavilion."

Gwalchgwyn looked at Ethan. "You?"

Ethan shook his head and pointed at Maelgoch. Gwalchgwyn rose and went to the commander's side.

"Thank-you, Maelgoch."

"I am sworn to protect our queen."

Gwalchgwyn smiled and nodded. "I'll get you something for the pain, then get that spear out of you."

"It would be appreciated."

Gwalchgwyn chuckled to himself and left the pavilion. Maelgoch glanced sideways at Ethan before leaning back and closing his eyes.

"I heard your voice in battle, Ethan," he said.

Ethan shrugged. "I didn't know what I was doing, really."

"Then why did you do it?"

"It was total chaos. It seemed the knights needed a direction."

"And you gave them one?"

"I didn't do much. There were two knights who took command of the left and right flanks, and then there was Joe. He fought like the Devil himself, you know."

"The what?"

"Uh… never mind."

"In any case, it seems Aerfyn was right, Ethan Cadfael. You have potential."

"Evans, my surname is Evans."

Maelgoch smiled. "It is our tradition, Battle Prince, that when a man is knighted, he is given a new name."

Ethan blinked. "Knighted?"

"Knighted."

"Are you serious? I'm… a… a knight now?"

"Welcome to the order."

Ethan's grin came slowly and in stages. "Ethan Cadfael," he said thoughtfully. "I like that."

Maelgoch grunted a laugh. "Well, Battle Prince, I cannot fight now, wounded as I am. I can command from a distance, but I will need someone on the field who can perform. You will be needed."

"Hang on. Wait. What? I can't…"

"But you can, Ethan. You proved it just now."

"Uh… right. Thanks. I think."

Maelgoch laughed. "You won't be thanking me during the fight. But, you're welcome. Aerfyn was right. You do have potential."

Ethan looked back at Aerfyn, who smiled at him.
"You'd best find your friend."

"Uh, yeah. Right. I'll do that."

Ethan left the pavilion, feeling strangely light despite his protesting muscles. He practically floated through the encampment as he searched for Joe.

In the pavilion, Aerfyn observed Maelgoch for a moment.

"You are a good man," she said.

"Hush," Maelgoch replied, smiling.

Aerfyn laughed quietly. The healers arrived, Gwalchgwyn immediately after. Aerfyn said no more, but her smile never faded.

****

"Yo, Ethan!" Joseph called.

Ethan turned and grinned. "Joe!" He walked up to Joseph and clasped his hand. "You made it through all right."

"Yeah, man. Man! That was amazing!"

"Terrifying."

"I know! What a rush!"

Ethan burst out laughing. "Man, you are twisted."

"Are you kidding me? Tell me you don't feel alive right now!"

"All right, all right. I feel alive. Now come on. Let's help with the cleanup."

Joseph grinned and the two reported to Cai to be given duties.

****

"Well, their stories all match," Officer Boulduc said. She sighed as she watched the monitor displaying the three witnesses sitting in their respective interrogation chambers.

Jazz toyed with her hair. Professor Davies had his hands clasped and they rested on the table before him, his eyes closed and a soft smile on his lips. Mitch chewed his lip, resting his cheek against his palm and looking thoroughly bored.

"They weren't all that detailed, though, were they?" another officer said.

"Yeah, well, there wasn't much to be said. Any word yet on whether they've found Ethan and the girl?"

"Not even so much as a shoe," the officer said. He shook his head. "It's as if they've vanished into thin air."

"Or another world, maybe," Officer Boulduc said thoughtfully.

"Pardon?"

"Hm? Oh… uh… nothing. Never mind."

"What do you think happened?"

"I think that Bill must have been right. Some sort of weird gang battle or something. Their first victims just happened to be schizophrenic. Then Ethan got involved with the first vic. and the rest is history."

"Those grey robes belong to the attackers then?"

"Probably."

The officer laughed.

"What?" Officer Boulduc demanded.

"Just... what kind of gang wears cloaks that look like they came from Lord of the Rings?"

"A cult, then. Maybe."

"Yeah. I can see a cult wearing robes."

"Maybe those poor crazy bastards were raised in the cult and turned insane."

"All right, detective. Calm down."

"It could be."

"Yeah. It could be a lot of other things too. Just wait for all the evidence before concocting wild theories."

"You're no fun, you know that?"

"Whatever."

Officer Boulduc's mobile buzzed.

"Message?"

"Hmm," Genevieve said. She pulled out the phone and flipped it open. The text read:

Out of hospital, sent home pending inquiry. Could use a beer. – Spiderman.

She smiled and flipped the phone shut again. "You reckon you can take over here?"

"Why?"

"Just... can you?"

"Sure."

"Good. My shift's over, I'm heading the hell outta here. Ciao!"

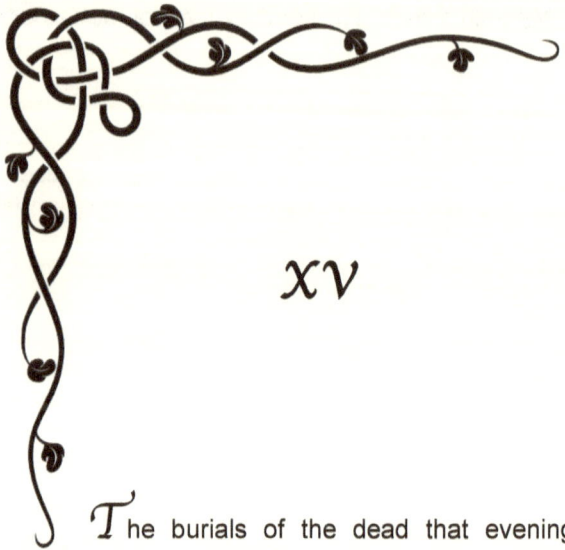

XV

$\mathcal{T}$he burials of the dead that evening were melancholic. Though Ethan did not know a single one of them, he felt the loss keenly. These were men and women who loved their queen and country so fully, they gladly gave their lives in defence of them.

Aerfyn had forced herself from her bed to attend. Though she looked very weak and pale, she stood bravely, not permitting assistance, throughout the burial ceremony. It was no wonder her people loved her. She was as devoted to them as they were to her.

"So much death," Aerfyn whispered. "It could have been avoided if I had simply accepted."

"Don't think on it, my Queen," Maelgoch said gently. "No one blames you."

"Perhaps they should."

Maelgoch smiled slightly. He bent over, wincing in pain as he did so, and kissed Aerfyn on her smooth, white brow. "All right, let's get you back into bed. You need your rest."

"What I need is to lead my people. I am the queen. These are my knights. I am useless in bed."

"There is no point killing yourself, or all we've fought for will be naught. Now off to bed with you."

At this, Aerfyn only sighed. She turned and, finally accepting aid, walked slowly and painfully back to her pavilion. Maelgoch followed shortly thereafter.

"I want you and Cai in the healer's pavilion at sunrise," he said to Ethan as he passed.

Ethan nodded. "Yes, my Lord."

The knights, battle weary and wounded, crawled into their beds. Joseph Bille and Ethan Cadfael shared a pavilion together. Though they each desperately wanted to talk out the night's events, they were far too exhausted. Sleep overcame them in just minutes.

Ethan's eyes fluttered open at first light. Having always needed an alarm before now, he marvelled at how he seemed to instinctively know that the day had begun. He sat up. Joseph snored fitfully on his bed, clutching his sheathed sword to his chest like a child holding a stuffed toy. The sight made Ethan smile.

"Nerd," he whispered. He slipped from the bed, and put on his breastplate and greaves. He'd slept in his mail shirt just in case there was to be another attack.
Stepping out into the cool morning air, Ethan smiled. Birds had taken up the joy of early morning, and sang it out throatily. The guard changed, for the fourth time that night, and tired sentinels marched smartly to bed. Ethan watched the small ceremonies at each brazier.

The knights bowed to one another. They grasped each other's forearms, exchanged news and then took up, or retired from, their positions as the case may be.

"Morning," one of the knights greeted Ethan as he walked past. He yawned.

"Morning," Ethan replied.

"Breakfast will be another hour or two yet," the knight said, turning.

"Thanks."

The knight nodded, eyeing Ethan curiously, before turning and resuming his march to bed. Murmured words caught Ethan's ear and he turned towards the noise.

The pages and squires of the knights were gathered in a broad, clear space near the centre of the encampment. They talked in low voices to one another as they piled wood into a pit. Some were grooming the rows of horses that had been tied to expertly constructed rails.

Others still were at wobbling tables, slicing vegetables, gutting fish, kneading dough or chopping large chunks of meat and skewering them on long metal spikes.

Ethan watched as those piling wood started a smoking fire. In a matter of moments, the small fire turned into a cheery blaze. The smell of wood smoke filled the air. Even when Ethan Cadfael, the knight of Caer Avallach, had been Ethan Evans, a lowly university student, he had loved the smell of wood smoke.

It poured from chimneys in Ottawa in the fall, filling the air with the smell of comfort. It was by far the best part of walking around the residential zones opposite Carleton University.

For a brief moment, Ethan was transported back to Ottawa and he realised, with a start and no small amount of guilt, that he didn't much care for it. He did not miss it and likely never would. Perhaps it was a symptom of continually being treated like a child there. Here, he was a man, and was expected to behave like one.

Given the opportunity to prove himself, Ethan had risen to his potential.

He took a long, deep breath in, relishing the scent of the wood smoke before making his way to rouse Cai. He needn't have bothered.

Cai was awake, fully dressed and scraping the nicks from his blade with a whetstone. He barely looked up when Ethan approached.

"Good morning, friend," he said amicably.

"You're up early."

"As are you."

Ethan shrugged. "Mind if I sit?" he asked, indicating the cut stump beside Cai.

"Please," Cai said.

"It's so weird. Before I came here, it would take a really loud, really annoying alarm to wake me up any time before the middle of the day. Now, I wake of my own accord, and it isn't even first light."

Cai smiled. "There is something to be said about being in the wilds. It awakens a man to his instincts. It is good you woke of your own volition. Natural and just."

Ethan grunted. "Maelgoch wants to see us at dawn."

Cai nodded. "I suspect it's about the upcoming battle."

"Do you think... I mean... He and Aerfyn...?"

Cai smiled. "Maelgoch and Aerfyn grew up together. They trained together. It is everyone's expectation that they would one day be married."

"Oh."

"Do not fret, Lord Ethan. Such a contract has not been announced. It remains Aerfyn's decision, at any rate."

"It does?"

"Yes, and it seems that Maelgoch has some fierce competition."

"Yeah? Who?"

Cai grinned. "You. Your affections can hardly be in question. You are not subtle, you know."

Ethan blushed slightly and Cai laughed.

"Do not be ashamed. There is not a man who has seen Aerfyn who has not fancied himself in love with her at one time or another.

"But she's going to marry Maelgoch."

"I said it is expected that she would, not that she would. Besides, I dare say she rather fancies you herself."

Ethan blinked in surprise. "She does?"

"She does. No one has missed her looks in your direction except, it seems, for you."

"Won't that make Maelgoch angry?"

"Maelgoch loves his queen. He will want to see her happy, whatever personal injury it would cost him."

"Oh."

"Come, I see the sun creeping over the horizon. We mustn't keep our commander waiting."

Ethan nodded. The two knights rose together and walked to the healer's pavilion. There they found Gwalchgwyn before the pavilion entrance, stretching.

"Good morning," he greeted as he dropped down to touch his toes.

"Good morning, Dryw," Cai answered, his voice made thick by barely contained humour.

The old man's eyes sparkled, and he said nothing. He smiled and continued his exercises as Ethan and Cai walked past and into the pavilion. Inside, Maelgoch's hip was being tended to.

Ethan grimaced when he saw the wound. "I'd wish you good morning," he said. "But I doubt you'd return the sentiment."

Maelgoch winced as the healers cleaned the wound. "I'd give anything to be able to," he agreed. He twitched savagely as one healer wiped the wound with a sharp-smelling liquid.

"You wanted to see us, my Lord?" Cai asked.

"I did. As you are aware, neither Aerfyn nor I can lead the troops into battle in our current states."

"Indeed."

"I need you and Ethan both. You are to select your lieutenants carefully. Then you will report to me, and I will go through the battle plan with you. Once we have engaged the enemy, I will rely on your judgement should things not go to plan and you can no longer hear my commands. They often do not go to plan, you understand."

Ethan's heart pounded in his chest. "I appreciate your trust in me, Maelgoch, but I..."

"You are a knight of the realm, Ethan Cadfael," Maelgoch said. "And you have proven yourself a leader. Men answered your call instinctively when the camp was under attack. That is enough."

"But I know nothing about this stuff!"

"You will be given objectives. It is up to you as to how you will achieve them."

Ethan swallowed. He nodded. Years of sitting in front of his X-Box playing R.P.G.s and strategy games in no way prepared him for the reality of an Iron Age style battle. Still, it was the closest thing he had to military training of this kind.

"Good," Maelgoch said. "Now find your lieutenants, and be quick about it. Meet me back here after breakfast."

"Yes, my Lord," Cai and Ethan said in unison.
They left promptly.

"You look pale," Cai remarked.

Ethan nodded. "I don't know if I can do this. I mean, you guys have trained all your lives for this. I played sport for a bit."

"That might be so, but Maelgoch and Aerfyn both have seen something of a commander in you, Ethan. They would not endanger their own people with the command of someone they didn't think could do what was required."

Ethan sighed.

"Come, cheer up. It is a great honour to be so singled out you know. Wake your friend and join me at breakfast."

Ethan nodded. The two new commanders parted ways at Cai's pavilion. Ethan jogged to the pavilion he shared with Joseph and went inside. Joseph still slept. Ethan grinned and shook him hard on the shoulder.

"Yo. Joe. Get up. Joe!"

Joseph stirred and rolled over. He blinked himself awake. "Yo, what time is it?"

Ethan shrugged. "Breakfast time. Come on. Get dressed, Lieutenant."

"Lieutenant?"

"Yeah. I've just had a chat with Maelgoch. Apparently I've been elevated to co-commander with Lord Cai. We were told to choose our lieutenants and report back to him after breakfast. So, congrats on the promotion."

"Oh man! That's... AWESOME!"

"Terrifying, you mean."

"Whatever."

"I don't know that I can do this, Joe."

"Don't worry, man. I got your back."

Strangely, those four words made a world of difference to Ethan. He felt a little better knowing that Joseph was behind him, and would be there when he needed. "Thanks, man."

"Help me with this, would you?"

Ethan looked across to see Joseph chasing his own tail as he tried to fix his breastplate on. He burst out laughing.

"Hang on, hang on," he said. "Hold still."

Joseph stopped moving. In a few quick minutes, Ethan laced up the steel and leather breastplate and the pair went to breakfast.

289

The warming air now filled with the rich scent of cooking meat and vegetables as well as wood smoke. The delightful fragrances awoke a savage hunger in the pit of Ethan's gut. His stomach growled with anticipation.

"Hungry much?" Joe noted as they threaded their way through the thickening crowd to find Lord Cai.

"Starving."

"Good," Cai said from behind them. "The last breakfast is always a feast."

"Last?"

"For many. It is the breakfast we eat before a major engagement."

"Appetite's gone," Ethan said.

Cai laughed. "Not for long. Come, Gwalchgwyn has invited us to sit at the table."

The table, Ethan and Joseph learnt, was a long, rough wood construction, with cut stumps and cushions for seats. As a man of immeasurable respect, Gwalchgwyn was afforded the best seat – the centre. Aerfyn, determined to break her fast with her knights as one of them, sat beside her aged father, Maelgoch beside her.

Two other lords took their seats beside them. Four stools sat empty on the other side of Gwalchgwyn. Cai, Ethan, Joseph and Cai's Lieutenant, a short, broadly built redhead named Ewan, took their seats beside the Dryw in that order.

"Gentlemen, and Aerfyn," Gwalchgwyn said. "Let us feast on this glorious morn in honour of those heroes with whom we now dine."

"In honour of our heroes," those who knew what to say murmured.

A series of pages brought food to the table, filled the cups of those seated there with metheglyn, and then dispersed to attend to the other lords. Ethan looked around him. Gathered around the fire, with no particular heed to class or title, men in armour sat or sprawled on logs or the grass, holding wooden plates and waiting patiently for their food and drink.

They talked and laughed easily, as if the thought of the upcoming battle disturbed them not. Ethan felt guilty and foolish for being so nervous surrounded by such care-free warriors as these.

Those that had food already neither ate nor drank, but sat patiently awaiting… something.

When all the lords had been served, Gwalchgwyn stood. Not long after, and with assistance, Aerfyn also stood. They both picked up their cups and held them out before them.

"We drink to you," Gwalchgwyn said, his voice carrying well in the cool air. "Knights and soldiers of Caer Avallach, who sit before us to slake your thirst on this, the day of battle. Your souls are all assured their place amongst the bravest and mightiest of us in the fragrant fields of Tir Heddychlon. Should you find yourselves there, my friends, smile and know that we, the living, shall not be long behind you."

"To our heroes," Aerfyn said, smiling a radiant smile that nearly stopped Ethan's pounding heart.

Everyone stood. "To our queen," they answered.
They all drank their cups dry.

"We break our fast with you," Aerfyn said, picking up a skewer of meat and vegetables. "Knights and soldiers of Caer Avallach, who sit before us to break your fast on this, the day of battle. You souls are assured great glories akin to the bravest and mightiest of us in the dawning of your new lives. Born anew, know that we, your friends, shall find you once more in the land of the living. Never could we be parted long from you."

"To our queen!" the gathering answered with enthusiasm.

Everyone tore a cut of meat from their skewer.

"All right," Gwalchgwyn said, a smile quirking the corner of his lips and setting his eyes sparkling. "Dig in!"

Ethan couldn't contain the laugh that escaped his lips. After all the pomp of the ceremony he just witnessed, an impish 'dig in' was the last thing he expected the Seer to say. Gwalchgwyn grinned over at Ethan as he sat.

"Liked that?" he asked.

"Very much."

"Good. I've been working on the delivery for the past two days."

Ethan laughed again, accepting more metheglyn from one the cupbearers that stood in waiting behind the table.

"Is there no such ceremony before battle in your world, Ethan?" Cai asked.

Ethan almost choked. "Uh... no. None. That I know of, at any rate. I mean, some seek blessings from their holy men, I suppose, but there's nothing like this. We certainly don't expect to see each other again after we've died. Well, Buddhists might."

"I'm confused. What?"

Ethan smiled. He launched into a detailed explanation of Christian and atheist beliefs, explaining Heaven and Hell, and the idea that there was no soul at all, that death was very final.

The horror that Cai expressed at the very idea of hell and eternal torment was outmatched by the horror he expressed at the idea of no soul at all.

"That is preposterous!" he exclaimed. "Of course there is such a thing as a soul! How could there not be?"

"Well, to be fair, there is no evidence of it."

"But of course there is! Have you never seen a loved one long dead? Or smelled their delicate fragrance when you know they could not be near?"

"Ghosts, you mean?"

"I am unfamiliar with that term."

"It's the same thing as a soul, I guess. It's just called a ghost when it no longer has a body."

"Then, yes. Ghosts."

"I've never seen one, no."

"But you've heard of them?"

"Well, yes... But there's no actual evidence..."

"How could the stories have arisen if there was no evidence? The stories are evidence."

Ethan shrugged. "Not scientifically, they're not."

"What is 'scientifically'?"

"Science. It's a process by which one acquires evidence, then forms a hypothesis, tests that hypothesis with experiments that can be duplicated by anyone following the instructions, and thereby produces a theory which is agreed upon by all because the results are repeatable."

Cai frowned as he tried to unravel the idea behind Ethan's words. "I can see the value, but ghosts, as you call them, are like people. They all behave differently. How can such a thing be tested?"

"It can't, so therefore ghosts are not real."

"That is foolish," Cai protested. "There must be a great many things that exist whose existence is denied simply because your 'science' lacks the scope to acknowledge them."

"I... well... I guess so. That's the thing about science, though. It is continually testing itself. We're learning about new things every day."

"So it might be that your science learns of ghosts yet."

"Well... it's possible, I suppose."

"Then how could they categorically deny the existence of the soul?"

"Uh..."

"And what does Ethan Cadfael believe," Gwalchgwyn asked. He'd been listening in on the conversation, fascinated by the views of Ethan's people.

"To be honest, I haven't thought much about it," Ethan admitted. "I can see the appeal of believing there is something more to life, but I can't see why there would be."

"And you must know why?"

"Well... no... Yes. I guess."

"I see. It is an interesting position to be in, to not believe in anything except to believe in the absence of anything worth believing in."

Ethan smiled after working his way through Gwalchgwyn's sentence. "And why do you believe there are souls, and in reincarnation?"

Gwalchgwyn smiled. "I have seen it."

"You've seen it." The tone of Ethan's voice indicated grave disbelief.

"I have."

"When? How?"

Gwalchgwyn grinned. "Goodness but your people are a cynical race!"

Ethan shrugged. "We've learnt that people lie."

"I see. Do you think I am lying now?"

"Uh... no. I think you believe that you saw what you believe you saw."

Gwalchgwyn laughed. "Indeed! Perhaps in time you will unlearn everything you know, so that you might be able to learn the truth."

Ethan shrugged. "Okay, Mr. Miyagi."

Gwalchgwyn cocked his head. "What is 'mister Miyagi'?"

"Never mind," Ethan muttered. "Cultural reference."

Breakfast went on until no one could fit another mouthful into their stomachs. They retired to their pavilions to strike camp and prepare.

Ethan was impressed with their efficiency. The camp was gone in a matter of minutes, the pavilions taken down and folded into neat piles. With much surprise, Ethan noted that one pavilion had been filled with nothing but rafts and odd, saucer-shaped boats, all still rigged up onto a cart. Two surprisingly small horses were hitched to the cart.

"Aren't they a bit small to be pulling that?" Ethan asked Cai as Cai showed him how to properly dress a horse.

"They are a very strong breed. From Bryniau Eira. You'll see."

Before midmorning, the entire army was on the move. Unable to mount, Maelgoch and Aerfyn rode in chariots, side by side. Both had donned their armour and carried with them javelins, war-darts and heavy bows with a chariot full of arrows. There were so many weapons in each chariot, there was barely enough room for the driver and passenger.

They rode at the head of the battalion of chariots. Twenty of them rumbled along in the centre of the army, just behind the light cavalry. Each chariot was pulled by a matched pair of the small mountain horses of Bryniau Eira. They trotted along at a good pace, their ears pricked forward.

Surrounding them marched the lancers. The rest of the infantry marched behind them, keeping the carts containing their war machines and boats surrounded.

Heavy cavalry at various intervals walked their larger plains horses in pairs on either side. Cai and Ethan led the main army, their lieutenants a step behind and a vanguard of swordsmen and archers ahead.

Ethan relaxed into his horse's gait, finding the rhythm soothing. The sun shone brightly over leaves that were just beginning to turn. Birds sang lustily from their perches, songs such that Ethan had never heard. They were hauntingly beautiful songs.

One bird, looking something like a brightly coloured chicken with an exceptionally long purple and red tail, flew overhead. Ethan watched it in wonder.

"One of Rhiannon's," Cai noted.

"Eh?" Ethan asked.

"Rhiannon's birds. A long time ago, one of the queens of Caer Avallach and Y Ynys Bendigaid kept and bred brightly coloured birds that sang sweet songs. At her death, the birds were released into the wild, and it seems to have suited them. They are everywhere now, surrounding Y Ynys Bendigaid with their songs from the first days of spring until the last days of the fall."

"In the winter?"

"They roost in Rhiannon's tower in Caer Avallach and are cared for by the royal bird-keeper."

"You have a royal bird-keeper?"

"Yes, of course. For the royal birds."

"I see."

"Is there no such thing for your people?"

"I don't know. Probably in England, where the queen lives. But in Canada, we don't really have stuff like that. The cats on Parliament Hill, maybe."

"You must tell me all about this 'Canada' of yours. It seems a fascinating place."

"Nowhere near as fascinating as this place, let me assure you. Though, like you, we do have a lot of wilderness, which is nice. Too many cities too close together turns a place ugly."

Cai smiled. "I also like the wilderness, though not as much as our chief lieutenant."

"Chief lieutenant?"

"Maelgoch. Aerfyn has returned and resumed command, so she is our commander now. Maelgoch is the lieutenant once more."

"Huh."

"In any case, Maelgoch was, before the war began, escaping the castle whenever he had the opportunity. His father used to call him 'his wilding.' It is true. There is something a little wilder in Maelgoch than in the rest of us."

"I didn't see it."

"Watch him in the castle. After a few days, he starts to pace like a caged cat."

"I'll keep that in mind."

"Do."

They rode on for a while in silence, Ethan enjoying the combination of a warm sun and a cool breeze as he rode.

"Man," he heard Joseph mutter from behind him. "This is chaffing."

He burst out laughing and turned back. "You okay, Joe?"

"Fine," Joseph answered, looking glum. "I can't wait to get off this horse!"

"Soon enough," Cai said, grinning.

Soon enough came sooner than expected. A low, crass horn sounded somewhere ahead as the vanguard sounded their warning.

"Forward!" Ethan shouted, kicking his horse into a run.

They came across the vanguard, some minutes later, struggling to hold ground against the attacking Dynion Gors. They fled the moment the Pobl Gwir cavalry thundered into view.

"Damn it!" Ethan hissed as he pulled his horse to a stop. "There goes the element of surprise."

He turned back and looked at Cai. Cai nodded.

"Form up!" Ethan commanded. "We attack now!" He turned to Cai. "You take the right, I'll take the left. Infantry down the middle. We've got to get them away from the docks."

"Done," Cai said. He kicked his horse. "Red riders! With me!"

"White riders!" Ethan bellowed. "With me!"

"Infantry down the line," Aerfyn said.

"Infantry down the line!" Maelgoch bellowed.

The army split into three. Half of the cavalry tore off after Lord Cai and vanished into the woods on the right of the road. Half followed Ethan to the left. The infantry broke into a run, heading straight down the road, the chariots quickly overtaking them.

Ethan hoped he knew where he was going. He had studied the maps with Cai, Maelgoch and Aerfyn and knew the plan fairly well. He and Cai would engage first, the infantry coming up through the middle.

It was likely that the Dynion Gors had managed to make a few rafts and were crossing Y Llyn Gwydr, the Glass Lake at this moment. The trick was to trap the rafts between two hostile shores. That meant taking control of the docks of Y Llyn Gwydr.

It would be no easy feat. The Pobl Gwir army had taken quite a beating during the course of the war, and the wiry Dynion Gors were a force to be reckoned with. More to the point, the Pobl Gwir were led by two commanders who knew little of commanding, one much less than the other.

"What would King Arthur do?" Ethan asked himself as his horse hurtled through the trees.

Before long before Ethan spotted the grey, heaving mass that was the army of Dynion Gors. There were so many, so closely packed at the water's edge, they looked much like rats scrambling over a rubbish heap.

"R.O.U.S.'s," Ethan mused aloud.

"What?" Joseph asked, his horse slightly out of control and almost over-taking Ethan's.

"The Princess Bride?"

"Huh?"

"Never mind," Ethan said. He drew his sword and held it aloft. "Now!" he roared.

Riders put spurs to horses and in a great thunderous cascade, slammed into the left flank of the enemy.

The Dynion Gors were prepared. Several horses went down screaming, pierced through their mighty chests by the waiting lances that bristled along the front line of warriors.

Ethan's horse had good instincts. It leapt high, clearing the lance. He had time enough to make two sweeping slices with his sword before his horse landed, taking three heads and two arms. It cleared the way for the riders following behind.

The commander of the white riders looked up only briefly to see Cai's red riders similarly engaged. Grimacing, he plunged forward, aiming for the docks, visible now on the clear, shining lake.

The brassy sound of a fleet of carynxes and rapid drumming announced the arrival of the infantry. They rushed forward with a mighty roar, while behind them, the chariots darted back and forth, launching javelins, darts and a hailstorm of arrows upon the Dynion Gors.

For a time, the Pobl Gwir had the advantage. Both cavalry commanders made good progress towards the docks. Ethan and his white riders made it there first, clearing the docks of the enemy. Once clear, he pulled out his white flag and raised it high, waving it to and fro.

A small victory, but it was enough to fill the hearts of the brave Pobl Gwir warriors. They pushed harder.

Then, as if pouring from a sinking ship, thousands more Dynion Gors flooded from the woods to the beach, tearing through the surprise Pobl Gwir with frightening ease.

"Hold the docks!" Cai yelled to Ethan. He turned his horse around to face the new threat. "Red riders, with me!"

What remained of Cai's force fought their way to him. "Caer Avallach!" he roared.

"Queen Aerfyn!" his men roared in response. They surged forward.

Ethan, struggling to keep the dock, watched Cai every chance he got. A short struggle took him away from Cai a moment, and when he next looked up, Cai had been separated from the rest of his men. Ethan watched in horror as a broad-headed spear pierced Cai's shoulder and dragged him to the ground.

"Cai!" he screamed. He turned to Joseph. "Hold the dock."

"Why? What are you...?"

Ethan turned his horse and kicked its flanks hard. The beast bolted forward with an irritated snort.

"Ethan!" Joseph yelled.

Ethan did not hesitate. He plunged forward, his eyes trained on Cai who, despite the spear skewering his shoulder, fought on. A sharp cut on the back of Cai's leg, and he collapsed onto one knee. Still, he fought on.

One of the enemy grabbed a hold of the broken spear shaft and twisted. Cai cried out in agony. He spun on his knee and cut the warrior down. Behind him, one enemy warrior raised his axe high and swung.

Ethan's blade caught the axe moments before it struck the back of Lord Cai's head. His horse's broad chest knocked the sinewy enemy to the ground and a few choice strikes of the animal's iron-shod hoof on the warrior's head ensured that he would not rise.

"Cai!" Ethan shouted down to the dazed man kneeling in the blood-slicked grass. "Take my hand!"

Cai looked up with hazed eyes. Not fully understanding but instinctually knowing what had happened, Cai grasped Ethan's outstretched hand and was hauled onto Ethan's horse. The commander of the white riders and his horse fought their way back to the dock. With the help of some archers who had managed to break through and join the white riders holding the dock, Ethan lowered Cai to the ground. He left his friend in the care of the archers and turned back to battle.

The fighting had moved away from the dock somewhat, allowing his knights to rest, and provide artillery support to those fighting on the beach. The hill that had previously been controlled by the Knights of Caer Avallach was swarming now with Dynion Gors.

"Where's Aerfyn?" Ethan asked.

"My Lord," a knight answered. "The hill was overtaken in the moments it took you to rescue Cai. Of Maelgoch and Aerfyn there is no sign."

Ethan let loose a string of curses that would have made his grandmother blush.

"There!" Joseph yelled, pointing his bloodied sword to the right hand side of the battlefield.

Aerfyn and Maelgoch as well as the few remaining knights assigned as the queen's guard for the battle held their ground in a fierce and desperate battle for survival.

"Abandon the dock," Ethan said. "We will win it back later."

"But…"

"Do as I say!"

Once again, Ethan spurred his horse forward.

"Knights to me! Knights to me!" he called as he and his men left the docks to rally at the front of battle.

One, crude blast of an unfamiliar horn caught Ethan's attention. He turned to find men and women on horse and on foot in crude but functional leather and mail armour gathering at the forest edge.

They were led by a long-limbed, muscular woman with deep copper hair tied back in a braid and wearing a braided leather circlet on her head. On one side, a twisted strand of hair hung loose, affixed with crows' feathers and boars' teeth. Bright, hard green eyes surveyed the scene.

Spying Ethan with the knights rallying to him, she kicked her horse. Ethan noted with some awe that the beast wore no saddle. Not only did she have a short sword strapped to her side, but a short-shafted, double-headed battle-axe strapped to her back, a long knife strapped to her left upper arm, and one on her right thigh as well as a short dagger tucked into each boot.

"My Lord," she said. "We are come to give Y Ynys Bendigaid our aid. I am Ceinwen of the Rhai Gwyllt."

"I am Ethan Cafael," Ethan replied, not bothering with formalities. "You take the left, I'll take the right, meet behind enemy lines to aid our queen in fighting back the Dynion Gors."

Ceinwen nodded. She raised her sword and pointed to the left. With no further words, the two parties split, cutting along the outside of the main battle and meeting behind Aerfyn and Maelgoch.

Together, Ethan and Ceinwen pushed forward, their horses and infantry now far outnumbering the army of Dynion Gors. The fight lasted all of fifteen minutes before one bellowed command from an enemy commander, and the Dynion Gors broke their lines and fled.

The combined armies of the Pobl Gwir and the Rhai Gwyllt returned to the hill where Aerfyn had collapsed to her knees, and Maelgoch lay unmoving.

"Ceinwen!" Aerfyn greeted the tall woman warrior, faint from blood loss and exhaustion.

"Cousin," Ceinwen greeted in return. The woman dismounted and went immediately to Aerfyn's side, helping her across to a boulder where she could rest.

"Maelgoch," Aerfyn whispered.

Ethan was already at Maelgoch's side. He pressed his fingers into the Chief Lieutenant's neck and paused. "He's alive," he said. "Just. Someone fetch a healer!"

Ceinwen, after making sure that Aerfyn was all right, left the Pobl Gwir queen in the care of her medics and went to Maelgoch. She carefully removed his helm, pausing ever so briefly at the swarthy, yet handsome face that was revealed. She quickly looked over the wounds on his head.

"These are not serious. He was likely knocked senseless," she said.

"He was fighting wounded. His hip was pierced through in the previous battle," Ethan said.

Ceinwen nodded. "A strong man." She motioned for her own lieutenants. Without so much as glancing at them, she began issuing orders. In a matter of minutes, an octagonal area had been cordoned off with screens and Maelgoch and Aerfyn both ushered inside.

Ceinwen looked around. "Where is my uncle? I need him in this."

"Here," Gwalchgwyn said wearily. He trudged up the slope of the hill, leaning heavily on his staff and holding a long sword. His white robes were covered in the thick blackish blood of the Dynion Gors.

"Wow," Joseph said to Ethan in a low voice. "That old dude is bad-ass."

"No kidding," Ethan murmured back.

"Hah!" Gwalchgwyn said, having overheard. "You should have seen me when I was a young man. I'd put all of you to shame!" His face grew serious and he turned to Ceinwen. "My daughter?"

"Aerfyn is all right, but needs treatment and rest. The pretty man is in dire need of your attention."

Gwalchgwyn turned to Ethan. "Ethan Cadfael, command falls to you. Across Y Llyn Gwydr, Caer Avallach is still under siege. I must stay with my daughter and her lieutenant. Go forth, break the siege and save our beloved Y Yny Bendigaid."

Ethan blinked. He nodded and turned to Ceinwen. "I would appreciate your assistance."

"You have it, Battle Prince. You were aptly named. You fight well."

If he were not so exhausted, Ethan might have blushed. He looked at Joseph. "Launch the boats," he said.

As the rafts and boats were unloaded from their carts, Ethan consulted with Ceinwen who, despite being queen of the Rhai Gwyllt and living in the wilds with her people, knew the fortress well.

Moments later, the rafts and saucer-boats were in the water, loaded with men and ammunition, and gliding silently across the lake. As they approached the island enshrouded in mist at the centre, the sounds of battle rang clear.

****

Lord Marshall Rhyddych bellowed his commands, but they were barely heard above the din of battle. Realising the Lord Marshall could not be heard, a brave squire ran across the walls, repeating the orders at the top of his lungs.

Rhyddych had never been a squeamish man. Still, he had to turn his head when that brave boy was struck through the throat by an enemy arrow. He gritted his teeth as the boy fell to his knees, blood spurting from his neck, mouth and nose before toppling, lifeless, over the parapet.

Vastly outnumbered, it had been a miracle Caer Avallach had survived this long, and it was owed to courage of its defenders, and the wise and calculated command of the Lord Marshall.

The ground beneath Rhyddych's feet shook as another section of the inner wall collapsed under the steady beating from the enemy catapults.

Rhyddych swore.

A pale, feathered thing swooped past his head, twittering. He turned to see a familiar barn owl turning gracefully in the air and swooping past his head again. His gaze followed the bird out and he spied on the misty horizon a large force of boats crossing Y Llyn Gwydr.

Fear gripped his heart.

"Please no," he whispered. "No more of these damned men of the marsh!"

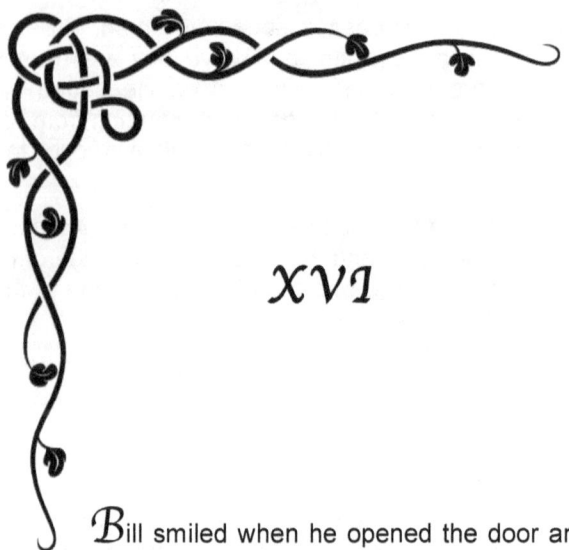

XVI

$\mathcal{B}$ill smiled when he opened the door and saw Genevieve standing there, a case of beer in her hands.

"Hey," he greeted opening the door wider.

"Hey. How are you feeling?" Genevieve entered the small but tidy apartment and dumped the case on the kitchen countertop.

"A bit like I've gone mad, actually. What's been happening with the case?"

Genevieve ripped open the case and handed Bill a bottle before taking off her jacket and retrieving a bottle for herself. She went to the living room and threw herself on Bill's ancient couch.

"Not sure. The girl and one of the witnesses are still missing. Ethan Evans. It looks like they got caught up in some pretty mysterious shit."

"Yeah?"

"Yeah. The place in the road where you said you ran over two of those hooded men…"

"What about it?"

"We found no one. No body, nothing to indicate they'd been dragged away by a hungry animal. Nothing, except the cloaks themselves."

"What?"

"Yeah. Just the cloaks. I mean, forensics said that the dents in the truck match up with your story, and there are cloaks, but no bodies. It's as if they just… I don't know… vanished into thin air."

"Jesus."

"Yeah, and it gets weirder. The surveillance camera caught the attack on H.Q. Well… they caught people's throats being slit, and skulls cracking, and furniture flying, but not the men doing it. It was like watching a scene from poltergeist or something. I watched you shoot into an empty room, hit something, and then a grey cloak falling to the floor."

"What? So in the interrogation room as well? There was only a cloak, no body?"

"Exactly."

"What the…?" Bill stood in the kitchen, his beer unopened, staring incredulously at Genevieve.

"That can't be possible. Gen, I swear on my grandmother's grave, I saw people. Tall, wiry, pallid-looking people. I killed them, I swear it."

"Hey, I believe you. I mean, something was tossing that furniture around at H.Q."

"So what's the theory? We were hit by a group of really angry ghosts?"

"Not a clue. I'm leaving this one for the detectives."

Bill grunted. He opened a drawer and pulled out his bottle opener.

"They're twist-tops, Spiderman," Genevieve said. She twisted the top of her beer off and took a swig.

"Oh." Bill threw the opener back into the draw and followed suit. Making his way over to the living room, he flopped down on his armchair and propped his feet up on the coffee table.

"I think I'm gonna quit the force," he said at length.

"What? Why?"

Bill smiled over at Genevieve.

"Okay," she admitted. "So you screwed up with this, but you're a good cop, Bill. One of the few honest ones left in the force. I mean, what the hell would you do instead?"

"Search and rescue."

Genevieve opened her mouth to protest, but clamped it shut again. "Actually, that sounds pretty cool."

"Yeah. I was thinking that would suit me better. Besides, after everything's in, I probably won't have a job."

"You never know. What did you tell them about why you abandoned S.O.P?"

"I had reason to believe that the victim was in immediate danger and the witnesses were the only ones who knew where she was."

Genevieve burst out laughing. "That might actually fly!"

Bill grunted. "Even if I'm cleared, I really want to do search and rescue."

"Why didn't you? When you were first starting out, I mean."

"I thought I wouldn't be able to handle it. After this though, I think I can handle just about anything."

"Yeah, bet you still couldn't handle a girl."

"Shut up. I could so."

"Dude, you could not."

"Are you challenging me?"

"Maybe."

Bill grinned. He put down his beer. Genevieve followed, slowly, her eyes scanning Bill's posture for signs, her legs tight and prepared for sudden, explosive movement.

Bill lunged. Genevieve dodged neatly and Bill landed on the couch with a muffled, "Oomph!"

"Told you! Come on, Spiderman. Let's see those super powers."

Bill rose and turned. The pair squared off like fighting cocks. Bill lunged again. Missed. He tried again. Genevieve dodged and turned, and ducked and danced, always just out of Bill's grasp.

"You see," she explained, breathless and grinning. "The problem with big guys in general, is they're too slo –"

A monstrous tackle put Genevieve on her side. Bill pinned her down.

"You see," he said in mocking tones. "The problem with women in general is –"

"Finish that sentence and I'll kill you."

311

"I'd like to see you try."

Genevieve struggled, using every trick her trainer had shown her. Bill, unfortunately, had the same training, and could counter every move she tried to pull. She slumped back, out of breath.

"Fine," she panted. "I yield."

"Good," Bill said.

Without thinking, he bent his head down and took Genevieve's lips in his own. Without thinking, Genevieve kissed him back. She pulled back and laughed, wrapping her arms around Bill's neck and pulling him close.

"Took you long enough," she said.

****

The mist parted slightly to reveal a motley crew. Tribesmen from the wilds surrounding Caer Avallach and knights both rowed their way across Y Llyn Gwydr. The Lord Marshall breathed a deep sigh of relief. Reinforcements they were and they were Caer Avallach's own, or close enough to.

Grinning, Rhyddych changed his battle plan. "With me!" he roared. "On the gate! With me!"

Stepping down from his position on the south tower balcony, he raced forward into battle. His personal guard ran with him. The fight on the walls withdrew, concentrating at the gate, which, as of the moment, was swarming with Dynion Gors.

The Lord Marshall kept a careful eye on the approaching forces. They would dock soon, and be at the inner gates of Caer Avallach shortly thereafter. All he had to do now was ensure that the knights and their tribesmen allies could get into the fortress safely.

Arrows flew wildly from both armies, filling the air with a buzzing hiss akin to the sound of a swarm of angry wasps. The tumult of tumbling stone dominated the lower register, the zing and clang of steel against steel answered in high countermeasure.

The air reeked of oil, and sweat, and dust, and blood.

A leader of men he might be but the Lord Marshall Rhyddych, like all the inhabitants of Y Ynys Bendigaid, was a man of peace. He hated battle.

He hated the Dynion Gors for bringing the battle to him. The passionate fire that hate enabled flooded through his veins in a hot rush.

No one fought harder than the Lord Marshall Rhyddych that day.

****

Ethan surveyed the scene from his raft. The outer wall of the city had collapsed near the dock, boulders strewn every which way on the rocky beach. The dock had been the only safe port on the island, and it lay in smoking ruin. The rafts and boats would have to try and make landfall on very inhospitable shores.

On either side of the dock, sheer cliff rose about four feet above the water. The narrow gap between, which once held the only jetty on the island, glowed red with embers. It was far too narrow to permit more than one raft to make landfall at a time.

The cliffs and the narrow beach dropped immediately into deep water. There was no gradual slope up to the beach. One misstep, and anyone disembarking would be drowned.

"I see a problem," Ceinwen noted from behind Ethan.

"No kidding."

"No."

Ethan turned. "It's just an expression... uh... never mind."

"Yo, look!" Joseph said. He tapped Ethan on the shoulder and pointed.

Three grubby faces peered out from the top of the cliffs. Children, street urchins by the look of them, had lined up on the cliff on their bellies, their little heads the only thing that could be seen from the lake.

Ethan smiled and waved. One child waved shyly back.

"I am Ethan Cadfael," Ethan called across the water. "The knights of Caer Avallach have come to lift the siege."

The children whispered amongst themselves. Then one vanished from the cliff and returned shortly thereafter with coils of heavy rope and fisherman's nets.

"Sweet!" Ethan said.

"I don't understand what flavour has to do with this," Ceinwen said.

"Uh... It's just –"

"An expression?"

"Exactly."

"You have queer expressions, Ethan Battle Prince."

More faces popped into view on the cliff, on the other side of the docks this time, similarly kitted with ropes and nets. Each child uncoiled the ropes and threw over the nets vanishing briefly to affix them to something. They reappeared just as the rafts bumped gently against the cliff faces. One raft made landfall on the smouldering beach and its passengers disembarked carefully. The rafts and boats that jostled against the cliffs were emptied with greater speed, the knights and tribesmen hauling themselves up the ropes and nets

The nets could hold as many as three warriors at once. The drivers of each vessel moved away from the cliffs as soon as the boats and rafts were emptied to allow room for the other vessels to approach and unload

It was all done with remarkable skill and speed

Ceinwen and Ethan reached the top together. Ethan smiled down at the tallest of the grubby boys, assuming he was the oldest and therefore in charge.

"Thank-you, young sir," he said.

"I'm not a boy!" the girl complained.

Ceinwen laughed. "Thank-you, then, young lady. What is your name?"

"Brynn."

"Well, Brynn, is there any secret way into the fortress that you know of?"

Brynn shook her head. "The passages have all been blocked in case the Bog Men found them. We helped blocked them up for the Lord Marshall. He promised us bread for a year if we did."

"A fine promise."

The girl nodded.

"We shall have to arrange apples as well, for your help getting us up here today."

The girl beamed. "That would be lovely!"

"We'll do what we can. For now, stay hidden. I expect a large number of Dynion Gors to be heading this way shortly."

"You think you can beat them?"

"Sweetheart," Ceinwen said with a knowing smile. "I am Ceinwen, queen of the Rhai Gwyllt, and I bring my fiercest warriors to battle. With me are the Knights of Caer Avallach, who are renowned throughout the lands. We will beat them."

The girl smiled and scurried off, her troop of grimey children along with them. They vanished from sight.

"I hope you're right," Ethan said, squinting up at the destroyed wall beside the thick gate.

"We don't have much of a choice, do we?" Ceinwen said in return.

Both commanders turned to find the last of the rafts being unloaded. Ethan turned to Ceinwen.

"You take the left, I'll take the right. Let's force these rats back towards the water, yes?"

Ceinwen grinned and nodded. The combined armies entered the city stealthily. Ethan led his knights up the city streets, keeping as much to the wall as possible. Every so often, he looked to his left and spied the wild tribesmen as they scampered along the left wall.

They reached the battle in under fifteen minutes. It took them two minutes more to form on either side of the wall of Caer Avallach.

"For Aerfyn!" Ethan roared.

The knights surged forward as one from the right, the wild tribesmen doing the same on the left.

Utter chaos followed. The Dynion Gors momentarily forgot their battle against the haggard defenders of the fortress and split down the middle to face each half of the allied army.

That was all the Lord Marshall needed. "Open the gates!" he commanded.

The massive reinforced iron gates swung open, and the defenders of Caer Avallach, led by the brave Lord Marshall, poured forth, taking each half of the enemy from the rear.

Ethan spied a taller than average Dynion Gors, wearing a crown of bronzed grasses.

"Hey!" he called to the warrior. "You're mine!"

"Beidh mé ag sracadh do cheann as!" the creature growled in reply.

"Sure," Ethan said. "Whatever the hell that means."

They engaged. The warrior before Ethan moved like lightning, the weight of his massive double-bitted axe seemingly nothing in his skilled hands. Ethan found himself on the defensive immediately. It was all he could do to duck. His attempts to try to directly block a strike from that weapon sent him reeling backwards.

The crowned creature threw a savagely powerful kick that landed square on Ethan's chest. Thrown off balance, the Battle Prince fell hard onto his back. Before he had time to recover his breath, the axe blade was falling towards his head. He rolled quickly to the side, the axe biting into paving just a hair's breadth from his ear.

Ethan rolled back, unleashing a kick of his own. It did not have the same effect. The Dynion Gors stumbled back, but remained on his feet. Still, it bought Ethan enough time to get back up and reengage.

Like the rest of the Dynion Gors, the crowned creature's armour was made up largely of stolen Pobl Gwir armour. Taller and more slender than the Pobl Gwir, armour designed for the Pobl Gwir did not fit the Dynion Gors well.

In a quick, calculating glance, Ethan spied several weaknesses in the creature's armour. The trick would be to get in close enough to take advantage of them.

It was a trick indeed. Ethan found himself dancing around his opponent, unable to move in. The frustration alone was enough to drive him to careless error. He moved in anger, earning him a sharp cut across his cheek. He moved his head just enough to avoid having his skull lopped open, but the strike that cut his cheek also sent his helm flying.

The cut stung like mad, but it hurt Ethan's pride much more. He stepped back and regarded his opponent, who took the moment to rest.

"You're the king, aren't you," he said.

"Cad?"

"You're the one who proposed to Aerfyn."

"Agus?"

"You sulky bastard. Do you respond this way to everyone who rejects you?"

"Cad a thuigeann thú? Nach bhfuil tú fiú ridire."

"Sorry, I don't speak monster."

The king of the Dynion Gors' eyes glinted angrily. With a bestial growl, he rushed forward. It was the foolish error Ethan had been hoping for. He stepped lightly to the side, spinning around to the creature's back. Dancing away, he cut low, the sword blade slicing through his opponent's calf with ease.

Tua Bhaill howled and stumbled, but kept his feet. He turned, his saucer-like pale eyes glinting savagely beneath his hood.

"Tough bastard," Ethan muttered.

The king charged again. Knowing he would not be fooled twice, Ethan danced to the other side, parrying lightly, then elbowing his opponent's cheek. The king stumbled sideways, straightening slowly.

The angry flash in his eyes became a savage glow. Ethan stepped back, for the first time genuinely afraid. With a snarl, the king attacked again. Ethan's heart froze as hope faded.

The axe whizzed through the air, quick slice after quick slice came at him, from seemingly every direction at once. He stepped back, to the side and backwards again, barely keeping his balance. Three savage blows he had no choice to parry cost him his weapon. The blade snapped at the hilt.

"Shit!" Ethan said.

Another slice forced him to roll out of the way.

"Ethan!" Ceinwen's voice shouted, stark and clear despite the din of battle.

Ethan turned briefly to see her unsheathe the short sword at her side and throw it to him, before turning once more to her opponent. She moved like a cat, despite the massive axe in her arms.

Ethan caught the sword deftly and rolled out of the way of another strike before coming to his feet.

"Fine," he grated. "Two can play at that game."

Losing all sense of precaution, Ethan grabbed the sword with both hands and rained strike after brutal strike upon the injured king.

At first Tua Bhaill parried and blocked efficiently, but a stumble over one of his fallen as he stepped back made him lose the rhythm. Soon he was back-pedalling wildly, his blocks and parries becoming desperate.

Fresh life flooded into Ethan's exhausted limbs. He applied greater speed, greater power to each strike until, at last, the king was disarmed, the axe pulled from his grasp by a skilled twist of Ethan's blade. The battle prince stopped short of lopping the creature's head off. Instead, the point of his sword came to a stop at the king's neck. He applied a small amount of pressure, and the king slowly fell to his knees.

"Liom teacht isteach," the king of the Dynion Gors growled.

The Dynion Gors had fought savagely, but they were now desperately outnumbered and their king had lost his weapon and knelt at the mercy of a knight.

One by one, having battled fiercely for hours, they surrendered. They threw their weapons down in defeat, their numbers more than halved, and fell slowly to their knees.

"Na Fir Bolg a thabhairt suas," the king said, his voice weary and melancholic.

"A bad day to be you," Ethan said. "For the record, you almost had me."

Tua Bhaill looked up and blinked in surprise. A slow smile spread across his face and he said, "I was ill prepared to face one such as you. You do not fight as the Pobl Gwir do."

"You can speak our language, you sly bastard!" Ethan said. "And thanks, I think."

The king of the Dynion Gors nodded.

Sounds of fighting died away to eerie silence as the last of the Dynion Gors realised they had lost and surrendered themselves.

"Victory!" Lord Marshal Rhyddych called, raising his bloodied sword high.

"Victory!" the allied armies cried in response. It became a chant. "Victory! Victory! Victory!"

"Yeah!" Joseph could heard yelling in the crowd. "No one messes with the Billes, yo! No one!"

Ethan grinned.

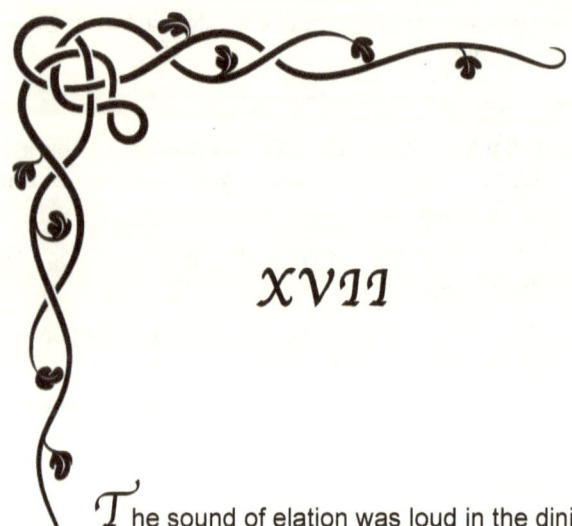

XVII

$\mathcal{T}$he sound of elation was loud in the dining hall of Caer Avallach. Gruff voices talked and laughed, filling the cavernous space with a great din. Ethan sat with Joseph, the pair being one of a surprising many whose wounds were not great. Joseph had his head bandaged and his arm reset and put into a splint.

Ethan suffered little more than severe bruising, a black eye and a cut cheek. His limbs, however, ached fiercely and he felt so fatigued that the possibility of falling asleep into his soup constantly worried him.

On Ethan's immediate left, sat Aerfyn, dressed in a beautiful gown of red silk, a rose gold circlet crossing her forehead, and garnets glinting from her pale hair. Though still wounded and weak, she refused to be kept to her bed. Instead, she elected to feast with her knights in celebration of a hard-won victory.

The hall in which they sat took almost all the ground floor of the fortress of Caer Avallach. The painted ceilings were three levels up, with galleries that ran the length of the hall on the second and third floors.

The ceiling's painting changed in accordance with the time of day. At the moment, it flushed in orange, purple, pale green and gold in a spectacular imitation of sunset.

Ethan stared at it, mesmerised by the shifting colours for, like the sunset outside, the colours never stayed the same, but changed and moved and deepened.

Tall, exquisitely sculptured columns supported the ceiling. The designs carved into the pink stone, of which the entire castle was built, were of natural things – vines and flowers, birds and boars. The edges of the leaves and flowers were gilded, their centres inset with brightly coloured stone.

That stone, Aerfyn told Ethan, changed colours to reflect the changing seasons. Now, they were golden yellow, some deepening in to oranges and reds. In the winter, they were stark white, changing to bright green for the spring. In the summer, when all the wild flowers were in bloom, the stones blossomed into a multitude of colours; some red, some purple, some white, some blue, some bright pink. Others still would be yellow, or pale lavender, or so deeply red they would appear almost black.

Ethan could not help but marvel at this. His mind leapt forward to the oncoming winter, eager to see the hall in pink and white. He imagined the following spring, when the white would give way, just as it did outside.

In his mind's eye, he stood in the hall, Aerfyn at his side. He sighed and looked over. She was talking and laughing with her father and her cousin, the wild Ceinwen of the Rhai Gwyllt. Adding his deep voice to the jovial conversation was the Lord Marshall, a great bear of a man who Ethan had earlier learnt trained the Knights of Caer Avallach.

Ethan turned from them and observed the hall still further.

The floor was polished rainbow moonstone, and it reflected the dying light streaming in from the floor to ceiling window that dominated the back wall. The view from the window was exquisite – the sunset reflected beautifully in the still waters of Y Llyn Gwydr. On the misty shore stretched the ancient forest as it had been thousands of years before the Pobl Gwir came to Y Ynys Bendigaid.

At the other end of the hall, above the beautifully carved red maple doors, an enormous stained glass window let multi-coloured light in. It cast its design on the moonstone floor as the setting sun burst through.

The feasting men were arranged in a stretched semicircle that covered the hall lengthwise. Aerfyn and her privileged guests sat at a separate curved table atop a platform that normally served as a dais for the throne. The centre of the hall remained clear for dancing, which was to come later in the evening.

Behind the dais stretched a tapestry that depicted the great siege of Caer Avallach by the Dynion Gors. Having only just won the battle, Ethan was certain nothing natural could have woven such a tapestry. A polite enquiry revealed that the tapestry altered to display events of importance and significance. The anniversaries of important events were remembered by the tapestry, even if the people living in the hall knew them not.

It was extremely old, Aerfyn said, first woven when Caer Avallach was little more than a simple wooden keep atop an Oppidum. It contained the memory of all the ages.

Aerfyn herself had studied the tapestry and admitted it sometimes displayed images depicting events of which she knew nothing about.

At the other side, just before the wall upon which hung three large embroidered banners, a large fire pit blazed cheerily. Above it, hanging from a fire-blackened tripod, a large cauldron bubbled merrily, filling the hall with the scent of spiced soup. The cauldron never seemed to empty, even when each man and woman in the hall had several helpings, it still bubbled away, full as it ever was.

Ethan smiled at a page as the boy refilled his goblet with clear, sparkling metheglyn. The boy smiled shyly in return, then scurried back to position. Ethan shrugged, and drank.

"You are something of a living legend," Aerfyn noted with a smile.

Ethan turned, surprised at being addressed. "I am?"

"Why yes, the strange warrior from the Otherworld who led the mighty knights of Caer Avallach to victory over the Dynion Gors. Look behind you, you stand the equivalent of seven feet tall on the tapestry."

Ethan turned. He spied a woven figure, a sword held to the throat of a smaller, darker figure. It did indeed look as though he stood a full head and shoulders higher than everyone else. He blinked.

"That's me, is it?"

"It is."

"I'm not really that tall."

"The legend states that you are."

"Does the tapestry make the legend?"

"No, it simply reflects it."

"Huh."

"Are you not pleased?"

Ethan smiled slightly. "I'm too tired to feel much of anything."

"Well, Ethan Cadfael, take heart. Here comes dinner."

Ethan followed Aerfyn's line of sight. Pages dressed in autumn brown and red brought in the main course – two roasted wild boars, still on their spits, on beds of roots and surrounded by wild mushrooms in some kind of garlic sauce. Behind that came platter after platter of steamed wheat, tiny roasted fowl of some kind, pheasant, and bowl after bowl of steaming vegetables fried lightly in butter.

Ethan's eyes lit up. "Wow!"

"Man, I am star-ving!" Joseph said, breathing deeply.

The dishes were paraded around the hall, with everyone cheering and clapping in appreciation and anticipation. At last, they were set on a table that had been especially brought out to hold them. The pigs were carved and large helpings of everything were put onto silver plates and presented to the head table.

Ethan took his loaded plate gratefully, taking a deep breath. The rich aromas of the food on his plate set his mouth watering. Once the head table had been served, the pages backed away, bowed and vanished. The rest of the guests were expected to fetch their own food.

The queue for food was orderly, though those therein must have been every bit as hungry as Ethan himself. The head table began to eat and conversation resumed.

326

"My Lord Ethan," the Lord Marshall said. "I understand that you've had very little experience in battle."

"Well, in this kind of battle, most certainly," Ethan replied.

"Is there another kind of battle?"

"Well, sports, I guess, would be ritualised battle. I play lacrosse."

"Lacrosse?"

"Yes. It's a game with a ball and the players have long sticks that have nets on the end. It's with these nets that we pass the ball to one another. The goal is to get it into the opponent's big net on the end of the field."

"It sounds interesting."

"I'll teach it to you if you like."

"Oh, that would be fun!" Aerfyn said, clapping her hands. "I love games."

"It gets pretty rough," Ethan said. He realised the moment he said it that it was a particularly stupid thing to say. Aerfyn was, in all likelihood, tougher than he was.

Aerfyn simply looked at Ethan, amusement tipping the corners of her mouth upwards.

"Sorry," Ethan mumbled.

Aerfyn laughed. "You are forgiven." Her eyes shone as she looked at him.

Ethan smiled, finding her humour infectious. "How are you feeling, your Majesty?"

Aerfyn waved her hand dismissively. "My name is Aerfyn, and I am well, to answer your question. Still weak and weary, but I shall recover nicely."

"Good."

"Nicely enough to beat you at lacrosse, at any rate." She looked across at Ethan slyly. He grinned broadly and said, "You're on!"

"Oh, this is going to be interesting," Gwalchgwyn said with a laugh.

"How's Maelgoch?" Ethan asked the old man.

"A little stunned still," Gwalchgwyn answered. "Slurring his words a little. The healers are waking him every so often to ensure he is well. He should be back on his feet a little inside a week."

Ethan could not help but notice Ceinwen shifting uncomfortably in her seat. He smiled at her. She frowned in return.

"Lady Ceinwen," he said. "Tell me about the Rhai Gwyllt."

"What do you want to know of us?"

"Well, and forgive me if I'm insulting you, but I've noticed some similarities between yourself and the Dynion Gors."

The others at the table grew uncomfortable, but Ceinwen simply grinned. "Like what?"

"Well, your eyes are large and pale green, your skin more golden than any of the residents of Y Ynys Bendigaid. And you are so very long-limbed."

"You are observant, Lord Ethan."

Ethan blinked. "You mean there is a link?"

"In my family, yes. My great, great grandmother was a Lady of the Dynion Gors, though they call themselves the Fir Bolg. In fact, most of the wild ones who live away from Caer Avallach are of mixed blood. Mine is more recent than most, however."

"That's very cool, actually."

"Another of your odd phrases?"

"Yes. It means it's actually good."

"Is it? Many would consider such mixing to be abominable."

Ethan shrugged. "We used to feel the same way about blacks and whites."

"I do not understand. There is no grey in your world?"

"No, there is plenty of that," Aerfyn said, a slight tone of disapproval colouring her voice.

"I agree," Ethan said. "We'd all be a happier people if we were surrounded by buildings as beautiful and colourful as this one, I'm sure of it."

"Then what do you mean?" Ceinwen pressed.

"Well, my lieutenant, Joe, here is black..."

"He is clearly brown," Ceinwen said with a snort.

Ethan laughed. "Yes, but we call them black."

"That's stupid. He's brown."

"Beside the point. Way back when, many white people, or my forefathers used to own black people, Joe's forefathers, as slaves. They were eventually emancipated, but racial relations remained contentious. Even today there are some whites who claim we're the superior race."

"Are you?"

"No!" Ethan and Joseph said together, Joseph much more emphatically.

Ethan laughed. "No. We're not. There is no superior race. It's just a stupid idea believed by stupid people."

"I see," Ceinwen fell back in her seat and grew thoughtful.

Aerfyn smiled at Ethan again. Ethan felt colour burn his cheeks and smiled in return. He turned away, and Aerfyn laughed.

"Yo, man," Joseph whispered to Ethan. "I think she likes you."

"Shut-up," Ethan said, pushing Joseph slightly.

Joseph simply shook his head and smiled.

The feast continued on well into the night. When the ceiling glittered with silver painted stars to match the sky outside, the musicians came. Candles were lit in sconces placed around the hall, and in their soft golden glow, people rose to dance to the music.

"Dance with me," Aerfyn whispered to Ethan.

Ethan twitched. He had drunk enough metheglyn to find the idea appealing, but not enough to be entirely unaware of the possible impropriety.

"A woman can chose her own dance partner in my kingdom, Ethan," Aerfyn said. She took his hand and led him onto the polished dance floor. Ethan wrapped his arms around her and they moved to the music as one.

****

Maelgoch heard the music drift into his room. Muffled and broken, it still sounded haunting and beautiful. He imagined himself down at the grand hall, dancing in celebration of their victory. A pang squeezed at his chest. It was not Maelgoch, son of the Lord Marshall, who led the knights of Caer Avallach to victory. His eyes fluttered open, clouded over with his guilt and shame.

He had lost Aerfyn, and now his position, to the stranger from the Otherworld, Ethan Cadfael. He wanted to hate the name with everything he had, but in truth, without him, Caer Avallach may have fallen and Aerfyn taken hostage by the king of the Dynion Gors. He was also genuine and good and though Maelgoch wanted to hate him, he found he could not.

It was not the boy's fault Aerfyn had taken a shine to him. Command was thrust upon him by Maelgoch himself. No, Ethan Cadfael could not be hated.

"We celebrate victory, yet you are almost in tears," a rich, feminine voice said.

Maelgoch turned his head. Large, pale green eyes observed him. He sat up rapidly in alarm, then grunted in pain. He'd sat up too quickly and now his head throbbed and the room spun. He squeezed his eyes shut and pressed his palm hard against his forehead.

"Easy now, Red Prince," the woman said. She sat on the bed and placed an elegant, though scarred hand on Maelgoch's shoulder.

He chanced another look.

The woman was not, as he'd first suspected, one of the Dynion Gors, but a woman of the tribesmen that lived in the wilds, away from the refined influence of Y Ynys Bendigaid.

She was slender, long of limb and wiry, but strong and strikingly beautiful. She smiled at Maelgoch.

"We have not met. I am Ceinwen, queen of the Rhai Gwyllt and Aerfyn's cousin. We came to lend aid to Caer Avallach when we heard she was besieged by the Fir Bolg."

Maelgoch frowned. "I do not recall…"

"You were knocked senseless defending your queen before we arrived. The Battle Prince had taken command and broke the Fir Bolg forces on the shore of Y Llyn Gwydr."

"Oh."

"Aerfyn speaks very highly of you and your actions that day."

"Does she? She is being kind. I am nothing." The bitterness Maelgoch felt could not be disguised.

Ceinwen laughed. It was a rich, musical sound. Her green eyes sparkled. "You, fighting wounded, defended your queen bravely, defeating more than ten Fir Bolg warriors before you were struck to the ground. That is not nothing, Red Prince."

"Then tell me why my heart feels heavy." Maelgoch laid back, he shook his head and turned away with a frown.

"Ah, you are heart-sore over Aerfyn."

Maelgoch turned and looked sharply at Ceinwen. She laughed again.

"It can be no great secret. You grew up together, and Aerfyn has always been the kind whose looks make her instantly loved."

"You are also beautiful," Maelgoch said.

Ceinwen smiled. "But not as beautiful as my cousin. No. My beauty is as the wilderness – untamed hillocks that rise from plains of tall grass and haphazard wildflowers, bracken and moss and overgrown forest. My beauty is as the craggy rocks of the north and the bitter, cold sea that pounds upon them. Aerfyn's beauty is refined, like a sculpted shrub, or flowerbed, like a tended garden – all pleasing lines and grace. Her beauty is as the planted lilies on a pond, or perhaps the stately, elegant architecture of Caer Avallach itself. What are the wilds compared?"

"Caer Avallach is beautiful," Maelgoch conceded. "And yet, I find myself often escaping to the wilds."

"And why is that?" Ceinwen asked. "Why trade a soft, dry bed for the hard ground and rain?"

"It gives me peace," Maelgoch answered.

He observed Ceinwen. It was true. Her beauty was wilder than Aerfyn's. Her skin was not as pale; her countenance not as serene. A small crease between her brows marked the hardship she bore as one of the Rhai Gwyllt. Her curves were more angular than Aerfyn's, as one raised without luxuries.

Still, it was those very things that contributed to her remarkable beauty. As one might appreciate the savage beauty of a lion or a wolf, so Maelgoch found he admired Ceinwen's beauty.

Ceinwen smiled at him. "Yes, in that we agree. There is peace to be found in the wilds. Even amongst all the hardship and peril, there is peace."

Mealgwyn nodded. "Yes," he slurred before dropping back to sleep.

A polite knock on the door and Gwalchgwyn stepped in, Tylluan perched on his broad shoulder. She twittered in greeting.

"My lovely niece. Why are you not down in the hall, dancing?"

Ceinwen shrugged. "My limbs are too tired for such revelry, and I find the music fearfully dull."

Gwalchgwyn smiled. He walked forward to stand by the bed and looked down at Maelgoch's sleeping face. "How is he?" the Dryw asked.

"Heart-sore for your daughter," Ceinwen answered with a smile. Gwalchgwyn was not easily fooled by Ceinwen's projected strength.

"And you are heart-sore for him."

"Don't be ridiculous," Ceinwen scoffed. "He's too..." she searched for the word. "Pretty."

Gwalchgwyn laughed. "It seems that not even the rugged women of the wilds are immune to a fair face."

Ceinwen screwed her nose up. "Any woman can love a handsome man, but there is a marked difference between handsome and pretty, Uncle."

"Is there?"

"Yes."

"And yet it seems..."

"Are you calling me a liar, Uncle?"

"Not at all, my dear. But do not deny yourself any joy for fear of the opinions of your ilk. For all his... prettiness, Maelgoch is a hardy man both in body and will. He would be a match for any wild one."

Ceinwen snorted, but Gwalchgwyn did not miss the fleeting expression of curiosity that passed across her face as shadow chases lightning. He tried hard not to smile.

And failed.

"Stop it!" Ceinwen fumed.

Gwalchgwyn laughed. "Oh, how like your mother you are! She was the favourite of my sisters, and you are the favourite of my nieces."

"I am your only niece."

"A small detail. Now, go downstairs and enjoy what remains of the feast. We bury our dead and begin our grieving on the morrow."

Ceinwen nodded, but she hesitated casting an unsure glance at Maelgoch.

"I will care for him. Now go. Aerfyn has been asking after you."

Ceinwen sighed and left the room.

Gwalchgwyn, grinning, closed the door carefully behind Ceinwen. He went to the window and opened it wide. Tylluan leapt immediately from his shoulder and soared off into the night. Gwalchgwyn watched her go, envious of her flight. This night was made for flying.

The moon hung high in the sky, full and close and glowing orange. It lit the ground with as much detail as the day, but the light bloomed softer, gentler. The air moved but gently, stirring only the lightest, most fly-away wisps on Gwalchgwyn's head. He sighed.

"I would follow you if I could, my love," he whispered.
Shaking his head, the ancient Dryw turned and walked to Maelgoch's bedside to take up the vigil abandoned moments before by Ceinwen.

"You, sir," he said to his sleeping patient. "Are lucky indeed. There has been no man before now who has caught the mighty Ceinwen's attention so. Just you take care to keep it, and you will find yourself contented for the rest of your days."

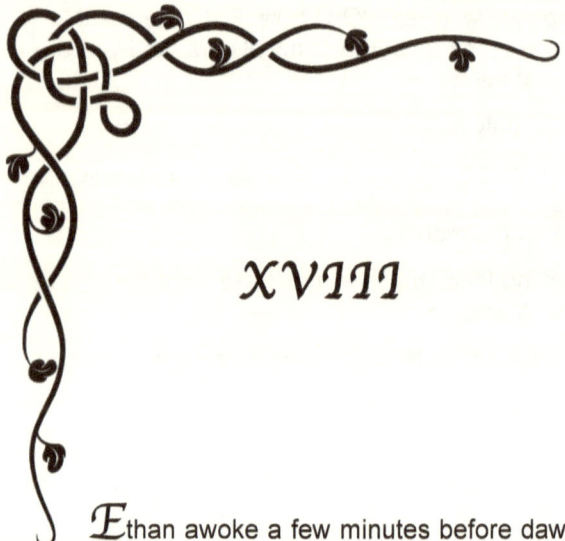

XVIII

*E*than awoke a few minutes before dawn. First light had already spread her glittering silver robe over the land. He shifted his weight, only to realise with a start that someone lay with their head on his chest. He looked down at Aerfyn's golden crown and frowned.

Slowly, through the alcohol-induced fog, Ethan remembered the events of the night. It started with a dance.

It always started with a dance.

Still, the newly made knight of Caer Avallach could not help but rejoice. His heart leapt at the sight of Aerfyn. The warmth of her body against his sent his skin tingling. A smile, unbidden and uncontrollable, spread across his face. He pulled her gently closer and she stirred, her eyes fluttering open in the dim light.

"What time is it?" she murmured.

"Don't know," Ethan answered. He ran his fingers through her silken hair and felt her smile.

Nothing more was said and the couple dozed off again until Gwalchgwyn awakened them. "It is time to be up. The dead need burying, and the trial must be conducted."

Aerfyn sat up and yawned. "The trial can wait," she said, shaking out her long tresses. "Thank-you for waking us."

Gwalchgwyn smiled. "But of course, my Queen."

"Stop that. Father?"

"Yes?"

"Maelgoch?"

"Recovering. He is anxious to leave his bed, but I have forbidden it. He will be up for the ceremonies, of course, but I cannot have him toiling in the sun in his condition."

"I will see him before the morning meal."

Gwalchgwyn nodded. "He would like that. Now up and dressed, both of you."

Ethan had managed to doze off while Gwalchgwyn and his daughter spoke. A soft pillow landed flush on his face. Ethan groaned, pulled it away and sat up.

"I'm up. I'm up." He yawned and blinked sleepily.

"Could have fooled me," Gwalchgwyn said with a smile.

Aerfyn hit Ethan in the face with another pillow. Ethan, too tired to retaliate, could only grunt in complaint. Aerfyn laughed.

Grinning from ear to ear, Gwalchgwyn bowed and left the royal bedchamber.

The burials took the better part of a fortnight. The knights and soldiers of Caer Avallach were buried in shallow graves and covered over with cairns of black and white stones. The warriors of the Rhai Gwyllt were cremated in a single mass grave, one enormous mound erected over them.

The Dynion Gors were buried by their kin, who were permitted the time they needed to bury their dead before they were placed back into the dungeons.

Much time and care was spent on the dead, each group buried where they fell. The battlefield, too, received the same treatment. The flower-strewn meadow soon bore the shapes of burial mounds and cairns.

It was hard, depressing work. Yet it was work that brought all the peoples of Y Ynys Bendigaid and the surrounds together. Knight and peasant worked side by side, digging the graves and lowering bodies into them.

Maelgoch, who refused point blank to be kept to his bed, worked amongst the rest. He helped the Rhai Gwyllt build their pyres – a task that was just as important but less taxing than digging graves and hauling bodies. Ceinwen worked beside him, silent and severe.

The ceremonies honouring the dead were profound. Song and dance, and feasting by the newly created mound accompanied the end of each day. Ethan found himself moved to tears as stories of friends now passed made their way to his ears.

The dead were remembered fondly and though the feasts were melancholic, laughter often rang out at the retelling of the lives of the brave warriors who now rested beneath the earth.

Pavilions were set up at the battlefield for such functions. The living stayed out there for three days burying the dead before making their slow way back to Y Ynys Bendigaid and Caer Avallach.

The city was in terrible condition. Many homes had been gutted. The beautiful wall surrounding the city was in dire need of repair. In this, the knights, soldiers and laymen of Y Ynys Bendigaid again worked side by side.

Ethan found himself much loved by all. Already a hero, he did not shirk work, nor did he pay much mind to class, treating each man and woman with the same respect regardless of rank. It soon ran through the city that Aerfyn had at last chosen a husband, and none were nearly as deserving as Ethan Cadfael. When the news reached Ethan's ears, he blushed furiously, but found he was not entirely opposed to the idea of marriage.

He turned to watch Aerfyn, who, though still wounded, ensured that all the workers were fed and rested, tending to them with her own hands. He noted how beloved Aerfyn was. Her people smiled and bowed to her, offered her their children for blessing, and tended her as much as she did them.

Aerfyn caught him watching and smiled at him. Ethan smiled in return before returning to work.

"You're a lucky man, my Lord," one toothless old farmer noted to him. "There's not a man in the kingdom who wouldn't trade places with you in a heartbeat."

"I am a lucky man," Ethan agreed.

For months, the city of Y Ynys Bendigaid crawled with citizens working to restore her to her former beauty. When the very last stone was placed upon the wall, a mighty cheer rose up.

That night, Aerfyn and Ethan arranged for a great feast to be held – a mighty celebration to honour every man, woman and child of the island city for their hard work. Music played on every street corner, with fire-eaters and jugglers performing in the spaces between.

People danced and drank and ate. Ethan and Aerfyn, along with Maelgoch, Ceinwen and Gwalchgwyn ate and drank in the street with their people. The Royal table set up in the central city round.

Talk that night was light and full of laughter. Ethan, having drunk a little too much, turned suddenly to Aerfyn.

"Marry me," he blurted.

Aerfyn blinked in surprise, then smiled. "I intend to," she said.

He laughed, wrapped his arms around her and pulled her close. Cheers and whistles from all those present to witness it accompanied their very public kiss.

Maelgoch, though he smiled, looked pained. He sat with his father, the Lord Marshall Rhyddych, who did not miss the slight slump in Maelgoch's shoulders or the involuntary twitch of his right hand. He placed one beefy hand on his son's shoulder and smiled at him. Maelgoch grinned.

"It is my pride that hurts, father," he said lightly.

"I know you better than that," Rhyddych replied.

Maelgoch grunted and buried his face in his tankard of metheglyn.

The following night gave rise to another festivity – the union of Aerfyn, Lady of Caer Avallach and Queen of the Pobl Gwir, and Ethan Cadfael, the Battle Prince. The union was something to behold.

Aerfyn wore a gown of crimson and gold, her long hair let down and a golden net studded with garnets adorned her head. Ethan's breath caught when he spied her approach, and Joseph, standing to the side had to remind his friend to breathe.

Ethan wore clothing borrowed from the Lord Marshall. Maelgoch offered clothing of his own, but he was wirier than Ethan, and the clothes were tight. His pants were navy and his loose-fitting shirt a dark blue trimmed in gold. Across his brow sat a simple circlet of yellow gold.

They were wed in a meadow just behind Caer Avallach, and the entire city came in their finest garments to bear witness.

Gwalchgwyn, dressed in new white robes trimmed in silver brocade presided over the union.

The couple stood beneath a woven wicker arch, laced with late summer blossoms and the multi-coloured leaves of autumn. The arch stood between two oaks, spreading their leaves in a majestic canopy of red and gold. All about them, the leaves fell, stirred from their branches by the gentle breeze.

The sun shone brilliantly in the late afternoon, lending precious warmth to what was otherwise a cool day.

"In the presence of these great oaks, whom our forebearers planted when they first came to this blessed isle; these great oaks who have borne witness to all royal unions since; Aerfyn, Lady of Caer Avallach and Queen of the Pobl Gwir and Ethan Cadfael, Battle Prince, now stand to be united as one," Gwalchgwyn intoned. "By the way, you look stunning," he whispered to Aerfyn with a wink.

Aerfyn smiled such a radiant smile that Ethan knees almost buckled. The look of alarm at his slight but sudden descent on Aerfyn's face forced Ethan to stand upright once more.

341

"I, Gwalchgwyn, Dryw and chief of the order of the oak, do hereby preside to give holy strength to this marriage."

The gathered crowd whispered to one another as Gwalchgwyn turned to the altar behind him. He knelt before it and lit powder in a small, black bowl. Sweet smelling smoke filled the air.

He then poured wine into two goblets. He whispered a short prayer over them both, waving the smoke over the mouths of the goblets. Picking them up, he turned and handed one to Aerfyn and Ethan each.

Following Aerfyn's cue, Ethan took a sip. Now that he had become used to metheglyn, the wine tasted sour in comparison. Still, he swallowed. Wine and nerves both worked against him. Once again, his legs gave up, and it was all he could do to remain standing upright.

Aerfyn placed her free hand on the bottom of her goblet and held it out to Ethan.

"I offer you this chalice, as it is my life, and all that is within it, to share without reservation, finding that in its emptying, I shall be ever full."

"Drink it," Gwalchgwyn whispered to Ethan.

Ethan did so, casting the Dryw a grateful look before he brought the chalice up to his lips. He drank deep. The wine in Aerfyn's chalice tasted sweet and rich. He handed the chalice to Aerfyn, but it was Gwalchgwyn who took it.

Mimicking Aerfyn, Ethan held out his chalice, holding the bottom as she had done.

"I offer you this chalice," he said. "As it is my life, and all that is within it... uh..."

"To share without reservation," Gwalchgwyn whispered.

"To share without reservation…"

"Finding that in its emptying."

"Finding that in its emptying…"

"I shall be ever full."

"I shall be ever full."

Aerfyn, smiling, took the chalice from Ethan and drank deeply.

"Thanks," Ethan whispered to Gwalchgwyn.

The Dryw simply grinned. He accepted the chalice from his daughter and placed them both back onto the altar behind him.

"Hold out your hands," Gwalchgwyn instructed.

Ethan and Aerfyn did, Ethan taking Aerfyn's hand in his own, stroking her pale skin tenderly. From the altar, Gwalchgwyn retrieved two ribbons – one pale yellow and the other dark blue. The pale yellow one he looped around their hands loosely twice.

"As the dawn follows night, as the sun brings light, as the spring arrives on the heels of winter, so it shall be that love follows love."

As Gwalchgwyn talked and looped, Aerfyn and Ethan fell into each other's gazes, barely hearing the words that were spoken.

The dark blue ribbon Gwalchgwyn also looped over their hands twice, going in the other direction. "As there can be no dark without light, as there can be no stars without night, as there can be no strength without love, so it shall be that one cannot be without the other."

Gwalchgwyn had tears in his eyes when he next spoke. "With this binding are thee wed, two made whole, husband and wife."

The crowd roared its approval. Aerfyn smiled and Ethan's shoulders fell in relief. Aerfyn pulled away, but Ethan pulled her back.

"Wait," he said.

Aerfyn looked surprised. The expression melted as Ethan pulled her in for a kiss. They kissed long and deep and the crowd roared with delight.

"So tame," Ceinwen sniffed, stepping up beside Maelgoch.

He glanced across at her. She did not wear a dress, but rather a purple and brilliant orange cloth imitation of her steel and leather armour. Amber beads and a single, brilliant purple tail feather from one of Rhiannon's birds had replaced the fetishes of boars' teeth and crow feathers that hung in her hair. The braided leather circlet she wore had also been replaced with a simple rose gold one, three small amethysts glinting from its centre.

In the crimson and gold of the autumn around her, she looked radiant.

"And what would you have done instead?" Maelgoch asked.

Ceinwen smiled at him, her large green eyes sparkling with wickedness. "Wouldn't you like to know?"

Before Maelgoch could give a reply, she vanished, moving through the crowd to congratulate her cousin and her new husband. Maelgoch's eyes were fixed on her as she moved, savage and lithe as any wolf.

Rhyddych, privy to the exchange observed his son with a smile.

"What?" Maelgoch demanded when he spied his father's expression.

"Nothing," Rhyddych said innocently.

The grand feast that followed the ceremony began with a chariot ride through the streets of Y Ynys Bendigaid. Crowds of common folk lined the procession way, calling out well wishes to the newly married couple. They would retire to their own festivities.

Ethan and Aerfyn danced as many dances as their feet would let them. Maelgoch danced only one. His courage fortified by the mead he had drunk, he crossed the dance floor to where Ceinwen sat, talking with her entourage, and extended his hand.

Ceinwen looked surprised, then a slow smile spread across her face. She took Maelgoch's hand and led him to the floor.

"No," Maelgoch said, pulling her close forcefully. "I am the man. I lead."

Ceinwen blinked, then smiled once more. "As my Lord wishes."

They danced a while in silence, Gwalchgwyn and Rhyddych looking on with secret smiles. They spied each other smiling and exchanged a curt nod of understanding. There would be another wedding before long. When the song ended, they pulled apart and Maelgoch began to lead her back to her seat. He stopped abruptly and turned.

"I would," he said.

"Pardon?"

345

"I would like to know."

Ceinwen released Maelgoch's arm and took his hand. "Come with me," she said.

Together, they escaped the fortress.

****

The king of the Dynion Gors had been, after some years in the dungeons, released to return to what remained of his people. Never during his stay was he or any of his ilk ill-treated, and for that he was grateful. Though his dark heart still raged at Aerfyn's refusal, he never again, during his long reign, attacked the Pobl Gwir.

Joseph rose to be Lord Marshall of Caer Avallach when Lord Rhyddych became to old to attend to his duties.

Maelgoch and Ceinwen were married the year following the union of Ethan and Aerfyn. Maelgoch resigned his position as a knight of Caer Avallach to be with the woman he loved. He reigned by her side as king of the Rhai Gwyllt.

The proud Rhai Gwylit were not welcoming in the beginning, but Maelgoch's skill at arms and intelligence soon established him as the single most valuable warrior the Rhai Gwyllt had. After the first month, none dared question his skill or courage and great warriors of many deeds stepped aside for him.

Though he often missed the company of his friends at Caer Avallach, the wilds filled his heart with peace, and his wife filled it with passion. In their first year of marriage, he and Ceinwen had a son. In honour of the brave knight who lost his life in the Otherworld, they named him Peredur.

Gwalchgwyn and Tylluan often visited the Rhai Gwylit stronghold. The ancient Dryw would amuse the child

Peredur long after both his parents had collapsed from the effort.

From a young age, Peredur proved a strong boy and a prodigy at arms. His shoulders grew broader than his father's, and his movements more lithe than his mother's. Wilder than both, he kept his parents busy as a youth.

Ethan Cadfael and Aerfyn, Queen of the Pobl Gwir, reigned for many, many years. The land prospered, giving her approval under their benign rule. Their first-born was a daughter, to whom Ethan had given the name Jasmina in honour of the young woman who had helped him on his journey in the Otherworld. As with the child Peredur, Jasmina proved unruly. A tough, free spirit, she became the youngest Knight of Caer Avallach, trained by the Otherworldly warrior, Joseph.

Upon her ordination into the order, she met Peredur. Three years later, they were wed.

The rest, as they say, is history.

Epilogue

Professor Davies smiled as he looked out the window. Today was Hallowe'en, exactly thirty-one years since he met Aerfyn and journeyed to the Otherworld. The case of the strange girl, as far as he knew, had been filed forever in the 'unsolved mysteries' drawer of the Ottawa Police Service. The brave men and women who had lost their lives to the Fir Bolg (though none but a precious few knew they existed) were honoured every year in a special ceremony in Ottawa.

Rain battered at the window, accompanied at times by sleet, as it was wont to do at this time of year in Canada's capital city. The sound of thunder filled the air with a resonant growl.

Inside, with a fire blazing cheerily in the fireplace by the sofa, Gwilym felt quite safe and contented. He checked his watch.

Jazz and Gordon, Bill and Genevieve, and their children should be arriving for dinner soon, though this weather was likely to make them later than usual. Tonight was their annual reunion. Wherever they were in the world, every Hallowe'en would find them back in Ottawa, sitting at Gwilym's table and reminiscing about their adventures into the impossible. In the kitchen, Gwilym's wife hummed as she prepared the roast. It was lamb this evening, and it smelled wonderful.

Gwilym took a sip of his schnapps and returned to the papers in front of him. Long since retired from academic life, he scrawled his name on the cover of his latest manuscript and smiled.

To the world, these were fantastic tales of journeys between two worlds. To the retired professor, however, they were truths – their fantastic nature fact. It filled his heart with joy to know this, and with sadness to know that there were few people in the world with whom he could share the secret.

He sighed, placed the manuscript on his table and leant back into his sofa. It took a few moments for him to realise that the tapping at his window matched neither the rain nor the ice. He turned to find a pale barn owl tapping her beak against the window and hopping along the sill.

He stood immediately and went to the window. The bird looked up at him expectantly. He opened the window, and she flew in, landing on the back of the armchair by the fireplace and shaking the frigid water from her feathers.

Gwilym stared bemusedly.

The doorbell rang.

"I'll get it," Gwilym's wife called from the kitchen. She trundled down the hall to answer the door. A few muffled words at the door and she appeared in the study.

"Gwilym, you have a visitor," she said, before showing the man in.

A tall old man walked through the door, a grey hooded cloak covering his long white robes. White hair and a white beard dominated his weathered features. Gwilym stared into the sparkling blue eyes; eyes that, with nothing more than their dancing light, told tales of mischief.

"Well, now," the man said in perfect Welsh. "I must say it is damp outside!"

Appendix A

Pobl Gwir Words and Phrases

A

A chi yw'r unig un sy'n gallu siarad?	And you're the only one who can speak?
A sut mae'n eich bod yn methu?	And how is it that you can?
A ydych yn Pobl Gwir?	Are you one of the True People?
Aerfyn mewn perygl	Aerfyn is in danger
Aerfyn yw ein brenhines	Aerfyn is our queen
Am rywle i guddio chi hyd nes y gall fynd â chi adref	For somewhere to hide you until he can get you home
Atal	Stop

B

Beth ddigwyddodd?	What happened?
Beth fyddech yn hoffi i frecwast?	What would you like for breakfast?
Beth oedd ei fod yn gofyn ichi?	What did he ask of you?
Ble mae Peredur?	Where is Peredur?
Bryniau Eira	Hills of Snow
Bwyd bore	Morning food
Bydd yn byw bendithio yn y byd a	He will live blessed in the afterlife

ddaw	
Byddaf angen gleddyf	I need a sword
Byddech yn gwybod y Pobl Gwir os oeddech	You would know if you were one of the True People
Byddwn yn dod pryd bynnag y gallwn	We will come whenever we can
Byddwch siarad fy iaith	You speak my language
Bore dda	Good day

C

Caer Avallach	Avallach's fortress
Caer Avallach o dan warchae	Avallach's fortress is under seige
Clwyf	Wound
Cwilsen	Quill
Cymorth	Help/Aid

D

Dangos i mi	Show me
Dim ond un yn siarad ein hiaith	Only one speaks our language
Ddewr	Courageously
Ddim yn eich pobl yn gwybod am y rhwystr?	Do your people not know about the barrier?
Dewch	Come
Dewch i gymryd i ni,	Take us, you evil

rydych drwg lyffantod	frogs
Dilynwch	Follow
Dim	No
Dim ond ei thad hi bellach yn cymorth	Only her father can help
Diolch	Thanks
Diolch yn fawr	Thank-you
Dryw	Seer
Dwedwch wrthyf eich bod yn deall	Tell me you understand
Dydych chi ddim yn dod o'r wlad hon	You do not come from this country
Dynion Gors	Bog Men
Dywedwch wrthyf amdanoch eich hun	Tell me about yourself

E

Eich mam yn gafr, ac mae eich tad yn llyffant	Your mother was a goat and your father was a toad
Ewch	Go

F

Fe wna i gynnal i ffwrdd	I'll hold them off
Ffoi	Run
Ffwl	Fool
Fy bobl galw eu hunain yn y	My people call themselves

Gymraeg; o Gymru	Welshmen; from Wales
Fy mhobl angen i mi	My people need me

G

Gadewch i mi wella fy merch	Let me heal my daughter
Gallai Rwyf wedi tyngu llw Clywais ymladd cleddyf	I could have sworn I heard a sword fight
Gwelaf	I see

H

Hoffech chi gael unrhyw beth gyfer y bwyd bore?	Would you like anything for the morning food?
Hyd	Up

I

Iachawr	Healer
Iachawyr	Healers
I ymolchi	To bathroom

L

Lliw	Colour

M

Mae angen i ni	We need to move

symud	
Mae e'n	Him
Mae gen i ddyledion i'w talu'n	I have debts to pay
Maelgoch yn gwersylla tu ôl i linellau'r gelyn	Maelgoch is camped behind enemy lines
Mae'n dim ond chwedl bell	It is only a remote myth
Mae'n edrych yn llwn	It looks grim
Mae'n rhaid i chi ein cymorth ni	You have to help us
Mae'n rhaid i ni ddod o hyd i Aerfyn ac yn chymryd ei chartref	We must find Aerfyn and take her home
Mae'n rhaid i ni ddod o hyd i'w	We have to find her
Maent yn ein gelyn	They are our enemy
Marw	Dead
Mynd â ni i Aerfyn	Take us to Aerfyn

N

Naddo	No
Ni allwn aros yma gyda chi drwy'r amser	We cannot stay with you all the time
Ni fydd hynny'n ei wneud	That will not do
Nid wyf yn deall yr hyn yr ydych yn ei ddweud	I do not understand what you are saying
Noswaith dda	Good evening

O

Ond nid yw'n gallu siarad eich iaith	But he cannot speak your language
Os gwelwch yn dda	Please
Os gwelwch yn dda yn mynd â ni i Aerfyn	Please take us to Aerfyn

P

Pa un ohonoch yn yr arweinydd?	Which one of you is the leader?
Pobl Gwir	True People
Pysgod	Fish

R

Rhai Gwyllt	Wild Ones
Rhaid i chi ddeall	You have to understand
Rhif	No
Rhydych yn gwybod am Annwfyn?	You know Annwfyn?
Rhydym yn chwilio am Aerfyn	We are looking for Aerfyn
Rwyf am i ymdrochi	I want to bathe
Rwy'n deall	I understand

S

Siwgr	Sugar

Sut mae hi?	How is she?

T

Tir Heddychlon	Peaceful Land
Twpsyn dewr	Brave idiot

W

Wyl yr Hydref	Autumn Festival

Y

Y Llyn Gwydr	The Glass Lake
Y Ynys Bendigaid	The Blessed Isle
Ydi hi yma?	Is she here?
Ydych chi'n dda?	Are you good?
Ydych chi wedi gweld hi?	Have you seen her?
Ydych chi'n gwybod sut i fynd yn ôl yno?	Do you know how to get back there?
Ymolchi	Bathroom
Yna byddwn yn trafod	Then we will discuss
Yna nad ydych yn	Then you do not
Yna byddwch yn gwybod unwaith, ond wedi anghofio	Then you knew once, but have forgotten
Yr wyf yn	I am
Yr wyf yn Gymraeg	I am Welsh

Appendix B

Fir Bolg Words and Phrases

A

Agus?	And?

B

Bastaird	Bastard

C

Cad?	What?
Cad a thuigeann thú?	What do you know?

D

Dearbhófar do chathair sruthán	Your city will burn

F

Fir Bolg	Stomach Men

L

Liom teacht isteach	I yield

N

Na Fir Bolg a thabhairt suas	The Fir Bolg surrender
Nach bhfuil tú fiú ridire	You aren't even a knight

R

Ró-dhéanach	Too late

T

Tá a fhios agam go bhfuil tú ann	I know you are there
Tá tú aon rud	You are nothing

Also Available from S.M. Carrière:

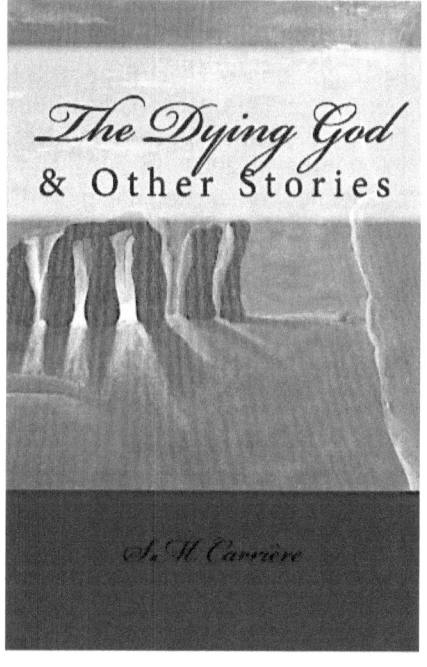

About the Author

Born in 1983 in Quito, Ecuador, S.M. Carrière has lived in five countries around the world including Ecuador, Gabon and The Philippines. The family moved to Australia from The Philippines shortly after the commencement of hostilities there in 1989.

After graduating High School, S.M. Carrière worked full time as an Office Junior at a law firm in Brisbane, Queensland before moving to Canada in 2001. In 2002 she began her academic career beginning in Criminology, but switching to Directed Interdisciplinary Studies (focusing on Celtic Studies) after her first year. She graduated with honours, earing a B.A. Hon from Carleton University in 2007.

It wasn't until well after graduation that writing found her. She hasn't looked back since.

S.M. Carrière now resides in Canada with her two cats and a growing collection of books.